LORD OF THE GOLDEN FAN

Of all the tales of adventure that have come down to us from the age of Elizabeth the First, the story of Will Adams is perhaps the most exotic and incredible. And yet it is true that this man of Kent, who sailed as pilot of five small trading ships on a twenty-one months' voyage to the fabled Spice Islands of Java and Sumatra, became not only the first Englishman to set foot in Japan, albeit more dead than alive, but the lifelong protégé and friend of the reigning Shogun, Iyeyasu.

This novel is a dramatic reconstruction of the tempestuous, exhilarating, gloriously colourful story of Will Adams among the Japanese—a people so different in all their thoughts, their beliefs and traditions that his life was constantly at stake. By his stature and intelligence he survived the many plots of his enemies and lived to become a Samurai, one of the Lords of Japan. And by his prowess and wise counsel he opened the way to Japan's first contacts with the learning and culture of the West.

Christopher Nicole's creation of seventeenth-century Japan is so splendid an achievement, his account of the adventures of this solitary Englishman amid that country's strange customs so full of excitement and suspense, that there can surely be few lovers of historical fiction who will not find their blood tingling and their hearts stirred by this portrayal of one of the great adventurers of the age of adventure. While Drake and Hawkins were creating their own legends at sea, Will Adams in so different a fashion carried the majesty of Elizabethan England to the other end of the earth and found there a civilization in many ways more enticing than his own.

LORD OF THE GOLDEN FAN

CHRISTOPHER NICOLE

CASSELL · LONDON

CASSELL & COMPANY LTD
35 Red Lion Square, London WC1R 4SG
Sydney, Auckland
Toronto, Johannesburg

First published 1973

I.S.B.N. 0 304 29190 0

Printed in Great Britain by
The Anchor Press Ltd, and bound by
Wm. Brendon & Son Ltd, both of Tiptree, Essex

F, 173

Contents

To Mike Legat
for his untiring advice and encouragement
without which this book could never have been written

PART ONE

The Sailor

Chapter 1

RICHARD HINE'S garden extended from the rear of the house down to the Thames itself. It aspired to no great elegance, lacked a maze and a sunken lawn, but was utterly beautiful on a June evening because of its endless beds of roses, reds and whites, pinks and yellows, separated by the neatly cut grass paths until at the end one could look beyond the topiaried hedge at the rushing brown waters of the great river, and remember how a year ago these empty reaches had been filled with ships as from every creek and every harbour between Windsor and the Medway the seamen of England had set sail to do battle with the Spanish Armada.

To the right of the rose garden stood the orchard, a meeting place for larks and nightingales on a summer dusk. This night they were absent; throughout the day there had been too much hustle and bustle about the Hine household, too much activity, and far too much noise. Now the garden was again empty, but the paths were sadly scuffed and littered with the relics of conviviality, gnawed chicken bones and discarded apple peels, with here and there even a shattered wine goblet. Tomorrow there would have to be a great cleansing; this night the festivities were just approaching their climax.

The winter parlour was crowded. It was not a large room, was intended for the family's comfort on the long January evenings, when the huge fireplace would be filled with leaping flame and the girls would roast chestnuts on the long iron forks. Now there was hardly room to breathe, as ballooning farthingale jostled against padded breeches, and many a tight-fitting, neck-irritating ruff had been pulled loose. The long table had been pushed against the wall; it resembled a battlefield, with the huge side of beef reduced to a few white bones and the dozen chickens picked clean, with gravy scattered across the white tablecloth and spilled ale dripping on to the floor. In front, the wedding guests gathered, a kaleidoscope of blues and greens and whites and pale reds, and ruddy pink flesh. There was little jewellery and no weapons; the Hines and their circle were merchants, not nobles, but they could enjoy a wedding with all the lusty boisterousness of Her Majesty's Court, with all the arrogant confidence of people who saw it their destiny to hold the balance of power in Europe.

The hubbub died, slowly. It was time for the toast, and Master Nicholas Diggines had taken his place at the end of the room, flanked by Richard Hine and his wife, by the vicar of St Dunstan's, and by the happy couple. Master Diggines wore his best scarlet madder doublet, and looked ill at ease. He was a tall man with thin features and slightly stooped shoulders, a result of his years over a shipwright's bench; clearly he would at this moment have preferred to be back in his shipyard than addressing this eager assembly. He took another swallow of beer, and inhaled, noisily. Richard Hine, small and bustling, clapped his hands for silence.

'I am no speechifyer,' Master Diggines confessed. 'And yet, on such a happy and auspicious occasion, and in the absence of my old friend Master John Adams, it is my bounden duty to sing the praises of my young friend Will Adams here. I have known Will and his brother since they were born, and when both John and his good wife Margaret succumbed to the plague it was my duty to assume the responsibilities of father to the lads, as well as a confirmed bachelor might undertake such an onerous task. But in the event it was a pleasure and involved me in more ease than labour. I know that Tom here will forgive me if I concentrate upon his brother for this moment. Will Adams, my friends, is a man of parts, and more than that, he is a man of fortune. I do not now speak of wealth in a physical sense. That were transient, like to disappear as rapidly as it were achieved, and leave the unlucky recipient poorer than before. Will's fortune, my friends, is in himself. Look at him there, towering above all of you, full two yards from toe to crown if he is an inch. Feel his muscles, ladies. Ah, not with his sweet bride standing close. You must choose a more private moment!'

There was a roar of laughter, and Will Adams flushed. Twenty-four years of age, he was as his foster father described him, a tall, strongly built man, with shoulders thickened by years of labour at the lathe and the saw, and more recently at the tiller. He wore mauve and crimson striped breeches under a brown madder coat, and the fashionable full beard, although it was uniformly clipped close to his chin rather than shaped to a point; like his hair, it was black. The moustache shrouded a wide mouth and clustered beneath a large, straight nose, above which two pale blue eyes frowned at the world. It was a face strangers found disconcerting in its aggression; intimates knew better. The hardness in Will Adams' features was the result of concentration; whatever he undertook in life, however small, however menial, he attempted with all his heart.

Now he smiled, a remarkable lightening of his expression, as he looked down at his wife. Mary Hine wore a plain white gown, the symbol of her purity, in mind no less than in body; her golden hair was lost in the white veil which descended from her cap, and her strong features with their clear blue eyes were isolated, a marvel of handsome serenity. The face, he would think, of a goddess, were such a comparison not blasphemy.

And now she was no longer Mary Hine, but Mary Adams. He thought he might have waited all his life for just this moment.

Master Diggines, having swallowed another mug of beer, was ready to resume his peroration. 'But there is more to Will than mere muscle. I apprenticed him at my bench when he was twelve. *I* sought no more for the lad than that he should in time succeed me in my business. This was never sufficient for *him*. His trade was the sea, and thus, with that singlemindedness which is his greatest characteristic, he set to work to master the sea. He will build you a ship worthy to set with the best. But he will also sail it for you. To be at the helm of a stout vessel was always his greatest love. At least, until now. I well remember his constant importuning, whenever a ship was launched and ready for delivery to her new owner, to be allowed a place amongst the crew. You will not credit this, my friends, but at eighteen I was happy to place him in command and now, why, there can be no more accurate navigator, no more capable shipmaster, in England.'

'You play the flatterer too readily, dear Nicholas,' Will said. But Mary squeezed his arm with pleasure. Her face was flushed. Not with beer, for she had drunk nothing save water. With excitement? And anticipation? They had known each other for years. Master Diggines did not only build ships, he sent them to trade with Holland, and Richard Hine, as an importer of Flemish wool, was one of his best customers. Will had spent many an evening seated in this very parlour, discussing politics and religion, business and gossip, with Master Hine. And watching Richard's daughter changing from a bundle of arms and legs into a woman. That they should marry had seemed the most natural thing in the world. And yet their relationship had always been that of brother and sister. Only now, as he looked down at her, was he realising what, in less than an hour, would be his; the skirt of her gown rested lightly on wide hips which moved upwards into a tightly packed bodice, and beneath the hips, what endless paradise would he there discover? Her eyes met his, and her flush deepened as she looked away. Excitement and anticipation, certainly, but apprehension as well. This night their friendship ended, and something else would begin.

'I speak the truth, Will,' Master Diggines insisted. 'For here again, my friends, how simple to master the trade of seamanship and navigation, and come to be known as a good fellow, a perfect boatswain, an able companion in storm or battle? But yet was he never satisfied. He has recently turned his attention to astronomy and gunnery. Why, lacking the benefits of an education at Cambridge, he has set to work to master the intricacies of the Latin language that he might more readily continue his studies. I confess, sweet Mary, that I know not whether you shall this night suffer an assault on your maidenhead, or a lengthy sermon from some learned book.'

Which raised another laugh. But Mary's lips were tight. She did not share his desire for learning, and did not understand any desire to possess books written by Papists. And yet, there was more than mere disapproval of Master Diggines' sally in the sudden relaxation of pressure on his arm. Her apprehension was growing. As was reasonable, on this night of all nights. But she also loved. He must remember this. When she had joyously consented to be his wife, she could have had no doubts as to what would ultimately be entailed. His requirement was to be gentle with her, and in this surely she could trust.

He found her hand, and squeezed, but still there was no response, and her gaze, as she stared at Master Diggines, was pensive.

'And this brings me to the point of the evening,' Diggines said. 'And Will Adams' crowning fortune. I could continue half the night, to relate how he conducted munitions of war to our fleet during their great and glorious victory over the Dons. I could relate how much in demand he is as a pilot. I could tell you of a vast venture now under discussion, in which certain Hollanders would have Will here investigate with them the secrets of the far north. But these are only incidences in a career which, granted a continuance of health and spirit, must inevitably arrive at greatness. Will's fortune is that he not only attracts to himself discerning *men* who would use his abilities. His goodness and the volume of his spirit also, it seems, attracts the best in the fair sex, and has at last brought him the love of the fairest maiden in all London Town, I do declare, surely saving only her gracious majesty, whom God protect. I avow it here with every confidence that no matter what conquests Will Adams achieves in the future, there will be none to equal his conquest of Mary Hine, and whatever joys are showered upon him as his days grow long, he will never know a happiness to equal tonight. So now, my masters, and my mistresses, join with me and raise your mugs to drink a toast to the happy couple, to handsome fortunate, Will Adams, and to beautiful, and equally fortunate, Mary Adams.'

At last they were alone. The crowd, seemingly redoubled in size in the narrow confines of the bedchamber, had laughed and shouted and sung, and told ribald jokes until Will himself had bundled them out, to shut and bolt the door. Now he leaned against it, panting, his heart throbbing, for he had been forced to drink a good dozen toasts in the last few moments.

Mary sat on the edge of the bed, her feet resting on the floor, a tall shadow in the half-light, for they had taken away the candle, and although it was still daylight outside the shutters were closed. He could make out only her hair, loosed now, and resting on the back of her nightdress.

'I thought they would never leave us.'

'I sometimes think,' she said softly, 'that of all those who attend a wedding, the bride enjoys the entertainment least.'

Will pushed himself away from the door. 'For fear, you mean?'

She made no reply.

'And do you think, sweet wife, that you have cause to fear me? We have been friends, good friends, for some dozen years.'

'True. And equally with my sister. But now we must separate, Joan and I, in our understanding of you. Must we not?'

He tiptoed across the room, sat beside her. 'Would you have it otherwise, sweet Mary?' His fingers slid down the arm of her nightdress; to touch her, as his wife, to know that in a few moments . . . but at least half the swelling beneath his nightshirt was caused by the beer. 'I must use the pot. I pray that you will excuse this weakness.'

'Weakness, Will? There can be no weakness in nature.' Her face was but inches away. He leaned forward and his lips touched hers. Her mouth remained shut, yet he kept his against hers, allowed his own to open, licked her lips, brought his hands forward, from her arms on to her nightdress, discovered ribs, ridged beneath her flesh. She was thinner than he had supposed. But above the ribs he found the softness he sought, billowing outwards. No disappointment here; softness punctuated by sword thrusts of hardness, stroking across his palms even through the linen, receding as her hands came up to his chest.

'You spoke of a natural call, Will,' she whispered.

Her mouth was opened. He drove his tongue forward, touched her teeth, her tongue, and she was away, rising, leaving the bed to reach the wall and stand there. 'Sir, you took me by surprise.'

'And that displeases you?'

She hesitated; her face was no more than a gloom in the darkness. 'No, Will,' she said at last. 'But we must be careful lest the lewdness inherent in mankind gains the upper hand.'

'The lewdness?' he cried. 'How can there be lewdness between man and wife? Did not the priest himself say we are now as one?'

'He meant our minds must be as one, Will. They shall be, with the passage of time, with the understanding that accompanies marriage . . . '

'Take off your nightdress, my sweet.'

'Sir? I have never undressed completely before any living soul. Not even my sister.'

'I am not your sister, Mary. I am your husband. And besides, it is dark.'

'Not so dark that I cannot see you, Will. And what does it matter, dark or light? To be naked is to be lewd, and there's an end to it.'

Will scratched his head; he nearly pulled the hair out by the roots in his impatience. But patience was all, here. The girl was terrified. Nothing more. True, she did not speak as if she were terrified. She argued reasonably and with obvious preparation. She had expected just such a confrontation, and had marshalled her defences. So he must just as reasonably disarm them. Certainly violence was not to be done here. Not to Mary. If only he had not drunk that last mug of beer. If only his hands were not still burning where they had stroked her nipples.

'Mary,' he begged. 'Did you not promise the priest to obey me?'

'As you swore to honour me, dear Will,' she said. 'Do not suppose me angry with you. I am well aware of your anxiety, of your manhood which importunes you into the most evil of ways, of the excitement of this day, of the headiness of the ale. I know these things will pass. It but remains our duty to see them pass without in any way injuring our love for one another. I love you, Will, most dearly and truly. I beg you to believe that. I love you now, and I shall love you always. And I shall gladly obey you in anything that does not force me to sacrifice my honour.' She left the wall and came towards him. 'Now, do you relieve yourself and then come to bed. I beg of you, dear Will.'

He got up, lurched across the room to the corner where the pot waited; a streamer hanging from a rafter brushed his face, and he angrily swept it aside. 'And what then?' he asked. How thick his tongue was.

'Now you are angry, Will.' He watched her climb into bed, slip her legs beneath the coverlet.

'No,' he lied. 'No. I am not angry, Mary. I could never be angry with you. I am but mystified. We are married . . . '

'And marriage involves a consummation, Will. It is our duty, just as it is our duty to have children. But I pray you, let us not approach the consummation in any spirit of levity or disgusting licentiousness, but rather as a duty owed to God, and blessed by Him.'

Will lowered his nightshirt, replaced the pot. The bedroom overlooked the garden; it was quite dark now, but he could hear the sound of revelry out there, and catcalls directed no doubt at this very window. So there would be no emptying the pot this night. And now there was no question of a full bladder interfering with his desire. And she had just consented to his assault. He stood at the foot of the bed. She had just consented to grant him what was rightfully his, to take by force, if he chose. There was magnanimity. But there, he realised, was the picture of the entire Hine household. Master Richard might speak as bluffly as he wished, and pretend to authority, but the ultimate fount of decision in the Hine family was his wife. And so, too, was it to be with the Adamses. Of course, Mary and Joan had been brought up to hold their mother's beliefs. But the whole country was inclined to matriarchy. And why not, with the past thirty years since Queen Elizabeth mounted the throne the most prosperous in history?

He moved round to the side of the bed. In the semi-darkness he could see her smile. 'Be quick, dear Will, that I may hold you in my arms, and suffer the pain with courage.'

And now she would play the martyr. So he was angry. And yet, how much he loved her. How little did he wish to hurt her. And above all, how much he wanted her body.

'Will?' she asked.

'I but wondered how much you understood of the consummation.'

'Enough.'

'It cannot take place through a linen nightgown.'

'I understand that, dearest Will. And so, as a good wife, I surrender myself into your hands. I but beg you to use me with honour, and with gentleness.'

'But you will not reciprocate?'

'I, dear Will? You confuse us, surely. My duty is to receive, not to give.'

'Your duty, surely, is to be sure you *can* receive, sweet Mary. Alas, I fear our difference just now has left me less of a man than I would have hoped. Perhaps, were you to assist me with your own soft hands . . . '

Her eyes were tight shut. 'Do it,' she whispered. 'Do it. Do it. Do not involve me in such a matter, Will. Play the man. Or if you cannot, declare it to the world.'

The anger welled up from his belly; there were still sufficient fumes from the beer to make his head swing, to dispel the normal reason which guided him. And yet the anger was itself overwhelmed by desire. For now she was his. However immobile, however dormant, she had just surrendered herself into his keeping.

His fingers trembled as he turned back the coverlet. She lay, straight as a corpse, with hardly the flutter of her belly to suggest otherwise. Tentatively he lifted the nightdress from her ankles, but it was caught beneath her legs. Gently he moved her body, to and fro, easing the cloth out. Slowly he moved it up. His eyes were by now fully accustomed to the darkness. As he had suspected, and hoped, she had the legs of which dreams are made, long and straight, and ridged with muscle which quivered as she shivered.

He laid the folded nightdress across her waist. God in Heaven, he thought; that I had the gift of poetry, for just one night. For just one minute, that I might capture this in words. Even Mary must surrender to beautiful words, beautifully uttered. The symmetry of the legs extended into the suddenly wide thighs, the softly flat and quickly moving belly, the high ridge of the pelvis, the soft pit of the navel.

And in the centre of this wondrous world the thickly matted pubic forest, no less symmetrical than the rest of her body, more extensive than he could have hoped with a slender avenue of paler hair leading upwards over the undulating whiteness. Of all the treasures in the world here was surely the finest, the most valuable, the epitome of all beauty. And thus surely Nicholas Diggines had been right in his speech. No matter what reserve clouded Mary's natural instincts, surely so long as she granted him access to this fount of all living matter he could have no complaints regarding his fortune.

His hands were on her knees, gently parting. They offered no resistance. She was his, surrendered. Use me only with honour, she had begged. How can a man, urged on by a gentle but insistent passion, and more, a passion ordered by love itself, ever use his wife with other than honour? The breath expelled from his lungs in a long sigh as he fell forward, reaching between her legs with his lips, his arms curling round her thighs to raise her from the bed, only to be lost in her scream as she in turn propelled herself upwards, turning and falling out of the bed, her sudden weight catching him off balance so that he fell back to the floor. For a moment she lay across him, and then she was on her knees and on her feet, rising above him, a vision of swirling white nightdress.

'Mary,' he gasped, throwing both arms around her ankles. She panted for breath, and stamped on his face to free herself, running across the room for the door, and checking there, her hand twisting on the bolt, yet without drawing it. There was the irrevocable step which would end the marriage before it could begin.

'Mary,' he whispered. 'Forgive me. I meant no harm. It was so beautiful. You are so beautiful. I was but afraid to lose you too soon.' He rose to his knees. 'I have dreamed of this for so long. My friends, old Nicholas, your father, all prate about my ambition and my singlemindedness, and know nothing of the matter at all. Throughout my life I have but sought one thing, Mary, the love, the true love, the *shared* love of a beautiful woman. Of a woman like you, my sweet. There is so much that can be shared, between husband and wife. You spoke of our minds. Those, of course. But our bodies, my darling. Can there be anything in existence more beautiful than the human body?

I seek to know yours, Mary, to explore it, inch by inch, to have you explore mine, inch by inch. I would do to you and for you everything that you have ever dreamed of, in your most secret heart, and I would have you do the same for me. What use can we have for secrets from each other? Is this not the true meaning of the marriage vows? Of marriage itself?'

He watched her shoulders move. 'Oh, God,' she whispered. 'Oh, God. What have I done?'

'Mary?' He started to get to his feet, and she turned, slowly, gazed at him.

'No, Will. Stay. I will come to you.'

She crossed the floor and knelt opposite him. 'On our knees were best, Will. For we are both suppliants before the Almighty.' She took his hands between hers, pressed them to her cheek. 'Can you not see, dear Will, that *this* is what I feared? Think you I feared your masculinity, your strength, dear Will? Think you I feared the bruises you might leave on my body? I am not such a coward. But I know more of men than you suppose. In our charitable expeditions Joan and I visit them, in their poverty and their loneliness, at least once in every week. I know, I have seen, the horror that can be man, alone. I have seen, and heard, enough to know that the secret depths of a man's soul is a terrible place, comparable to hell itself. And you would have me enter there? That would be to turn my love to hate. Will, Will, you must believe me when I say that I love you, that I have always loved you, for your handsome face and manly body, for your openness, for your humour. But I know too, as you have adopted the sea for a profession, that the devil has already cast his bid for your soul.'

There was a likely beginning to a lifetime of marriage. She could not understand him, because she did not wish to understand him. And who was he to say that she was the mistaken one? At the least she was certain of her ground, where he knew nothing but confusion.

'Alas, sweet Mary,' he said. 'No doubt all you say is true. But the sea, Mary, if you blame the sea, then am I lost. It is all the trade I know."

'Blame the sea? Why, Will, how can I blame that purest of the earth's constituents? I *blame* no one. To apportion blame is not my task, here on earth. I pity those lonely men who confound their hopes of salvation with deeds and thoughts of the gutter. I pity you, for having suffered so. But now that we are married, now that we have reached such an understanding of ourselves, now I know the depths of despair in your soul, why, we shall reach upwards together, for the truth and beauty that awaits us in marriage, and then, the sea, and even the men who sail upon the waters, can no longer harm you. For when you are at sea, you will ever be thinking of me, of the home we shall soon have, of the peace and comfort to be found there, and these thoughts will keep you strong. Now come, Will, let us complete this business as the Lord would have us.'

He shook his head. 'I cannot, Mary. Oh, God, how I acknowledge the truth of your words. But God, no doubt seeking to punish us, has taken away the muscles from my loins, the strength from my manhood. Fear not, no one will ever learn *that* secret. And who knows, by tomorrow morning my vigour may have returned, and then . . . '

'It must be done *now*,' she gently insisted. 'And you blaspheme, dear Will. Oh, how much you have to learn, of God and all His works. Your present weakness is but a result of your earlier haste. Now come, Will, lie on this bed with me. Put your head upon my shoulder, dear Will, and gird up your shirt as I gird up my dress, and let our bodies rest one against the other, and be sure, Will, that in due course God will call us together, and make us one.'

Chapter 2

'AND THEN the Strait.' Timothy Shotten took a long swallow of beer and sighed. His eyes gloomed over the crowded alehouse as if he were still at sea, searching the waves from the masthead; his fingers clutched his pewter mug as if they still needed to grasp the shrouds to steady himself against the rolling of the ship.

'What time of the year was it by now?' Will asked.

Shotten shrugged. He was a massive man, better than six feet tall, with huge shoulders which seemed to dwindle not at all as they reached downwards to a thick waist and legs like tree trunks. He wore sea boots even when ashore; it was said there was no hose able to stretch around his tremendous calves. 'Into February, Will, lad. But summer in those latitudes.'

'And cold, even then,' Tom Adams said. 'We have spoken with a man who sailed with Drake.'

'Not too cold, yet, although certain to become colder. It was the wind. It was fair, but strong. A full gale. We took our chance. In those latitudes, a chance must be taken.'

'A gale, in the Strait of Magellan,' Will whispered. 'I wonder you are here to tell of it, Timothy.'

'I doubted such a pleasant future myself, Will. The seas, man, you'll never have seen seas like those. Coming up astern they were, long, long, a ship's length and more, curling, with a hanging crest, like an old man sporting a full beard. But these weren't old, Will, lad. They were young and angry. Six men on the helm, lads. Six strong men. I was one of them. And it was devil's work. Had we broached to, and taken one of them curlers on the beam, we'd have been rolled up like a child's toy on the beach. And all the while the wind was plucking at us like the fingers of death itself. By God, it was not an experience I'd repeat.'

'Forgive me,' said a high-pitched voice. 'I could not help but overhear, my masters. You have a singularly dramatic turn of phrase, sir.'

The three seamen looked up at a young man, in his early twenties, like Will, but looking older, for all that his beard was nothing more than a wisp of fair hair. His face was thin, but already lined with dissipation, and his considerable height was lessened by the stoop to his shoulders. Only his eyes were brilliant, gleaming from one to the other of the seated men, dark pools of glowing, anxious intelligence. His eyes, and his clothes which seemed out of place in a dockside alehouse. His cloak was Venetian red, with a deep yellow border, and was worn over a tunic and breeches of black and yellow stripes. His cap was black with a white feather, and his hose a dull orange. His shoes were a similarly dull yellowish brown. He wore a sword, a thin Spanish blade, suspended from a crimson belt, but the hand resting on the hilt was so slender and fine, with every blue vein so distinctly delineated, and ending in fingers so long and delicate, it was difficult to suppose it had ever grasped the weapon in anger.

'A butterfly,' Tim Shotten remarked. 'Blown in by the wind.'

The young man smiled. His smile was as anxious as his eyes. 'Indeed, sir,' he agreed. 'An apt simile. I repeat, you choose your words well. May I join you?'

The three friends exchanged glances.

'Our pleasure,' Will said. 'This is Master Timothy Shotten, and this is my brother, Master Thomas Adams. I am William Adams.'

'And you are a man of Kent, sir.'

'Why, yes,' Will agreed. 'I am from Gillingham.'

'Then doubly well met. I hail from Canterbury itself.' The young man shook hands with each of them in turn. 'My name is Marlowe. Christopher Marlowe, although my friends call me Kit. Saving those who prefer Kitty.' He uttered a nervous giggle, and glanced from one face to the next, but finding no reaction, clapped his hands. 'My good landlord, these gentlemen are drinking with me. Beer, is it? Beer for my friends, good Master Tomwyn. But beer, alas, does not agree with my stomach. A glass of wine if you please, Master Tomwyn.'

'You are known here, Master Marlowe?' Will asked in surprise.

'Oh, Kit, please, Master Adams. And I will make bold with Will. For I have no doubt that we shall be friends, you and I. Why should I not be known here? A seafarer's house, you say? Why, sirs, I love the district for that, as well as other reasons. I write poetry, sirs. For that, I need the breath of fresh air, of fresh minds, even the fart of fresh bellies. Like an alchemist, Will, I take the raw faeces of life itself, the dribble from your drooping tool, and crush them together within myself, and send it forth as beauty from my mind, through the agency of these fingers.' He laid his hands on the table.

Timothy Shotten took the mug of beer from the tray, held it up. 'We'll drink your health, Master Marlowe, and then take ourselves off.'

'You do not like me, Master Shotten?'

'No, Master Marlowe. I do not like you. And should you seek your blade I'll break this mug over your head.'

Marlowe's laugh was as effeminate as his giggle. 'What violence, sir. You exude violence, like a wild animal. Mistake me not, good sir, I beg of you. I admire violence, being myself the most timid of creatures. Why, sir, I *love* violence. I have written a play, acted in it myself, whose theme . . . but no matter. I did not inflict myself upon you in order to sing my own praises.' He sighed, and drank some wine. 'But violence is my theme, good sir. So do not take yours away. Nor yours, good Will.' His left hand raised from the table, and flopped across Will's, for the shortest instant, before being withdrawn.

Tom Adams chuckled. 'You'll find none there, Master Marlowe. Will is the most reasoned of men, except when aroused.'

'Then I must treat him with caution. But, good Master Shotten, you spoke of waves, longer than a ship, higher than a house . . . nothing you have witnessed in the Channel, I'll be bound.'

'Off the southernmost tip of America,' Will said. 'The Cape they call the Horn. Tim here sailed with Candish.'

'Then, sir, we must have another round. Master Tomwyn? My friends are thirsty. Candish. I have met him. Once. And some time ago, before he earned himself fame and fortune, when he was as like as not to touch a passing acquaintance for his last penny. Tell me, Master Shotten, is it true you returned with a mainsail made from cloth of gold?'

'We flew a sail made from damask, Master Marlowe. For when the last of our canvas had rotted, why we had no material of less value left on board. And there was gold enough. That was the *Great St Anne*, November 1587. A prize to remember, I can tell you that. The richest ship ever taken. Or ever will be taken, I'll avow.'

'But she was only one of many,' Will said.

'Nineteen, all told, Will. On the Great Sea they sail without a lookout, so safe do they count themselves. It was like a fox discovering himself in the middle of a pack of blindfolded geese.'

'How romantic,' Marlowe murmured. 'The very name is sufficient to stir the blood. The *Great St Anne*. Laden with gold, and jewels, and fine clothes . . . from whence, do you suppose?'

'Why, Master Marlowe, she came from Manila. A city in the Ladrones, a group of islands off the southern coast of Asia, and claimed by Spain. Their ships come from there, laden with all the riches of the Spice Islands, and cross the entire vast ocean in preference to risking the Cape of Good Hope and the Indian pirates, and unload their cargoes in Acapulco, in New Spain. Thence it is carried by mule train across to Nombre de Dios, to be loaded on the flota for Havana, and back to Spain. Once landed at Acapulco they are beyond the reach of chance encounters. In Nombre de Dios they accumulate men of war for their protection, and in Havana they become part of a large fleet. But in the South Sea, Will, ah, there, as I said, they sail on their own, and are easy prey. This one was already in sight of the coast, blown but a few miles north of her course and beating down to safety, when we espied her. It was like picking an over-ripe apple.'

'There were women on board, Master Shotten? Tell me there were women aboard.' Marlowe leaned forward, his eyes sparkling.

'Females, Master Marlowe. Females.'

'Not beautiful?' Marlowe demanded. 'Not to be seized? And perhaps even wooed? Forgive me, friend, but I have a romantic imagination.'

'Well, sir, as to that, perhaps they were to be seized, or wooed, upon some other occasion. But consider, sir, if such a thing is possible, that these people had recently crossed the Great Sea. Seven weeks on the oceans, sir, with scurvy already rampant. How do you think we found her so easy a prey? There were men on that ship could scarce lift a sword.'

'And yet this was a crossing you yourselves had then to undertake,' Will said.

'It was an easy decision for us. Better scurvy than the rack and then the flames. The whole coast was armed and waiting for us to attempt to return to the Atlantic. It is said there was a man of war even waiting in the Strait itself.'

'And so you crossed the South Sea,' Marlowe whispered. 'What *devils* you seamen are. On, on, across the mighty waves, to Cathay and Cipangu.'

'No, sir,' Shotten said. 'To the Ladrones and Java, and then the Cape of Good Hope.'

'Not Cathay? No temptation to visit the Great Khan?'

'Our temptation was to return home while we breathed, Master Marlowe.'

'And yet, to be so close . . . was there no man on board this ship has read Marco Polo? I will not suggest your captain. Tom Candish never read more than an unpaid accounting in his life. But surely someone . . . '

'I have read Marco Polo's travels,' Will said.

'You, sir?' Marlowe exclaimed in surprise.

'Oh, he is not quite so ordinary a seaman as he seems,' Tom said smiling.

'Indeed, sir, I had never supposed that there would be anything common about your brother,' Marlowe protested. 'Alas, Master Will, you were not with Candish, there's the pity. Ah, Cathay, Cathay. Fabled Peking. The Great Khan. The slant-eyed women. Zenocrate, lovelier than the love of Jove, brighter than is the silver Rhodope, fairer than whitest snow on Scythian hills. Forgive me. Lines from my play. Did I not tell you I had a play produced, but a few months gone? It concerns Tamburlaine. Have you heard of Tamburlaine, Master Will?'

'A Mongol conqueror of the fourteenth century,' Will said.

'Sir, you are too good for your profession. And yet, not good enough. A Mongol conqueror, you say? A devil in human form. They called Attila the Scourge of God. The name is far better suited to Tamburlaine. I used it in my play. The man was lame, you'll understand, Master Shotten. Of noble birth, certainly, but not born to power. And yet conquest was in his blood. Central Asia, Persia, Turkey, even India, if you would believe it. He had Europe at his mercy, fifty years before the cannon played upon the walls of Constantinople. But he turned east. For what was Europe, Master Shotten, compared with the great empire of Cathay?'

'And this man conquered Cathay?' Tom Adams asked.

'He died,' Marlowe said sombrely. 'Journeying to watch the Great Wall itself crumble into dust before his tempestuous assault. A great man. A man of violence, Master Shotten. Sometimes the two are synonymous. Providing the rest of the character is so formed. But Tamburlaine: Why, sir, with Nature's pride, and richest furniture, his looks do menace heaven and dare the Gods.'

'Sir,' Shotten said. 'You blaspheme.'

'Why, so I do. A thousand pardons. Another line from my play. They stick in my head like wine. But to say truly, I blaspheme, and often. Oh, I am a very devil, Master Shotten. With words. With words I have the destructive urge of Tamburlaine himself. Words, and ideas. Master Tomwyn, some more beer for my friends.'

'No,' Shotten said. 'We have drunk enough, and the hour is late.' He stood up, swayed for a moment, and sat down again. 'We'll bid you good night, Master Marlowe. We are grateful for your hospitality. But I will not drink with a blasphemer.'

'It is time, Will.' Tom Adams also stood up, and remained on his feet. 'Mary will be wondering what has happened to you.'

'Oh, let them go,' Marlowe whispered, leaning across the table. 'You are a companion such as a man might dream of, Will. You have brawn, and yet brains. You have sailed the oceans and risked your life in battle with the elements, and yet you have read of other men's travels and adventures as well, which is all the excitement poor sods like myself may ever hope for. Spend another hour with me, Will. Oh, not here. Come with me, and let us find new fields to conquer.'

'Leave the lad alone, Master Marlowe,' Shotten growled, once more struggling to his feet. 'He has the sweetest wife in all the world awaiting his return. While you, sir, I know you, for what you are. Drunkard, lecher, atheist; he is a man of evil, for all his intelligence, Will. And they say worse things of him than that. Now, sir, draw your sword, and receive my fist in your face.'

'Why, Master Shotten, why should I take offence at your words? They are nothing but the truth. I am a poet, sir. A man of ideas. Now, sir, I would but ask you this: You are a sailing master, and indeed you have circumnavigated the world. Now, sir, was your course planned, from Plymouth to Plymouth? Or were you not exploring, investigating, risking disaster at every step of your journey, but driven ever onwards by a determination to *learn* about this world of ours? I, sir, lack your courage, and yet I venture forth in my own small way. My world is my mind, and the mind of man. So I explore. I venture where others fear to tread, where they fear even to look, lest they be repelled. So I am repelled sometimes. But every time I am the wiser for my experience. I seek nothing of your friend, save to learn something of the seamen who have raised this country of ours to greatness. I wish to speak of their customs, their fears, and their beliefs.

Perhaps I shall write a play about the sea. Why, then, I need to be a sailor myself, at the least at second hand.'

'Spoken like a man, Master Marlowe,' Will said. 'And I accept your invitation. Go home, Tom. Go on. Take Tim with you. Tell Mary I am delayed on a business matter. They treat me like a child, you know, Master Marlowe, and this is my younger brother. You'd not suppose I had a head on my shoulders.'

'I doubt you have,' Timothy Shotten remarked. 'It is that sodden with ale. In any event, it is not the head on your shoulders we worry about. Yet leave him be, Tom. As he said, he's old enough to care for his own peccadilloes.'

Marlowe waved his hand. 'Let them go, Will. And in the name of God call me Kitty. We shall be friends, you and I. Now, what say you to some food? I could eat the backside out of a horse.'

'Indeed, sir, an excellent idea,' Will agreed.

'Kitty.'

'Kitty.' He wished his head *was* a trifle less active, swinging to and fro, thickening his speech. Marlowe might be a very odd fellow, but there could be no doubting his intelligence. It was a learning, and a sharpness of wit, which needed to be matched. 'They serve a good dish of mutton here.'

'Here, dear Will? Here, in these unsavoury surroundings? You'll walk with me to my lodgings, it is not far, and I shall provide you with a meal fit for a king. Nay, an emperor. A Tamburlaine. You shall be Tamburlaine, and I shall be your slave. Your concubine, if you will. Your Zenocrate. Ah, fair Zenocrate, divine Zenocrate, fair is too foul an epithet for thee.' He pushed back his chair and stood up. 'But first we must find ourselves a suitable cook.'

They ran down the darkened street, tripping over cobbles, laughing like schoolboys. Marlowe's sudden bursts of humour were as entrancing as his sudden flights of fancy. Now he checked, without warning, stooped to seize a rounded stone from the ground and hurl it through the air. It disappeared into the darkness, but they listened to its progress, crashing into the tiles of a roof, rattling down, striking the ground with a thud.

'You'll have a storm of apprentices about us,' Will said. 'We'd best take to our heels.'

'If they come, I shall fight them.' Marlowe drew his blade, and whirled it round his head before starting to dart here and there with his point. 'Oh, I can be a devilish fellow, dear Will, for all my soft words.'

'I do not doubt that in the least,' Will laughed, retreating to the safety of an alleyway. 'Be sure you do not injure yourself.'

'Myself. Myself. As for myself I walk abroad o' nights and kill sick people groaning under walls; sometimes I go about and poison wells.'

'Poetry again? Is that also in your play?'

'No. No,' Marlowe said, suddenly thoughtful. The sword rasped as he replaced the blade in its scabbard. 'A thought which suddenly sprang to mind. I shall use it. Certainly, I shall use it, to describe some terrible fellow. Yes. An idea comes. Paper. I must have paper. We'll to an inn . . . '

'We'll eat, if you please, Master Kit,' Will insisted, seizing his arm. 'I am starving, and I cannot remain away from home all night.'

'Of course, your wife awaits you. Mary. But she is a shrew.'

'Sir?'

'Oh, forgive me, Will; I had no thought to insult you. I but attempted to reason, thus: You are young, therefore Mary must be young; you are handsome, therefore Mary must be beautiful; you are intelligent, therefore Mary must be at least witty; and you are a seaman, bound to spend many long months away from your bed, and yet you are in no haste to gain that bed of a night. Ergo, for all her youth, beauty and wit, Mary is not to your taste.'

'And you, sir, seek to pry into a most private matter.'

'For which I again ask forgiveness, dear Will. Nor will I pry again. But tell me this; do you spend many long months at sea?'

'Indeed I do. We sail in a week, as a matter of fact.'

'With your friends? In a week?' Marlowe's arm went round his shoulders. 'Then you were commiserating.'

'Lord no. We were celebrating. I have the master's ticket. And ships are hard to come by. Ships that I will berth on, at any rate.'

'There is a mystery here,' Marlowe said. 'A mystery I would investigate. We shall talk, you and I. But first, as you say, our supper. We must hurry. That way.'

'You spoke of a lady who would cook for us,' Will panted at his elbow.

'A lady.' Marlowe gave his high-pitched giggle. 'A lady.' His fingers closed on Will's arm, and he drew him into the deeper shadows at the side of the alleyway. 'I hear one approaching now.'

'But . . .'

'Ssssh,' Marlowe said. 'Do you not feel like a slice of cake, dear Will, just to whet our appetites? It will be soft, and yielding, and you may dig your fingers in . . . it is the wine. The wine and the heady company of you hardy seafarers. Why, Will, at this moment my rod is hard enough to do me honour in a duel. Come, feel for yourself.'

Hastily Will withdrew his hand. 'I'll believe you, Master Kit.' But Marlowe, with that marvellous gift of his, had formed the thoughts in his mind. Untrue. The thoughts, the wishes, had been there from the start. The devil, which lurked in his belly, seeping upwards whenever excitement or an excess of beer allowed it the chance. This was Mary's diagnosis. Her answer was prayer. But here was Marlowe confessing to possessing a similar demon.

'I see you there, young masters,' said the girl. 'Hiding from me? Have you no penny for a simple maid?'

'A penny?' Marlowe cried. 'A penny for you, sweet child? Come here and let me look at you.'

She stood immediately in front of them, a short, plump creature, with untidy red hair and surprisingly good features. She wore a yellow skirt and bodice, set off by her scarlet flounce. Her head was bare, and so were her feet.

'A penny, sweet child,' Marlowe said again. 'I have here a shilling, should you please me.'

'That were wasted, Kit,' Will muttered. 'And we shall need another.' For certainly there could be no turning back now. Hard enough to fight a duel. There was a simile. The clash of flesh . . . God in Heaven, he was sweating. But too often he played the Onanist, and hated himself in the morning. So why not hate himself, with even more reason? He would be at sea for perhaps a year, with no one but himself for comfort.

'Nay,' Marlowe said. 'Not another.' He took the coin from his pocket. 'A shilling, mistress, should you humour my friend and I.'

'A shilling,' she whispered, and reached for the coin, but Marlowe as quickly whipped it out of her grasp and dropped it in his pocket.

'Should you humour us.'

Her head flopped up and down. 'That I shall, sir. And your friend.'

'But surely . . . ' Will said.

'This night you place yourself in my hands,' Marlowe insisted. 'This sweet child . . . ' His hands came forward again, rested lightly on her thighs, and then stroked upwards, fingers pointed down, over rib cage and breasts to lodge under her chin. 'She shall be our assistant. But first my lodging.'

'Your lodging, sir?' the girl asked, in some alarm. 'I know of a field, just down the street. And it is a warm night.'

'No harm will befall you, sweet child,' Marlowe said. 'You see here two men of honour. But do not come if you are afraid of us. A shilling will not take long to find an eager owner.'

'Oh, I will come, sir. I will come. Is it far?'

'Not far at all. But first, your name.'

'Maggie, sir.'

'I do not like Maggie. I will call you Meg. And as we are now friends, you will know me as Kit, and my companion here is Will. We are friends, Meg?'

'Oh, yes, sir,' she said. 'Kit.'

'Good. Then let us go home. But mark me well; we walk as two gentlemen might escort a lady, arm in arm, but nothing more.'

Will shrugged, and took the girl's left arm. 'You are an amusing fellow, Kit.'

'Why, not at all. I *think*, Will. There is the secret of my genius. It could be yours, were you to practise it. Now take Meg here. She is no beauty.'

'I did not claim to that, sir,' Meg protested.

'And I honour your honesty. You are nothing more than a woman, and so possess certain attributes that we this night would borrow. Now is that not a mundane statement? I close my eyes, and I can see your breasts, the pout of your belly. I can part your legs and count the hairs, in my mind, while you, in fact, could be a thousand miles away. So, the reality might be a trifle different, in detail, but never in substance, and as my imagination is at *my* command, and not that of nature, be sure that anything *you* possess different to my imagining of it, sweet Meg, can only disappoint *me*. So then, why *not* close my eyes, and use my hand, and save my shilling? Only that that also loses its variety, its attraction, given time. And so I must make do with you. But, fearing disappointment, I must heighten your value. As, to be sure I enjoy my drink, although parched as the very desert, I place my cup upon the table, and then fold my arms, and gaze upon the beautiful liquid for fully half an hour before even considering a sip. And so you see, I lure you to my chamber, that I may consider you, enjoy your company, discuss with you, this and that, all the while regaining my earlier ardour, only by now it will return with redoubled vigour and anxiety, until, when I embed myself in your charms, dear Meg, be sure that we shall both be aware, to the limits of our understanding, just what we are about.'

She giggled, a sound almost like Marlowe's own laugh. 'Why, sir,' she said. 'You do talk strange.'

But she was already anxious; her fingers were tight on Will's. To be sure, he thought, Tim Shotten was right. I am out with the devil. What an exciting prospect it was.

'Ssssh,' Marlowe warned, as a stairboard creaked beneath Will's weight. 'My landlord considers that to entertain a lady in one's chamber is no different to inviting the devil to dinner.'

'A lady?' Meg burst into laughter. 'Oh, sir, you are droll.'

'Ssssh,' Marlowe said again, and opened the door on the landing. 'Not much, but I call it home.' He stepped into the darkness. 'Stay a while. I will find my tinder.'

A moment later a candle flared, and Meg stepped inside, Will at her heels. The room, although large, was bare of furnishings, or even comfort, beyond the tent bed against the wall. There was a table, covered with sheets of paper, all higgledy-piggledy, in the midst of which, somewhat dangerously, the candle glowed, and two straight chairs, one laden with clothes, which Marlowe was at this moment dumping on the floor. Against the far wall was another mass of papers, some bound together, others loose and slowly slipping down the pyramid like the beginnings of an Alpine landslide, and the whole intersected with various books, their spines protruding from amongst the parchments, again suggestive of boulders penetrating the snow. There was a cupboard in the corner, and beneath it a full chamber-pot. The window was grimy, and the air had a sour smell.

''Tis the paper rather than the piss,' Marlowe pointed out. 'And yet the piss has been here long enough.' He opened the window, emptied the pot. 'Now then, Miss Meg, we shall eat before anything. In yonder cupboard you will find cheese, bread, and a bottle of wine. Only one plate, but we are all friends here, are we not? And there are two cups, at any rate.'

'You promised me a banquet.' Will sat on one of the straight chairs.

'And a banquet you are having, dear Will. For what is food? It is the wine, and the company, that matters. This wine is excellent, and as for company, why, there are you and I, the best of friends, and pretty little Meg, here.' He caught her wrist as she set the bottle on the table. 'You *are* pretty little Meg, at that.'

'Why, thank you, sir,' she smiled; she had apparently reconciled herself to an unusual evening.

'Then give me a kiss. A good kiss, sweet Meg. A long kiss. A slow kiss.'

She bent her head towards his, her tongue extended. Will ruffled the papers. And yet it was stimulating, as Marlowe no doubt intended, to watch them.

'Now one for Will,' Marlowe said, and got up. 'You must play double for your shilling.'

'At least there's room for three in the bed,' she agreed, and bent her head towards Will in turn.

'But no touching her, Will,' Marlowe commanded. 'No touch beyond the lips and tongue. Else the pattern is broken.'

Meg laughed as their mouths met, and her breath accompanied her saliva into his mouth. She had eaten raw onions for lunch. And yet even this excited him; it was all he could do to keep his hands at his sides. I am bewitched, he thought. Bewitched by this madcap, just as Tim Shotten prophesied. But to leave now were to play the coward. Even supposing such a thing were possible.

Kit Marlowe was locking the door. 'And now,' he said, 'let our banquet commence. You'll strip, sweet Meg. And you, dear Will. It is a warm night. Oh, fear not,' as he saw the surprise on their faces. 'I shall lead the way.' His sword clattered on the floor, and Meg gave a shout of laughter, and twisted away from Will, her fingers already loosening her bodice. Not to be outdone, Will took off his doublet, dropped it on the floor, dragged off his shirt, and found himself confronted by the pair of them, each quite naked, a strange contrast, for where Meg was plumper than she had seemed and older too, with large, drooping breasts, a pouting belly, and wide thighs, Marlowe was even thinner and younger than *he* had appeared, with narrow shoulders and protruding rib cage, slender hips and spindly legs. In the midst of which emaciation his genitals seemed twice a normal size, and he held them in his left hand as he jumped up and down.

'Tempered by battle, Will,' he cried. 'Oh, they are the very devil himself. He is slow, sweet Meg. A very Puritan. Come, we'll have at him together.'

Will put up his hands to ward them off, and the chair teetered for a moment on its rear legs before crashing over to the floor. The entire building shook; shrieking with laughter, Meg slid up Will's chest and across his face, while Marlowe knelt, suddenly serious.

'Ssssh,' he said. 'Wait.'

A stick rattled against the floor from beneath. 'You'll cease that rumpus, Master Marlowe,' bawled a voice.

'Oh, aye, Master Crowe,' Marlowe called. 'I but fell from my bed.'

'Are you alone up there?' the voice demanded. 'I'll have no lewd women in my house.'

'I have a friend,' Marlowe confessed. 'A sea captain. Say something, Will.'

Will sat up and rubbed the back of his head; Meg came up with him, her arms round his neck as she scraped her nipples up and down his back. 'A good night to you, Master Crowe,' he called.

'Less noise, sir. Less noise. There are people sleeping in this building.'

Marlowe held his finger to his lips. 'We must be careful. It would be sad to have to continue our revelry in the street. Leave him be, sweet Meg. That was a preliminary tumble. You'll pour the wine and cut the bread. Up you get, Will, and we'll eat. But first, a toast to our company.' He sat down, cup in hand. 'You'll share mine, sweet Meg. Now, Will. Gillingham, you say? The village school, no doubt. And then which university?'

Will slowly picked himself off the floor, took the other chair. It was the first time he had ever sat down to a table, naked. Meg was slicing bread on to the plate, and Marlowe had already seized a piece of cheese; Will doubted that he would be able to digest a morsel. He was too aware of his own body, too aware of the breasts moving to and fro only inches from his nose, of the enormously stimulating scent of unwashed bodies. 'No university, Kit,' he muttered. 'I was apprenticed to Master Diggines at twelve years old.'

'A shipbuilder, at twelve.' Marlowe drank some wine. 'While I wasted myself on study. And you are less ignorant than I. You are not drinking.'

Will sipped his wine, cautiously. It was the first he had ever tasted and he was not sure he liked it. Meg seized the cup from his hand and tossed it off with a giggle; liquid spurted from the corners of her mouth and ran down her shoulders. When she ate cheese, it squelched in her open mouth.

'Only on matters pertaining to ships and the sea,' Will pointed out.

'Which is sufficient for most men. So perhaps you know little Greek. My own is considered poor. But in mathematics, astronomy, and it seems even knowledge of the world, you are at least my equal. Having wasted my years at labour, with very little reward, or indeed, prospect of reward, I find myself inferior to a fledgling sea captain.'

Meg was refilling their glasses; she had perched one plump white thigh on the edge of the table, and rested her foot on Marlowe's knee. She faced Will, smiling at him, constantly allowing her legs to fall apart. He was seized with a tremendous yearning to take a thigh in each hand and thrust his face into the curling dark hair. Bewitched. He drank half the cup without thinking.

'Surely your reward comes in the immortality of your poems,' he said. How incredible to be seated here, naked, opposite a naked man and woman, discussing commonplaces. Surely he must be dreaming, and would awake to find Tom and Tim Shotten shaking him by the arm.

'Bah,' Marlowe said. 'Immortality. Of what use will that be to me, or even to the worms chewing on my tool? Even should it ever come, which is unlikely. You have not heard those gentlemen who think they understand literature discussing my words. Nay, my very ability. But you, Will, yours will be a name to set alongside those of Drake, Frobisher, Hawkins . . . '

'Never.'

'What? This ship you join next week. You do not sail against the Spaniards? I have heard Drake himself fits out an expedition. Norris will command the troops.'

'I'll not sail with Drake.' Will held out his cup. 'I'll not sail with any of them.'

'Aha, the mystery I scented, earlier. Dear Will, in your own way your attitudes are almost as blasphemous as mine. They say mine will bring me to the stake. Yours will certainly cause you to be stoned in the street should they become widely known. You do *not* sail against the Spaniards?'

'I sail with a Dutch fleet, owned by a company of Amsterdam merchants; our intention is to make our way north, and attempt to reach the Spice Islands by travelling east around the top of Europe and then Asia.'

Marlowe stood up so suddenly Meg had to seize the table to stop herself falling to the floor. 'With Hollanders, and not Englishmen? You'll tell me why, Will.'

'The reason is very simple. I am a sailing master. I know more about the sea than Francis Drake himself. I could navigate any ship on the water around the world and back home again, with scarce an instrument. But I cannot command, Kit. I am not a *gentleman*.' How easily the words flowed in this company. How simply the sentences formed themselves, the statement of all that was pent up inside him.

'I suspect you are something of a Lollard,' Marlowe observed. 'And will the Hollanders give you command?'

'Perhaps not. But that is a matter of nationality, not birth and property. There is not a gentleman, by English standards, in our fleet.'

Marlowe nodded, thoughtfully. 'I had thought you a seaman, with some learning. Now I begin to understand that you are a man as well. With dangerous sentiments, certainly. But attractive. And you have ambition. Tell me that you have ambition, Will.'

'I have ambition,' Will said. 'To *do*. Can you understand that, Kit?'

'Oh, aye, that I can. I share it. But is not fighting the Spaniards *doing*?'

'Any fool with the ability to steer a course can lick the Spaniards and take their gold.'

'I'll not argue with that.' Marlowe took the bottle, stood with legs apart, the bottle held above his head, and poured the wine into his opened mouth. 'Tom Candish is surely a bigger fool than the average. Brace yourself, sweet Meg. I feel a powerful urge coming over me. See how he rises; I swear the wine does fill my veins. I will bargain with you, dear Will; allow the first penetration to be mine. To be sure, I am the more ready.'

'By all means,' Will said. 'I will sit here and drink another glass of wine.'

'Sit there?' Marlowe cried. 'Sit there? Now, where is the enjoyment in that? We must have at her together. So, while I do assault the more natural orifice, you may possess her mouth. Or let her mouth possess you.'

'Indeed, I like that arrangement best,' Meg said, and before Will could decide what she intended, she had parted his legs and knelt between them.

With a tremendous lunge he threw himself backwards, catching the chair to prevent it striking the floor, but leaving poor Meg falling forward on to her face.

'Ow,' she cried. 'You damned rascal. Now I have cut me lip.'

'Will?' Marlowe asked, replacing the empty bottle.

'No woman's lips shall touch my tool,' Will declared. 'It is indecent.'

'Indecent?' Marlowe seemed genuinely bewildered. 'But, dear Will, supposing the act of love to be undertaken in the first place, how can anything connected with it be considered indecent?'

'It is sinful, too,' Will said, panting for breath.

'Well, there too, dear Will, fornication is itself sinful, according to certain ill-informed people. Having met that hurdle, without hesitation, all other sins surely must fall by the wayside.'

'Sinful,' Will said, sitting on the bed in dejection. 'It is a measure of our lowness, as men. But there is no need to compound the deed. The act is for the procreation of our kind, after marriage. Being lewd, we seek enjoyment where there should be none, just as too many men find pleasure in fighting and killing, where such things should always be considered nothing more than a ghastly necessity. But to compound the crime, why, Kit, would you, with a man helpless at the end of your sword, and knowing you must kill him, first cut off his ears and nose for your enjoyment?'

Marlowe appeared to consider. 'Well, as to that, I might, did I not abhor the sight of blood. 'Tis little enough enjoyment we have in this life of ours, and none at all promised afterwards, as there can be no man not born a eunuch who has not at some time thrust his weapon into an illicit hole, or at the least, wished to most heartily, which must surely amount to the same thing.'

'Christ in Heaven.' Meg climbed to her feet and picked up her gown. 'You brought me here for a long tumble, Master Kit, not a debate. I'll have my shilling and take my leave.'

'Without fulfilling your task?'

'Task?' she asked scornfully. 'What task, kind sirs? I have poured your wine and served your food. Were I to lie on my back now it would surely be for nothing more exacting than sleep. Why, look at the pair of you. You'd not get those two drooping plants stiff with wooden splints. My shilling, if you please.'

'You'll whistle for that, sweet Meg.'

'You mistake me, *sweet* Kit,' she said. 'Be sure I'll scream for it so loud I'll have the dead in here.'

'God save me from indignant woman.' Marlowe reached for his breeches, fumbled in the pocket, tossed her the coin. 'At least leave quietly.'

She held the coin to the candle for a moment. 'No treason,' she muttered. 'There's a pleasant surprise. Don't forget to include me in your prayers, Master Will. This night I have surely taken another step towards hell.'

'Now there's a pity,' Marlowe said. 'You have cost me a shilling, and all for nothing, dear Will. But no matter. Women are nothing but nuisances in any event. They are too impatient. All must be hurry, hurry, hurry. Whereas man, being more positive of his ultimate achievement, may approach the business in a more leisurely fashion.' He held up the bottle. 'Empty. Still again, a blessing in disguise. Alcohol dulls the senses, Will. So a little is useful, for slowing the vital processes. But too much will spoil an evening.'

'I fear I have already spoiled yours,' Will said, gathering up his clothes. 'I am, after all, nothing more than a common seaman, Master Marlowe, incapable of dallying with the less obvious pleasures of life. My objective, when I desire a woman, is to plunge my weapon into her body as quickly as I may and as far as I may. I am a low fellow.'

'Do not sell yourself short, dear Will. And what are you doing now?'

'Why, dressing. You would not share your bed with nothing better than a man.'

'Will, Will.' Marlowe held his shoulders. 'Think you I fancied sharing it with that whore? She was but to set us up, so to speak, to whet our appetite for the beauties that lie ahead. You have but to place yourself in my hands, and look upon me less as Kit than as darling Kitty. Did I not promise to be your mistress? Your Zenocrate? There is only one woman for me; the one I created. But even she must pall beside the beauty of true manhood. I have the lines for you, dear Will. How unseemly it is for my sex, my discipline of arms and chivalry, my nature and the terror of my name, to harbour thoughts effeminate and faint. Save only that in beauty's just applause, with whose instinct the soul of man is touched; and every warrior that is rapt with love of fame, of valour, and of victory, must needs have beauty beat on his conceits. Now, if Tamburlaine could say such things, understand such things, where are mere men such as you and I to gainsay our instincts?'

Will dropped his shirt over his head. 'You confuse me with your eloquence, Kit. I fear you are too high for me. You drink wine, I exist on beer.'

'Then tell me this, dear Will. 'Tis a thought which has often taxed my brain. You seamen, who spend long years at sea, with only hairy men for company, how do you make ends meet?'

Will frowned. 'I must confess I have never considered the matter. I have not been at sea for longer than a few months at a time. I am content to await my return to the shore.'

'Then it is Master Shotten I should have up here? Think of it, Will. Two years and more at sea, and the only women found to be shrivelled with scurvy. Be sure that by the conclusion of that voyage every man had his mate. As I have mine. Will, Will, dear, dear Will.' His arms went round Will's chest, his hands drove downwards, fingers reaching for the already fluttering prize . . .

Christ in Heaven, Will thought; I cannot sit here. I cannot submit to this . . . this monster. I must drive him away, and force myself away. But God, how I am bewitched.

And Marlowe was himself away, moving round to kneel in front. 'Now there is a rod,' he whispered. 'It stands aloft like a battle flag, challenging all. Mine . . . ' he gave his penis a distasteful flick, 'is indeed a puny thing. Nay. Do not move, dear Will. Not a muscle. Sit there and let me look at you. I would kneel here forever. Will. Do you know what I would do were you mine? I would pluck out every hair from your belly. Pluck each out, one by one. What exquisite torture. And then when I was done, your beauty would stand alone.'

'By God, Kit.' Will closed his legs. 'You live too deep in your own imaginings. My breeches . . . '

'No, wait. Tell me of Mary. I break my promise, I know. But I seek to help you, Will. Look at you, man, tall and strong and brimming with health and energy, handsome to boot, and talented, and intelligent, and ambitious. And miserably unhappy. For the love of a wench? You do love her?'

'I married her, Kit.'

'Hardly an answer, dear Will.'

'I have loved her for years. I did love her for years.' Will sighed. 'I love her still. My fingers itch for the touch of her body. But she regards physical desire as unclean, and hardly to be tolerated.'

'And you, Will, a man such as you, tolerate such an attitude from your wife?'

'You would have me commit endless rape in my own bed?'

Marlowe giggled. 'It is at least amusing.'

'And believe me, Kit, I have practised it often enough. But to what end? She lies there, lifeless as a corpse, while I follow my fancy. And when I am exhausted, she gets on her knees beside the bed and prays for the salvation of my soul. And indeed I am damned. For she is right. The Bible itself expresses her opinion.'

'Confound the Bible, Will. If God had not meant us to use our tools be sure He would have devised some other means of impregnating the womb. But yet you have not told me all. To possess a beautiful woman, who *must* submit, however unwillingly, would satisfy many a man. But not you.'

Will gazed at his body. How his heart pounded, as he knew he would not leave this room until Marlowe was done with him. For how much he wanted to stay. Not for Marlowe. Not even for Marlowe. And in the full knowledge that tomorrow would be a hateful day. But to submit, in turn, to willing fingers.

And how he wanted to tell of his misery. How he had wanted to do so ever since his wedding night. But to whom? Tom? Tim Shotten?

'To conquer,' he muttered. 'Endlessly. Like your Tamburlaine, Kit. There would be a sterile existence.'

'Ah,' Marlowe said. 'Now we have it. As I suspected. You would share.'

'Not only the body, Kit. I swear that. I would share the mind utterly. I would share hope, and fear, pain and ecstasy, ambition, and disappointment.'

'But the body comes first, Will, because it is the fount of all our hope, all our fear, all our pain and all our ecstasy, all our ambition and all our disappointment. Indeed, to feel a woman's soft hands, or better yet, her lips, reaching for such a treasure as you possess; and yet you refused Meg.'

'A common whore? Is it sharing to purchase for a short hour?' Will sighed, picked up the empty bottle and looked at it. 'Besides, it is clearly sinful. As Mary says, woman's task is to receive, no give.'

'Ah,' Marlowe said again. 'You have spoken to her on this subject.'

'Fool that I am. I thought sharing could come from discussion, from an understanding, each of the other. But ever since she has looked upon me with something close to horror.'

'And she speaks for her sex, here in England at the least. In Europe. In all the world, dear Will. Which is why we must make do with each other. Women are women and men are men, and there's an end to it. To obtain more we must enter our dreams. Thus Zenocrate. She is mine, Will, because I created her. When I use my hands, they are transferred to her keeping. When I accept other hands, they are hers. Imagine such a woman, Will. Imagine such beauty as you have never supposed possible reaching for you, eager, dominant as yourself. She can be yours, Will, every time you close your eyes. I give her to you. Close your eyes now, Will, and let me become her.'

'And know lonely disappointment whenever I open them again?'

Marlowe shrugged. 'Is that not man's lot? We can only pray that on our arrival in Heaven we are not similarly disappointed. But tonight, Will, tonight I will make you a heaven of your very own, when Zenocrate, knowing your desire, and knowing, too, your strength, shall conduct you to the very portal of paradise before releasing your spirit.'

Chapter 3

ON A winter's evening it was good to be ashore. The icy wind rattled through the pantiles and sent draughts whistling down the corridors, and the black smoke welled up in the grate like a wave at sea, threatening the room with obliteration before slowly finding its way up the chimney, but inside the house all was secure.

Mary played on the dulcimer. She played well, the notes clear and accurate, the result of hours of practice. Her skill at music was at once a testimony to her industry and the emptiness of her life. No woman could work harder or with more reward; the house was cleaner than any palace, and every garment was embroidered and darned to perfection. Nor could her meals be criticised. Her neighbours spoke of her as the perfect wife.

As she seemed. She sat before the music stand, her long fingers resting lightly on the reed, frowning slightly, for the light was poor. But frown apart her face was serene. And beautiful. She wore her hair up, concealed beneath her cap, as befitted a matron of past thirty, and her face was as handsome as ever it had been upon her wedding night. And this evening she played with more confidence than usual. Whatever crisis might lie in the next few hours, this night would surely mark the beginning of another long period of peace. If the Hollanders were coming to visit Will Adams, it could only be with offers of further employment.

Will knelt on the floor, over his charts. Deliverance sprawled on her stomach beside him. She wore her nightdress, and was ready for bed the moment the guests arrived. Indeed, she would have been asleep long ago, but it was one of Will's delights to spoil the child. He knew so little of her. He had been at sea the night she was born, and he had been at sea for five of the seven years since then. He delighted to look at her, for her resemblance to Mary, so strangely set off by her possession of his own black hair. He delighted to talk with her, because of her obvious intelligence. She was his friend. He knew it was said that Will Adams only smiled in the company of his child.

'And so we turned back,' he said. 'The ice was so thick the ships could go no farther.'

'And was it cold, Father?'

'Aye. So cold it froze the breath in front of your nose. Beautiful, mind. But no place for men. And no passage to the East, either.'

The music died. 'There are people at the door, Will.' Mary stood up. 'You'll come with me, Deliverance.'

The little girl glanced at her father, and then scrambled to her feet.

'Kiss me, child.' He bent his head for her lips. 'And you'll rejoin us, madam?'

'If you wish it, sir.' She held out her hand, waited for her daughter, and left the room.

Will folded up the charts, straightened his doublet, and went to the door. 'A cold night, gentlemen. You'll come in, please.'

There were four men, wrapped in their cloaks to muffle themselves against the wind. Now they stamped their feet free of snow, and slapped their hands together as Will closed the door.

'A good night to be off the coast of Africa, eh, Will?' Cornelius Houtman said. 'It's good to see you again, I'll swear.' He was a short man, with round, flushed cheeks, and wore a velvet doublet, in brilliant red, an indication at once of the confidence which drove him through life and of the prosperity it had brought him. 'My friends, this is Master Will Adams. Will, I wish you to meet Sir Jacques Mahu. Sir Jacques will be our general.'

A tall, thin man, with an attractively strong face. 'My pleasure Master Adams. I have heard much good of you.'

Will shook hands. '*Sir* Jacques?'

'Knighted by your Queen herself, Will, for his services against the Spaniards. And this is Jacob Quaeckernaeck, Sir Jacques' quartermaster.'

Another tall man, but much younger than the general, and with brilliant yellow hair.

'Master Quaeckernaeck. Welcome to England.'

'And Melchior Zandvoort,' Houtman said. 'Melchior is my nephew, Will, and will travel with the fleet as factor.'

Zandvoort was hardly more than a boy, not yet twenty, Will estimated, short like his uncle, with a similarly round, happy face. 'My uncle has told me so much about you, Master Adams,' he said, 'that I feel I have known you all my life. He says there is no better pilot in all Europe.'

'And no more determined pilot, which is equally to the point,'

Houtman said. 'Why, my friends, when on our voyage to the North a few years ago we ran into ice so thick it was almost worthy of description as a continent, Will was yet for continuing, meaning to hurl our prows against the floes until they disintegrated.'

The Dutchmen looked suitably impressed. But what else had Houtman told them? Will wondered. How his pilot was a strange, solitary man, who drank little and laughed less? How he kept to his own quarters when not on duty? How he dreamed? Surely that was plain to all. For of what value was a man who could not dream? Thus Marlowe. But of what value was a man who did nothing *but* dream? Houtman knew nothing of his dreams. An entirely practical man, the merchant no doubt supposed all others the same, presumed that his pilot dreamed of capturing Spanish galleons, of piloting Dutch and English fleets to the remotest corners of the globe. Would Houtman continue to employ him and praise him were he even to suspect the glowing hell which raged in that so competent mind?

No risk of that. Had Marlowe lived . . . but Kit had been cut down in a tavern brawl, five years ago. A brawl such as could easily have developed on that night in Limehouse, had he not been of a mood to restrain Tim and indulge the madman. A talented poet, they now said of him. A man of strange opinions and beliefs, and stranger behaviour, but of talent. A wasted life. And Kit had been no more than nine and twenty. What would they say of Will Adams, already six years older, should he drop dead this instant? Why, nothing at all. The world did not know he existed.

The Dutchmen were exchanging glances. 'My apologies, gentlemen,' Will said. 'I am a poor host, to be sure. You'll come into the parlour and take a mug of ale. And tell me whence we aim on this occasion. The Barbary Coast?'

'Nothing so mean, Will, nothing so mean.' Houtman bustled into the parlour to take his place before the fire. He was clearly in a state of high excitement. 'This is the culmination of all my ambitions, Will. All my hopes. The Spice Islands, Will. Java. Sumatra. Who knows, perhaps even India. The Portuguese have possessed those pearls for too long. 'Tis time we took our rightful share.'

The charts were spread on the floor, the men knelt around them. Mary Adams sat in the corner and watched them, her eyes sad.

36

However courteous their greetings to her, she was now forgotten as they prodded with their fingers and drew imaginary course lines through the air.

'You'll go by the Cape of Storms,' Will said, half to himself. 'And then the Indian Ocean. By God, Master Houtman, you'll require a fleet of war.'

'Not Africa, Will. I agree, that would be to challenge Lisbon throughout the journey. Cape Horn. We'll follow Magellan and Drake. And Tom Candish.'

'I suspect the Portuguese will be less formidable than the Spaniards, Master Houtman.'

'The Dons will not even know we have sailed until we are in their midst, Will. And it will be all to the good, for then we shall be supposed on a piratical expedition, whereas we shall already be on our way across the South Sea.'

'We?' Will asked.

'I have five ships, Will. The *Hoop* will be flagship, and Jacques here will command. She is two hundred and fifty tons, and carries one hundred and thirty men. A stout ship, Will. The *Trouw* is one hundred and fifty tons and carries one hundred and nine men. Simon de Cordes will command, and he will be admiral and second-in-command of the fleet. The *Liefde* is one hundred and sixty tons, and carries one hundred and ten men; Pieter Benninghen is captain. The *Geloof* is one hundred tons, and carries eighty-six men. Sabalt de Wert is captain. And the *Blijde Boodschap* is seventy-five tons, and carries fifty-six men. Jan Bockholt is captain. Each ship will be armed and equipped to withstand any action by the Spaniards, you may be sure of that.'

'Aye,' Will said. 'Around the Horn, and across the South Sea. We are speaking here of not less than a year, Master Houtman.'

'I have the provision lists here. Bread, salted meat, wine . . . '

Will glanced down the scrawled figures.

'And there will be places to trade, Will, in America,' Houtman added. 'The Indians there do not all acknowledge the rule of Madrid.'

'It is a most carefully considered venture, Master Adams,' Mahu said. 'How carefully, you may consider from our decision to come here to speak with you. Master Houtman is determined to have the best men available and it is his decision that *you* are the best navigator to be found. We offer you the position of pilot major. You will sail in the *Hoop*.'

'And the others?'

Mahu glanced at Houtman.

'We had thought of Tim Shotten, and your brother Tom.'

'Good men,' Will agreed. 'If I say so myself.'

'And there is Tom Spring, as well. I have heard good reports of him.' Houtman slapped Will on the shoulder. 'Naught but English pilots for my fleet, Will. Only the best for Cornelius Houtman. I would I could accompany you, myself.'

'But you will not?'

'A year, and perhaps longer, is too much for me, Will. I have my business to be seen to. But I shall await your return with the more eagerness, you may be sure of that. You will carry cloth. The natives of the Spice Islands are eager to yield their pepper for our patterned fabrics. I tell you, Will, this will be the voyage of your life. Of all our lives. I feel it in my bones.'

Will gazed at the chart, and seemed to see the tavern in Limehouse and the faces of Tim Shotten and Kit Marlowe. Around the Horn, and across the South Sea. To fabled Cathay? To Tamburlaine and Zenocrate? No. To Java and a cargo of pepper. And yet, how his blood tingled at the thought of merely being in those waters. For had he not spent too many years dreaming of them, and of what he might find there?

'You accept the post, Master Adams?' Mahu asked.

Will gazed at them; Mahu, serious but anxious; Quaeckernaeck, no less serious, but more confident, perhaps because of his youth; and young Zandvoort, smiling and eager. These would be his companions through eternity. 'Oh, aye, Sir Jacques,' he said. 'I accept the post.'

'Are you there, Thomas Spring?' Timothy Shotten elbowed his way through the throng crowding the waterfront to shake the young man by the hand. 'Welcome to you. You've met Will Adams?'

'That I have, Master Shotten.' Spring held out his hand; for all his youth his face was sufficiently weatherbeaten to suggest many long weeks at sea. 'I'm glad to be in your company, Master Adams.'

'You speak of me as if I were famous. This is my brother, Tom.'

'My pleasure, Master Thomas.' Spring gazed at the waiting dory, at the onlookers, not one so excited as himself, then up at the brilliantly blue June sky, half turned his head to feel the gentle breeze on his cheek. The hot sun gave colour even to the turgid waters of the Thames, helped to alleviate the foetid squalor of the decrepit, grimy warehouses which lined the river bank, picked out the women's bright flounces and the reds and yellows of the men's breeches. 'A good day for it, eh, Master Adams?'

'A good day for the commencement of a good venture,' Will agreed. 'You'll have sailed with the Hollanders before, Master Spring?'

'No, sir, I have not,' Spring confessed. 'But I have heard nothing but good of them, as seamen.'

'You'll find that to be true enough,' Tom Adams said. 'Providing that you remember they expect the best from their pilots.'

'The tide is turning now, Will,' Tim Shotten said. 'We'd best be on our way.'

Will nodded, and crossed the dock, the spectators parting to let him through. Mary waited with her daughter. 'Well, sweethearts. The tide is right for our passage down the river.'

Mary nodded. 'Now, look, I am about to weep.'

'You, dear wife? Now tell me this, how many times have we not said farewell at these very steps, and made an even heartier greeting on my return?'

'I know not how I stood any of them,' she said. 'When I was younger I was less concerned about the future. And then, what is a voyage to the Barbary Coast, into the Mediterranean itself, or down the coast of Africa, compared with this venture?'

'A matter of a few more miles? Besides, I have Tom and Tim to look after me. What man could be in better hands. And look, they are all embarked. You would not have the pilot major be the cause of our missing the tide?'

She rested a hand on each arm, and her fingers ate into his flesh. 'You chide me gently, Will. You have always been uncommonly patient with me. And yet I swear you have not always felt so.'

'I am a man, and therefore given to changing moods.'

'And therefore given to passion, you mean. Oh, Will, Will, when will you return?'

He shrugged. 'A year. Perhaps two.'

'Or never?'

'What nonsense.'

'Is it, Will? As you say, you have been away from my side so often in the past, yet never have I felt such foreboding. Perhaps it is this which calls our life to mind. I have been happy, Will. This I swear. I wish you could do the same.'

'Then I shall, willingly.'

'I said could, Will. Not would, or shall. I would not have you lie to me. Hurry to your voyage, husband. Come back with your pockets filled with gold. And go to sea no more.'

Will gazed into the cool grey eyes. When she spoke like this, she was again the maid he had courted, nine long years before. When she looked like this she could reawaken all the passion he had once felt for her, and still experienced in the loneliness of his mind. But this was a delusion. She had consented to his embrace last night, because he was leaving her for upwards of a year. That had been her duty, and it had been so performed. Her duty, to yield herself up to such of her husband's desires as could not be mastered by commonsense and prayer.

'Husband?' Mary Adams asked. 'You will not grant me that wish?'

He kissed her on the cheek. 'We'll talk of it when I return, sweet Mary. God watch over you and the child.'

———◆———

A whisper seeped through Osaka Castle. 'Hideyoshi is dying,' it said. The lords in the antechamber heard it first, and exchanged fearful glances; except during the last ten years, Japan had known no peace for five centuries. Now Toyotomi Hideyoshi was dying, and suddenly the horizon was again clouded.

The guards heard it as it crept along the corridor, and insensibly stiffened to attention. Many of them were veterans. They had followed Hideyoshi for close on forty years, watched him rise by sheer merit from the ranks to a command, and by sheer determination from a mere general to dictator of all Japan. He had aspired to no other title than Kwambaku, or Regent. Regent for the defunct Shogunate, the military rulers who had held Japan in fief for so long? Regent for the Emperors in Kyoto? Or Regent for the gods themselves? The soldiers preferred the last.

The whisper reached the women's quarters, and Asai Yodogimi.

No veteran here; Yodogimi was not yet thirty. But hardly less of a veteran in the intrigue that surrounded Hideyoshi's bedchamber.

The whisper reached her as she slept, and she sat up to gaze at the officer in disbelief. Disbelief, firstly, that a captain of the palace guard should be here at all, attending the bedside of the Kwambaku's lady at so early an hour in the morning. Disbelief at what he said came afterwards.

Yet for the moment his presence was the more important. He was younger even than she. Not tall, although far taller than her master, he had small, delicate features, which fitted well with his small, delicate hands. His body was that of a boy. Perhaps he was no more than a boy. A boy who worshipped the Moon, and had now found his way into her chamber, as a harbinger of death.

She moved the heavy black hair from her forehead, allowed it to rest on her back. And what did he see in her? She was without paint, without protection of any sort, only the quilt pulled to her neck. He saw her as no man save Hideyoshi had looked on her since she had left her father's house. He saw the beauty that was truly there, the beauty, it was said, that had driven Hideyoshi from his mind, turned him from the rightful paths of both domestic and national policy, made him disown his legal son in favour of what he could extract from this woman's loins. Hideyoshi had been fifty-seven when he came to her bed, already exhausted with more than thirty years of continuous campaigning, and continuous fathering, and yet within a year she had been pregnant.

She knew what was said of her. Her enemies had sought her lover amongst the lords, amongst even the guards. Yet Hideyoshi had never doubted, and had claimed his son. But the boy was yet only five years old, and now his protector was dying. Or would the terror of his name live on?

In any event, she would need every possible friend, within the palace and without it. So what did this boy see, now? The most beautiful woman in Japan? The high forehead, the small straight nose, the tiny eyes which seemed no more than window slits in the smooth brown flesh, the suddenly wide mouth which could smile with such looseness, the pointed chin? Or merely the mistress of his lord?

She half smiled. 'You are too bold, Ono Harunaga.'

He supposed she had not heard him. 'My lady, the Kwambaku is dying. The last fit all but extinguished life, and it is said he will not survive another. And so I came to you, my lady.'

Or did he wish more? The quilt slipped, before she had intended it. The smoothest shoulder in all Japan, Hideyoshi had said. Once. How long ago. And beneath that, the sweetest breast.

The quilt was hastily restored to her throat. 'He has sent for me?'

'He murmured your name, my lady. It could have been a summons.'

'Then I must go to him.' The quilt was forgotten around her waist as she clapped her hands. But boldness deserved reward. She would remain mistress of these surroundings only by obtaining the unswerving loyalty of Hideyoshi's captains, and the young ones, being the most pliable, were also the most important. 'Remain, Ono Harunaga.'

'Yes, my lady.' The soldier bowed from the waist. Yodogimi was already surrounded by the three girls, raising her from her mattress, escorting her to the far end of the chamber, removing her sleeping kimono. She crouched on the slatted wooden floor beyond the tatami mats, and shivered as the cold water was emptied over her shoulders, the soap applied to her back. For even if her lord might die at any moment, no lady could begin her day without first purifying herself from head to toe.

Another bucket of cold water, to rinse away the soap, and she was ready for the bath itself, waiting, steaming, sunk into the floor at the very end of the chamber. Yodogimi entered the near boiling water with a slight shudder; the heat brought the blood to the surface of her flesh, seemed to fill the small breasts. Her hair had already been piled on her head. This was the work of Magdalena. Sweet Magdalena. The half-caste girl was seated on the lip of the bath, also naked, up to her knees in the water, kneading her mistress's scalp with her strong fingers. 'What will become of us, my lady?' she whispered.

Yodogimi leaned back, her head resting on Magdalena's knees, her own legs outstretched and floating. She closed her eyes, waited for the other two girls to massage her limbs, slowly inhaled as their fingers stroked up and down between her thighs, between her toes, awoke her muscles and soothed her spirit. No questions from them. They knew their places. Magdalena, because of her Portuguese ancestry and her belief in the Christian God, had a different, even a dangerous concept of a woman's place in the order of things, because she carried her concept to every woman and not just those ordained by fate and the gods to be above the rest. Yodogimi supposed that in her heart the girl even presumed herself the equal of her mistress. A fault of youth; Magdalena was but sixteen years of age. And yet . . . she moved her head, parting the girl's thighs so that she could rest against the softness of her belly, felt the instinctive hardening of the muscles on either side of her ears before they too relaxed with pleasure . . . who could say for sure that the girl was wrong? Again, because of her European grandfather, she *was* different. Yodogimi tilted her head, working it against the stomach behind her, looked up. She could see little beyond the high, pointed nipples. Different. All different. In this case, perhaps grotesque. A woman, to be beautiful, should possess breasts just large enough to fill a man's hand; not so large and thrusting as to hold a garment away from the body. But if Magdalena's breasts were abnormal, there could be no gainsaying the beauty of *her* face. Here the contrast between her and the other girls was no less marked, but all to her advantage; the enormousness of her liquid eyes matched the colour, green like the sea, and perhaps as deep; the surprising tint of red in the darkness of her hair, like sunlight drifting through a cypress wood, fitted the smooth cheekbones and rounded chin, which gave her face the shape of a heart. Scarce a man saw the girl but looked at her twice; soon it would be time to find her a lover. Even the young officer, presented with the prospect of a glimpse of the Princess Yodogimi as she left her bath, kept allowing his gaze to stray to the beauty already displayed behind her head.

Of course, Magdalena's body would continue to be a problem. The swelling breasts were but a symptom of the whole. She was far too tall, and her legs were far too strong. It was a body which might provide great comfort, but could scarcely be called beautiful.

And now she was afraid. They were all afraid. But only Magdalena would show her fear.

Had the captain heard her whisper? Or did he just seek to improve his position? He moved round the bedclothes, although carefully remaining on the far side of the room. 'You must be present, my lady Yodogimi, should the Kwambaku die.'

'He will not die,' she said softly. 'Except in my presence. Has the Tokugawa prince arrived?'

'Prince Iyeyasu has not yet arrived, my lady. But he has been summoned.'

Yodogimi sat up, extended her arms to be assisted from the

bath, was immediately wrapped in her robe. For just a second the boy had achieved his objective, and even across the room she could hear the whistle of his breath. Magdalena, also on her feet, glanced at the officer and flushed. She did this whenever a man gazed at her, even when fully clothed. The Christian in her. A strange teaching, certainly. One of more appeal to women than to men.

'It is to Prince Iyeyasu that we must look for support, my lady,' the boy whispered. 'He is more powerful than all the other daimyo together.'

Yodogimi glanced at him; the girls massaged her body through the thick drying robe. '*We*, boy?'

'I pledge my fealty, my lady Yodogimi. Unto death. There will be perilous times ahead.'

Yodogimi walked across her bedchamber, leaving damp patches on the mats, turned at the end, and looked at him. 'The Tokugawa prince is *the* most powerful daimyo, Harunaga. But even he cannot oppose the will of the rest, if they remain inspired by my lord Hideyoshi. We must first see what my lord has ordained for me. And for my son.'

Of what does a man think, when is dying. Of what *may* a man think, when he is dying? Especially such a man.

The room was dark, the floor was hard. 'Who is there?' Hideyoshi whispered.

'Ishida Mitsunari, my lord Hideyoshi.' The man's head lifted from the ground. A thin face, with a thin moustache. A proud face. No great lineage here, but a good Chief of Police. 'My son is with me.'

The other man also raised his head. 'Ishida Norihasa, my lord Hideyoshi.'

A youthful voice. He served his father. Policemen, at the deathbed of greatness. Was this to be his monument?

'My lady?' Hideyoshi whispered.

'Your lady wife awaits, my lord.'

'I wish to see my lady Yodogimi.'

'She has been summoned, my lord Hideyoshi; and Prince Iyeyasu is also on his way.'

'Iyeyasu.' Hideyoshi fell back on his wooden pillow, his mouth open, so that the policemen bent forward, supposing the moment come. 'Listen to me, Mitsunari. Remember my words. Iyeyasu would destroy my son.'

'My lord, have you and the prince not fought shoulder to shoulder for thirty years? Have not . . . ?'

'Listen to me, policeman. With me dead, there will be no one able to stand in the way of his ambition. I know it is said that the prince is lazy, and cares nothing for power, because he eats and drinks and whores to his heart's content. But tell me this, policeman: Does not eating and drinking and most of all, whoring, require vast energy? Is this not merely the behaviour of a man who has not yet found the proper outlet for his energy? Mitsunari . . . ' The small, wizened hand closed on the policeman's sleeve. 'Listen to me. Guard my son. And his mother. Guard them with your life.'

'This I swear, my lord Hideyoshi.'

'And you?' Hideyoshi's eyes flickered to the young man.

Norihasa bowed. 'I also, my lord Hideyoshi.'

'But wait,' Hideyoshi whispered. 'You think it will be a simple matter, of swords and arrows, of seppuku if you fail. But I will tell you this, policeman: Should you fail, then will I come back from the grave to rend you. Do not suppose the belly cut will absolve *my* vengeance.'

'While Princess Yodogimi and Prince Hideyori live, my lord, so shall my son and I in their service.'

'So listen. Prince Iyeyasu will not oppose my son by force, at least without careful preparation. Yet must I appoint him to the regency. The other four lords I shall name are as nothing, by themselves. Together they may oppose him. But they must act together, and for my son, always. This will be your responsibility, Mitsunari.'

'I understand, my lord Hideyoshi. But I wonder if it would not have been better . . . '

'To have given you a place amongst them, Mitsunari?' Hideyoshi's twisted face almost appeared to smile. 'Beware, policeman, beware. You are a man of much talent, much ambition. Thus I made you what you are. But you are still only a blackbird, flitting from tree to tree, and Iyeyasu is an eagle, soaring above the common plain. He would destroy you in seconds, Mitsunari, were you ever to oppose him openly. And yet, the blackbird is not so helpless as he seems. Unlike the eagle, he moves close to the earth, unseen, unnoticed. And who knows, a thousand blackbirds may yet suffice to bring down one eagle, should their attacks be co-ordinated. Remember my words, Mitsunari. Whatever I say from now on, whatever I promise, whatever I instruct, the future of Prince Hideyori is in your hands.'

'And I shall not betray your trust, my lord Hideyoshi. This I have sworn. And my son, should I fail, will swear to do the same. While your son lives, so shall we, to fight for his honour.'

'This I swear,' Norihasa said.

'And for the honour of his mother,' Hideyoshi whispered.

'And for the honour of the lady Yodogimi, my lord Hideyoshi.' Mitsunari half turned his head as the doors to the chamber slid open, and the majordomo bowed from the waist.

'My lord Tokugawa, Prince Minamoto-no-Iyeyasu,' he said, speaking more quietly than usual.

As befitted the Kwambaku's oldest friend, Iyeyasu had left his armour and long sword in the antechamber, and donned the crimson ceremonial robe. He did not look like a warrior; his features were too jovial, and his body too plump, although this day he was looking suitably solemn. He advanced half way across the room, and then dropped to his knees, placing his hands flat on the tatami mats which covered the floor and bending forward from the waist until his head almost touched the rice straw. But for the Tokugawa chieftain the kowtow was merely a formality. Scarcely had he inclined than Hideyoshi was motioning him upright again.

Iyeyasu advanced to the side of the dying man and lowered himself to the mat. He glanced to his left, at the two Ishida.

'Leave us,' Hideyoshi whispered.

Mitsunari and his son bowed, and withdrew to the screen doorway. From here they watched Iyeyasu bend forward to catch Hideyoshi's words, his expression unchanging.

'My lord father,' Norihasa whispered. 'What my lord Hideyoshi said was true. With him dead, Prince Iyeyasu *is* the obvious ruler of Japan. Nor can we deny that he alone has the power, and the wisdom, to keep the peace. To attempt to destroy him in favour of a five-year-old boy is to do no favour to our country.'

'Yet have we sworn,' Mitsunari said. 'And we shall keep our oaths. Hideyoshi spoke no more than the truth when he called us his creatures. We can only transfer our allegiance to the princess now, for be sure that as we dream of destroying Iyeyasu, he has already determined to destroy us.' He stepped round the screen, into the antechamber. On the far side of the huge room there waited a group of ladies; the consort, Sugihara, and her entourage. But they were no longer of importance. Hideyoshi had made his wishes known throughout the land; his action, in elevating a concubine above his wife, had been criticised by many, but there was no man in all Japan would openly oppose the Kwambaku, living. And Mitsunari, with all the vast information at the disposal of his police system, did not think there would be many interested in opposing *that* decision, even after the Kwambaku was dead.

More dangerous was the group of young men at the rear of the room. These were the Tokugawa princes, Iyeyasu's sons and sons-in-law; the true secret of his strength. Each of the six was an acknowledged territorial lord, with possibly thirty thousand men on call.

A vast rustle filled the room, and all heads turned. The Princess Asai Yodogimi entered, her son beside her. Her face was painted white, her teeth dyed black; her kimono was white silk, and she carried a matching fan in her left hand; her hair lay in a black shawl on her shoulders and down her back, all but brushing the floor. Hideyori also wore white, the colour of grief; his tiny shoulders were hunched and his face tightly closed, less perhaps with sorrow than with uncertainty.

The pair were followed by Yodogimi's three women and two soldiers. Men she had chosen? Or men who had chosen her, already? Mitsunari's eyes narrowed as he identified them. Two brothers, named Ono. Officers of the guard. They commanded no forces other than their regiments. Surely of no account in what might lie ahead.

Yodogimi motioned her women to halt, and herself advanced, her son still clutching her hand. Mitsunari bowed from the waist, and his son followed his example; but the young man's gaze searched the gloom beyond the princess, seeking the height of Pinto Magdalena.

'The policemen,' Yodogimi remarked, with faint contempt. 'Does my lord Hideyoshi await me?'

'He asks for you, my lady Yodogimi,' Mitsunari said. 'But for the moment the Tokugawa is with him.'

Yodogimi half turned, her brows knitting, a careless expression of concern which threatened to crack her paint. 'Should this not encourage me to enter with more haste?'

'I should counsel waiting, my lady Yodogimi,' Mitsunari said. 'My lord Hideyoshi may well have words for your ears alone.'

'You are a wily fellow, policeman. But then, I suppose cunning is part of your profession.' Yodogimi gazed across the room at her rival. 'And she? Does my lord Hideyoshi have no words for his wife?'

'No, my lady Yodogimi. You have nothing to fear from *that* quarter.'

Yodogimi glanced at him.

'Prince Iyeyasu leaves,' Norihasa whispered.

Iyeyasu slowly left the Kwambaku's chamber, pausing in the doorway. His sons moved forward, protectively. The prince bowed to Yodogimi. 'My lady, you will understand how heavy is my heart this day. There can have been no greater disaster in the history of Japan.'

Yodogimi's nostrils dilated. Did she fear him? Mitsunari wondered. Or was there more? The Tokugawa chieftain was the most renowned lecher in the country. And Yodogimi was the most beautiful woman in the country. Strange, that they should never have done more than look at one another. No, not strange, so long as Hideyoshi lived and ruled. But with Hideyoshi dead . . .

'No doubt, my lord Iyeyasu,' Yodogimi said, 'my lord Hideyoshi bestowed upon you some last words of advice and recommendation.'

'Indeed, my lady Yodogimi.' Iyeyasu raised his voice, to make sure it was heard by everyone in the chamber. 'My lord Hideyoshi vouchsafed into my keeping a grave responsibility.' He rested his hand upon Hideyori's head. 'He knows the danger of minority, the risks of a resumption of the internicine warfare which has bled Japan white for five centuries. This must not happen. My lord Hideyoshi will not have it happen. And so he said to me, I bequeath the whole country to you, Iyeyasu, and trust that you will expend all your strength in governing it. My son Hideyori is still young. I beg that you will look after him. When he is grown up, I leave it to you to decide whether he shall be my successor or not.'

PART TWO

The Soldier

Chapter 1

A GREY MIST, a grey sky, a grey universe. Because it was dawn. Another dawn, bringing an end to another night. Last night had been clear; Will could remember the stars, seeming so low in the heavens he had felt he could reach out and grasp them in his hands, thrust them into his pockets to warm him, and keep out the cold, to resist the fingers of death. But this morning there was mist. His instincts, his long-forgotten knowledge of the sea, told him this had meaning. Mist, creeping across the surface of the sea . . . but he was too tired to consider the matter, too exhausted in body and spirit to try to remember, to try to calculate. To try to do.

Yet, as it was grey, and therefore dawn, he must once again drive himself onwards. For how many dawns had he done this?

He sat up, slowly. He was not aware of any pain, beyond the dull grind in the pit of his empty belly. His belly, and his head. His head swung so much it hurt. His head was a strange place, nowadays. A place of fantasies and nightmares, but of good things, too. A place so bedevilled with memory that it was sometimes difficult to separate fact from fancy. Last night, for instance, had been spent with Mary. Not the Mary he remembered. This Mary had been the girl of his dreams, tall and strong, large-breasted and wide-hipped, and anxious, to give. It had been a night to remember. Except that when he had reached for her, he had fallen flat on his face, too weak to move any farther.

And on his face he had remained. Slowly he pushed himself up. How the damp clung to his bones. It seemed inside his bones. He cleared his eyes, slowly. His every movement was too slow. Thus he had slept on deck. It took too long to get below, and it would take far too long to climb back up the ladder, should there be cause during the night.

But his brain was also an endless court of law, every dawn, when he was at his freshest. Where, how, when had disaster struck, the first time? The death of Jacques Mahu. By God, that was all but two years ago. They had put into the Cape Verde Islands, for fresh meat. And taken aboard more than meat. Some kind of fever, which had destroyed too many men, amongst them the general, and left them to the hasty decisions of Simon de Cordes.

Yet it had been Mahu's dying wish that they should make Cape Lopez, on the south-western coast of Africa. He had been there before, remembered a safe anchorage, and a supply of fresh food. Poor Jacques Mahu. Already no doubt he had been delirious. Cape Lopez had been a disaster, where the natives had attempted ambush, and where again there had been fever. Thus Annabon. The Portuguese island was only a day's sail from the African coast, and there at the least had they been sure of sustenance. Annabon had been Simon de Cordes' first decision. And it had been taken simply enough; the Portuguese and their African women had preferred to abandon their township and take to the woods rather than oppose so strong a fleet. Yet had de Cordes not been satisfied, but must mount an expedition into the forest to chastise the hated Papists, only once again to encounter an ambush and lose nine men, amongst them poor Tom Spring. In revenge the Hollanders had burned the town. Will thought the sight of those flames, clinging to the eastern horizon, would follow him forever. With all their food stolen, with their houses destroyed, and with winter coming on, the settlement was doomed. That was hardly even piracy. That was wanton destruction.

From that moment the expedition, already dogged by misfortune, had turned sour. They had fought their way across the South Atlantic, against invariably contrary winds, and had yet made the Strait of Magellan just before the onset of the southern winter. And here the winds had been fair. Two, three days, and they would have been in the South Sea. But de Cordes must drop anchor, and repair his ships, and search for water and fresh meat. So the men had been so hungry they had been gnawing the leather baggywrinkles intended to stop the sheets chafing on the rigging; hunger was preferable to remaining a winter in the Strait. For within a week the snow had started falling, and the ships had been iced in. They had stayed on Penguin Island from April to October, buffeted by icy winds, no less hungry, assailed by savage Indians, quarrelling amongst themselves, and dying. Only the dying had been consistent, inevitable, unchanging.

And yet the weather had changed. With the coming of spring they had set forth once again, with some confidence, only to be greeted by a tremendous storm on the far side of the Strait, and scattered for the last time. They had at least had the foresight to arrange a rendezvous, on the coast of South America at the forty-sixth latitude. But only two ships, the *Hoop* and the *Liefde*, had made the rendezvous. What had happened to the others? To the *Geloof* and the *Trouw*? God alone knew, if He still cared. The American natives, so quaintly called Indians by the Spaniards, had told them that the *Blijde Boodschap* had been taken, and in her capture had alerted the entire coast to the Dutch presence. But by then, did it matter? For by then Simon de Cordes was dead, killed in an assault upon the island of Mocha, in the endless search for food. And by then, too, Tom Adams was dead. He had fallen to the American Indians, and twenty-two others with him, ambushed and destroyed while their comrades had looked on helplessly from the decks of their ships.

He had thought then that no other disaster could, or would, matter. Tom and he had not been as close as some brothers, perhaps. Tom had not approved of his friendship with Marlowe, and in recent years had found him too withdrawn and unsociable. He had spent more time in the company of Tim Shotten. Yet had he followed his elder brother with utter faith, on voyage after voyage after voyage. To be torn to pieces by savage Indians scarce deserving the name of humans.

He had, no doubt, still been too affected by grief to play his proper part in that unforgettable conference in the great cabin of the *Hoop* when the two ships had at last found each other, off the island of St Maria, some twenty miles from the Peruvian coastline. Eight men had assembled then, representing the combined ships' companies of fifty-four. Fifty-four, where four hundred and ninety-one had sailed from Rotterdam. There was the price of pepper.

They had faced each other, across the table, the two newly elected captains, Max Hudcopee and Jacob Quaeckernaeck, the two mates, Derrick Gerritson and Gilbert de Conning, the two factors, Jan van Owater and Melchior Zandvoort, and the two remaining pilots, Tim Shotten and Will Adams. And they had debated, not the prospect of saving their lives, for that had no longer seemed possible, but the prospect of ending them in the least disagreeable manner.

And they had elected to continue on their way. Where? Across the ocean, certainly. There had been no question of turning back; no man on board either vessel would face the Horn again. So, Java? Too weak to fight the Portuguese, or even to load the pepper? Supposing the Javanese would trade. Gerritson had spoken of a place called Cipangu, an island kingdom off the coast of China. He had been to the Spice Islands before, round the Cape of Good Hope, and while there had taken passage in a Chinese junk which had been wrecked on the southernmost coast of this fabled place. Cipangu and Cathay were at continual war, he had said, and yet the disabled seamen had been granted every care, and finally returned to Java on one of their own junks. In Cipangu, according to Gerritson, they would find succour.

And what else? What of the dreams with which they had started this voyage? Will Adams in particular. A dream of wealth, certainly. Of fame. For the man who could pilot a Dutch fleet around the world and back into the mouth of the Texel would never again lack for reputation. And of what else? Gerritson had used names he had not heard since Kit's death. Cathay. Fabled Peking. The Great Khan. Cipangu? Marlowe had known nothing of Cipangu. As Gerritson had known nothing of Zenocrate. Because she did not exist. So then, Will Adams, confess it, you have sailed half way around the world, and seen better than four hundred men die, for love of another man's creation. Could any man be that honest? Or that mad? And yet, could he deny that? Could he honestly claim to wish more than that? Would he not forget all, fame, fortune, the world of men, to gain such a love as Marlowe had described?

Cipangu lay close to Cathay. That was sufficient. There remained only the getting there. The crossing of six thousand miles of terrible ocean, in ships already leaking and rotting, with scarce sufficient men to man the sails, much less the guns.

They had debated burning one of the vessels and combining in the other. And decided against it; Hudcopee would not burn the *Hoop*, and Quaeckernaeck would not burn the *Liefde*. Stubbornness was so often a prescription for disaster. They had quarrelled, and parted on bad terms. Hudcopee had cursed at Will, and Will had cursed back, with the result that the pilots had exchanged ships, Will taking Quaeckernaeck and the *Liefde*, and Tim, Hudcopee and the *Hoop*. Tim had been for burning *both* ships and taking to the shore as buccaneers. But the others, with the memories of the screams of Pieter Benninghen and Tom Adams as they had died, still fresh in their ears, had refused that suggestion. So they had sailed.

He reached the hatchway, after what seemed an eternity, and

looked down at the deserted tiller. But the ropes still held, and the wooden bar moved to and fro, brought up by the restraining lines, maintaining the bow of the ship before the wind. The wind, since the great storm, had remained true. At least, it remained astern. As if that mattered, now. It came from the south-east, and therefore drove them to the north-west, endlessly. He picked up his log board, gazed at the scrawled figures. It took him several seconds to establish the fact of them in his brain. Because they, too, were meaningless. According to the chart, Cipangu lay in the thirty-second degree of north latitude. He had read off that sight from his astrolabe two days ago. But still no land. Oh, there had been that island on the horizon. But that had clearly been only an island, so small and barren as to be unable to support life. Yet would he have put in there for the sake of the catchments of water he might find had he the strength to alter course, to trim the yards himself, to drop and then raise the anchor himself. Failing that, he must let the *Liefde* plough onwards, for ever and ever, until she ran into the snows and ice of the Arctic. How remarkable if, having failed in his attempt to discover a passage from Europe to the East by way of travelling east around the North Cape, he returned to Europe by travelling west, around the North Cape. Truly was he being fanciful this morning.

Melchior Zandvoort dragged himself to his feet holding on to the gunwale, disturbed by Will's perambulations. He also had slept on the poop. He stayed close to Will. They were the strongest. De Conning and van Owater might still be able to move, and one or two of the others, but only Melchior and himself could risk going aloft. As if they had any reason to go aloft.

Melchior slowly extended the telescope, swept the horizon. He did this every day. For no man could tell, one morning the *Hoop* might be there, proudly riding in their wake. So thought the Hollanders. They were more optimistic, and less experienced than himself. The *Hoop* had been taking water even before the great storm. So had the *Liefde*, but not sufficient to overwhelm the pumps. The *Hoop* had ridden low in the sea. He remembered that evening, exchanging his usual wave with Tim Shotten, and remarking to himself how she seemed to have sunk into the waves. And those waves had still been small. Not calm. The wind had already been whistling, and whipping the crests into spin-drift. But not a storm, then. Only the horizon, black, black as midnight, wherever they looked, had promised disaster. And the *Hoop* had already been low in the water.

'There is nothing, Will.' Melchior Zandvoort let the arm holding the telescope droop, and drooped with it. He was most optimistic of them all. Perhaps because he was strongest of them all. Will thought he was stronger even than himself. Who would have thought it, of such a diminutive lad? But then, perhaps he needed less sustenance to maintain his strength. He remembered Melchior calling him from his berth, that night, with shouts of pleasure. The wind had dropped, suddenly, remarkably. Not the sea. The swell remained, huge, running from the south-east, so high that the lights of the *Hoop* disappeared entirely in each trough, only to reappear triumphantly on the top of the following mountain. A swell such as he had never seen before, and prayed that he would never see again. For now he knew what it foretold.

But then, he had been as pleased as Melchior, had gone back to his bunk with an easy heart, and been awakened again, an hour before dawn, when the end of the world had come close upon them. Why did seamen fear the Strait, when there was *this* beyond? Because the Strait was always bad, the great ocean only occasionally? But necessarily at least once, in a crossing.

So they had driven on, for five days, with not a stitch of canvas set, yet running as fast as on any previous occasion in his life, hurtling through day and night, unable to move, unable to eat, unable to speak, sometimes, he thought, unable to breathe. And at the end of it all, they had been alone. So Melchior searched the horizon every morning, for a sight of a sail. Only Melchior now. The others knew better, if they knew at all. Will had known from that first night. The *Hoop* lay at the bottom of the sea, her crew grinning cadavers, her masts coral-encrusted pillars of eternity.

If they knew at all. They had known then, those others, that they were doomed, and they placed their situation at the door of but a single man. He had not had the heart to resist them. For indeed was he damned. Tom was dead, and now Tim. And some four hundred and fifty others.

How much of this truly lay at his door? His spirit alone was driving them onwards. Onwards and onwards and onwards. Perhaps, had de Cordes acted on his advice and kept on through the Strait last April—*last* April, a full year ago—this might have been avoided. Or might have arrived sooner. Certainly he had voted for the decision to stand for Cipangu. He shared that responsibility with Derrick Gerritson, and poor Derrick was now dead, lost with the *Hoop*. As was Tim. Tim had always warned against attempting the crossing. He had done it once, and had no wish to repeat the horror of that experience. He had said so, on that long-forgotten night in the alehouse, when they had been interrupted by Marlowe. Marlowe. For how much of what had happened had he, with his flights of the utmost fancy, in reality been responsible? A poet, a man who knew nothing of the sea, nothing of life, really, save the squalid pleasures he could find in and around London Town—the pleasures which had ultimately killed him—but who had possessed the inestimable power to dream, and to inspire others to do the same.

But even Marlowe, for all his crimes, had no effect now. Even his shipmates had turned against him. He had been saved by Melchior, and by Quaeckernaeck. When de Conning and van Owater and the rest would have seized him and thrown him after the *Hoop*, these two had stepped between. Melchior's intention had been no more than to die with his friend, if need be. Quaeckernaeck had negotiated. 'However much Will is to blame for our predicament,' he had said, 'you cannot deny, my friends, that as we *are* in a predicament, none other than Will can possibly extricate us.' Quaeckernaeck had saved his life.

He lurched down the ladder, bent over the water barrel. There were four of these on deck now, because sometimes it rained, or sometimes there was an accumulation of dew. This morning there was an accumulation of dew. Not enough to fill a cup and take below, to where the others lay, dying or perhaps already dead. Enough to wet his lips, as he drew his finger round the edge. Enough for Melchior's lips as well. He must send him down.

He knew better than to try the galley. They trailed lines astern and had caught fish, from time to time. To be eaten raw, as they had long since run out of fuel, or indeed of the strength of mind to resist food while it cooked. But yesterday they had caught nothing. He must try the lines, now. Try the lines. How simple a phrase. For him it would mean an endless hour of agony as he willed his muscles to work, as the tarred rope cut into his fingers, as his brain spun and his blood turned to water.

He climbed the ladder once again. His daily duty. Down the ladder—that was simple enough; it was a matter of checking his slide at the bottom—and then up again. A long process this, hand over hand over hand, resting every third step, clutching the balustrade, panting as if he had run a mile. And all for what? Would it not be simpler to give up and die? Would it not have been simpler to do this yesterday? Last week? Last month? Would it not have been *better* to do this, last year?

Melchior Zandvoort knelt, leaning against the gunwale, staring up at the mast. Perhaps he was praying. Praying for what? There was nothing up there, save the sky. There had never been anything. For all of their lives, they had been deluded by the dream of protection from the heavens. Now they knew better. But what of the untold millions of others, who would not share their knowledge until it was too late?

Or perhaps Melchior was dead. Certainly he never moved.

'Melchior?' Will whispered.

Melchior's head turned, slowly. 'Will,' he said. 'Tell me I am not blind. Tell me, Will.'

Will shrugged, reached the poop deck, and sat down. How exhausted he was. Why, already this day he had covered all of thirty feet, coming and going. 'It is the emptiness of your belly which induces fantasies.'

'Such as that?'

Will looked aloft. A bird sat on the mizzen yardarm, looking down at them. A bird. Just a bird. But it sang, gently. 'Great God in Heaven,' Will whispered. 'That is a lark.'

'A lark, Will,' Melchior shouted. 'I had thought so. A lark, Will. They do not fly far.'

Will crawled across the deck, reached the gunwale, pulled himself to his feet. Nothing out there. The mist hung close, scarce a cable's length in front of the ship, blanketing them in a grey half-light. But it was a sea mist, only to be found when there was a considerable temperature difference between nearby land and the surface of the sea. *This* was what he had sought to remember, earlier. The sea mist, and now the lark. And now . . . he leaned over the rail and gazed at the water. How green, how cold. How *green*. No longer the tremendous unending blue of the bottomless ocean. Green. Pale green. And momentarily growing paler, except where he could see patches of purple seaweed clinging to the bottom. The bottom.

Will swung away from the rail. 'Melchior,' he shouted. 'Melchior. On your feet, lad. Quickly, now. We must anchor.'

'Anchor?' Melchior stared at him. 'Are you demented, Will?'

'Maybe. But not so demented I will run us upon some reef. We have no strength to swim ashore, lad. We must stop ourselves. Come on.' He slid down the ladder, his muscles miraculously regaining at least some of their former power.

'Master Adams? What is the trouble?' Jan van Owater emerged from the forecastle like a sleep walker.

'Land, Jan, land,' Will bellowed. 'Not just an island. The sea is too shallow, and for too great a distance. We must anchor, and quickly.'

He clambered up on to the bows. Melchior staggered behind him. And now men came out of the forecastle. Van Owater and Gilbert de Conning, and even two others. Who'd have thought there were six men left able to move on board the ship? But there they were, helping him heave on the windlass. And a moment later there was a splash as the anchor cut through the waves; still carried onwards by the gentle breeze, the *Liefde* rode over her chain, which continued to pay out until Will snubbed it with the brake, estimating a good thirty fathoms had gone. The ship then came round in a circle, facing up to the wind, the sails now drooping from the yards, and the yards slapping the shrouds.

''Tis certainly shallow.' Gilbert de Conning peered into the mist. 'But where is your land, Master Adams?'

'It is there, man. There. And surely this mist will lift, when the sun is properly high. Now aloft with you and furl that canvas.' Will ran down the ladder, all but fell at the bottom, regained his balance and staggered towards the aftercastle. He tore open the door and burst into the great cabin. 'Jacob. Jacob. Are you there, Jacob?'

There was movement from the bunk, and a bag of bones and tight-drawn flesh, surmounted by a few wisps of strawlike hair, rolled to face him. 'I heard the cries. Land they say? What land, Will?'

Will sat down, so suddenly that his backbone jarred his brain. He put up his hand to clutch the pain, and found himself scratching his head instead. 'Why, as to that, Jacob, I have no idea at all. But should it be heaven, or should it be hell, it will be better than the empty ocean.'

Heaven, or hell? He feared the latter. For surely these men came from no heaven. He stood at the gunwale with the six Hollanders able to keep their feet, and watched the boats approaching. Strange boats, indeed, relics of some bygone age, galleys such as were to be found in the Mediterranean, but scarce fit to traverse an ocean, with never a cabin or suggestion of a sail other than a single square sheet of canvas, indicating that should the wind be exactly right they, like the ancient Greeks and Romans, might be enabled to run before it.

And lacking, Will estimated, even a keel to prevent the leeway forced upon them by the wind.

Even the oars seemed too short. But this was not strange, for the men themselves were little fellows scarce larger than school-boys, with crisp black hair and hard-muscled, yellow-brown bodies. Those who pulled the oars wore little except a cloth around their loins, but in the stern of each craft were half a dozen warriors, each wearing a suit of iron scales, with an enormous flattened helmet, complete with nose-piece made in the replica of some hideous monster, and fashioned with false moustaches, also made of iron, so as to give their faces an aspect at once fearsome and faintly comical. There was nothing comical about their weapons, however, even if they seemed somewhat primitive to European eyes. Each man carried two swords, a long and a short, both stuck through the multicoloured sash around his waist, and in addition a spear and a bow of odd design, shaped not like the continuous powerful English yew, one piece of wood from tip to tip, but rather composed of several pieces, joined together, but yet as tall as the men themselves, and no doubt as powerful.

'What manner of people be those?' Gilbert de Conning whispered. 'Should we not load a cannon?'

'To what purpose?' Will demanded. 'Even supposing the six of us possessed the strength to run one out, and so could drive these creatures away, are we not all starving for lack of food? We must pray that they are less devilish than they appear.'

For certainly the land beyond was promising. The sun had now risen far enough to dispel the worst of the mist, and he could see the brown sand of the beach and then green fields which rose in gentle cultivated terraces to hills in the background, no less green, while away to the right he thought he could make out the roofs of a township. And what roofs. Even at this distance he could tell their strangeness.

'In any event,' Melchior said, 'have we anything to fear?' He pointed, and they saw the banner on the foremost vessel, a cross enclosed in a ring.

'Christians,' muttered Jan van Owater. 'Let us pray they are not Papists.'

For the brown men were bringing their fragile little galleys alongside and swarming up the chain plates.

'I like this very little,' Melchior whispered, standing close to Will. 'Shall I at least load a firepiece?'

Will glanced up the deck. Gilbert de Conning and Jan van Owater stood by the forecastle hatch with another man. The other twenty-odd members of the crew were below, most of them helpless. And there were more than fifty men at this moment appearing on the gunwales. Did they plan murder, then it was already done.

'Just be patient,' he muttered. 'And confident, Melchior. Nothing repels aggression better than confidence.'

He sucked air into his lungs, wished that his muscles possessed just a little strength and that his head would stop swinging for an instant, and faced the armour-clad figure which was first across the rail. At least this man had not troubled to draw either of his fearsome-looking swords, and he had raised his visor to reveal a young and remarkably pleasant countenance, with softly rounded features, at this moment looking suitably severe, but betrayed by the perpetual twinkle of the black eyes. And yet, the eyes themselves were unlike any Will had ever seen; they almost seemed to possess two lids, which made them appear narrower and larger than European eyes, mere slits in the smooth brown flesh.

'Right glad am I to see you, sir,' Will said. 'Welcome on board the *Liefde*, out of Amsterdam. You see us, sir, battered by an overlong crossing of the great sea. Our captain, Jacob Quaeckernaeck, lies below too weak to move. I am his sailing master, William Adams of Gillingham, in the county of Kent, England.'

The soldier stared at him, and in turn said something, speaking very quickly and with a somewhat high-pitched tone. His followers crowded the deck, running to and fro with excited cries, and already starting to investigate the hatches.

'Why not try him in Portuguese, Will?' Melchior whispered. 'They are reputed to have sailed these waters.'

'Fool that I am,' Will said, and repeated his speech in Portuguese.

The officer held up his hand. 'Speak slowly,' he said, also in Portuguese. 'You are from the empire of the Pope?'

Will glanced at Melchior, but as his friend did *not* understand the tongue there was no advice forthcoming there. And yet, to fly under false colours must necessarily soon betray them. He shook his head. 'From an even greater empire, sir. That of men owing allegiance only to God Himself.' How easily the words came to his lips. Words he no longer believed?

The officer gazed at him for some seconds, his brow slightly knitted. Then his face cleared. 'I am Shimadzu no-Tadatune.'

'My pleasure,' Will said. 'I am Will Adams.'

'Will Adams,' Tadatune repeated, and frowned as he saw Will shudder. 'You wish food?'

'Food, yes. And water. All our company. Many are sick.'

'They will have food,' Tadatune promised. 'You will accompany me.'

'But the others . . . '

'Will be looked after in turn. Now, please.'

'He wants us to go with him,' Will said in Dutch.

'Better not to argue,' Melchior suggested. 'He at least appears to be civilised.'

Will nodded, and glanced aft. The Japanese sailors were returning on deck, bringing clothes, belts, hats, boxes, brushes, combs, everything, it seemed, they could find.

'You'll excuse me, Master Tadatune,' he said. 'I must bid my captain farewell.'

Tadatune inclined his head, and Will hurried down to the great cabin, where Quaeckernaeck had contrived to rise on his elbow. 'God in Heaven, but I am glad to see you, Will,' he gasped. 'What manner of men are these?'

'Now that, Jacob, I cannot tell you as yet. But we are most certainly in their power, and they have promised to feed us and care for us.'

'And meanwhile they loot our ship,' Jacob grumbled.

For there were several men in the cabin, examining everything, and removing everything that could be removed.

'Not my charts, jackanapes,' Will growled, and ran to his berth. The man there was already fingering the astrolabe, holding it up to squint through the eyehole. 'Avast there,' Will bellowed in Portuguese, and the man dropped the instrument in surprise, turning round and reaching for his sword. 'I meant no harm,' Will assured him. 'But if you draw your weapon I'll be forced to break your head.'

The man clearly did not understand him, but he also obviously realised his meaning, and more, that in the confined space there was no room for him to display any swordsmanship. He backed and Will hastily seized his canvas wallet and stuffed into it a clean pair of drawers and a shirt, his charts and astrolabe, as well as his logboard and the parchment upon which he had kept his tally of daily reckonings. More than this he could not accumulate at such short notice; but here at least were the tools of his trade, was he ever to be allowed to practise it again.

He came on deck, where Tadatune and Melchior waited. The officer nodded and climbed over the gunwale and down into the waiting galley, beckoning them to follow. He gave a command, and the oars dipped into the water. Seated in the stern, Will glanced over his shoulder at the *Liefde*. It was the first time he had left the deck of the little vessel for four months. A long, terrible four months, coming upon a long and terrible year. Yet the *Liefde* had never failed them; suitably attended to, she was entirely capable of returning them to Europe. My God, he realised, this was the first time he had considered any future beyond surviving from day to day since leaving Penguin Island. Europe, once again, and Mary, and Deliverance. And there his pleasurable anticipation ended. For there was no possibility of the *Liefde* regaining the Texel with a mainsail of damask. He would return poorer than when he had set out, alike in wealth and reputation.

'A strange ship,' Tadatune remarked.

'Have you not seen her like before?' Will asked in surprise. 'And yet you speak the Portuguese tongue?'

'Portuguese ships are different,' Tadatune pointed out. 'Portuguese ships are large.' He held out his arms. 'And high.'

'And unwieldy, save well before the wind,' Will agreed. 'And what of your ships, Master Tadatune?'

The young man smiled. 'These.'

'These cockleshells? Now that is strange, Master Tadatune. A people living by the sea, and having no ambition to sail upon its waters? And yet you must be well acquainted with the world. As a Christian.'

'*I* am of the Faith,' Tadatune said. 'But my people, no.'

'But the flag?'

Tadatune glanced up. 'That is the crest of my family, the Shimadzu of Satsuma. We are the greatest lords of the southern island. It represents a horse's bit and bridle, not the cross.' Once again the ready smile. 'The priests also have been confused.' The galley, which had made remarkable speed, grounded in the shallows, and Tatadune leapt over the side, to turn, with his arms expanded. 'Welcome to Japan.'

Slowly and painfully Will clambered over the gunwale. 'And where might that be, Master Tadatune?'

'You will know it as Cipangu,' Tadatune said. 'That is from the Chinese, Nippon, which is in itself a corruption of Japan. The words mean "where the Sun rises". Here, Will Adams, on the shores of the ocean which houses the great lady of heaven herself, the sun goddess, is the beginning of all life. In the name of my uncle the Satsuma, in the name of the Kwambaku, Toyotomi Hideyori, son of the great Hideyoshi, and in the name of the Mikado himself, I bid you welcome.'

They walked along a road bordering the beach, towards the distant houses. There were other boats on the beach, but no suggestion of a breakwater, or even the rudiments of a harbour. And now the weakness was becoming unbearable. And yet he could not demean himself by stumbling and staggering, for now there were people, men, poorly dressed with bare feet and great flat hats, like upturned plates, on their heads, and women too, similarly clad, all solemnly dropping to the earth and touching it with their heads as the procession approached.

'Are these, then, slaves?' he asked Tadatune.

'They are farmers.'

'And count themselves so low? In my country a yeoman would scarce bend his knee to Her Majesty.'

'Yours must be a strange country, Will Adams,' Tadatune said. 'I am a samurai, the nephew of a daimyo. I am as far above these people as is the sun you see there above us as we walk here below. They have their place. They are certainly superior to any artisan or merchant, and far above any eta or honin.'

'What are they?'

'The eta are those unhappy beings who are forced to handle the flesh of dead animals.'

'Now that I do not understand at all,' Will confessed. 'How else do you live?'

'To take life, from any living creature, is a mortal sin, Will Adams,' Tadatune pointed out. 'Certainly from any animal. Perchance we seek to vary our diet, weak vessels that we are, by eating birds or catching fish; yet those who are obliged to kill these creatures will surely not be forgiven by the gods, and therefore must be counted lowest of the low.'

'And yet I observe that you carry two swords, Master Tadatune, and look as if you would use them well.'

'I, my friend, will never take life, except in battle, where it is honourable to do so. For indeed, how else may a samurai die? Like a dog in his bed? Thus the honin, that I mentioned. They are lower even than the eta, for it is their unhappy lot to handle the death of humans, either the execution of the criminal or the burial of the dead.'

Will scratched his head. 'And where, sir, should I come into this hierarchy? I am a simple shipmaster. Should I then crawl along upon my hands and knees beside you?'

Tadatune smiled. 'That we shall have to see, Will Adams. It will be ordered in due course. But everyone must have his place in society, and must *know* his place in society.'

'You mean that *you* would acknowledge a superior?'

'But of course. I am better than a mere samurai, that is to say, one entitled to bear arms; I am a hatamoto, which means literally a flag bearer. I command a regiment of men, who march beneath the flag of my uncle the Satsuma.'

'The daimyo?'

'That is correct. The word means a lord who holds lands in fief. Every daimyo in turn acknowledges the superiority of the Kwambaku, who is regent for the Shoguns, who in turn govern the empire in the name of the Emperor, the Mikado. I must yield in rank and property to any daimyo, just as any daimyo, even the Kwambaku, must yield in rank to the kuge.'

'Some sort of god, no doubt.'

Tadatune shook his head, and this time he did not smile. 'Do not joke about your betters, Will Adams. The kuge are the nobles of the Mikado's court in Kyoto. They have no land, but because they are the oldest families in the empire they are inferior only to the Mikado himself.'

'And the Mikado?'

Tadatune bowed towards the sun. 'The Mikado is the descendant and therefore the viceregent of the gods, and as such holds the entire empire in fief. Now come, we have arrived.'

They had entered the village he had seen from the ship. If it could be so called, for anything less like a street in London or Gillingham he could never have envisaged. The road itself was wide and unpaved, and therefore dusty, and yet lacking the ruts he would have expected. There was the apparently inevitable crowd of people gathered on each side in front of the houses, all wearing the loose gowns he had noticed earlier, and the wide hats, so that at first glance it was difficult to separate women from men. And what houses, if indeed they were houses, with deep sloping roofs erected over walls made of the thinnest wood, merely lacquered to give them at once a splendid appearance and some semblance of strength; but he never doubted that with a single blow of his fist he could enter any of them.

'You will find comfort here, Will Adams,' Tadatune said.

The largest house, certainly. But no more substantially built than the others. And how narrow; the doorway itself occupied almost the entire frontage of the street, suggesting enough space within to allow perhaps four men in the front hall. 'Your house, Master Tadatune?'

The young man smiled. 'I do not live in this village. This is the inn. There is an inn in every village for the comfort of weary travellers, and surely there can be no more weary travellers than yourselves. Now come, Magome Kageyu is anxious to bid you welcome.' He led the two Europeans up a short flight of steps, and here paused, stepping out of his sandals as he did so. 'You will take off your boots, Will Adams. And tell your companion to do likewise.'

'Sir?' Will demanded, glancing over his shoulder at the crowd which had now accumulated behind them.

'Street wear, Will Adams, especially when it is of such weight and size as your own, is not permitted within our houses. Come, the young lady wishes to assist you.'

Will realised that the door of the inn was open, and a girl knelt there, holding in each hand a pair of slippers. He could see nothing beyond the glossy head of raven hair, longer than any he had previously beheld, lying in a vast black cascade over her shoulders and down her back, where at last it was fastened in a tress which swept the floor. Beneath this the deep blue kimono suggested the sea at midnight. The entire picture was one of such grace and beauty he felt his weariness lifting from his shoulders like a cloud. Hastily he pulled off his boots, arranged them as Tadatune had done his sandals, and motioned Melchior Zandvoort to do the same.

The girl was already sliding soft slippers on to Tadatune's feet, and now she did the same for Will, with the most marvellously gentle hands he could imagine, and at the same time allowed not the slightest movement to indicate what must have been terribly apparent, at least to her nostrils, that the boots had not left his feet for three weeks.

Tadatune had already removed his breastplate, to show that

he wore a garment similar to his less distinguished countryman, although of far better quality than any they had seen in the street, in deep crimson. Now he took off his helmet as well, to reveal a strange hairstyle, for his scalp was shaved in two wide swathes on either side of the crown, to leave only a patch of hair in the centre; this had been allowed to grow until it was clearly as long as the girl's, but instead of lying loose, it was bound up in a large knot on top of his head. He replaced his two swords in his sash and smiled at Will's obvious interest. 'You must go with this young lady.'

She raised her head to give them an anxious smile. Oh, Marlowe, Marlowe, rise up from your grave and come to my aid, Will thought. For here was a perfectly oval face, thickly coated with white paint to which had been added a trace of rose on each cheek; the paint seemed to delineate every feature, a straight, high nose, a small but perfectly carved mouth; slightly thin lips; and above all a narrow forehead, perfectly framed in the arch of black hair. And then the eyes, black, soft, and utterly welcoming. And then? The robe hid all else. But the roundness of her neck, the delicacy of her small hands and feet, which for the first time became visible as she rose to bow, promised nothing but delight.

'By God, what a vision,' Will muttered in Dutch.

'Oh, indeed, Will,' Melchior agreed. 'And will this young lady show us to some food and drink? I fear that I am close to collapse.'

Will relayed the request to Tadatune.

'But of course,' Tadatune said. 'Once you have been purefied.'

'Purefied?' Will demanded. 'I do assure you, sir, that dirty we may be, but it is of far less import than the empty condition of our stomachs.'

Tadatune shook his head, still gently smiling. 'You people from across the ocean are all the same, Will Adams. Barbarians once in the presence of food. But no man may eat until he has bathed. The young lady will look after you.'

Will sighed. But they seemed to have no choice. 'And her name, Master Tadatune?'

'Her name? Why, she is Magome Kageyu's daughter. Her name is Magome Shikibu.'

Chapter 2

'WE'D BEST follow the custom of the country, Melchior,' Will decided. 'Lead on, Miss Magome.'

The girl glanced at the hatamoto, who said something in Japanese. Now she smiled, and rose to her feet, hands tucked into the sleeves of her gown. She walked in front of them, noiselessly, and Will realised that the inn, if narrow, was by no means small, but stretched inwards from the street for an interminable distance. They followed a corridor, on the right of which were a succession of small rooms, as strange as the house itself; every one seemed devoid of furniture, save for the mats which covered the floor.

After they had passed several of these, Magome Shikibu halted before a closed door, and said something, surprisingly loudly, her voice high and with a delightful lilting quality. The door opened and they were greeted by two more young women, who bowed almost to the ground. They had arrived at the rear of the inn, and found themselves entering a small garden, surrounded by a white wall. There was no topiary work, and no flower beds; instead, a series of orderly shrubs, separated by a path, not paved, but composed of smoothly rounded stones; farther off, in the corner, there were several dwarf trees, but all of a variety unknown to Will.

Yet a great deal of work, and upkeep, clearly was needed here. As they followed their three guides through the shrubs Will saw that the trees were planted upon a raised embankment at the far end of the garden, and this embankment was landscaped like any park, although scarce measuring twelve feet across, with the model of a building nestling amidst the trees and a stream flowing through the centre to cascade into a pool at their feet.

'How beautiful,' Melchior muttered. 'Truly, Will, I wonder at the fortune which has guided our footsteps here.'

Quite beautiful. And yet Will was so conditioned to suspicion, to fearing some disaster in every occasion, he could not help but suppose there had to be such an event lurking around every corner.

They reached the end of the path, and found themselves

before two sheds, both low and small. One of the girls opened the door on the right.

Will glanced at Melchior. 'Well, having come this far, I suppose we'd better see what is meant by this cleansing. It's sure we'll obtain no food unless we humour them.'

He ducked his head, and stepped inside; the ceiling was too low to permit him to stand upright. But the room was large, and very hot; it was like stepping into an oven, and steam rose from beneath the floor. The floor itself was composed of wooden slats, laid somewhat apart from each other to form a grating; beneath it there was a deep trench cut in the earth. At the far end of the room, let into the floor, there was a huge steaming tub of water, big enough for several people at the same time.

Melchior brushed his shoulder as he entered, and to their surprise the three young women also came in, and the door was closed.

''Tis some indecency here,' Melchior whispered. 'I like it not.'

Will watched Magome Shikibu, who had gone past them to dip her hand into the tub. Now she shook it dry, and faced them, smiling, and bowed, her hands once again disappearing into her sleeves. She said something in Japanese, gazing at their clothing.

'It seems we are to share the same tub, Will,' Melchior said. 'The water looks warm enough, to be sure. And we could certainly do with a wash.' He smiled, and bowed in turn, and moved to the door to open it and allow their guides out, only to discover to his consternation that it was bolted, and that one of the young women was there before him, also smiling like her mistress, and reaching up to remove his shirt.

'Will,' Melchior bellowed. He also was being attended. 'What means this, Will?'

'Means? Why it means . . .' Yet the girls went about their duties with no hint of lewdness or levity, but with a grave and persistent concentration, carefully removing each garment and rather distastefully dropping it on the floor before turning to the next. 'Truly,' Will said, 'I doubt we have the strength to resist them, Melchior.'

'Then we are damned. Damned,' the Dutchman groaned.

And still Magome Shikibu stood before the tub, gently smiling. She disturbed Will more than the two girls, who were obviously servants. For now he was naked. No doubt it was, after all, a good thing that he was so weak that his reactions were less than normal. But still, he decided, it were best to take refuge, and quickly. He ran for the tub, but was stopped by Shikibu, who put her hands on his chest and shook her head.

'Eh? Are we not supposed to wash, young lady?' Will demanded.

Still she smiled, and inclined her head towards his right shoulder.

'Will,' Melchior bellowed. 'Will.'

Will turned, watched the girl standing before him. She had removed her gown, and anything else she might have been wearing, and held a pitcher of water. Girl? Or angel descended from heaven? She was very young, short and with slender arms and legs, even narrower thighs and shoulders, flattened belly and breasts which were hardly more than enlarged nipples, the whole shrouded in the endless black hair. Scarcely nubile, he realised, and wondered that he could think such thoughts without feeling immediately sinful.

He looked back at Shikibu, who slowly lowered herself until she knelt, pointed at him, and rose again. He hesitated, but it was necessary to do something, and quickly. He knelt as instructed, and the girl knelt beside him. On the far side of the room Melchior was doing the same, gazing at his attendant like a petrified rabbit.

The water was emptied over his shoulders; it was distinctly cold and made him shiver. But then the girl's hands were at him, filled with sweet-scented soap, caressing his shoulders and thighs.

'I do assure you, Miss Magome,' Will gasped as the fingers slid between his legs and round his buttocks, 'that we can manage.'

Shikibu smiled at him.

'Will?' Melchior gasped. 'Will? By God, Will, *surely* we are damned.'

Damned? Or blessed? His body moved, involuntarily, and the girl cast him a hasty, anxious look and was as quickly reprimanded by her mistress for any inconvenience she might have caused. God in Heaven, not so weak. But she was away again, leaving soap dripping from the end of his penis, washing his legs and toes, while he stared at the smiling Shikibu.

The soaping finished, they were again rinsed and then at last allowed into the tub. Here the water was so hot it took Will's breath away. But how wonderfully relaxing. He allowed his head to sink back, while he gazed at the three girls, standing in a row, anxiously watching them. He could lie here forever, remembering what had just happened, anticipating what might yet be going to happen. But now Shikibu was beckoning them again, and a moment later they were encased in warm, soft towels, while the girls rubbed them dry, inducing at the same time a tremendous tingling of blood and muscle, a feeling of well-being which almost made up for the emptiness in his stomach.

Shikibu smiled at him and indicated the garments she had brought. These consisted of a band to be worn around his waist, with a separate piece to be passed between his legs and secured at the front, and on top a loose robe, rather like her own but made of cloth rather than silk, and secured with a girdle instead of a sash. It was utterly comfortable, even if it made him feel vaguely sinful to be standing so clad, his feet thrust into slippers, instead of encased in tightly buttoned doublet and close-fitting hose.

Shikibu inspected him, her head on one side, and then bowed, and laughed, the sweetest sound he thought he had ever heard, and took her hands from inside her sleeves to clap them together. He wished he could be sure whether she was expressing admiration or amazement. But now she turned away to inspect Melchior in turn. He experienced a sudden pang of jealousy. Of Melchior? Over a girl he had only just seen, and could hardly be described as having yet met? What was there about her, beyond the fact that she had just seen more of him than any woman, including his own wife? Zenocrate, Zenocrate, fair is too foul an epithet for thee; how Marlowe's words stuck in his brain.

The girl who had washed him, having dried herself and regained her robe, opened the door for him. He stepped into the garden. But what a different place it was, on a sudden. And now he was to be fed. In the same style as he had been bathed?

Shikibu hurried forward to lead them back to the house, along the corridor, and into one of the rooms he had seen while passing earlier. Here Shimadzu Tadatune was seated, cross-legged, on a mat, his long sword resting on the floor beside him, his short sword still in his sash. 'Ah, Will Adams,' he said. 'Now truly you are ready to eat. Perhaps you will reassure your countrymen.'

For Gilbert de Conning and Jan van Owater were also in the room, standing awkwardly, staring at Will and Melchior, at their clothes, and at the women, with amazement.

'You'll have to be washed,' Will said, and smiled at Shikibu. 'Who'll take *them* in hand?'

She smiled in turn, and bowed. She would, of course. And the two girls. For a moment he was angry. Would she, then, superintend the cleansing of the whole ship's company? By the end of that she would have forgotten him entirely.

'Now come, Will Adams, sit down,' Tadatune said. 'Here on my left and tell your companion to sit on my right.'

Wondering at the honour paid to Melchior, Will obeyed, motioning his friend to do the same.

'Now we can talk, while we eat.' Tadatune clapped his hands, and three girls, no older than the two who had washed them, entered the room, bearing three tables, each about a foot square and raised on short legs. One of these was placed in front of each of the men. The girls bowed, and withdrew.

'Food, Will, food,' Melchior said. 'My stomach can hardly wait.'

'What does your friend say?' Tadatune asked.

'He looks forward to our meal.' Will inhaled. 'What is that delightful smell?'

'Do you think the room is sufficiently heated?' Tadatune asked.

'Why, yes, it is a warm day.'

'It is the period of the Clear Day. But soon enough it will be the time of the Seed Rain, and then it will be damp. So Magome Kageyu warms his house. There is a hole in the floor, over there beneath that mat, filled with live coals, suitably scented, which give off at once the heat which fills the room and the odour. Tea.'

The three girls had returned, each now bearing a tray on which was a small, handless cup of steaming green liquid.

'What's this?' Melchior demanded.

Tadatune looked at Will.

'My friend wishes to know what it is we are to drink.'

'Tea, Will Adams. It is the essential accompaniment of any meal.' Tadatune raised the cup, held in both hands, and inhaled rather than sipped.

Will copied him, and seemed to have scalded his upper lip. He heard Melchior spluttering, and watched the girls withdraw through the screen door. 'It is good,' he said. 'Very warming.'

'It will sharpen your appetite,' Tadatune said. 'But your companion does not like it?'

'He waits for it to cool.' But his curiosity, perhaps mingled with jealousy, was getting the better of him. 'He is also over-whelmed with honour at having been placed upon your right hand.'

Tadatune raised his eyebrows. 'He is less used to civilised company than you, perhaps, Will Adams. The post of honour does not seem to concern you in the least.'

Will drank some more tea to hide his confusion; the liquid seemed to carve its way down his gullet and into his stomach.

Tadatune was smiling. 'Of course. I had forgotten; the priests have told us that in Europe the right hand is the side of honour. But how can that be so, Will Adams? My left hand is the side on which I carry my sword. Can there be a more honourable place than that?'

The girls had returned with their trays. Now they bore plates, containing two long slices of some brown, cake-like dish, covered with a dark sauce, and scattered over with ginger.

'This is called manju,' Tadatune said.

'Oh, what would I give for a slice of beef,' Melchior muttered.

'You'd best eat what you can while you may,' Will suggested. 'You value your sword, Master Tadatune?'

The samurai frowned, and then smiled. 'Is it not said, there is nothing between heaven and earth that a man need fear, who carries in his belt this single blade?'

Will made to carve the food with his knife, discovered to his surprise that the girl still knelt beside him, two small sticks, perhaps nine inches long, held in her right hand. Using these as if they were extra fingers, she expertly broke off a piece of the cake, rolled it in ginger, and held it to his mouth. An exclamation from beyond Tadatune told him that Melchior was being similarly attended, as was the young nobleman. And the food was extremely tasty, if unlike anything he had had before; his saliva was almost painful, as it poured into his mouth. He glanced down at the sword which lay beside him. 'Truly it is a splendid weapon, Master Tadatune. May I look at it?'

Once again Tadatune frowned, and once again his forehead cleared. 'Certainly, if you wish. No,' he cried, raising his voice for the first time as Will reached for the hilt, which was richly decorated with a variety of designs representing animals, and also studded with several semi-precious stones of a sort he had not seen before, and from its length clearly intended to be grasped in both hands. 'No, my friend. No man may touch another's sword, without joining him in combat. Allow me.'

From his girdle he took a silk napkin, which he folded around the hilt before gripping it. He then carefully turned the weapon over before drawing it, so that the reverse of the blade was presented to Will as it slowly left the scabbard. And what a splendid blade it was, quite matching the hilt in splendour, although a good deal more purposeful. Not much over two feet long, and single-edged, it tapered from the quarter-inch-thick reverse to a blade with the sharpness of a razor, and obviously hardened with steel, for Will could discern the difference in the metal over the last half-inch. The reverse was straight, but the blade was very slightly curved, until at the end it was rounded to indicate a cutting rather than a thrusting weapon.

'A work of art,' he said, and looked up as the girls removed the remains of the manju and offered instead small cups of thin, clear liquid, warm rather than hot.

'Saké.' Tadatune carefully replaced his weapon in its sheath, which was a brilliant red colour. 'Wine made from rice. Very strong.'

Will drank, and discovered his cup to be empty before he had properly tasted the liquor. The girls were now serving skewers on which there were small fish, apparently fried.

'And the small sword?'

The fish was much more to his liking, and the saké was starting to fill his body with well-being. 'For defence at close quarters?'

'No, no, my friend. A man's short sword is the ultimate guardian of his honour. For no samurai may surrender his person, following upon a defeat. In that eventuality, only death can absolve the shame.'

'Only death . . . ' Will swallowed some fish before he intended. 'You mean that should you be defeated in battle, you would take your own life?'

'Defeat is not in itself dishonourable,' Tadatune said. 'Providing one can withdraw one's forces in good order from the field, in the hopes of renewing the contest on a later occasion. But should one be forced to surrender, then certainly. Am I not a samurai? Would you not do the same?'

The girl was kneeling before Will, pouring more saké.

'No,' Will said. 'It is not the custom in my country.'

The remains of the fish were removed, and in their place was a dish of two thin slices of goose, roasted and warm.

'Now here is *food*,' Melchior said.

The girl smiled at Will as she conveyed the first piece to his mouth.

'As I thought,' Tadatune remarked. 'The customs of your country are very like those of the Portuguese, Will Adams. I hope you have not lied to me. There is no crime lower than a lie.'

'I have not lied to you, Master Tadatune,' Will said. 'My country is not far from Portugal, to be sure, in the context of the distance we have travelled to reach you. But truth to say, we are enemies.'

Tadatune nodded. 'Your lord would destroy the lord of Portugal?'

'My ruler is far superior to a lord, Master Tadatune.' The goose was finished; he drank some saké, watched the girl as she withdrew to the door, still smiling at him. How good he felt, at once warmed and filled, and delighted by the wine fumes which circulated in his brain. How delightful the company. He could sit here forever.

And then he thought of Gilbert de Conning and Jan van Owater, in the tub with Magone Shikibu standing next to them.

'You will have to explain your hierarchy to me,' Tadatune said. 'The priests say there is one superior to their lord, and he is the Pope of Rome, who they say approximates to our Mikado. There is no Shogun, in their country of Europe.' He sighed. 'There is no Shogun, in our country of Japan, now, either.' Then he smiled, as readily as ever, gestured at the goblet just placed in front of Will by the girl, and raised his own. 'Wine made from the plum. It is good.'

Indeed it was, Will decided, after a sip. But European politics was something to be thought about, if the Japanese believed that Europe was all one country, ruled by the Pope. 'What does the term Shogun signify?'

'The correct term is Sei-i-tai Shogun,' Tadatune said. 'It means the general who repels the barbarians. This was his original function, many centuries ago, when first the Emperor found his sacred duties as viceregent for the gods consumed too much of his time to permit him to look to the nation's defences. In time the Shogun came to rule the country, as regent for the Emperor himself. But then the great lords would no longer obey him, and Japan was rent with endless civil wars. These were ended, after five centuries, Will Adams, by the great general Oda Nobunaga, who conquered all Japan and restored the rule of law. He died not twenty years ago, and was in turn succeeded as ruler by *his* greatest general, Toyotomi Hideyoshi. But Hideyoshi, being of humble birth, could not take the title of Shogun, and so called himself, as I have told you, Kwambaku, or regent for the Shoguns. Now, alas, Hideyoshi is himself dead, but recently. He willed the empire to his son, Toyotomi Hideyori, but as Hideyori is still a child, the government is in the hands of a regency of five lords.'

'And yet he will rule,' Will said. 'So now, Master Tadatune, explain this. You told me outside that the people here, as farmers, were as far below you as the earth is below the sun. Yet you say this Hideyoshi was of humble birth, and came to rule the land.'

The meal was coming to an end; the girl had produced another cup of boiling tea.

'Lord Hideyoshi was originally lower even than a farmer, Will Adams. A wood cutter, who became a soldier. But with a sword in his hand, and the knowledge of how to use it, there is no limit to the power a man may gain, even if he may not adopt the title.'

'No limit,' Will said. 'But it must be done by means of blood.'

Tadatune frowned. 'You are not afraid of blood, Will Adams?'

'Afraid? No, Master Tadatune, I can honestly say that I am not afraid of blood. And yet it is not in my nature to spill it without some good cause. My religion teaches otherwise.'

Tadatune nodded. 'You will have to meet the priest. He comes often enough. Then you will also meet my father. But before then you must rest. This room is yours, my friend. Yours and your companion's. These girls will bring you anything you wish.'

'I must confess that all I really wish at this moment is to sleep,' Will said. 'And I would say my friend feels likewise. So if, perhaps, you would be good enough to ask the young ladies to show us to our beds . . . '

'Beds, Will Adams?'

'Couches for sleeping, Master Tadatune.'

'These are for sleeping, Will Adams.' Tadatune gently tapped the mats on which they sat. 'The girls will clear away these eating utensils and provide you with pillows, and a blanket, should you need it.'

'The floor?' Will sighed. 'And these pillows, Master Tadatune? What might they be?'

Tadatune smiled 'You people from across the ocean seek to ruin the strength of your bodies with too much softness. But fear not, Will Adams, the pillows will be more to your taste. They are fashioned to fit your neck and head, and the wood is of a special quality.'

'The wood?'

'But of course.' Tadatune rose to his feet, picking up his swords as he did so. 'You did not suppose we rest our heads on stone, Will Adams?'

Heaven, or hell? His instincts told him the latter. In which case why was man so afraid of death? But how could it be heaven, in the absence of God, of priests, of any apparent consciousness that there might be evil surrounding all men, leading them to damnation? In the heathen belief that strength was all, strength, and the determination to use that strength. In the suggestion that by the use of his sword a man might rise from the lowest peasant to the highest station in the land?

So, then, where was the punishment? Will walked the garden, his feet slopping in their slippers, his mind and body refreshed under his robe. His kimono; the very word sounded sinful. He had just bathed. Or to be more precise, he had just been bathed. But now there was no longer any sexual gratification to be gained from *that* adventure; he had been bathed morning and evening, by a different girl each time, on every one of the five days he had been in this place. Bungo. A strange name. Bungo. But then, no doubt, England, Holland, France, would seem as strange to the Japanese.

To be bathed, by a naked young woman, without guilt. Without enjoyment, of other than the warmth and the feeling of well-being which followed the immersion. Could this, then, be hell? An absence of sexuality? But that was nonsense. By the priests' own declaration, such a state must be bliss. And in any event he was far from achieving it. The girl who bathed him might already be nothing more than a pleasant servant, who also brought him his food and swept the floor of his chamber. But Magome Shikibu. He saw her seldom. She no longer attended the baths, and of course as the daughter of the innkeeper she was too superior to attend their meals. She had her other duties, for the inn was often busy; it seemed that this town lay on the main road through Bungo.

Indeed, he had spent only two further periods in her company since they had landed. Once when she had returned their European clothing, every stitch laundered and darned and very nearly as good as new; then she had smiled and bowed at their pleasure. And the second time yesterday, when she had supervised the cutting of his hair and beard, which had grown to an untidy length. And then she had stood behind him, only now and then issuing instructions in that clear, melodious voice. But once she had touched him; her fingers had stroked the back of his neck as she had indicated some point to the girl wielding the razor-edged knife. His flesh still tingled to that caress, and last night he had dreamed of her fingers again, but no longer on his neck.

Sinful? Oh, yes, there was sin even in paradise.

'A pleasant day.' Jacob Quaeckernaeck sat by the artificial hill, watching the water cascading down the slopes. 'But then, there can be no such thing as an unpleasant day, here.'

Even Jacob was all but recovered from his ordeal, while Will felt as strong as ever before in his life. How strange, to have endured such hell and to be so swiftly recovered that it all seemed nothing worse than a dream. It had not been so for them all. Three men had died the day after being brought ashore, and had been buried with due ceremony. However lacking in outward evidences of religion, the Japanese were at least disposed to treat death with solemnity. But no more would die now. No men could have received better treatment than they had over the past five days.

And yet, they were not happy in themselves, nor in their relationship with their pilot. Some remembered how he had promised them that they should arrive, as they had. They were embarrassed. Others, like Gilbert de Conning and Jan van Owater, were jealous of that achievement, and remembered only, or so they claimed, the disasters of the expedition, and the warning issued by poor Tim Shotten. They would say, endlessly, had we but remained on the coast of America, with fifty men and a large store of arms and ammunition, why might we not have succeeded in capturing a Spanish vessel, and thus made our way back through the Strait? And might that vessel not have contained a store of gold and silver? Might we not all by now have regained the Texel, and be wealthy? Instead of still having such a voyage in front of us?

'I have been to the shore,' Will said. 'The ship still rides at anchor. And yet, I would be unhappy to see her there should the weather change.'

'Does the weather ever change in this enchanted place?' Quaeckernaeck said. 'In any event there is nothing to be done at the moment. I thank God that I am so much better than a week ago, and yet it will be several weeks before I can consider taking to sea. And most of the men are weaker even than I. I would suggest you cease to worry, Will, for just this season. Else will you consume yourself with anxiety.'

Will sighed. 'No doubt you are right.' He watched Magome Kageyu leave the inn and come across the garden towards them. The innkeeper had the same sunny disposition as his daughter; his face was usually wreathed in smiles, causing him to appear like some happy attendant on St Nicholas at the festive season. But this morning the smile was absent.

He came up to them, and bowed. 'Honourable gentlemen,' he said in halting Portuguese. 'I must ask you to accompany me.'

'What's this?' Quaeckernaeck asked.

'It appears that we are being removed,' Will said. 'Where do we go, Master Magome?'

The innkeeper bowed again. 'Lord Shimadzu Takanawa wishes your presence, honourable sir. He would speak with the crew of the ship *Liefde*.'

'But Master Quaeckernaeck here can scarcely walk.'

'I am to provide the litters necessary for the sick, honourable sir. Nonetheless, it is the wish of the lord Takanawa that all are present.'

Will translated.

'I like it not,' Quaeckernaeck muttered. 'I had thought they were too kind.'

'The young nobleman who attended us when first we landed is the son of this fellow,' Will said. 'He indicated then that before long his father would wish to see us.' He turned to Kageyu. 'You will give us time to put on our European clothing?'

'It is what my master wishes.'

'Then shall we not be long.' Will frowned. 'The thought of this meeting disturbs you, Master Magome. Are we not welcome in Bungo?'

'You are welcome in this house, honourable sir, and indeed in all Japan, to my knowledge. But there has this day arrived a priest from Nagasaki.'

'A Portuguese, you mean?'

'That is so, honourable sir. I beg you to observe caution. That priest was grave indeed when he saw your ship at anchor. And, honourable sir, I must inform you further, that this priest has engaged in conversation members of your own company.'

'Which?' Will demanded.

'The man called de Conning, and the man called van Owater.'

Grave indeed. 'Aye, good Master Magome,' Will said. 'I will pay heed to your suggestion.'

They walked up the hill beyond the village, the sea and the sun at their backs, for it was early in the morning. It was slow progress, both because of the steepness of the road, and because more than half of the crew still had to be carried in litters. There was no other means of transport available. There were horses, certainly, for Will had seen them on the street outside the inn, but few and far between, and apparently not to be possessed by common folk.

Yet the walk was pleasant enough. Had he not worried about what might lie ahead he would even have enjoyed it. They first of all passed the high wooden torii, the simple gateway to the Shinto shrine outside the village, the only obvious symbol of religion in these people's lives. But even their religion was conducted with a personal freedom which seemed impossible to Western eyes; there seemed to be no set days or hours of worship, but each man or woman visited the shrine as his or her conscience dictated, without compulsion or persecution. Beyond the shrine were terraced fields, swamped with water so as to allow only a few blades of grass to show; yet this was not grass, Kageyu informed him, but rice, which was the staple vegetable of the land. The fields were presently empty, but soon they would be filled with men and women, Kageyu said, for the harvesting was a matter for all the Shimadzu tenants. The fields were not their own, but held in fief from their lord, or daimyo, in this feudal society; at this distance from his seat of power he was represented by his hatamoto, Shimadzu Takanawa.

The nobleman's house crowned the hill, and the road ran absolutely straight from the village. At the top they faced a high wooden palisade made of timbers lashed together and cemented in place with earth and mud, in the centre of which a gate opened as the Europeans approached.

But apparently their time was not yet. Magome Kageyu motioned them to halt, slightly to one side of the road, and to wait, for there was already business being conducted before the lord.

'Is this, then, a court of law?' Will asked.

'It is the duty of the daimyo to dispense justice to all his tenants,' Kageyu agreed. 'But he will not keep you long.'

'What is the case being heard?'

'That of a wanton woman, Will Adams,' Kageyu replied. 'While her husband was away from Bungo on business for my lord Takanawa, she did entertain at her house not one, but two men, at various times. As it happened each of these learned of the other's visits, with the result that they quarrelled, and would have fought each other. Thus they are brought to justice. But it is finished.'

Will turned. From inside the wall there came a piteous wailing.

'Whatever can the sentence be?'

'Why, they are to be executed.'

'Executed? You mean all three of them?'

'But of course, Will Adams. What other punishment can you inflict on criminals?'

Will pulled his beard. 'The punishment must surely depend on the crime, Master Magome. Now adultery is serious enough, to be sure, and the woman should be whipped, but surely the men were accepting what was offered to them, and should be exposed to nothing more than a term in the pillory? To take a man's life for doing what comes naturally is surely harsh.'

'Truly the ways of your country are strange, Will Adams,' Kageyu said. 'These men are not being executed for adultery. That is a matter between a man and his wife. Their crime is seeking to fight one another to the death, and the woman's crime is incitement to such an act. Even samurai may only fight either in battle or in pursuance of a blood feud.'

'And for this, death? No blood was spilled.'

'Surely the only just punishment for *any* criminal act must be death? For that is the only punishment which affects young and old, man and woman, prince and pauper alike. To adopt another system, to attempt to differentiate between crimes or between ranks, would be to initiate injustice.'

Will scratched his head, watched the group leave the gate. It had taken on the form of a ceremonial procession, grim enough in view of what he had just heard. First there walked a man with a pickaxe, and then another with a shovel; clearly the gravediggers. Then walked another man, carrying a long scroll, on which was written a series of Japanese characters, no doubt outlining the offence for which the punishment was being inflicted. Then came the three condemned, their hands bound behind their backs with lengths of silk; thrust down the back of each kimono was a thin pole, at the top of which, waving above their heads, was a little banner of paper, again bearing Japanese characteristics. The men seemed unconcerned; the woman was a most distressed-looking creature, her hair untied and loose upon her shoulders and back, her shoulders bowed, her eyes red with weeping.

Last came the executioner. He wore his sword at his side, and in his right hand, like reins, he held the ends of the cords binding his victims' hands. On either side of him there walked a soldier, in full armour, carrying a pike, the head of which rested on the shoulder of the prisoner in front. The woman, in the centre, was spared this indignity, but tears streamed down her face as she passed the dumbfounded Dutchmen. There could be no doubt that she anticipated her fate.

'How will she be done to death?' Will whispered.

'Oh, by beheading, of course,' Kageyu replied. 'There is no other custom recognised for common malefactors. Watch.'

Will turned, and gasped in horror, for the sentence was about to be carried out. The procession had stopped at the edge of a shallow pit, only fifty yards to the right of the Europeans, and the three victims were being made to kneel. There was little preamble, and no prayers. The huge sword swept above the executioner's head and crashed down on the first exposed neck. The head disappeared into the pit, carried onwards by the impact; the trunk remained upright for what seemed a full second while blood pumped upwards, cascading down on to the shoulders. Then it slumped forward. But by then the executioner had already moved round to stand by the second man.

'God in Heaven,' Quaeckernaeck whispered. 'Can this be true?'

The second man was dead. Even at this distance they could see the woman's shoulders shaking as she wept. But neither her constant movement nor the profusion of scattered hair seemed to concern the executioner. Once again the blade, no longer gleaming but instead dark with blood, swept through the air. The executioner stepped down into the grave beside her still shuddering body.

Will licked his lips. 'Must he also bury them?'

'No,' Kageyu said. 'That is the duty of the honin. But as this is a particularly iniquitous crime, my lord Takanawa has sentenced their bodies to be cut into little pieces after death.'

'Cut into . . . ' Will found difficulty in swallowing. But the sword was already rising and falling with rhythmic power. And half an hour ago he had been considering himself in a perfect heaven, where his only discontent was the absence of Shikibu.

'Now come,' Kageyu said. 'My lord Takanawa awaits you.'

Will found himself walking forward. Within the gate was a courtyard, but before gaining access the Hollanders had to pass scrutiny by a dozen heavily armed soldiers, helmeted and with fearsome mask-visors in place. This done, they entered the yard, and were escorted towards an open porch which fronted the main building, but Will was for the moment distracted by the large number of people gathered on either side, so as to allow an avenue up the centre. He saw women as well as men, and no peasants, these. The females wore brightly coloured silk kimonos, and carried dainty little fans, and the men's robes were hardly less brilliant, while every one of *them* had tucked into his girdle the two swords which marked the samurai, as well as the other marks of his office, the shaven scalp, and above everything else the tremendous air of arrogance they seemed able to project even when standing still. Incongruously, each man also carried a fan.

But these were the onlookers. On the porch, facing them, were the principals. Will was relieved to see Tadatune seated in the peculiar Japanese fashion, half kneeling on the floor next to his father. Shimadzu no-Takanawa was grim-faced and scowling as he surveyed the mariners. Yet even he was pleasanter to look upon than the black-robed priest who stood at the foot of the short steps, and just to one side, his right hand resting on the large wooden crucifix which hung from round his neck.

'That man means us ill, Will,' Melchior Zandvoort growled.

'Perhaps. But the law is in the hands of the magistrate here. And Tadatune is our friend.'

He attempted to catch the young man's eye, but Tadatune was looking extremely solemn. And only now did Will realise that there were yet other nobles behind the hatamoto, seated on the floor in the shadows to the rear. Interested spectators from some neighbouring fief? Or more judges?

Tadatune was on his feet. 'Will Adams,' he said. 'I speak to you because we understand the same Portuguese tongue. Are you prepared to act as representative of your fellows?'

Will stood beside Quaeckernaeck's litter. 'They wish me to act as spokesman, Jacob.'

'But of course, Will. The rest of us have little Portuguese.'

Will pulled his beard. 'You are aware that we are on trial?'

'I am aware that this priest means to misrepresent our presence.'

'And should we lose the coming argument, or rather, should *I* be outspoken, then we shall all likely be beheaded before lunch.'

'That is absurd. We have harmed no one.'

'Nonetheless, Jacob, I beg you, give me your prayers.' He straightened. How he sweated; no doubt it was the sun, now assuming a position immediately above the courtyard. And yet, it could do them no good for their inquisitors to see that he was apprehensive of the possible outcome of this event. 'I will speak for my comrades, my lord Tadatune.'

'I am glad, Will Adams,' Tadatune said. 'I speak for my father. He wishes to say that when your ship was discovered off our coast we visited you, with friendship in our hearts, and brought you to our country and our town, and tended your sick, and grieved when they died, and did all in our power to bring succour to you. Do you acknowledge this?'

'Willingly. My comrades and I can never show sufficient gratitude for the goodness you have bestowed upon us.'

Tadatune bowed. 'This we understand and appreciate. Yet now we must ask the question, what purpose did you have in venturing into our waters?'

'We sought to trade, my lord Tadatune.'

'To trade, Will Adams? And where were these goods with which you would trade?'

'Our holds are filled with cloth . . . '

'Cloth,' said the priest, contemptuously. 'I have seen no cloth on board that vessel.'

The hatamoto addressed Will for the first time. 'This is so, Will Adams. I have visited your ship, and have seen no cloth.'

'Why, sir, that is because your people here in Bungo have removed it. Indeed, they commenced removing our goods before they even brought us ashore, and but for the good offices of your son I doubt we should have received any comfort whatsoever.'

'He is lying, my lord Takanawa,' the priest said. 'As I have said, theirs was a piratical expedition. I have often told my lord

Takanawa of how the great King of Spain, the mighty Philip, revered by Heaven and Earth, rules not only his land in Europe, but the entire continent of the Americas as well, and seeks to educate his peoples in the way of the One True Church, just as my compatriots and I have sought to educate your people here in Bungo. But constantly has he been forced to resist incursions into his domains by these cursed heretics of Holland and England, countries like your own offshore islands lying south of here, which breed only pirates.'

'We are no pirates,' Will declared. 'We came across the ocean to trade.'

The hatamoto gazed at Will. 'For a man to lie is to put himself beyond not only human justice, but human respect.'

'We came to Japan to trade,' Will insisted. 'This I swear.'

'But what of your purpose in coming to the South Sea at all, Master Englishman?' the Jesuit demanded. 'Oh, we have purposefully given you sufficient rope to hang yourself. Master de Conning. Master van Owater. Stand forth.'

There was a moment's hesitation, and then Gilbert de Conning and Jan van Owater stepped out of the group of Dutch sailors.

'What means this, Will?' Quaeckernaeck whispered.

'That we are undone by a pair of traitors,' Will muttered in reply. 'What mean you, Gilbert?'

'Why, to save our necks,' de Conning replied. 'The priest has assured us that you will all be executed as pirates.'

'But *he* will save *you*, for betraying your comrades? You are a fool, Gilbert de Conning.'

'Now, Master van Owater,' the Jesuit said. 'Tell my lord Takanawa what duties you fulfilled on board the ship *Liefde*.'

'I am, sir, a merchant of Amsterdam,' van Owater said, 'who did ship my store of cloth on board this fleet, and took passage in this ship, for the purpose of opening a trade between my associates and the island of Java, far to the south. To this end I inquired as to what goods would be most acceptable in these parts, and was told woollen cloth, which was indeed shipped in the hold of the *Liefde*. It was not until we were past the Strait of Magellan, and in the South Sea, that I overheard sailors who had ventured into these waters on a previous occasion discussing our expedition, and laughing at the subterfuge indulged by their captains, in carrying cargoes of woollen cloth when we intended not to venture away from the equatorial regions. For these sailors declared that our true purpose was piracy, and our intention to raid and destroy the Spanish settlements in the Americas.'

Will stared at the man in astonishment.

'Well, Master Englishman?' demanded the Jesuit. 'Has guilt struck you dumb? My lord Takanawa awaits your answer.'

'Why, sir, as to the cargo, I am not qualified to speak. I can but say that far from having any intention of attacking the Spaniards, our one objective was to leave the Americas undiscovered lest they attack us.'

'We scarce expected you to adopt a different tone, Master Englishman,' the Jesuit said. 'But will you also oppose the word of Master de Conning?'

'I cannot until I discover what it is he has to say.'

'Well?' demanded the priest of de Conning.

'I feel it is my bounden duty to support the confession of Master van Owater,' de Conning said. 'In my capacity of boatswain on the *Liefde* I had too often to attempt in some small way to prevent our captain, Master Quaeckernaeck there, encouraged by this Englishman, Will Adams, and others of the crew, from attacking defenceless Spanish settlements on the coast of America. Indeed, sir, I will confess that I had scant success, and that those settlements escaped was due to a lack of courage amongst the pirates themselves. But then, sir, they decided that the Portuguese settlements in the East Indies were less well protected, and so decided to cross the great sea, always with murder and rapine in their hearts.'

The hatamoto made an aside to his son, and the priest was frowning.

'Your intention was to make war upon the Portuguese?' Tadatune asked.

De Conning realised his error. 'By no means, sir. Nothing so simple. For our two nations are not at war. We intended piracy, sir, not only upon the Portuguese, but upon your own good people, and the people of Cathay and of the Spice Islands themselves. There, sir, have I confessed my iniquity, and may God have mercy on my soul.'

'Now make you a good reply, Will Adams,' Tadatune said gravely. 'This man's confession is a most serious affair putting as it does his own life in jeopardy.'

'Why, Master Tadatune,' Will said, 'I can only plead the honesty of our intentions. It was the wish of our masters in Holland that we trade with the Spice Islands. This voyage, sir, necessarily takes upwards of a year, or more as in our case, and it is impossible for any ship to carry sufficient food and water for a journey of such duration. Thus from time to time we sought to purchase these necessities of life from the various European settlements in Africa and America, and were invariably rebuffed. We were desperate men, who daily saw our comrades dying on every side. Reduced to such extremity, perchance on one or two occasions we took where we could not buy. A guilty act, no doubt, but one which I hazard any commander, including yourself, Master Tadatune, would have undertaken.'

Tadatune gazed at him for a moment, and then turned to his father.

'Let not this man's words addle your brain, lord Takanawa,' the priest cried. 'Why else do you think he was elected spokesman of these pirates in their hour of need? Whatever he says will be lies, my lord, and for a very simple reason. He claims that this ship, this entire fleet of which this ship was a part, left Europe only intending to trade with the East. Then have him tell you this, sir: have him explain the eighteen cannon which line the ports of this ship. Have him explain the five hundred matchlock fire-pieces, this for a crew of perhaps a hundred men, mark you. Have him explain the five thousand ball, for the cannon. Enough, sir, to destroy a town, or even a city. This was required for trade? And to fire them, five thousand pounds of gunpowder. And worst of all, sirs, have him explain the three hundred and fifty fire arrows, weapons of the strictest offence, my lord, meant to destroy by burning, to drive an enemy from his encampment. These things are there, and I have counted them, there. Should you wish to see them, they are there now. No, no, my lord, this man lies. This ship, these men, are all part of a piratical expedition, intending mayhem and murder wherever they might find themselves, and prevented only from inflicting death and rapine upon the coast of your own fair land by the goodness of that God I have so often invoked to your aid. They will claim to be Christians, sir, but they worship a different deity to myself and my comrades. Yet, as heretic criminals, let them suffer. Let them be crucified, my lord Takanawa; hang their bodies high on wooden crosses, set along the shores of this land of Bungo, and leave them there to serve as a warning to all future heretics who would dare risk themselves upon this land.'

He paused for breath, panting, clutching his crucifix, his face mottled red and white, his eyes blazing, his right finger pointing as if, Will supposed, he was posing for a painting representing himself as the angel of God.

'And you call yourself a priest, a man of piety and charity?' he asked.

But the damage was done. Takanawa and his son were talking in low voices, heads close together. Those of the assembly who understood Portuguese, and there seemed to be several, were translating the events to their neighbours, who were in turn passing them on, no doubt adding their own comments and ideas, so that a vast rustle seemed to surround the enclosure. Even the three men seated behind the hatamoto seemed alarmed and upset by the news, and were in earnest consultation.

At last Takanawa looked up, and the whispering slowly ceased.

'Will Adams,' Tadatune said. 'It would serve no purpose to require you to answer the priest's accusation. I will but say, do you deny or acknowledge that these weapons of war are concealed in the hold of your vessel?'

'They are there, Master Tadatune, but . . . '

'Then his words are proved true, and yours false. There can be no purpose in attempting to discover upon whom you meant to practise this piracy. Having lied once you will certainly lie again, and again, for such is the mind of the liar. As pirates you came to Bungo, and as pirates you will die, here upon the coast of Bungo, as the priest wishes.'

Will stared at him in horror. To have undergone so much, survived so much, and now to be executed like a common criminal? But what to say, what to do? How to tell Quaecker-naeck and Melchior, and the others, that he had failed them?

He became aware that a voice was speaking. Passing sentence? For a moment he could not discover whence the quiet sound came. But certainly it was a voice of authority. Both Tadatune and his father had turned their heads, and the priest was also gazing behind the two hatamoto, his face losing its anger in an almost comical expression of consternation.

Takanawa spoke in reply, seeming to be remonstrating, but the other man, the centre of the three figures seated behind him, shook his head and repeated his earlier words. Takanawa hesitated, and then glanced at Tadatune and issued some instructions.

'Will Adams,' Tadatune said, not less sternly than before, 'your proper punishment must be deferred to a later occasion.

It is the wish of no less a person than the Kwambaku himself, the mighty Toyotomi Hideyori, lord of Osaka, to hear your words, and no doubt decide your sentence. Hence it is decided that you will accompany this gentleman, Kosuke no-Suke. You may take one of your companions with you. Haste now, for Kosuke no-Suke wishes to return to Osaka immediately.'

'Will?' Quaeckernaeck whispered. 'What is happening, Will? Truly during the declamation by that Papist I supposed our hour had struck.'

'So did I, Jacob. But now, it seems, we are being allowed to appeal to a higher court. I am to visit the emperor, or at least his regent, in Osaka, a place some leagues distant, I fancy. They say I must take a companion.'

'Would that I could accompany you, Will. But I fear such a journey is beyond my strength at this moment, and in any event, I must remain with my ship and my men. You may take whom you choose.'

'Then it shall be Melchior Zandvoort.'

'A perfect choice, Will. Aye, take Melchior and go with God.'

Will nodded. They would need every bit of His protection now. If it were there for the using. He gazed at Tadatune, very grave, at the man Kosuke no-Suke, now slowly rising to his feet, careless, it seemed, of the consternation he had caused, at the priest, muttering with frustration, and then at the people, standing close, whispering amongst themselves, the men behind their hands and the women behind their fans.

All except one, who stood by herself, quite close to the porch of the house, and next to her father. Magome Shikibu's fan hung at her side, drooping from the end of her fingers, as she gazed at him. But when she saw him in turn looking at her, the arm came up, and the fan extended, almost as if it were an extension of her fingers, to cover her face, and then drooped again. Will silently cursed the sunlight, which still half dazzled him as he cursed the variety of colour and movement on either side of him. It was almost impossible to make out the expression in her eyes, to determine what she had intended by raising her fan and then lowering it again. Certainly his blockheaded stare had at once confused and concerned her. The fan was back in place, and now she turned away.

Magome Shikibu.

This was, at the least, a pretence at a ship, Will reflected. The galley was some forty feet long, propelled by a single bank of oars, a dozen to a side, and slid through the calm waters at considerable speed. Because the waters were calm. They had not been so immediately on leaving Bungo; then the swell coming in from six thousand miles of open sea had caused the boat to dip and sway, and the spray to fly high over the fragile bow, and the oarsmen had hunched their shoulders and gripped their blades in grim determination. But within an hour they had ducked behind a rocky shore, and found themselves in a world of islands, separated by the reefs from the rollers outside, where the water was as calm as a lake, and of the deep blue colour which suggests eternal depths. For these waters had such boats been created, just as the Phoenicians had found their galleys all that were needed for the Mediterranean, and only when venturing beyond the Pillars of Hercules had they deemed it necessary to look for more seagoing qualities.

Now the men sang, as they dipped their blades in the water, and now the samurai had once again taken their positions in the bow, while the wind played with the brilliant paper pennants fluttering from their helmets, and the sun glinted from their armour. Fine armour it was, too, painted in a variety of colours with red and black and gold the principal choices. They seemed to wear no distinguishing marks, although they uniformly carried their long swords in white scabbards, and he did not doubt that they were members of one military force.

Excepting their leader. Kosuke no-Suke had not donned armour, nor had he undertaken to travel in the bow, but rather in the place of comfort and safety in the stern, his arms folded into the sleeves of his kimono, which was made from extraordinarily rich silk, with a flowered design depicting a circle containing three flowers rather resembling the mallow, their stalks resting on the edges of the circle, their tips meeting in the centre. A peasant's wide hat shaded his head from the sun, and beneath its brim his long, thin face, elongated by the drooping moustache and thin beard, was relaxed and peaceful. And yet he carried the two swords which marked the samurai.

Interesting people, Will thought. Inhabiting an interesting and utterly beautiful country. For the placidity of the lake over which the galley raced was in startling contrast to the mountains which surrounded them on every side, reaching up and up and up towards the sky, many of them still crowned with snow, despite the month. And beautiful people, as well. Some of them. He could not get the face of Magome Shikibu out of his mind, the pleasure with which she had realised that he was not, after all, about to be raised on the cross to die in torment and humiliation. But mingled with that memory was the earlier one of her standing with utter composure next to the tub while he had knelt, naked, being washed by a naked young woman. And of all the other members of the crew whose cleansing she had similarly supervised. This memory was indeed a mixture of nightmare and delight. For on the one hand, there was the unthinkable thought that naked humanity and all that might follow, and should follow, was of no account to her; while on the other hand there was the almost equally unthinkable suggestion that if naked manhood meant nothing to her, it was necessarily because she had seen so much of it, for starting from such a premise, and carrying it to its logical conclusion, where then would she begin to be disturbed, or shocked, by the appearance of sexual desire? Where, indeed. And over it all, he could still feel the touch of her hand.

But how to reconcile Shikibu with the suggestion of savagery which lay around him, the decision to cut a poor adultress into pieces?

'Your companion sleeps soundly,' Kosuke no-Suke remarked in Portuguese.

'My faith, sir, but you took me by surprise,' Will said. 'I had no idea that you understood Portuguese.'

Suke bowed, slightly. 'It is my duty, Will Adams, to know all things, and endeavour to understand all things.'

A double-edged remark? Will nudged the snoring Melchior, without effect. 'He is happy to be afloat again.'

'And this ship travels well, does it not?'

'She has a rare turn of speed. In smooth water.'

'As you say, our galleys are not suited for traversing the open sea. But why should we wish to do so, save for the purpose of piracy?'

A trap? 'Piracy, Master Kosuke, despite the imagination of the Jesuit, is the least of all reasons that men take to the ocean,' Will said.

'So tell me of the others.'

'Well, sir, first and foremost there is the desire to trade.'

'Why?'

'Why? Well, sir . . . ' Will scratched his head. 'To reduce it to a parable, supposing I own a handsome cow, and you a run of fat chickens, it would be to our mutual advantage for me to offer you my milk in exchange for your eggs.'

'Here in Japan we have everything that we desire, or require.'

'And yet you suffer the Portuguese.'

Suke nodded. 'They hunger for gold and silver. They obtain these things to the south, and yet they seek them here as well.'

'And is there gold and silver in Japan?'

'Of course.'

'And do we of Europe have nothing you would possess in exchange?'

Suke appeared to smile. 'The Portuguese offer us, in exchange, the love and protection of their God.'

'But this is not to your taste?'

Suke looked up at the sky, and then over the side of the ship at the water racing away from the hull. 'Their God, they say, is more powerful than any other, but yet is a God of peace, and brotherly love, and piety, and more, a God who regards only prayer as truly good, and bids man neglect the requirements of the flesh in order to pursue those of the spirit. Do you believe in such a God, Will Adams?'

'I was brought up to do so, Master Kosuke,' Will replied cautiously.

'But now you are a man you see the world differently?'

'Now I am a man I have sometimes doubted, and felt sadly guilty for doing so.'

'Know you the use of a sword, Will Adams?'

'I would say that compared with your samurai I am a novice.'

'You are a man of strange honesty, Will Adams, and I hold honesty greater than any other virtue. But I would look far to find a Japanese who would admit to such a lack of swordsmanship as you have just done. The Portuguese God is truly a God of children. I ask you this, Will Adams: Show me His strength that is greater than the sun, more terrifying than the sea when aroused, which can be more irresistible than the wind, more devastating than the earth when it opens.'

'The Portuguese will say that their God is responsible for all of those things,' Will said.

'A point which can hardly be proved,' Suke remarked. 'And which can be disproved in relation to their other claims. For if indeed He places love and honesty above all other virtues, then explain to me that priest's animosity towards you? Indeed, these priests' animosity towards all who do not profess their faith. He would have had you crucified, Will Adams. Can there be a more cruel fate than that?'

'It occurs to me that death is itself a cruel fate,' Will said. 'And you practise it in this country without discrimination.'

'How do you say that? Is not death the ultimate end of every man, daimyo or eta? But it should be done quickly, and without suffering. To take off a man's head is the purest method of execution. To leave him bound to a cross, slowly to perish of hunger, thirst and exposure, is inhuman. But this is what these priests would do, and what they claim to do in their own land. We at the least will not permit such brutality. If we raise a man upon the cross, then immediately he is pierced with a lance to put an end to his suffering. No indeed, Will Adams, the Portuguese God may be mighty, although I take leave to doubt this; He may be merciful, although a brief study of nature will persuade any thinking man otherwise; and He may be chaste, although it has long been known that the observance of chastity goes hand in hand with cowardice and dishonour, whereas he who will take his pleasure as he chooses is nearly always your man of courage and honour. Here in Japan we make do without Him.' He pointed. 'Osaka.'

Will raised his head, gazed at the approaching shore, for the inland sea over which they had come was now narrowing to a gulf, and the mountains themselves were dwindling, to present before him a plain which seemed to stretch for as far as his eye could see to the north, and through which there meandered a large river, splitting itself into a delta as it reached the shore. Some way inland there was a forest of houses, and these quite put to shame the tidy villages of Bungo, for the streets seemed to wander in every direction and contain several buildings of considerable size, although even at this distance he decided that in the main they were of no greater substance. But in addition to the houses there were several spectacular temples, thrusting their tiered roofs towards the sky, and to the west, on the banks of the river itself, he could see a fortress, and one, he realised, which would make many a European citadel seem like a mere stockade, unless the walls which from the sea appeared so thick and strong were also composed of little more than lacquered paper, and the towers which dominated at once the keep and the city below were of no more than wood.

'A sizeable city,' he remarked.

'Have you any to compare in your own land?'

'Perhaps one,' Will admitted. 'And is this the seat of your emperor?'

Suke shook his head. 'The Mikado is to be found at Kyoto, which is some miles to the north of here, on the shores of Lake Biwa. Osaka is the residence of the Kwambaku, the regent for the Shogun. As we no longer have a Shogun, Osaka is the seat of all temporal power in Japan.'

'And I am to be taken before this Kwambaku?'

Suke smiled. 'Toyotomi Hideyori is but seven years old, Will Adams. He has inherited the appearance of power by the wishes of his father, the great Hideyoshi. The country is governed by a regency of five daimyo.'

'Shimadzu no-Tadatune explained that to me. And these lords would have words with me?'

Once again the slight smile. 'Those lords do not know you exist. Indeed, only two of them are presently in Osaka, and it will be best for all if one, at the least, never discovers your presence.'

'Then, Master Kosuke, you have befuddled my understanding,' Will said. 'Have I undertaken this journey to no purpose?'

'You have undertaken this journey on my responsibility, Will Adams. When I learned there was a ship at once strange and yet not from Portugal off the coast of Bungo, I made all haste to see for myself, and learn for myself. And when I had done so, I decided that I must take you to Osaka to see my master. He is a great man, Will Adams, and will be greater yet. But should you speak fairly with him, and prove to be of service to him, he may be the cause of much profit to yourself.'

'But this is not the boy Hideyori we are discussing.'

'By no means, Will Adams. My master is the prince, Tokugawa Minamoto no-Iyeyasu, greatest of daimyos, mightiest of warriors, lord of Edo and the eastern coast. Please him, Will Adams, and your future is assured.'

Chapter 3

'YOUR COMPANION will remain here, Will Adams,' Kosuke no-Suke said. 'And you will accompany me. You will please imitate me in all things, however strange to you.'

Will nodded, and motioned Melchior to wait. He doubted Melchior understood. He was himself a little beyond understanding, he thought, his brain a whirl of conflicting emotions and half-appreciated wonders. Where then was your London or Paris or Amsterdam, or even Lisbon and Madrid? He suspected that he could even include Rome in the débâcle, and Osaka, according to Suke, was scarcely the greatest city in Japan.

They had landed at a dock filled with more craft than he had ever seen before. Granted they were all small and hardly seaworthy; they were also all heavily laden with produce of various kinds, proceeding up and down the river above the city, or heading out into the inland sea.

And then, the city itself; warehouses which might include Her Majesty's palace and not know it was there; endless houses, all with the narrow fronts he had noticed in Bungo—for the simple reason, Suke had explained, that property tax was paid on the amount of street frontage taken up—all, to be sure, of the utterly flimsy construction he had earlier observed, but nonetheless splendidly decorated, and if no stronger structure was required, then why build in stone just for the sake of it? What impressed him even more was the extreme order and cleanliness of the streets no less than the people, just as the fact that each street ended in a gate, watched over by an armed guard, filled him with a certain foreboding. It being day the gates were now open, but according to Suke they were shut at night, and a permit was then needed to pass from one street to the next. How then would a Marlowe survive to write immortal lines when he could not wander freely of an evening? Did Japan have no Marlowes? Or was that amount of freedom for the individual not considered necessary?

Soon enough they had come to the castle itself. Suke had referred to it as one of the strongest in the land, without awe, which suggested that it was, after all, no more than one amongst many. But certainly neither Melchior nor himself had seen anything like it, anywhere in the world. No lacquered wood here; by means of a drawbridge they had crossed a deep moat to pass through a barbican set in a high wall composed of immense blocks of freestone, laid without cement or any other binding compound that he could see, and yet embrasured at regular intervals. But this was only the outer defence. Three hundred paces farther in there was yet another wall, no less formidable, and beyond this yet another, this time twelve feet high. Within this final gate there was a large courtyard, with stables on one side and armaments and barracks on the other. But these were themselves small villages, and from the numbers of men he saw on duty, all armed, even those lounging, not to mention their women and children, Will calculated that there might well be several thousand people permanently stationed within the fortress, were such a thought possible. But when he had asked Suke, the Japanese had merely shrugged, and said, 'The regular garrison is twenty thousand men.'

Twenty thousand men. A lie? Heaven, or hell? The entire army of Queen Elizabeth did not number twenty thousand men; to encamp them permanently would pose an insuperable problem of feeding and health. Yet here was this number enclosed within one fortress and the air smelt as sweet as any in Bungo.

But the strength of the fortress, the numbers of the defenders, seemed irrelevant once the keep was reached. It stood within yet another moat-enclosed bastion, on a higher level than the rest of the castle, in the centre of a courtyard not less than a quarter of a mile across and containing numerous outbuildings and storehouses. The keep itself rose six storeys high, each storey fronted and overhung by the many-tiered, slightly upturned roofs which made the building seem like a gigantic pagoda, although the windows were embrasured for defence. Most remarkably of all, however, the keep was made of wood. Immense, thick planks, and doors which might well contain a cannon ball, to be sure, but still of wood. Was there no risk of an enemy ever penetrating to this heart of the Kwambaku's defences?

The true reason, he decided, was that this was less of a last stronghold than a palace. The first apartment they entered was entirely covered with rich ornaments, carpets, stuffs, velvet and gold, the walls were hung with hunting scenes, and as usual there were large numbers of people about, men as well as women, each richly dressed in a patterned silk kimono which made so graceful and so comfortable a garment.

Now, leaving Melchior staring around himself in utter bemusement, Will followed Suke into the next room where, if anything, the decoration was even more splendid, although, incongruously, like every other house he had seen, there was an absolute absence of furniture. Would the prince himself be seated on the floor?

The moment had come. Suke paused before a huge screen, guarded by two soldiers, lances in hand. 'Now be your best, I pray of you, Will Adams, and all will be well.'

The screen slid open, and Will sucked breath into his lungs. Here there were no mats; the floor was covered in a blue carpet, and the room itself was fully forty feet across. By the door was the usual gaggle of men, supported by several more guards. But in this room there were no women to be seen. At a distance, exactly in the centre of the room, Will estimated, the carpet changed from blue to crimson, and at the same time mounted two shallow steps to a small dais. On this platform the carpet was edged with gold, and in the centre, on a woven mat, there sat the prince. More than this he could not immediately make out, as Suke was already moving forward, slowly and carefully, one hand making fluttering gestures at his side to indicate that Will should do the same.

Will followed him, his bag of charts and instruments under his arm, wishing that his clothes were not so threadbare, despite Magome Shikibu's efforts. They approached the steps. He would have raised his head to scrutinise the prince, but Suke was now dropping to his knees, and then slowly inclining his body forward, resting the palms of his hands on the carpet and lowering his head until it was all but touching the velvet. It was a humiliating posture, to Will's eyes, and yet he had been warned to follow the minister in everything, and so he did the same, understanding at least one of the reasons for the kimono, as there was no question but that with his breeches drawing tight over his backside, and his tattered stockings clinging to his legs, he looked far more ridiculous than the Japanese.

They knelt for several seconds, the room entirely silent, and then the prince spoke. His voice was low, and not very loud, but in the vaulted chamber it seemed to travel forever.

'Go forward,' Suke whispered in Portuguese. 'Rise, and go forward, Will Adams, but kneel again before the step.'

Will climbed to his feet, sucked in his waist, threw back his shoulders and approached the dais. Now he could see more clearly. The Tokugawa chieftain sat, like all the Japanese, on his knees and toes, his outer kimono spread around him. There seemed to be three of these altogether, each in green, with the outer one shorter than the others, and in a paler shade. In his sash there were two swords of the samurai, and his head was shaved except for the topknot. But Will was held by his face. It was a square, hard face, plumper than he had expected, and yet still sufficiently firm-fleshed to prevent the hint of a jowl. The mouth was wide and flat, and accentuated by the thin moustache which drooped at the corner of each lip. Chin and nose were not prominent, but the high forehead gave a promise of tremendous intelligence, just as the carefully clipped, short beard, clinging only to the very point of the chin, suggested the dandy. It was the eyes which were totally surprising. They were brown, and soft, seeming to possess an even more liquid quality than most of his countrymen. The Tokugawa appeared to be perpetually smiling at the world, or at the very least at peace with it, and yet . . . Will went to his hands and knees at the bottom of the steps, placed his hands on the floor, and lowered his forehead. He felt the eyes sliding over him like warm water, taking him in, sucking him in, learning about him although he had never said a word.

He was aware of a tingling in his veins, a feeling of destiny. A feeling he had not known since the night of his wedding. Then he had faced crushing disillusionment. But now? He had the strangest conception that he had lived for thirty-five years, and sailed half way around the world, for just this moment, this meeting in time, to kneel here before this one man, Tokugawa Minamoto no-Iyeyasu.

The Tokugawa said something in Japanese. Will raised his head, and slowly brought his body upright. There could hardly have been any other meaning in the words.

Again the prince spoke. Will shook his head, slowly.

Iyeyasu's gaze went past him. Will waited, and a moment later Suke knelt beside him.

'The prince lord Iyeyasu wishes to know from whence you have come, Will Adams,' Suke said. 'And what purpose brought you to this land.'

'Tell him I come from a country called England, which is

itself an island kingdom off the coast of the continent of Europe, which is far, far away across two oceans. Our purpose in coming hither was to trade with the peoples of Japan.'

'Trade for gold?' Suke asked, in reply to Iyeyasu's next question.

'Tell my lord Iyeyasu that we do not seek gold alone,' Will said. 'I represent the peoples of England and their neighbouring state of Holland. In those countries we produce many things which you do not have here in Japan, but which are of great use. And I observe that here in Japan you have a great number of things which we do not possess in Europe, but which we would find useful. A trade between our two countries would be of great benefit to both our peoples.'

'These goods you produce,' Suke said. 'My lord Iyeyasu asks if they are mainly firearms and powder.'

'We make firearms and powder, for our defence,' Will said cautiously.

'And there is much of this stuff on board your ship,' Iyeyasu said through the interpreter.

'For our defence, my lord Iyeyasu.'

The Tokugawa paused, gazing at Will for several seconds. 'This England of which you speak; does it war with other nations?'

'Yes, my lord Iyeyasu,' Will said. 'We are often at war. But not with our friends, or those in whom we know we can trust. Our wars are only with Spain and Portugal, for they seek to impose their rule upon us.'

Iyeyasu nodded, thoughtfully. 'What gods are worshipped in this England, Will Adams?'

'Not gods, my lord prince. We worship the one God who made heaven and earth, and rules all things.'

Iyeyasu and Suke engaged in a short conversation, no doubt, Will supposed, repeating what had been said on the galley.

At last Suke turned back to him. 'My lord Iyeyasu would have you tell him about your journey here. How many days did it take?'

Will did a hasty calculation. 'Over five hundred, my lord.'

Iyeyasu frowned, and his eyes lost some of their softness.

'It is not good to exaggerate,' Suke whispered.

'It is the truth,' Will insisted. 'If your lord will look at these charts I have with me I will explain it to him.'

Suke translated, and Iyeyasu nodded, and beckoned Will

closer, apparently a great honour, for a whisper of comment ran round the room, as hastily subdued. Will mounted the dais, taking care to sit on the step lower than the prince, and spread out his charts. He took the Tokugawa, who appeared to be interested, through the entire voyage. He seemed to be talking forever, and still Iyeyasu listened, with obvious attention, while Suke translated, in his low, dry tone, never moving from his crouching position although it occurred to Will that he must be suffering agonies of cramp. And throughout the lecture, as the hour grew later and later, and his own belly rumbled with hunger, the other nobles and guards standing around the room waited just as patiently, hardly moving, never speaking.

At last it was done, and Will paused for breath, and to rest his throat. He felt he could drink the ocean dry.

'My lord says that you have told a marvellous story,' Suke remarked. 'Story-telling is an art much practised in Japan, and you will do well in the profession.'

'Marvellous it may be, Master Kosuke, but you may tell the prince that every word is true.'

Suke translated, and Will was once again subjected to that embracing stare. At last Iyeyasu nodded, and gave Suke an order.

The minister frowned, and replied rather than translated.

Again the softness left Iyeyasu's eyes, and he repeated his earlier words, not raising his voice, but yet changing his tone.

Suke bowed. 'The hour is late, and my lord Iyeyasu says you have spoken enough. We are to withdraw. Do as I do.'

The minister made the kowtow and then straightened, and rose to his feet. Will did likewise. Iyeyasu spoke again.

'My lord says to wait,' Suke said. 'He wishes you to tell him what your ship carried. Everything.'

'I have the cargo list here,' Will said. 'It is lengthy, but, if your lord is prepared to grant me another hour . . . '

'My lord wishes it.'

Will thereupon went through the ship's inventory of goods, while Suke translated, and Iyeyasu listened. He finished with the list of arms and ammunition which had caused such a stir at Bungo, and watched Iyeyasu nod to himself.

'My lord says it is good,' Suke said. 'Now we will withdraw, Will Adams. But my lord wishes you to leave your papers and instruments.' He saw Will's concern. 'They will be safe, and returned to you in due time.'

Once again the kowtow, and then he followed Suke backwards across the floor, as if they were in the presence of a ruling monarch, until they reached the door which was opened by the guards to let them out.

'By God.' Will dried his brow on his sleeve. 'What time can it be, Master Kosuke? We seem to have been in there forever.'

'It is the hour of the rat,' Suke said. 'Which is to say, it is the beginning of a new day by the Portuguese reckoning.'

'Past midnight? Poor Melchior will have fallen asleep.'

Suke nodded, and led him across the room, his face unusually grave. The next doors were thrown open, and they reached the first of the antechambers, abandoned by all its courtiers, so that the room was empty save for the two guards. Suke made to lead Will across this room in turn, and checked. From a doorway on the far right-hand side there emerged three women.

'Down,' Suke whispered. 'On your knees, Will Adams. Quickly.'

Will hesitated for just a moment, and slowly sank to his knees, and then forward to lower his head. He listened, to an almost noiseless rustle, inhaled a gentle scent, and watched a pair of exquisite sandal-clad feet come up to him. The kimono was white. All their kimonos were white.

The woman closest to him said something, and Suke replied. 'You may raise your body, Will Adams,' he said. 'But do not stand.'

Will got himself upright, gazed at Asai Yodogimi, reached for breath. He had not been prepared for so much beauty; Magome Shikibu was an entrancing child, but yet of distinctly Eastern flavour in appearance. No doubt this woman was also of an Eastern flavour in appearance, in her general smallness, but her beauty, crystallised by the glistening white of the paint which covered every inch of her flesh from her chin to her forehead, transcended race, and colour, and, he suspected, creed.

And, as with Iyeyasu, he felt himself in the presence of something bigger than he had known before. And harder. There was a suggestion of steel emanating from the black eyes. He had once stood in a crowd close to the road upon which Queen Elizabeth had passed, on horseback, and, no doubt entirely by chance, she had glanced at him as she drew abreast. There had been no beauty there; he had felt a distinct disappointment. But the imperiousness of her stare, the utter confidence in her manner, had done much to atone for any lack of looks. She had been so obviously mistress of all she surveyed. He knew the same feeling now. This woman *owned* this castle, and all in it. And *she* was beautiful into the bargain.

The woman next to her was clearly her sister; slightly shorter, no less perfect in feature. But lacking the aura of power.

Suke was speaking again, but Yodogimi stopped him with a gesture from her fan, and said something else.

The third woman, who had been standing behind the two princesses, now moved forward.

'God in Heaven,' Will whispered, before he could stop himself. Surely he was dreaming, now, had fallen asleep while relating his adventures to Iyeyasu? And thus included one of his dreams. For this girl was clearly no more than half Japanese. Taller than her mistress, her loose black hair heavily streaked with reddish tints, her face was everything any man might have wished in his sweetest midnight encounter; although she was very young there could be no arguing about her womanhood. Where the princess's kimono shrouded everything from her shoulders, the girl's hesitated at her breasts, and rested lightly on her hips. And she had long legs; that much was obvious. Woman. The epitome of everything woman should ever be, or could ever be, standing here before him, after thirty-five years of unfulfilled desire.

And did she ever stand next to a bath in which a naked man soaked? Christ give me strength, he thought.

'You are the man from across the ocean,' she said in perfect Portuguese. 'My mistress, the princess Asai Yodogimi, bids you welcome to Japan in the name of the Kwambaku.'

Will licked his lips. How dry was his throat. 'It is my great good fortune to be here,' he said. 'I would thank your mistress for her kind words.'

The girl translated, and Yodogimi smiled. Will's mouth fell open in surprise, for her teeth were painted black. Hastily he glanced at the girl. Hers, too? But she was not smiling.

Yodogimi spoke.

'We had heard that you came to Osaka,' the girl said. 'But you have not been before the Kwambaku.'

Will glanced at Suke, who replied in Japanese.

Yodogimi's gaze drifted to him, and she frowned, and spoke quickly.

'What is your name, please?' Will whispered.

'Pinto Magdalena is my name,' the girl said.

'Then you are Portuguese?'

'My grandfather was Portuguese. He was the first European to land in Japan.' She gave an anxious glance to her right as she realised that her mistress and Suke had stopped speaking, and were listening to them. Hastily she explained their conversation in Japanese.

Yodogimi gazed at Will for several seconds, and then smiled again, and made a remark to Suke.

Once again his reply caused her to frown; indeed, she looked for a moment angry, and as before, her speech quickened.

Suke replied stubbornly.

Yodogimi tossed her head, and made a remark to Magdalena.

'My mistress says to you, Will Adams, that you must have patience and all will be well. She further wishes me to tell you that you must learn the Japanese tongue, should you intend to remain amongst us.'

'I should like to do that, Senhorina Pinto,' Will said. 'Providing I could discover someone with the patience to teach me.'

Again the anxious glance at her mistress. But now Suke was bending forward once more in the kowtow, and Will followed his example; the ladies swept past and were gone, only their scent hanging on the still air.

Suke stood up. 'Come, it is late.'

'I look forward to a bed, and that's for certain.'

Suke said nothing, but hurried through the next room, at the far end of which they saw Melchior, seated on the floor, his back propped against the wall, snoring loudly.

'That lady,' Will said. 'She is the wife of the Kwambaku?'

'His mother,' Suke said. 'The princess Asai Yodogimi was the favourite concubine of the great Hideyoshi; her beauty is such that he elevated her above all other women, and her son above his other children.' He clapped his hands, the sound echoing in the huge, empty chamber.

'Certainly she is very pretty,' Will agreed.

'There is none more beautiful in all Japan.' The doors opened, and half a dozen guards came in; Suke addressed them in Japanese.

'And the other lady?'

'The princess Asai Jokoin. Yodogimi's younger sister.'

'I meant the Portuguese girl.'

Suke shrugged. 'She is one of the princess's maids. I know nothing about her. Osaka is not Prince Iyeyasu's normal residence. Now, Will Adams, you and your companion must go with these men. Believe me, I am sorry this had to happen; I can but beg of you, as was recommended by the princess, to exercise patience, and trust in the future. And in Kosuke no-Suke; be sure that I shall be working for you.'

He hurried off, leaving Will staring after him in amazement.

'Eh? Eh?' Melchior yawned and struggled to his feet. 'Will? Is that you? I had given you up for lost.'

'We seem to be in the care of these fellows,' Will said. 'What would you, sir?'

But there was no pleasantry in the faces of the soldiers. Their captain merely pointed to the doorway, and kept his hand on his sword.

'No doubt we are to sleep with the garrison,' Melchior said, as they followed the guards towards the great door of the keep. 'Did you notice the richness of the hangings in there, Will?'

'And that was nothing compared with the prince's reception room,' Will told him. 'There is great wealth here, Melchior. Greater, indeed, than any I have heard tell of in England, not excluding the palace of Her Majesty herself.'

'And yet it does not pervade everywhere,' Melchior remarked. They had left the keep itself and crossed the courtyard to enter a doorway let into the outer wall. Now they followed hewn stone steps downwards between walls of undressed stone and lit by flaring torches set in the crevices. ''Twas ever thus; in this world one must either be a prince or a pauper, and we are limited to the latter region.'

The good fellow was still half asleep, and, no doubt, still bemused by the unvarying kindness they had been shown since their arrival in Japan, Will supposed. For his part he was becoming a little concerned. The stone steps reached a landing, from off which branched a corridor, lined with what he could not help but regard as cells. And yet they did not stop here, but followed the steps ever downwards.

'Will?' Melchior asked. 'A strange distance for the garrison.'

'I very much fear that in some way I angered the prince,' Will said. 'Or he has chosen to believe the Portuguese opinion of us.'

The steps came to another landing, but this contained no corridor, only a hatch set in the wall. And here, suddenly, they had left the sweetness behind them. The air was fetid, and filled with *sound*, of an indescribably ugly sort, like a herd of pigs wrestling together. But the sounds were human.

The commander of the guard nodded, and three of his men presented their pikes at the hatch, while another stood to one side, and with a quick movement threw it open.

Stench and noise blared at them, and hands and feet immediately came thrusting out, but what hands and feet. Here was none of the neat cleanliness Will had already begun to associate with these people, but rather limbs such as he would have expected to find in one of the London gaols, covered in dirt and festering sores. The pikes were busy driving the monsters back. The officer jerked his head.

'By Christ, Will,' Melchior cried, 'are we to go in there?'

Will glanced at the guards. Six men, and armed. No wonder Suke had been distressed. But so had the princess Yodogimi, when she had learned of their fate. And they had both counselled patience.

'It seems we have no choice, dear friend.'

'I would rather die.'

'Patience,' Will said. 'I beg of you, Melchior. I do not know what brought this upon us. But I am sure we have friends.'

The officer's gestures had become imperative. Will sighed, dropped to his hands and knees, the pikes thrusting on either side to clear a way for him. He could hardly breathe, so terrible was the stench; it seeped around him like a living thing, seemed to strike at his body; he could feel his clothes becoming filthy as he moved. He got through the hatch, his eyes dimly making out more than a dozen forms, twisting and writhing as they were driven back, dimly hearing the groans and grunts and shrieks and cries, and then moved to one side as Melchior joined him. A moment later the hatch dropped into place and the cell was once again dark. Which in one way was a blessing, he supposed; it hid the hideousness of their situation. But in another was more desperate than ever, for now hands came at them out of the darkness, seeking their clothes, tearing and scratching, stroking their faces, rifling their pockets, and doing far worse, as they sought nipple and genital, like hungry beasts on heat.

'God in Heaven,' Melchior shouted. 'Will? Will? Surely we have been consigned to hell.'

Will clasped his hands together, swung them left and right. If he angered them and so was murdered, well then, this was best. He encountered flesh, felt it moving to and fro. A body dropped on his neck, hands thrusting downwards like some decayed and disgusting Marlowe. Will reached behind him, hurled the man across the room and listened to an echoing howl of pain. He forced himself backwards, found the stone of the wall. 'Melchior,' he shouted. 'Melchior, are you there?'

'Here,' the Dutchman grunted from close at hand.

'Come against the wall,' Will said. 'Stay close, Melchior. Stay close. We will resist them yet.'

But already the onslaught was subsiding. The arms no longer flailed the darkness, the scraping fingers no longer scoured obscenely. He realised that these savage creatures were actually too weak to do more than react to what went on around them. They had been aroused by the guards, and so they had attacked, blindly and without reason, those who had entered their hell. But already their interest had waned, and they had retired. They knew not whether it was night or day; they merely existed, groaning, howling, talking amongst themselves, chattering and twisting, rustling and stinking.

'Will,' Melchior said. 'These men must be condemned.'

To death? This indeed would be a merciful thought. But supposing they were only condemned? Locked in this hole to rot? Patience, Will Adams. Patience. Yodogimi had said that. The most beautiful woman in all Japan. Not true. Christ, how he dreamed of those breasts. But more, of that cleanliness, of that exaltation. Had Pinto Magdalena known where they were being taken? No matter; she would know now. Would she care? Would she understand such horror, having lived all her life in the brilliant light above? Would she ever, could she ever, again look on him as other than a piece of filth, contaminated through all eternity? Would she ever have the opportunity?

'Will?' Melchior said. 'Are you awake?'

'Aye.' But how tired. How exhausted. It seemed that he might never have slept before in his life.

'I must sleep, Will. And yet I fear for our lives.'

'You sleep, Melchior. I'll watch for a spell. Then you may take my place.'

Although he supposed there was little enough to be afraid of. He could see nothing in this blackness, even now that his eyes were accustomed to it. He could scarce make out his hand in front of his face. So the other prisoners were hardly likely to be better off in that respect. An assault would mean a resumption of that fumbling, grasping obscenity, and at the first touch he would be sufficiently awake to repel them.

He closed his eyes. His head drooped, and became buried in

the softness of breasts, and fell lower, to meet long, strong legs. Mary had such legs. Mary Magdalena. Mary Magdalena.

A rasping sound, bringing them upright. And not only them. That ghastly howling, wailing noise came from all around them. He feared it now. He had seen more, too much, of what his companions in distress looked like. That had been when they had been fed. He was not sure of the hour. He would never be sure of the hour again. But the hatch had been opened and a vast bowl of rice had been pushed in, and in the second before the hatch had been closed again he had seen the naked bodies, the running sores, the slavering mouths, the erected genitals, of men who were no longer men.

They had not eaten, Melchior and himself. Hungry, certainly, but to venture into that cesspool of humanity, not knowing, in the dark, what you might touch, what might touch you, was an inconceivable thought. So, they would sit here and starve to death. But even that was a horrifying thought. For in the brief moment of light the others had also looked at *them*. And understood their defeat of the previous night. They had known they were no match, even nearly a score of them, for two large and strong young men. But starvation would bring weakness. Even incarceration in here would bring weakness, quickly enough. And then how would they resist those questing fingers?

And now, what new disaster was to be inflicted upon them? The bowl of rice had not been so very long ago. There would hardly be another meal already.

The hatch swung open, and the pike butts came snapping in, cracking on bone and fingers, driving the howling creatures back into the darkness.

'Will Adams,' Kosuke no-Suke called. 'Bring your companion and come. Quickly, man. But call out as you approach the door.'

'Melchior.' Will shook his friend. 'Come on, lad.' He crawled forward, re-entered that forest of flailing horror. 'Now, Master Kosuke. We are coming now. Do not stop, Melchior.'

He hurled himself at the hatchway, tumbled out into the flickering light of the torch, fell across the passage and collapsed against the wall, watched Melchior also come out, accompanied by two of the other inmates. But these were met with the pike staffs, and driven back, shrieking and snarling. There were six guards, and Suke. And the hatch was dropping back into place. 'Come, my friends,' Suke said. 'Let us escape this place.'

'By God, Master Kosuke.' Will helped Melchior to his feet. 'Do not tell me that is a fair sample of a Japanese prison?'

'Indeed, Will Adams, for such malefactors as those. You have been in hell.'

'We'd already deduced as much.' He followed their friend, for such he certainly counted Suke now, up the stone steps.

'Not a Portuguese hell, Will Adams. It is the name of the cell. In our language, gokuya.'

'And yet I was informed in Bungo that the only punishment meted out to criminals in Japan was death.'

'Indeed,' Suke agreed. 'But those men are not being punished. They are awaiting trial. They are suspected, with good reason, of being robbers, but as they have always murdered their victims, there are no witnesses against them. It would be unjust to condemn a man without proof, and so they are placed in the hell until they are ready to confess. They have been there for some time.'

'And if they do not confess they must rot there forever? Truly, in each country justice takes on an entirely different concept.'

'They must stay there, certainly, until they confess. Or until their friends can prove their innocence. I am sorry you were forced to suffer with them. It was the will of the lord Iyeyasu. He found it difficult to credit your remarkable tale, and was thus angry. But this morning I succeeded in interesting him in your charts again, and attempted to show him that all of what you said could very well have been true. With the result that he considers the matter further. So now, here is your new cell. This is known as a roya, or cage; you will be comfortable here.'

The door was barred, certainly, and Will estimated they had not yet regained the ground level of the palace; but the room itself was large, and the air was fresh. Most important of all, it was empty, and there was a window, also barred, but let into the outer wall of the keep and looking over the moat and the next defensive level. 'Master Kosuke, this is a palace, compared with the other.'

Suke bowed. 'And even this, I hope, will soon be but a bad memory, Will Adams. Now you will wish to remove your clothes and cleanse yourselves. I will send people to you.'

'Food, Will,' Melchior said. 'Ask him about food.'

Will translated, and Suke smiled. 'You shall be fed, never fear.'

The door closed. Will remained at the window. There was a sight he'd never expected to see again. But it was early in the morning, and there was little activity in the fortress. Could they really have spent better than twenty-four hours in that hell? Truly, he realised, this was an all or nothing country.

Footsteps outside the door. He turned, and watched Melchior also rise in anticipation. They were to be bathed. What delights would this have in store for them? The door swung open; there were guards out there, pikes at the ready to discourage any attempt at a break-out, and four very young men, hardly more than boys, two of whom carried between them a huge tub of steaming water, while the others had towels and Japanese clothes and the pitchers of cold water which were necessary for the actual washing; there was the usual grating in the corner of the room, connected to a drain in the castle wall.

'This day we have to attend to our own wants,' Will said. 'There's the penalty for being in gaol.'

'I'd settle for a swim in the sea,' Melchior declared, stripping off his clothes. 'What's this?'

For the boys were also undressing.

'They mean to share our bath,' Will said. 'We'd best ignore them.' He knelt, and one of the boys emptied a pitcher of water over his shoulders; he reached for the soap, and found it was already gone—it was being applied to his back.

'Will?' Melchior asked uneasily. 'Will, I like it not.'

For whereas Magome Shikibu's young women had preserved a total disinterest in what they did, the boys seemed unable to do so.

'I fear me,' Melchior said, 'that for all the appearance of civilisation, this is a most devilish country. When condemned criminals are hacked into little pieces, when prisoners not yet condemned are confined in such surroundings as our recent cell, when we are forced into close contact with two such hardened lances as these . . . two? I am dreaming.' For of course there were four boys.

'Stop that,' Will growled. 'I will finish myself.' He shook his head violently, for his attendant obviously understood no Portuguese, and made a gesture for him to go away as the youth would have carried his ministrations to the front.

The boy stared at him, eyes wide, face a picture of dismay.

''Tis certain they *mean* no harm,' Will muttered. But what were they doing to him as well? 'Leave off,' he bellowed, rising to his feet in defence, and hastily climbing into the tub, covered in soap as he was, for sheer shame.

The boy gazed at him, water running down his legs, his thrusting penis but typifying the combination of passion and anxiety which seemed to fill his entire being.

'But they have done enough.' Melchior joined Will in the tub. 'And by God, here are some more.'

For the door was opening again, to admit Suke and two more youths, these now carrying bowls of rice.

'Ah, my friends,' Suke said. 'You will feel better for your bath, I have no doubt. Now sit you down and eat your fill.'

'I doubt we could manage a morsel, Master Kosuke.' Will climbed out of the bath. 'These young fellows are shameless creatures, and I trust you will take a stick to their backsides and then dunk them in cold water, to settle their ardour.'

Suke spoke to the boy who had bathed Will, and then to his companions, and turned back to the Europeans, his face a study of concern. 'Do they not please you?'

'Now there's a question,' Will said. 'We are men, Master Kosuke. As are they. To be pleased by boys like these is to be damned.'

Suke smiled. 'For all your protestations, Will Adams, you have much in common with the Portuguese. They too call it sinful for one man to couple with another. But then, they call it sinful for a man even to couple with a woman, save within the bonds of marriage. A strange people, and indeed, often I wonder that there *are* any Portuguese, if they regard the natural act as such a duty, rather than a pleasure. But from you, Will Adams, I had expected more. I selected these boys myself. They have been carefully educated to do nothing but please.'

Will scratched his head. '*You* selected them, Master Kosuke? Boys?'

'Would you rather have had girls? Then it shall be so. I but sought to make amends for your miserable night in that hell.'

'And you thought boys would please us best?'

'It never occurred to me otherwise, Will Adams. Oh, a pretty girl is nice to look upon, but they are changeable creatures; should they fail to like a man they will tease rather than please, and even to beat them makes little change in their demeanour. But a pretty boy, now, and these are pretty boys, would you not agree?'

'Oh, indeed,' Will said. 'As pretty as any I have ever seen.'

'Well, you may believe me when I promise that their hands will be as soft as any girl's, and that they will seek only to please you, and more, to have you please them, and that, being well versed in the art of love, they will make that easy for you as well.'

'No doubt,' Will said. 'And you would not consider it unmanly for one man to take another?'

Suke frowned in genuine bewilderment. 'Unmanly, Will Adams? Manhood is proved, or lost, with a sword in your hand. It can be gained in no other way, and it can be lost in no other way. Indeed, to this end it is far better for man to couple with man, when each will understand his true responsibilities to his own and his lover's honour, than with woman, who too often would sacrifice honour for comfort and survival. Now come, if these lads displease you, I will send them away. But you must eat in haste. My lord Iyeyasu wishes to hold another conversation with you. And this time, I beg of you, Will Adams, to be careful. At least part of your recent misfortune was caused by your insolence.'

'My insolence?' Will demanded. 'To the prince? By God. I performed the kowtow. What else would you have me do, Master Kosuke?'

'It is your manner, your way of speech, the very look in your eye. Indeed, no Japanese would dare to meet the prince's gaze at all. Think on these things, I beg of you, for your own protection.'

Think on these things, for your own protection. The Tokugawa was smiling at him. 'My lord says you are more suited by Japanese clothes, Will Adams,' Suke said.

Too insolent. But when addressed, it was not in his nature to do otherwise than look into the eyes of the man to whom he spoke, prince or not. 'Tell my lord Iyeyasu that I am flattered by his compliment.'

'My lord wishes to know the history of your land. The course of your wars, Will Adams.'

Will gave as good an account of English history as he could, going back to the Norman Conquest, touching on the Hundred Years' War with France, and then entering into the rivalry between England and Spain. As before, Iyeyasu listened to Suke's translation with a grave, thoughtful expression. But the last time the expression had, apparently, hidden disbelief.

'My lord says that in many ways the history of your country and the history of Japan are similar,' Suke said. 'Except that Japan has never been conquered by a foreign invader. The Mongols attempted to land here, many years ago, but they were defeated, and a great storm wrecked their fleet, much as you say happened in your fight with the Spaniards. And only eight years ago the mighty Hideyoshi embarked upon an invasion of China, much as your King Edward sought to impose his will upon France.'

'And met with a similar failure?' Will asked.

'By no means. Korea was conquered without difficulty, despite assistance from the Chinese. And China would have fallen as easily, despite the warnings of the Chinese themselves, who told us we might as well seek to empty the ocean with a spoon, as send our armies into the world that is China.'

'But the war does not continue?' Will asked.

'Alas, Will Adams, the lord Hideyoshi died, a year and a half ago, and the counsels of the country have since been divided, with the result that our armies were brought home. Our generals wait for a use for their skill and valour. My lord Iyeyasu asks if those eighteen cannon mounted in your ship can be used on land as well.'

'Tell your lord that they can, provided some means of transport is found for them.'

Iyeyasu nodded, more thoughtfully than ever.

'And can you, Will Adams, fire those cannon?'

Will hesitated. But he had studied gunnery, and there was no question as to the answer Iyeyasu wished. 'Yes, my lord Iyeyasu.'

Iyeyasu nodded.

'My lord has been considering your voyage, Will Adams, with the aid of your charts. He wishes to know if all such ventures are so costly in men and ships, and if so, why do your people undertake them?'

Once again Will realised that the prince had already decided what answer he required. 'All are costly, certainly, my lord, but ours was more so than most.'

'Why?'

'Our leaders were uncertain as to their purpose, and our counsels were divided.'

'Yet you are yourself one of the leaders.'

Will opened his mouth to protest, and then changed his mind. The prince was not interested in excuses, he was sure. 'I take my share of the responsibility for the disasters of the voyage, my lord. I think I would have done better had I been in sole command. Instead I had to try to persuade, not always with success.'

Iyeyasu said something, smiling.

'My lord remarks that it is good, and wishes you to return to your quarters. He hopes you are comfortable.'

'My comfort has increased, my lord Iyeyasu. I hope it may continue to do so.'

Once again Iyeyasu smiled.

'My lord has one more question to ask you, Will Adams,' Suke said. 'What will you do with your time before he calls for you again?'

Think, think, think. There would be one answer above all others, now, which would matter. Will sucked air into his lungs. 'I would endeavour to learn the Japanese tongue, my lord Iyeyasu, so that when next we meet I may converse with you as man to man.'

Iyeyasu gazed at him for several seconds, and then nodded.

'My lord is pleased,' Suke said. 'And so am I, Will Adams. I will myself teach you our language. Now come, we must withdraw.'

From the window of the cell, the courtyard of the next level was a constant wonder. Even after several weeks. How many weeks? He had almost lost touch with time. But always there was so much to be watched, the soldiers of the garrison exercising, with much shouting and stamping of feet, practising their archery, which was superb; great nobles arriving and leaving, each accompanied by an endless troupe of followers with gifts for the Kwambaku; messengers from various parts of the empire; strange beings who were apparently Buddhist monks, although they seemed to have as many sects and subdivisions as Christianity—but never a sight of the Kwambaku himself. Or more important, of his mother. And her ladies-in-waiting?

Perhaps they never went out. So perhaps he would never see them again. There was doubt, all the time. Prince Iyeyasu had been pleased with his replies, so Suke had said, and true to his promise, Suke had laboured to teach him the Japanese tongue, for several hours in every day, exchanging Japanese for lessons from Will in Dutch, much to the amusement of Melchior. Now Will could manage a passable speech in Japanese, although reading the language remained a problem. But for what purpose? Prince Iyeyasu had *appeared* to be pleased. But then, he had not appeared to be displeased on their first meeting. And so they waited, uneasily. For in addition to the endless spectacle and procession in the yard there were regular doleful lines of condemned criminals, much like the ones he had seen at Bungo, making their last sad walk to the gate and beyond. Who could say they would not one day make that journey? For there were Portuguese priests too, far more than he would have expected, often to be seen in the courtyard.

He had asked Suke about this, but the minister had been reticent. The Jesuits had started coming about sixty years ago, led by Francis Xavier, of whom even Will had heard. Oda Nobunaga, the great general who had begun the reunification of the country, just about the time, Will supposed, that Her Majesty had mounted the English throne, had welcomed the Christians, because he had been opposed by the immense Buddhist priesthood, and had found the Christians useful allies. Nobunaga had broken the power of the Buddhists after a long siege of this very castle, then a Buddhist stronghold, but after his death Hideyoshi had decided that the Christians were equally a menace to strong government, and had instituted a persecution which had led to the crucifixion of more than one convert. Strangely, now that Hideyoshi was dead, Suke said darkly, the priests were always welcome at Osaka. Of course, Hideyori was still only a boy, entirely under the rule of his mother. And Yodogimi was not a Christian, at least openly, but there were many in her train who were, men as well as women.

Including Magdalena?

'And what of Iyeyasu?' Will had asked.

'Prince Iyeyasu judges each man, each creed, on its merit, Will Adams,' Suke had replied. 'He will not hold it against you that you are of the Christian faith.'

Not Iyeyasu, but who else? Perhaps himself. For Suke had done more than teach him to speak Japanese. Seeing that neither Melchior nor himself had seemed pleased with the idea of being served by boys, he had cheerfully offered to send girls, and indeed their twice-daily bath was now superintended by various young women. But they had refused any other service. At least, he had refused it, and Melchior, a little grudgingly, had followed his example.

Now, why? God, how he wanted. How, indeed, he tore at

himself, on occasion. And here there could be no sin. *Here*. But where was here? A physical place? Or an eternity inside the human mind? What did he fear? He would have taken off after any Limehouse whore without a second thought. Oh, no, he would have had a second thought, and then done it just the same, and spent an agonising week wrestling with his conscience.

Was that what he feared? That there would be no conscience, here? Merely a joust with the devil which would leave him damned? What nonsense. For what was conscience save an invention of mankind? Of Christian mankind. At least in matters of the flesh. How stupid that man, with so much to do, should spend so much of his time engaged in mental wrestling, in some cases to the ruination of his health, over what to do about a part of his body which developed an appetite. He did not so brood on the call of his belly, on the thirst he could slake with a glass of wine.

So why? Because he feared the women themselves? If nakedness meant nothing to them, if even the touch of a man's body, the intimate stroking that accompanied the bath, meant nothing to them, what would, or could, turn them back into women? Did he fear his own inability to meet their demands?

Or did he fear to become Japanese himself? Now why? In so far as he could see, everything about these people, and most important, their way of life, their attitude to life, was superior to anything in England. To anything in Europe. So perhaps theirs was a totally material existence. Perhaps they *would* never produce a Marlowe. Were they not the more fortunate for that? Certainly Marlowe had not been happy. Of what good was it to call a man a genius after he was dead?

So why? Did he continue to punish himself, for having survived the voyage, where all the others, Tim and Tom, young Spring, Jacques Mahu, had not? What nonsense. Would he, then, deny himself for the rest of his life? Or was it truly, because he was English, alien to this culture, he still dreamed of the one above all, his Zenocrate. As he had dreamed of Mary, so many years ago. And now he had seen the one, the only woman there could ever be for him, and so, belonging to a nation of dreamers rather than doers, he preferred to dream instead of to act?

How Suke would laugh. And Tadatune. And Magome Shikibu.

And Pinto Magdalena? He turned away from the window as the door opened, for there she was.

Chapter 4

MAGDALENA DID not enter the room, but instead gave it a quick glance, and then half smiled at Will. Today she was unpainted, and her cheeks were flushed; she was even more beautiful than he remembered. 'My mistress, the Princess Yodogimi, wishes to speak with you, Will Adams,' she said, in hardly more than a whisper.

Will's heart was pounding so much he found difficulty in speaking. 'And my friend, here?'

She shook her head; the heavy, dark red-tinted hair swayed gently. 'We must be careful,' she said, and stepped back into the corridor, which, surprisingly, was empty of guards. She waited, while Will stepped outside, and then carefully closed the door; the catch dropped into place by itself. He stood at her shoulder, inhaled her perfume, was almost touched by her hair as she turned. She wore a similar white kimono to when he had first seen her, although on this occasion there was a faint flowered pattern upon the silk. Now she glanced at him, and the colour spread upwards from her neck. 'Quickly,' she said, and moved down the corridor.

Will hurried at her side. 'I do not understand,' he said. 'Is this not the Kwambaku's palace, and is the princess not the Kwambaku's mother?'

'Nothing is as it seems in Japan,' she said and checked at the stairs, throwing out her right arm to stop him. Perhaps deliberately, he was slow to react, and so brushed into her arm, and closed his fingers on her hand. Again the quick glance, this time accompanied by an even quicker frown. Then she gently pulled her hand free, and to his surprise, hurried down the steps. At the bottom she turned into another corridor, which he estimated carried them beneath the courtyard, until she reached another very narrow flight of stone steps. Here she paused, listening.

'Then perhaps you would explain the situation,' Will said. 'I would not have you risk your life for me.'

'My life, Will Adams, is at the disposal of my mistress,' she told him. 'Nor do I think it is in danger at this moment. But my mistress would not have Prince Iyeyasu know she has spoken with you.'

She set off again, up the steps. Soon they changed to wood, although remaining very narrow, and he gathered they were in the palace itself.

'I had assumed that Prince Iyeyasu was a guest here,' he panted.

She nodded.

'But then . . . '

Again she checked, and this time turned to face him, so suddenly he all but ran into her, and stopped before he actually intended to, cursing himself for a slow-witted dolt. 'There is much intrigue in Japan, Will Adams,' she said. 'And more in Osaka than anywhere else. The Kwambaku is but a child. The empire is governed by a regency of five daimyo, of whom by far the most powerful is Prince Iyeyasu. But the prince has many sons of his own; he would make one of them ruler of Japan. Or perhaps he would take the power himself.'

'Your mistress *knows* this?' Will demanded. 'And yet entertains him in her home?'

'My mistress is reluctant to provoke an end to the peace. For three centuries before the great Hideyoshi there was nothing but war in Japan. Besides, the Tokugawa are too powerful. It is better for us to wait, and watch, and perhaps force *them* into an overt act.'

How seriously she spoke. How serious she was. This was no idle gossip she repeated. How unlike any comparable English girl.

'And is your time entirely taken up with affairs of state, Magdalena?'

This time she did not flush, and her green eyes were cool. 'There is a time for all things, Will Adams,' she said. 'And we are presently engaged upon affairs of state.'

She made to lead him on, and he touched her arm. He would have held it, but she turned with such evident surprise that he should dare to lay a finger on her that he hastily let her go. 'And perhaps you also look upon me as an enemy of your people?'

'How can you, Will Adams, be an enemy of my people? At least as yet. It is your intention that my mistress would discover.'

'I meant the Portuguese. I am a Protestant. In the eyes of your priests, a heretic.'

Pinto Magdalena smiled. Her teeth, to his relief, were gleaming white. 'I am a Christian, Will Adams. As are you. I do not understand the differences made by the priests, nor do I wish to do so. That we worship the same Christ is sufficient to make me your friend, if you will have it so. As for Portugal, that was the land of my grandfather. My country is Japan, and there can never be another.'

She walked away from him, and he hurried behind her to another narrow staircase, now obviously set in the outer wall of the palace itself. This they climbed until at last Magdalena parted a curtain to admit him into a surprisingly small chamber, although as richly decorated as the one in which Iyeyasu had received him, and with the same raised dais, although this time it was at the far side rather than in the middle. Here she dropped to her knees in the kowtow and he followed her example.

'You may rise, Magdalena,' Yodogimi said in Japanese. 'And tell the foreigner to do likewise.'

Will raised his head. 'I understand Japanese, my lady. I have learned the tongue these past six weeks.'

'Then we have no need of an interpreter.' Yodogimi sat on an embroidered mat on the dais, and, like her servant, she wore no paint today; her features were even more flawless than he had supposed. 'Leave us, Magdalena.'

He wanted to turn his head, but dared not. There was a momentary rustle, and then silence. By God, he thought; I kneel here, alone, with a princess.

'Come closer, Will Adams,' she commanded.

He stood up, moved to the edge of the dais, knelt again. She gazed at him without blinking.

'Tell me,' she said, 'of what you speak, when with the Tokugawa.' This day her teeth, too, had been neglected; the black had faded to an ugly brown.

'He asks about my country, about my voyage here, about my god, my lady.'

He watched her hand emerge from the sleeve of her kimono, and slowly come towards him. He felt hypnotised, unable to move, aware only of a sudden swelling in his groin. But surely that was impossible. *That.*

Her fingers touched his cheek, slid down on to his beard, thrust into it. 'Such hair,' she said. 'No man in Japan has hair like this. Nor do the priests. Magdalena's grandfather. But that was so very long ago.' The hand was withdrawn. 'You see me dressed for the bedchamber, Will Adams. Magdalena has told me this is how the women of Europe appear, even in public. Is this true?'

How he panted, or wished to do so. If only he could read the expression in her eyes. 'Yes, my lady.'

'Then it will not appear strange to you, Will Adams. Am I a beautiful woman, to European eyes?'

'I have never seen such beauty, my lady.' Oh, Magdalena, Magdalena. Had she known? But he still did not know, himself. He could not believe.

'As you are a beautiful man,' Yodogimi said. 'For where a woman should be small, a man should be large. I have never seen a man of such size. I would look more closely, Will Adams. Disrobe. And stand.'

May God have mercy on my soul, he thought. But resist this, Will Adams, and you are more than a fool. Resist *this*? Had he been made of purest steel, that were not possible.

He rose to his feet, released the girdle at his waist, thrust back his shoulders, and the kimono fell to the ground.

'And the other,' Yodogimi said, without changing the expression of her voice or her face.

He had known, from the moment he had entered, that she would wish this. And he had known that he would obey without question. Perhaps all his life he had looked forward to be thus commanded, by a woman. The loin-cloth fell on top of the kimono. He trembled although it was warm inside the apartment. God, to stand here, in such anxiety, before so much beauty.

'Yes,' Yodogimi said. 'I have never seen such a man. Are all the men in your country like you, Will Adams?'

He watched her move, slowly uncoiling her legs as she rose to her knees.

'Not all, my lady,' he whispered. 'But enough.'

'Then are your women blessed.' Her hands started at his buttocks, came round his thighs, slowly cupped underneath his testicles, extended along the penis itself. 'Such wonder,' she said. 'Such wonder.'

'My lady . . . '

She frowned. 'And are they similarly impatient, your people?'

'It is your beauty, my lady. Your touch. And I have been without a woman for too long.' How simple to say, to a princess.

To be stroked, where no woman had ever delved before, save in the sexless luxury of the bath. But this was no serving girl. The Princess Asai Yodogimi, mother of the Kwambaku, mistress of Toyotomi Hideyoshi.

Her forehead cleared. 'Then you are forgiven. But yet, I do not wish you to fade away from me, Will Adams.' She rose to her feet, effortlessly, seemed to glide away from him, across the room to a small cupboard set in the wall, and then turned and came back to him. In her hand she carried a small cloth ring, very carefully and indeed beautifully made, with a decorated fringe. This she placed over his penis, rolling it down the flesh until it reached the base. It seemed to grip him tightly; he felt his belly was about to explode.

Yodogimi stepped away from him, released her own girdle. Her kimono lay on the floor. What beauty. What beauty. Except for the teeth. But the teeth were not relevant when in the presence of the body. How small, and delicately formed; but flawlessly proportioned as well. She walked on to the dais, and there knelt on the mat. 'Do I, then, displease you?'

He followed her, knelt beside her, put his arm around her shoulder to lower her on to her back, and was once again warned by the quick frown.

'Are you, then, a savage creature, Will Adams? Do you seek to ravage me?'

'My lady, I know nothing save desire, at this moment.'

'Nor I,' she whispered. 'Nor I. But for a moment I thought you meant to lie on me.'

'To lie on you. But how else . . . '

'As is truly said, Will Adams, Europe is a country of barbarians. Should not your weight bear me, rather than otherwise?' She had *his* shoulders, and gently eased him on to the mat, while still kneeling herself. Sinful. How sinful. There was only one way of love, surely. That ordained by Church and custom. Christ in Heaven, what is happening to me?

Yodogimi straddled his knees, one of her legs on either side of his, slowly lowered herself until she sat. For a few seconds she amused herself, exploring him with her fingers, and then slowly came forward. Her body slid over his thighs and belly. Her eyes were half closed, and her flesh seemed filled with a pinkish glow. Her small breasts rose and fell rhythmically. And yet he had not properly touched her. But she came ever closer, her knees spreading as she slipped upwards. Now she sat on his chest. His arms came up to allow his fingers to grip her shoulders, but lightly, now. He was learning with all possible speed. There was no risk of withdrawal here, of denial. There was only the risk of too hasty a conclusion; he could feel the semen pounding against the restraining band. He was, indeed, being tortured in the most delicious possible manner. And tortured in more than one sense. Did Pinto Magdalena make love like this also? God, to have *her* here. To have those breasts, for his hands were sliding under the princess's armpits to come round to the front, and gently encourage the nipples into hardness. Would he then never be satisfied? To hold Asai Yodogimi in his arms, and yet wish for more? Now *there* was hell.

And yet he had not sampled a fraction of what she had to offer, of what she wished to offer. This was plain. She waited, and yet she would not wait forever. But for the first time in his life, here was woman actually wanting to be possessed, without payment or fear, but merely for the desire of it. His hands moved down to her thighs, and behind, to cup the tiny buttocks. For this, apparently, had she been waiting. Her body moved forward again, to command his face. For how long had he waited for *that* from willing woman? He seemed to be seized by a convulsion as his arms wrapped themselves around her waist to bring her yet closer, to be swamped by a sweet-smelling world of dampened hair. And then she was gone, as she half fell over, thrusting down her hands to check herself.

'Barbarian,' she said, but she was smiling. 'Do they not teach gentleness in your land, Will Adams?'

'Yodogimi,' he whispered, reaching for her again. 'Yodogimi . . .'

But now she frowned. 'I am a princess, not a slave girl, Will Adams, and must be properly addressed. I forgive your rudeness, for your lack of knowledge. But it were best finished, I think, before you do me an injury. Just now I felt your teeth, where I should have known only lips and tongue.' She made him lie down again, and took her position across his thighs. Like this? God in Heaven. How sinful. How sinful. But the restraining band was being withdrawn by those unforgettable fingers, and a moment later he was imprisoned, her body slowly rising and falling, seeming to stretch away forever above him before gently, oh so gently, returning to touch his thighs.

How strange, he thought; we have not kissed each other.

She rose, as effortlessly as ever, and clapped her hands. Instantly the room filled with young women. By God, Will thought; they were there all the time, just behind the curtain. And yet, how solemn, and courteous, where English girls would have been a mass of giggles and excited whisperings. Even Magdalena. Or was Magdalena merely sad?

They carried bowls of warm water, with which they attended to their mistress and to him at the same time. How soft, how gentle; their hands reinvigorated him, and he felt once again capable of doing justice to his manhood. And more than that, for it was Magdalena herself attending to him, kneeling beside him, her head bowed, her kimono rising and falling as she breathed. Oh God, that this could be his one day. Now he knew what she could offer, what she would offer, this had to be. Some day . . . but why not soon? Why not now? Unless the princess again required him.

The girls wrapped Asai Yodogimi in her kimono, and she sat on the dais. Will found himself removed, almost without knowing it, to the lower level, and Magdalena was girding his cloth around his loins, before in turn thrusting his arms into the sleeves of his gown.

'Boast not of this affair, Will Adams,' Yodogimi said. 'For I have found you to be handsome and able, and I would meet you again. Now, go with Magdalena.'

Will started to rise, and was stopped by the girl. Hastily he lowered himself into the kowtow, remained there for several seconds.

'It is good,' Yodogimi said. 'You have pleased me, Will Adams. Be sure that fortune will smile upon you.'

Magdalena touched his arm, and he rose, and followed her to the curtain. They stepped through, entered the corridor.

He chewed his lip, watched her shoulders moving beneath the thin silk, her hair swaying as she walked. There was no expression on her face. There had been none when she washed his genitals. But now he knew better than to suppose it would always be absent.

'Your mistress is a remarkable woman.'

'She is a princess, an Asai, and she was the favourite mistress of the lord Hideyoshi.'

'Which makes her irresistible?'

'She is also very beautiful. There is no one more beautiful in all the land.'

He caught her arm, checked her. They had now descended two of the flights of stairs, and were far enough removed from the hearing of the princess. 'Saving you, Magdalena.'

Her head turned as she looked at him. But she did not frown. 'I? I am ugly, Will Adams. It is said that I have the body of a man.'

'No,' he said. 'No.' Now one of his hands was on each shoulder. Did they dare move? She gazed at him, her face emotionless.

'I would have you know, Magdalena, that just now, while I was with the princess, I wished she could be you.'

'For those words, Will Adams, you could lose your head.'

'Yet it is true.'

'Would you, then, wish to have at me also? Truly, you English are men of great appetite.'

Contempt? 'I desire you, Magdalena. I have desired you from the moment I saw you, six weeks ago. I have dreamed of you, every night. But there must be nothing unwilling in your response. I want your love.'

She gazed at him, and her lips parted, very slightly. 'You speak of love,' she said. 'Without discovering whether I can make you happy?'

'In Europe, it is more usually thus,' he said. 'Did your grandfather never tell you of this?'

'My grandfather died before I was born, Will Adams. You wish to be my lover. I am flattered, but I must ask you to remain bathed in the glow of the sun, and not demean yourself by seeking the feeble light of a star.'

'She commanded me, Magdalena. As is her prerogative. She commanded my body. She cannot command my love.'

'Where Yodogimi commands, all obey.'

'Even the Tokugawa?'

'Who knows, Will Adams. Is the Tokugawa a mere man?'

'You fear him?'

'All in Osaka fear the Tokugawa.'

He sighed. Her answers were always so carefully framed. 'And the princess has also commanded you to love, Magdalena?'

She nodded.

'Will you tell me his name?'

'He is a samurai. Do you know what that means?'

'What we in England would call a knight.'

'I do not know what your word means, Will Adams. But a samurai lives only for the honour of his name and his sword.

Fighting and bloodshed are all his life. He knows no fear. And no pity. It were best for you not to know his name.'

'Meaning that he would kill me.'

She glanced at him. 'Yes, Will Adams. He would kill you. Europeans are not trained to fight as are samurai. More than that. It would mean the death of you both, for duelling is forbidden, unless sanctioned by the laws of the blood feud, and that would be too terrible to contemplate.'

Because she also would die, he thought with sudden horror, as he remembered the weeping woman of Bungo.

She stopped at the top of the stone steps. 'Go down there, past two landings, and you will come to the corridor leading to your cell. You may unlock the door from the outside; it will close itself. Wait.' From inside her kimono she took a small clay ring, and with a twist of her fingers broke it into two pieces. 'My mistress would have you keep this,' she said, handing him one of the halves. 'If someone, anyone, Will Adams, should bring you the matching piece, be sure he comes from the princess.'

So, her interest had not been merely in his body. How disappointing. And how utterly irrelevant, at this moment.

'Tell me one thing, Magdalena. These samurai: Do they also know how to love?'

How dark were her eyes, how sad her face. 'Yes, Will Adams,' she said. 'They also know how to love.'

The door to the cell was open. Will hesitated, and then boldly entered. Kosuke no-Suke was there, looking through the window, while Melchior paced the floor.

'Thank God you're back,' he said. 'Old Suke here is upset.'

Will nodded. 'Well, Master Kosuke?' he asked in Japanese.

'Should I not ask you, Will Adams? Well?'

'The door was open, so I went for a walk.'

Suke shook his head. 'Never utter falsehood, Will Adams. It is worse to lie than even to play the coward, and I know that you are neither. You have been with the Princess Yodogimi.'

Will felt his cheeks burning and cursed himself for a fool. 'In my country, Master Kosuke, it is not called lying to guard a woman's honour.'

'Women have no honour, Will Adams. Yodogimi least of all. I do not wish to know what she pretended. I would like to know what she asked you concerning Prince Iyeyasu.'

'She asked of what we spoke, certainly. I told her of the voyage, of myself, and my God, of Europe and its history.'

'Nothing else?'

'Not that I recall.'

'Good. In any event, it matters little. You and your companion will come with me. Quickly, now.'

'You mean we're being set free?'

Suke smiled. 'You are being released from this cell. As to freedom, no man is free, in that he serves his lord. And even his lord serves the gods.'

'Come, Melchior, we're leaving,' Will cried, and checked. To leave now? *Now*, when he wanted to sit down and think, and recall every movement, every touch, every sensation? When he wanted to dream, of what might happen again? He hurried behind Suke, who was already started down the corridor. 'You mean we're now in the employ of Prince Iyeyasu?'

'No greater honour can befall any man,' Suke assured him. And then they were in the courtyard; they had, after all, been only a few feet away all these weeks. How good it was to feel the sun on their heads, to look around them at the bustling people, to stare, and to be stared at. But there were great preparations all around them, men assembling, and men such as the guards who had first brought them to Osaka, who marched under the three mallow banner and wore white scabbards. The Tokugawa.

'Is the prince then leaving Osaka?' Will asked, in Portuguese.

'He hurries back to Edo, his city, to take command of his armies. The lord Uyesugi of Echigo has declared that he will tolerate the regency no longer, and has taken up arms in the north. Our prince must march against him.'

'And we are to accompany him on this campaign?'

Suke led them through the gates of the castle, into the teeming streets of Osaka, turned towards the dock area. 'Not on this occasion.' He glanced at Will. 'You do not wish to take the field?'

'I have little experience of soldiering, if that is what you mean.'

'And perhaps you would rather stay in Osaka, and visit the Princess Yodogimi again?'

'The princess commanded me, Master Kosuke.'

'Oh, indeed. Beware, Will Adams. Nothing is as it seems in Japan.'

'You are the second person who has said that to me this day,

Master Kosuke. I am well on the way to believing it. Yet, if I am not to take the field with the prince, where do my duties lie?'

Suke held out both hands towards the river, which now came in sight as the street ended. 'There, Will Adams.'

'By Christ,' Melchior shouted. 'The *Liefde*.'

The ship rode at anchor, like a whale amidst minnows.

'Master Kosuke, you are a sly fellow,' Will said. 'How came she here?'

'By our master's command. Especially to greet you, Will Adams. Your charts and instruments have been placed on board for you.'

'And our companions?'

'Are on board also. All fully recovered from their exertions.'

'Including Master de Conning and Master van Owater?'

'Ah, no.' Suke smiled. 'They preferred to remain in Bungo. But look, this boat waits to take us out to the ship. I will give you the prince's orders now, while we are yet alone. I will not accompany you on the voyage itself, but you will find on board a guard of Japanese soldiers, and also several of our fishermen; now you understand our tongue you will be able to converse with them. They will assist you to navigate the ship round the coast to Edo.'

'And suppose I do not wish to leave Osaka?'

Suke's smile faded. 'You have no choice, Will Adams. Only the Prince Iyeyasu stands between you and the cross. Serve him, and serve him well. Take your ship to Edo, and await him there. But beware, it is a treacherous coast.'

'So long as your pilots know the currents, we shall be all right. And once in Edo, Master Kosuke?'

'With fortune, my master and I will also be there, Will Adams. But whether we are or not, the Prince Tokugawa Hidetada, my master's heir, will be waiting for you, and he will know his father's mind. You will unload the guns and ammunition from the *Liefde*, and you will see that the cannon are prepared for moving on land. This can be done by means of carriages and wheels; we have been shown pictures of this by the priests.'

Will nodded. 'I can do that for you, Master Kosuke. This is for the northern campaign against this lord, how is he called, Uyesugi?'

'Who knows, my friend. Who knows.'

'You have a trusting nature, Kosuke no-Suke. What is to prevent me and my fellows, now we are recovered in strength, from overpowering your guards and fishermen and once again putting to sea?'

'Very little, Will Adams. Except that it would a grave mistake. The ship is not provisioned for a long voyage, and there is nowhere you may land in these parts where you will be as well received as here. Not even Bungo, now. But there is more. You have been looked upon with favour by the greatest man in Japan. You have but to prove a faithful servant, and as he rises so will you.'

'And should he fall, Kosuke?'

'Then you will also plunge into hell, Will Adams. As will I and many, many others.'

Will pulled his beard. 'Then answer me one more question, Master Kosuke. Can your prince and the Princess Yodogimi rise together? Or must one fall if the other is to remain supreme?'

Suke's eyes were opaque. 'The decision must rest with the princess, Will Adams; my prince does not willingly make war upon women.'

'Will.' Jacob Quaeckernaeck looked as if he was seeing a ghost. 'And Melchior? God in Heaven. We had heard you were dead. And when they brought your bag of instruments on board, we were sure of it.'

'Aye,' said another of the crew. 'Crucified, by God. We imagined you hanging on the cross, Master Adams.'

'Instead of which you see us fat as pigs for the table,' Will cried. 'Thanks to Master Kosuke here.'

The secretary bowed.

'But you also look in the best of healths,' Melchior said.

'Oh, we are that,' Quaeckernaeck agreed. 'But yet we are utterly destitute. This ship has been so looted it is a miracle she still has halliards to set the sails, and be sure that if the people of Bungo had understood what they were about those also would have disappeared.'

'But the munitions in your hold?' Suke demanded anxiously, in Dutch. 'They are still there? I see your cannon are in place.'

'Oh, they are all right, Master Kosuke. It seems your people of Bungo considered them no more important than our rigging. But I would take it kindly, sir, were your master to find us at least some clothes other than those in which we stand.'

'My master understands your situation, Master Quaeckernaeck, and regrets it. He does not have the power, as yet, to force the people of Bungo to make restitution of your belongings, but he has authorised me to say that the sum of fifty thousand golden pieces is to be paid to you and your men, to enable them to purchase the necessaries of life.'

'Fifty thousand golden pieces?' Quaeckernaeck cried. 'God in Heaven, but the man must be a prince.'

'He is,' Will said. 'You never mentioned this to me, Master Kosuke.'

'I did not think you were so interested in money, Will Adams, as you possess the favour of the prince himself, beside which money is of no value whatsoever. The sum will be paid upon the arrival of this ship in Edo Harbour.'

'I understand your drift. You take no chances, Master Kosuke.'

'All life is a great chance, Will Adams,' Suke said. 'The wise man reduces the odds against him whenever he has the opportunity. Not that I supposed you would be tempted to desert my lord's service. But it will be so much better if these friends of yours set to with a good heart.'

'And they shall do that, I promise you,' Quaeckernaeck said. 'But where is this place, Edo?'

'The seat of the Tokugawa power,' Will said. 'Some distance round the coast. We are to take the ship there with all despatch. So, if you will accompany me, Jacob, we'll see to our plans for the voyage. You'll excuse us, Master Kosuke.' He seized his friend's arm and hurried him below into the great cabin. 'Now tell me straight, you are as well as you look?'

'Indeed, I am, Will. From the moment your Master Kosuke interfered with our fate, the people of Bungo have treated us like lords.' He slapped Will on the shoulder. 'And you? You are better than you look.'

'I will tell you this, Jacob. Since coming to Osaka I have entered a world I did not know to exist, anywhere on this earth. This man, this Prince Iyeyasu, *is* a prince, Jacob. Make no mistake about that. He traces his descent through an unbroken line for over a thousand years, back to the Empress Jingo and beyond, and she claimed descent from the gods themselves.'

'And you believe such a mythology?'

'No. Not yet, at the least. But I can tell you that in one of his apartments he has more wealth than in all of Whitehall, in my estimation. Yet he is but a noble, the head of a powerful clan. He is only one of five regents who rule the country in the place of the Kwambaku, who is himself regent for the Shogun, who in turn only acts for the Emperor, the one they call the Mikado, in Kyoto. Can you imagine, Jacob, what wealth must exist in Kyoto, what splendour, if this far from the throne there is so much?'

'You have been bewitched,' Quaeckernaeck sighed. 'By a heathen warlord.'

'Heathen? Who can say what is heathen and what is Christian, Jacob? The Christians in Japan would have crucified us. The heathens offer us shelter. These people exist by a simple philosophy, one which depends upon their merits as men, not on some complicated metaphysical argument. Give a man a sword and let him know how to use it, and he may conquer the world. Give a woman beauty, and let her know how to use it, and she may conquer that man, and thus own the world.'

'Bewitched,' Quaeckernaeck said. 'Ah, well. Your head has been turned, dear friend, and I doubt you will have use for this.'

'For what?'

From the table Quaeckernaeck took what might have been a small book, but which, on closer inspection, Will discovered to be just two pieces of polished wood, joined together with thongs passed through holes in the edges to form a solid piece.

'Open it,' Quaeckernaeck suggested.

Will untied the string, parted the boards. Between them was a flower, dead now, but still preserving much of its beauty and colour, although the scent was long gone.

'Miss Magome asked me to give it to you, Will. She approached me privily, and said that she had been sorry not to be present at your departure, and hoped all was well with you. And she wished to give you some keepsake, to remind you of where you first came ashore in Japan.'

Will gazed at the flower, so like the child, in its gentle loveliness. No power and domination here; no thrusting beauty. Just a girl, who wished only to please.

Magome Shikibu.

The huge building echoed to the sound of hammers, the chatter of voices; heat and noise seeped upwards to the roof, brought sweat rolling out on arms and shoulders, although not a man in the warehouse wore more than his loin-cloth, Will included. But he sweated more than any of them, and it was the time of the White Dew, to use the more picturesque Japanese description of the weather, rather than the English month. It approximated to early September and was so called because the nights were becoming chilly. But not yet the days.

He pushed damp hair from his forehead, surveyed his men. They worked with tremendous gusto, for all that they chattered constantly. They worked because the guns remained a source of wonder to them. The day they had been unloaded, the entire population of Edo had assembled at the waterfront to watch them. A great number of people. He remembered the disappointment with which he had viewed the town itself; it had seemed no more than a delta of mud flats through which a sluggish river found its way into the huge gulf which began some thirty miles to the south-east. Beyond the mud flats there had been streets and houses, but far too few when compared with the teeming thousands of Osaka. And the castle, situated in the very heart of the town instead of to one side, while surrounded by a moat, lacked the air of grandeur. Had he then elected to follow a lesser star? The fact was, he had not elected to follow any star at all; his heart remained in the women's apartments of Osaka Castle, and more than just his heart; too often he found himself dreaming of the Princess Yodogimi, of those silken legs sliding up his body, of that sweet-smelling love forest. All his life he had dreamed of such possession; strange that now it had belonged to him, he could only want for more, and other, such forests. Because, of course, still he had not possessed. He had *been* possessed, by an exceptional woman.

Yet he followed the Tokugawa, and wondered why. They had been greeted upon their arrival by Prince Hidetada, Iyeyasu's heir. Not his eldest son, though; one older had died, and the real first-born, Hideyasu, had been given in adoption to the late Hideyoshi. As a hostage? Who could say, but it was a measure of the ruthlessness with which the Tokugawa seemed to be slowly strengthening his power; now Hideyoshi was dead, Hideyasu had rejoined his father's standard, but in a subordinate capacity. Because he could no longer be trusted? There was so much to be considered.

He had not cared overmuch for Prince Hidetada, as if his opinion was of any importance. But the prince had thin lips, and a habit of gazing over your left shoulder when speaking, rather than into your eyes. In these respects he differed from his father. It was difficult to say in how many others. For Will was realising day by day how little he knew about this man who so strangely had taken control of his destiny. He was not even sure if he liked the prince; if indeed the Tokugawa was determined to be the enemy of the Princess Yodogimi and her entourage, then he might very well come to hate the old man. And yet he had not really considered refusing to work for him. There was the coward in him. To refuse the Tokugawa was unthinkable, short of death.

And besides, there remained Kosuke no-Suke. Suke he trusted, absolutely, and Suke had apparently not yet found cause to doubt the Prince. Suke had taken him on a tour of inspection of the town, ostensibly to discover a warehouse big enough to take the cannon and their carriages, for, as he explained, espionage was such a fine art in Japan they could not risk anyone seeing why the guns were being brought ashore but were giving out that the pieces were to be mounted in defence of the citadel.

Yet at least part of Suke's purpose had been pride. He had taken Will to see the outer wall. There had been a wall, certainly, but to what purpose? Inside the barrier there were the same acres of unhealthy swamp; the nearest houses were a mile away.

'Oh, yes, Will Adams,' Suke had said. 'They all laughed when my master built this wall. But Edo will grow. Edo will become the first city in all Japan. More than that. Edo will become the first city in all the world.'

When Suke spoke with so much conviction, there was no arguing with him on a point of belief. But perhaps on principle.

'With an emperor on the throne and a regent in Osaka, in my country we should call such talk treason,' he had suggested.

'Treason, as you say, Will Adams, can only be offered to the Emperor, and he is in no danger.'

'Your prince has no ambition to take the highest seat in the land?'

'How could he, Will Adams? That would be more than treason; that would be blasphemy. My lord would rather receive the humblest token of esteem from the Mikado than own all the wealth in Japan. But below the Mikado there is no position which could not be his, which *should* not be his. And more than that, he recognises as do all that in the absence of the Shogunate the country declines into anarchy such as afflicted us for five centuries before the coming of lord Nobunaga. There was peace in Japan, Will Adams, during the great days of lord Hideyoshi. He has been dead but two years and already warfare breaks out in the north. It will spread.'

'And yet your lord wishes to replace Hideyoshi's son.'

'They were friends, Will Adams. The friendship of mutual greatness, mutual ability, mutual respect. I do not think there was ever mutual love. And that respect was given to the father, not the son. Where there is no imperial blood, ability must rest on the individual, not the possession of a parent.'

'The Princess Yodogimi told me that Prince Iyeyasu had sworn to protect the boy Kwambaku until he was old enough to take power himself.'

'Beware the Princess Yodogimi, Will Adams. You do not have to tell me more of her than you wish; I know both the woman and the beauty, and I think I know the man, as well, now. She has sought you out and given her beauty to you, but you would do well to forget such a gift. If she held you to her breast, it was as she might have held a pigeon, bringing news of some far-away event. For that moment, I have no doubt at all, she loved the pigeon. But should she ever grow hungry and only the pigeon be available, she would herself pluck the feathers from his flesh, and suck the flesh from his bones. As for what transpired between lord Hideyoshi and my prince, at the end, who can say? My lord admits that the Kwambaku was given into his care but with the proviso that he alone must decide, when the boy is of a proper age, whether or not he is to rule. Now go to, Will Adams, and carry out the task he has chosen for you.'

Suke had been angry. It seemed that in Japan loyalty to one's employer was everything. But not between those of equal rank? Hideyoshi must have looked upon Iyeyasu as a loyal supporter. On how many daimyo did Iyeyasu so look, without sufficient reason?

And always there was the haunting thought that these cannon, when they began to roll, might one day be turned on the towers of Osaka Castle itself. But then, he reflected, they would do so, now, whether he agreed to command them or not. With him there, he might be of some assistance to those inside.

And certainly he was the fortunate one in that he was busy as long as there was light to see, and the moment there was again light in the morning. Not the others. It was disagreeable even to consider the *Liefde*, now, and her crew. The prince had been as good as his word, and fifty thousand golden pieces, the Japanese called them kobans, had been delivered to the Hollanders. Quaeckernaeck would have kept the money in a common fund, to buy food and clothing, and more important than that, to revictual the ship for the voyage back to Europe. The crew would have none of it, but insisted upon dividing the money there and then, and were now scattered throughout Edo, drinking saké and sampling the delights of the Japanese bed-chamber. Certainly he had no right to criticise, as these joys had also been his. And certainly he could not help but suppose there was method in their madness; there was very little prospect of the ship being allowed to leave Edo for the time being, at least not fully armed and equipped. And who would be so bold as to face the voyage home without guns?

But now they would never sail. Not *those* men. Not any man who had once held a Japanese woman in his arms, or, more to the point, had her hold him in hers. Even Melchior had sunk into something hardly better than a debauchee. The exception was Jacob, who remained on his ship, paced the deck, surveyed the growing town and the restless sea, fretted and grew older day by day, where all the tribulations of the voyage from Amsterdam had added not a grey hair to his head, not a wrinkle to his cheek. There was the strength-sapping responsibility of command.

But he had his work to do. He massaged his neck with a towel. And while he worked, he could dream. Of whom should he dream? Of Princess Asai Yodogimi? Oh, certainly. It was impossible ever to forget so much beauty, so effortlessly, so magnificently, taking possession of his body. But whose face did he put on that delightful flesh? Magdalena Pinto, or as she would have it, Pinto Magdalena? Or the childlike wonder of Magome Shikibu?

And how long could a man exist on mere dreams?

Until his work was finished. The men were laying down their tools, and dropping to their hands and knees. Will turned to the door, and himself bowed; there was no mistaking that short, plump figure, that distinctive green kimono, that white scab-barded sword, any more than there was a possibility of mistaking the myriad guards, the anxious Suke, the supercilious Hidetada at his shoulder.

'Rise, Will Adams,' Iyeyasu said. 'And come forward.'

Will advanced. No change, here, except perhaps a slight suggestion of fatigue. The prince's eyes drifted over him like a warm bath. It was the first time he had seen Will virtually naked; instinctively Will sucked air into his chest and brought his shoulders back.

'You have worked hard and well, Will Adams,' Iyeyasu said. 'I congratulate you. Are these cannon ready to take the road?'

'Twelve of them, my lord prince. The other six yet need some work.'

'Then they shall have to await a future occasion. Twelve should suffice. I will provide the horses, Will Adams, and you will prepare the cannon, and yourself, for a campaign. Upon the events of this next month will depend all our futures.'

Chapter 5

THE ARMY marched by the sea for several days before turning inland, through a pass in the mountains, following a highway such as Will had never seen before, wide enough to take three carriages abreast, lined with trees, marked by post houses, all eager to feed and rest the generals, and the prince. They numbered, Will supposed, forty thousand here, an endless column of armour-plated warriors, the sun flashing reds and greens and golds and whites from the colour of their breastplates, or being absorbed into those who preferred black; it picked out the tips of their lances, just as the wind flicked the pennants which rose from the commanders' helmets, to create the effect of an endless kaleidoscope. But over all there rose the single banner, repeated time and again, a white flag embroidered with hollyhocks, and containing as its emblem a golden fan— the battle standard of Prince Iyeyasu; just as every man in the army wore his long sword in a white scabbard. The Tokugawa were on the march.

And with them, Will Adams, of Gillingham, Kent. An incredible thought. Certainly Melchior and Jacob had found it so. 'To die, in this far-off land, fighting for a heathen prince who is in revolt against his rightful lord?' Quaeckernaeck had cried. 'Truly, you are demented.'

But in this land, warfare, courage, honour, were the only roads to fortune. And he had been given a sword. Only one, as befitted a common man, but it hung at his side in a white scabbard, like all the others; the feel of it slapping his thigh made his blood tingle. No armour; there was none in Japan would fit his chest. But his task was not to enter the cut and thrust of battle; he marched at the very rear of the army, and behind him rumbled the guns, manned now by an eager pack of hastily trained gunners. They were not yet ready, in his opinion. He did not know if he was himself ready. But his instincts told him he was approaching the watershed of his life.

He had also been given a horse, as captain of artillery. He had little knowledge of riding, and he did not wish to disgrace himself before the Tokugawa nobility. So he walked his mount immediately in front of the first pair of oxen, inhaling the dust raised by the myriad company in front of him. Captain William Adams. But this was unimportant, now. This victory could be followed by a world of dreams . . .

Would it be a victory? There was sufficient confidence and resolution in the Tokugawa army. They expected soon to be joined by the other great clans, the Kato and the Asano who supported Iyeyasu in his march on Kyoto. Yet this was but a sham. Their true destination was Osaka. Not to assault the castle, not to destroy the Kwambaku, meaning only to honour his mother and her ladies. This was the official policy. Iyeyasu sought but to rescue the Kwambaku from the advice of evil men, those who feared the Tokugawa power, who sought to govern themselves in the name of the boy Hideyori. For the revolt in the north had been nothing more than a ruse to lure the Tokugawa away from the centre of power. Once their armies had been engaged, the lords who were discontented with Iyeyasu's rule had declared *him* to be the traitor, made public their fears that he sought to claim the Shogunate. Many of the great nobles had taken up arms in defence of the boy Hideyori, amongst them the powerful Mori clan, the famous general, Ikeda of Bizen, and the rulers of the southern island, the Satsuma. Would Tadatune and his father ride with their lord? How strange, to be marching against them. Would one of his cannon balls kill Tadatune? He remembered the boy with pleasant gratitude, however clouded their parting.

But more than ambition was involved, now. The inspiration of the conspiracy against Iyeyasu was the one they called the policeman, Ishida Mitsunari; he had been Hideyoshi's chief minister, and now sought to prolong his grasp of power, even while an inferior daimyo to any of the generals who followed his star. In pronouncing Iyeyasu an outlaw, Mitsunari had attempted to seize the wives and families of four of the Tokugawa generals, in residence for the summer at Osaka, and hold them as hostages. Most had escaped, but the wife of the lord Hosokawa, discovering her house surrounded, had killed her children and herself rather than fall into the hands of the policeman. If there was true hate in the hearts of any of the Tokugawa, it was directed against this one man: Ishida Mitsunari.

So this was a fight to the death, at least amongst the daimyo. The generals sought vengeance, no less than advancement. Whoever lost, when the armies met, need expect no mercy.

How different to Europe where it was the common soldiers who were massacred, and the lords, and their ladies, who could expect to be treated with the respect due to their rank, and in time be ransomed. Here it was the common soldier who could expect to survive, and his captain who must fight to the last, or failing that, ceremonially cut open his belly. A horrifying thought.

And into what category did Will Adams come? He was no samurai. Yet he had no doubt that he was well known to the generals of the Western army, as Mitsunari's forces were designated in contrast to the Eastern Tokugawas. Imagine being hauled before Asai Yodogimi and her women, a helpless prisoner, a man who having enjoyed the best she could offer had gone off to fight for her enemy. The thought chilled his blood, and then heated it again almost as rapidly. Not only because behind Yodogimi there would surely stand Pinto Magdalena, but because of the other side of the coin. Imagine Asai Yodogimi and her women being dragged before Iyeyasu, prisoners.

What thoughts. What thoughts. Thoughts to be thought without guilt. There was the most amazing thing of all. Where was the doubt-tormented man who had sailed from England to join the Dutch fleet in the Texel? Why that man was dead. Perhaps he had been dying before he had even kissed his wife goodbye. Certainly he had died some time during that terrible journey across the South Sea. So now, was he reborn? Or merely transported to heaven? Or hell? Yet the doubts had been there at the beginning. Perhaps they still lingered, only temporarily lulled by the enormity of what he was doing. He marched to battle, the only European in an army of strangers. Time enough to doubt the moment before he died; or the moment before he lived forever.

But would the Princess Asai Yodogimi ever permit herself to be taken alive? Would she not follow the example of Hosokawa's wife and commit seppuku (the soldiers called it hara-kiri) rather than fall into the hands of her enemies? And with the princess her women? A knife, cutting into the soft pale brown flesh? He discovered himself to be sweating.

And the army was stopping. The dust cloud in front of him was settling and the caissons behind him were grinding to a halt. The road continued to feel its way through the low hills which limited visibility, but in the distance Will could see the roofs of houses, enough to indicate a town. And from that distance there came the wailing of conch shells, and the screams of men.

'Wait here,' Will told his gunners, and rode up the column. The soldiers gazed at him without interest; they muttered amongst themselves, listened to the sound of combat.

'Will Adams.'

'Master Kosuke.' The secretary looked incongruous in armour. 'Dismount, man, quickly.'

Will slid from the saddle, dropped to his knees. He had not noticed the prince, seated on a folding stool beside his horse, surrounded by his officers.

'Rise, Will Adams,' Iyeyasu said. 'Why do you hurry?'

'I heard the sounds of conflict, my lord prince, and . . . '

'Rode towards it. That is good, Will Adams. But here is a messenger.'

The samurai's horse was a lather of sweat; the man threw himself from his saddle at Iyeyasu's feet. 'The Western outposts, my lord Iyeyasu. Our advance guard has been worsted, and seeks orders.'

'And that town is Ogaki?' Iyeyasu said. 'Why, let them make camp. As shall we all.'

'But my lord prince,' protested one of the generals, Kato Yoshiaki, lean visaged and with angry eyes, a veteran of the Korean campaign. 'They will say we were forced to halt.'

'I am parched,' Iyeyasu said, and held out his hand. Quickly Suke handed his master a persimmon to suck. Iyeyasu took the fruit, looked at it, and smiled. 'There is your future, my lords. Ogaki will be ours, this night.'

He dropped the fruit on to the ground, and with a shout his guards seized it, to share amongst themselves.

'Now, that I do not understand at all, Suke,' Will whispered.

'It is simple, Will Adams. That fruit, in Japanese, is ogaki also. The men will take it as an omen.'

It rained, a steady, persistent drizzle, obliterating the hilltops, clouding into the valley, settling the dust and then turning it into mud. The Eastern army huddled in its encampment around Ogaki. A last rest, before the battle? Will hoped the rain had not come to stay. It was the twentieth of October, in the year 1600. Thus European reckoning. To the Japanese it was the twelfth day of the Cold Dew, in the Year of the Rat, in the reign of an emperor no soldier in this army, saving only the daimyo, had ever seen, or would ever follow into battle. More to the point, as the term Cold Dew was proving singularly accurate, it was worth remembering that it ended in three days' time with the Fall of Hoar Frost. Either way, his guns would hardly be seen at their best advantage.

And they were, apparently, considered of great importance. He stood at the rear of the inn which had been appropriated as the army headquarters. In the centre, Prince Iyeyasu sat on the floor on an embroidered mat, his sons and officers kneeling on either side of him, back through the crowded room. Kosuke no-Suke was speaking, gathering the threads of information which had come in, depicting the scene on the large, coloured map spread on the floor in front of his master.

'Our advance guard has reached here, my lord prince,' he said, placing his hand on a cluster of hills some twenty miles to the north-west of Ogaki. 'They had sought to go farther, through the passes and on to the Moor of the Barrier, but they send word that the enemy are gathered in force opposite to them.'

'How many?' Iyeyasu asked, his voice, as ever, quiet.

'Many men, my lord Iyeyasu. My lord Hosokawa sends that it is difficult to estimate their numbers, but surely there cannot be less than eighty thousand men under arms.'

Eighty thousand men. An army which would strain the resources of any European kingdom; and this was a civil war.

'Is there news of Kobayakawa of Chikuzen?' Iyeyasu asked. 'Has he yet joined the Western army?'

'Not yet, my lord Iyeyasu. But it is said he moves to do so.'

Iyeyasu nodded. 'We will march tomorrow, to join the advance guard.'

'Will the Westerners not fight in front of Ogaki, my lord Iyeyasu?'

'It were best for them to do so,' the prince said. 'But they will withdraw to the mountain pass. The policeman is no general. He is one who lurks, not one who fights. Kosuke no-Suke, keep me informed of the whereabouts of my lord Kobayakawa. Now leave me.' His hand lifted. 'You will remain, Will Adams.'

Heads turned, and they were as quickly set straight again. The captains performed the kowtow, and withdrew, firstly to the door, and then along the corridor without; Will could hear the whisper of their feet as well as their voices. The room was empty, save for the Tokugawa, and himself. For what purpose? How his heart pounded.

But the screen was sliding again, and a boy entered. A very young boy, hardly in his teens, Will estimated. His presence did nothing to cool the heat in the air. He carried a tray, on which there was a small bottle of saké, and a cup. He knelt beside his master, remained motionless.

'Are your cannon ready to fire, Will Adams?' Iyeyasu asked.

'I believe so, my lord Iyeyasu,' Will said. 'Although the rain is not good for firearms.'

'The rain will cease. Come closer.'

Will crossed the floor, knelt beside the prince. The boy faced them both, his eyes half closed, hardly seeming to breathe. He wore a kimono, but no loin-cloth, and his girdle had already been loosed. His eager youth made an unforgettable picture.

Iyeyasu filled the cup, sipped. 'I have spoken with my secretary, Kosuke no-Suke, regarding you, Will Adams. And I have thought much of you, during these months.' He refilled the cup, handed it to Will. 'Drink.'

Cautiously Will sipped the warm liquid. Each man continued to stare at the raised penis, no doubt aware of his own. Christ in Heaven, Will thought; I am mesmerised.

'What would you be doing now, in your own land, Will Adams?'

Without thinking, Will took another sip of saké, uninvited, and was rewarded with a flicker of the boy's eyelids. 'No doubt I should be at sea, my lord Iyeyasu, but eager to regain the land. Our weather in October is much like yours.'

'October?'

'It is the name for the month, my lord Iyeyasu.'

'And what does it mean?'

'It is very simple, my lord Iyeyasu. It means the eighth month of the year.'

Iyeyasu refilled the cup, sipped, and smiled. 'Your people are entirely mathematical in their approach to life. I would have you teach me mathematics, Will Adams. We do not use enough of it, in Japan.'

'I will do what I can, my lord Iyeyasu.'

'And the stars. Kosuke no-Suke tells me you know of the stars, can name them, and even predict their positions in the heavens.'

'It is part of the science of navigation, my lord Iyeyasu, in which a seaman must be trained.'

'This too, I would learn. I would learn more about the sea, and ships. You will build ships for me, Will Adams.'

'I, my lord? It is many years since I built a ship, and even then I was not the designer, merely the shipwright. I doubt such a thing is possible for me.'

The boy was losing his power. Iyeyasu stretched out his hand, touched the glans with his forefinger, and it came upright again. The hand was withdrawn, and for the first time Iyeyasu glanced at Will's face. 'Nonetheless, you will build me a ship, Will Adams, without fearing my wrath, should you fail, but in every certainty of my favour, should you succeed. Ships are the future of my people, Will Adams. We lie here in the ocean, entirely surrounded by water, and yet we have no knowledge of those waters. When Hideyoshi set forth to invade Korea, ten years ago, his plans were all but set to nothing by a few Chinese junks, and I observe that the ship in which you crossed the ocean is larger and better than any Chinese vessel.'

'You are ambitious for your country, my lord Iyeyasu.'

'Which man is not, Will Adams? And remember, it is your country now. Although what we shall do for it depends upon the outcome of the next few days. You march with me, for what reason?'

The boy was breathing harder now, and the tray was trembling. His entire body seemed swollen. Merely with the power of suggestion?

'I march at your command, my lord Iyeyasu.'

'No other reason?' Iyeyasu held out the cup. 'You do not like this boy?'

'My lord . . . ' Will could feel his cheeks catch fire. 'I am a stranger to your customs.'

'You are like the Portuguese priests, who carry their insidious doctrines of dishonour throughout my land,' the prince said. 'They call us sodomites, and say we are damned. But we have no use for empty words. I have put down the words of the priests to ignorance, for they are men who have foresworn the flesh. Yet my secretary tells me you are married.'

'Yes, my lord Iyeyasu.'

'And have a child. That is good, for a man. But, having married, what more can you achieve, with woman?'

'My lord . . . '

'Beauty, to look upon,' Iyeyasu said. 'Is not this boy beautiful? He will soon achieve perfection. It is a pity it will last for so short a time. But you will have none of it. You wish for a woman.'

'My lord . . . '

The perfection was reached, and as the prince had prophesied, was over in a second. The boy caught his semen in his left hand, while his right all but dropped the tray. He gazed at his master with wide eyes. Iyeyasu waved his hand, and he backed to the door.

'Now, you see,' the prince said, 'he has served me well. To watch him, for this short time, has caused the blood to tingle in my veins.'

'In mine also, my lord Iyeyasu.'

'But you are a young man, and so easily aroused. I am an old man. Not so much in terms of years, perhaps. But I have lived too long. Do you know how many times I have led the Tokugawa into battle, Will Adams?'

'No, my lord Iyeyasu.'

'Eighty-seven times. That is very nearly twice for every year of my adult life. Do you know how many women I have loved?'

'No, my lord Iyeyasu.'

'Neither do I. Nor how many children I have fathered. But it is the battles which count, now. Have you ever fought in a battle?'

He had been no more than a trader in the fight against the Armada. But at Annabon he had marched with the Hollanders. 'One, my lord Iyeyasu.'

'Were you afraid?'

'I think I was, my lord. I marched, with my companions. There did not seem anything else to do. When they ran away, I did too.'

Iyeyasu gazed at him. 'You are a man of strange honesty, Will Adams. No Japanese soldier would ever admit to having run away. But you were nothing more than a common soldier. As you say, there is a communion of spirit to be obtained by marching shoulder to shoulder towards the enemy. Oh, naturally, it is a communion of fear as well as courage. It is the duty of the commander to make sure the courage is uppermost and remains there. But commanders also know fear. So do generals. Try to imagine the fear that can be known by the general in command of an army, Will Adams.'

'I can understand that, my lord Iyeyasu.'

'It is a fear which must be overcome by inspiration, by an

inspiration which can be communicated. So I must make my blood tingle, like a young man's. And yet, what have I to do with the flesh? There is no corner of a woman's body, no corner of a woman's soul, that I have not explored. They are cloying creatures, who entwine a man's legs like a thicket, and prevent freedom of movement. Men, boys, are more pure. They can also be approached in a different spirit. That boy just now could reveal his heart to us just by kneeling there, in a way no woman could do, because she is turned inwards, lacks the external evidences of her arousal. So, my blood tingles. And yet, not enough, perhaps. Perhaps, sometimes, I crave something more. Do you understand me, Will Adams?'

'I am not sure, my lord Iyeyasu,' Will said uneasily.

Iyeyasu smiled. 'Because your desires are restricted. You are strange to me, in a way no man has hitherto been. You are so large. Almost a giant. The priests are not so large. Nor even the men of Portugal. And you have a way of standing, and speaking, which is not becoming for a common man.'

'Then I must apologise, my lord Iyeyasu. I have been called arrogant even by my own people.'

'So you see, Will Adams, that you present me with a problem. Your arrogance, as you call it, is insufferable to me. Should I, then, cut off your head? Yet you yourself are attractive to me. Should I, then, raise you above your fellows?'

'My lord . . . '

'Should I say to you, remove your cloth, would you obey me?'

Will sucked air into his lungs. For, of course, he had known this was coming. For how long? Yet had he cast himself adrift on this particular ocean, and these waves were not for the fighting. And besides, his blood did still tingle. 'If you should command me, my lord Iyeyasu.'

'And if I wanted more than from that boy?'

Will licked his lips. 'I will obey your command, my lord Iyeyasu. In all things.' Christ in Heaven, he thought; what have I done?

Iyeyasu continued to smile. 'It is good. But I will not force you, Will Adams. I have forced men before. It is often amusing, and always stimulating. But I think, having forced you, I would have nothing left but to cut off your head. I think we shall let the future dictate our course. Yet there are things I would know. You visited the Princess Yodogimi in her chamber.'

'Yes, my lord Iyeyasu.'

'And did she also command you?'

Will gazed into liquid eyes. There was no time for relaxation here; every question, every word, was as barbed as any arrow. The prince's brain was every bit as sharp as Marlowe's. 'She did, my lord Iyeyasu. But I was happy to be commanded.'

'You would love the Princess Yodogimi?'

'It would be an easy thing, my lord Iyeyasu.'

'And for that, also, should I remove your head, Will Adams. The Princess Yodogimi is as far above you as is the moon above the earth. You think of her as the concubine of Hideyoshi, but she is an Asai, a princess in her own right, given to the Kwambaku to cement a friendship, because then he would not divorce his wife Sugihara.'

'This I understand, my lord Iyeyasu. Yet I would count myself scarcely a man did I not admire her beauty. I am not so foolish as to suppose I can aspire to more than her passing favour. Besides, I would not wish it. My heart is already given.'

'To your wife?'

Will hesitated. 'Alas, my lord Iyeyasu, my marriage has not been blessed with happiness.'

'The half-caste?'

Will's head jerked in surprise. 'I had not suspected you knew of her existence, my lord.'

'It is my business to know, Will Adams. Is *that* why you follow my banner? In the hopes of Pinto Magdalena?'

'I believe this must be a cause, my lord. At least in my heart.'

Iyeyasu smiled. 'She is unobtainable, Will Adams. Certainly as things are at present. And for you, she should remain so. She is Yodogimi's creature, and you are yourself a good judge of the power the princess can exert when she chooses. Now let *me* tell *you* why you march behind my banner instead of starving in the hell at Osaka. I am a Minamoto, which is to say that my earliest ancestor was Minamoto Yoshiiye, son of the Mikado Seiwa, and next in line to the throne. This was many centuries ago, but yet I remain the second prince in the land, as the head of the Tokugawa clan. The Shogunate has always been mine, by right. I have known this, from birth, known that it was my duty to overthrow my cousins, the Ashikaga usurpers. And yet of what use is duty where fulfilment is impossible? Should your duty call you to the other side of an unscalable mountain, where would your fulfilment be were you to perish crawling up snow-clad precipices? Duty requires responsibility, Will Adams, the responsibility to succeed, and not to dissipate your strength in useless gestures. My father, and his father before him—excellent men, for if a man should not honour his father, he is himself without honour—were yet men of no ambition, content to hold what they had. Their mighty allies thus drifted away from them, and I began my duty with no more than the Tokugawa at my back.

'And so I took service with Oda Nobunaga, and with Toyotomi Hideyoshi I conquered all Japan for him. Nobunaga died and the empire was left to Hideyoshi. I opposed him, with only my clansmen, while his army was as numerous as the sands on the beach. Yet could he not defeat me. I married his sister, and we became friends.

'Hideyoshi was a great man, Will Adams. I respected him. But I cannot respect a woman, who although a princess has the instincts of a whore, or a boy who is reputedly half-witted. And yet, because I am the Tokugawa prince, my friends remain few. The jackal will always band together to bring down the tiger, and the tiger finds his own kind hard to come by. We march now with every man I command, save the garrison at Edo, and yet I tell you this, Will Adams, the army of the West will amount to nearly twice our numbers. Does this make you afraid?'

'I have heard it said, my lord Iyeyasu, that you are the greatest general this land, this world, has ever seen.'

'For the first time I think you play the flatterer, and this I do not like.'

'Nonetheless, my lord, I have heard it.'

Now Iyeyasu's head turned. Clearly he was unused to the slightest opposition, even in thought. 'I am a great general, Will Adams. Had I not been so, and still fought eighty-seven battles, I would surely have been forced to seppuku by now. But greatness in a general does not come on the field. To draw one's sword and inspire one's men is the task of every commander of a hundred. A general's greatness must come before the battle, in the steps he takes to ensure that he does not lose. I have studied this matter for years, always knowing that I must be outnumbered when the time came, and that, as now, my enemies would have choice of ground. *I* must defeat *them*, and so they are content to wait. And so I have waited. I have had faith in my star, in my name, in my destiny. And destiny brought your ship and her cannon to me. And perhaps, even yourself, Will Adams.'

'Eighteen cannon, my lord Iyeyasu?' Will asked. 'Of which only twelve are with us? And in the rainy season, when the ground will be soft? I trust you have not misplaced your confidence.'

'Twelve cannon,' Iyeyasu said. 'That is more than in all Japan. There will be one, perhaps two, on the Western side. These will have been supplied by the Portuguese. You see, Will Adams, while I know as well as you that twelve cannon will not win me a battle, should I be outfought or outmanœuvred, twelve cannon will win me the battle by the mere possession of them.'

'I do not understand you, my lord Iyeyasu.'

Iyeyasu nodded. 'I have kept you talking for a purpose. Listen.'

There was movement in the corridor outside, and a moment later the screen slid to one side, to admit Kosuke no-Suke. 'A messenger from the West, my lord Iyeyasu.'

Iyeyasu nodded, and another man entered the chamber. His clothes were wet and his feet splashed with mud, but his two swords denoted the samurai. He lowered himself to the floor, and was brought upright again by a flick of Iyeyasu's fingers. 'Speak.'

'I come from my lord Kobayakawa, my lord Iyeyasu. He wishes me to inform my lord Iyeyasu that Ishida Mitsunari will withdraw from Ogaki tonight, and fall back towards Lake Biwa. He will join the rest of the Western army at the pass above Sekigahara, the Moor of the Barrier, and await you there.'

'Why will he abandon Ogaki, without at least a rearguard action?'

'Because, my lord Iyeyasu, at Sekigahara the road runs in a valley, as my lord is aware, thus there is no means by which you may outflank the Western army, but must decide the battle on a narrow front, where it is hoped your cannon will be less effective.'

'And my lord Kobayakawa?'

'Commands the right wing of the Western army, my lord Iyeyasu. He will be on the high ground to the south of the road, and the village of Sekigahara itself. From there he will prevent any attempt you may make to turn the Western flank.'

'Yet will he respond to *my* command. Tell your lord that when a fire arrow is shot straight into the air above my standard, he will engage the Western forces on his left.'

'Yes, my lord Iyeyasu.'

'That is good. Now tell me this. You speak of my lord Mitsunari as if he is in general command. What of Mori Terumoto?'

'My lord Terumoto has returned to Osaka for the protection of the Kwambaku and his mother. But the general command has devolved upon my lord Ikeda of Bizen, not Ishida Mitsunari. It is his orders that my lord Mitsunari should evacuate Ogaki.'

Iyeyasu smiled. 'Then give my lord Kobayakawa this message: Tell him my enemies have delivered themselves into my hand, that all he must do is play his part, and the day will be ours. Now go.'

The messenger performed the kowtow and withdrew. Kosuke no-Suke waited, watching Will.

'We will move forward at first light, Suke,' Iyeyasu said. 'Inform the generals. The rain has stopped?'

'Indeed, my lord Iyeyasu. But now there is mist, and the clouds remain low.'

'Thank you, Suke. Alert the commanders.'

The secretary bowed and withdrew.

'It is as I feared, my lord Iyeyasu,' Will said. 'This is no weather for cannon.'

'Your cannon have already fired, Will Adams. For without them I doubt that Kobayakawa would have agreed to desert to my side. This is what I meant earlier.'

'And without him, the battle would have been lost?'

'Without him, the battle would not be won so easily.'

'And you do not fear, my lord, that as you have negotiated with one of the Western commanders, their general may have negotiated with certain of your followers?'

'All warfare is a matter for negotiation, and treachery. But there again, the cannon will play their part. For who would be so foolish as to desert the general who commands twelve cannon? At least before he has been defeated. And if I am defeated in this battle, Will Adams, it will mean the end of my life. Of yours too, if you are wise. It is not good to be taken prisoner after a defeat. A defeated warrior is a man without honour, without the right to exist, save as the slave of his conqueror. But this is not so in your country.'

'No, my lord Iyeyasu. Providing he has fought to the best of his ability.'

'Ah, but, Will Adams, if he is beaten, then surely he has *not* fought to the best of his ability. Either that or he should never have fought at all. A man must choose *before* the battle, not during its heat, whether or not he is the best man. But for those who do, Will Adams, and win, the world is not large enough. Remember this. I undertook this campaign because of your ship, and thus because of yourself. I count you my star, my sign from heaven, that sign for which I have waited for so long. After the victory, Will Adams, ask, and it shall be yours.'

'I am overwhelmed by your generosity, my lord.'

'Then do not forget the responsibilities which accompany it,' Iyeyasu said. 'You wear only one sword. Suke will give you another. Be prepared to use it, Will Adams. Now, leave me. Come again at dawn.'

The sound of the bugle blared through the night, brought Will upright to a long shudder. It rained, steadily and persistently, blanketing the darkness, penetrating even the wooden shelter which had been erected for him by his gunners, soaking the ground, turning his body into a clammy mass, entering his very bones to leave him chilled.

He rose, reached out for his two swords. His *two* swords. This day might be his last on earth. God in Heaven; he had never before awoken to quite such a realisation.

'The cannon are ready, Will Adams.' The man stood just inside the doorway. Kimura was his name. A good soldier, Kimura, a man of far greater experience than his captain.

'And the army?'

'The advance guard is already on its way.'

'I must go to my lord Iyeyasu,' Will said. 'I will return with our orders.' He put on his helmet, the one piece of armour he had been able to obtain to fit himself, and hurried through the darkness; the iron plate, for all its weight, at least kept off the worst of the water. But his feet squelched on the soft earth, and all around him there was the gigantic stealthy bustle of men moving, punctuated by bugle blasts and the haunting wail of conch shells. Every moment the ground was becoming more like a bog; fire cannon into that and the ball would be absorbed like water into a sponge. This was supposing they could even light their matches. And the arquebusiers would be hardly more useful.

A man lurched against him. He glanced down; the Japanese wore the armour and carried the two swords of a samurai, and his scabbard was the Tokugawa white. Yet, unlike the samurai, there was no instant angry reaction, but instead an apologetic half-smile. 'It is the mud caused me to stumble, Will Adams.'

'And I, also, stumbled,' Will said. 'Good fortune to you this day.'

'Good fortune to all our friends. I looked for you, last evening, but you were always too close to the others. Now the time is short. The Princess Yodogimi bade me give you this.'

Before Will properly understood what was happening, the broken half of the clay ring was pressed into his hand; there was no need to compare it with the piece in his possession. And he had supposed his next summons would again be to her bed-chamber.

'I must leave while I may,' the samurai said. 'So I would know this; from which Western daimyo did the messenger come to lord Iyeyasu?'

The most beautiful woman in all Japan. And at her side, Pinto Magdalena, with all that *she* promised. Against whom? An ageing debauchee, with his eyes on a throne. And his dreams? There was the question. The dreams of a man's penis were for a night; the dreams of a man's country were for eternity.

'I serve the Tokugawa,' he said. 'Now and always.'

The Japanese glanced from left to right and his hand closed on the hilt of his sword.

'Draw that and I shall throttle you before it is clear of your scabbard,' Will said. 'I have no need to fight like a Japanese.'

The man hesitated, gazed at Will's size, at the strength in his hands and slowly released his weapon. His tongue stole out and circled his lips.

'I shall not condemn you,' Will said. 'Leave the camp as you entered it. But I shall not betray lord Iyeyasu.' He hesitated. 'Wait. Tell the princess . . . tell her that I honour her, and my memory of her, and that I shall always do so. Tell her that I intend her no harm, and neither does Prince Iyeyasu. Tell her that I beg her forgiveness, for this, but that Prince Iyeyasu gave me my life, and returned to me my purpose in life. And tell her also that I believe he is the man best fitted to rule this country of ours. Tell her these are my reasons, and ask her to understand.'

The samurai stared at him for several seconds. 'Fine words,' he said at last. 'In Japan, Will Adams, we save our fine words, our fine thoughts, for the poetry competitions, to be uttered before the Mikado. But that is a game. In life, it is deeds which matter, not words. You may not choose to fight like a Japanese,

Englishman, but be sure you shall die like one.' He stepped backwards, into the rain, and disappeared around the corner of the building. Was it rain, or sweat, on his neck? Certainly the morning, so chill a moment ago, had become warm.

He was before the door of Iyeyasu's house; the guards presented their lances. But as ever, Kosuke no-Suke, wearing full armour, was just within. 'Enter, Will Adams,' he said. 'My lord Iyeyasu awaits you. Have you bathed?'

'Eh?'

'It is our custom to bathe before battle,' Suke said. 'It is too late for you, now. But my lord has just finished his bath, and is dressing. He will see you now.'

The inner door was opened, and Will dropped to his knees before inclining his forehead.

'Rise, Will Adams.' Iyeyasu was already half dressed in his armour, being assisted by the boy who had been present the previous night, and another, busily tying the straps of his breast-plate, arranging his sash, adjusting the iron greaves on his calves. 'You will make yourself a target, with your height, and your lack of armour.'

Should he tell him? But the enemy had learned nothing, and the Tokugawa plans were as viable now as yesterday. He sought no compliments which might well carry the seeds of suspicion. 'Perhaps your men will look upon me as a flag, my lord Iyeyasu.'

'A flag? That is good. But more than that. You are a pilot, are you not? You shall pilot us to victory. That is good. I have wondered about a name for you. Will Adams is too strange. And now you are one of us. You will be our pilot, Will Adams. I name you Anjin Sama, Master Pilot, and from this day shall you be so known. Now, Sama, my first command to you is to ride up to the front and choose a place for your guns. My army already advances.'

'Yes, my lord. I am hoping that the rain will stop before long.'

'It will stop, Anjin Sama. At this time of the year, it will stop. Now go, and then return and report to me. We shall be on the road soon enough.'

One of the boys knelt, with a helmet; the prince was fully armoured.

'No helmet,' Iyeyasu said. 'Bring me that white handkerchief.' The boy obeyed.

'Now bind it round my head.'

The boy obeyed.

'No helmet, my lord Iyeyasu,' Suke remarked. 'Surely this is unwise.'

'One helmet is too much like another, Suke,' Iyeyasu remarked. 'By this handkerchief shall my men know me. White is the colour of the Tokugawa. Let them rally to the head of white.'

The road was crowded with men, marching onwards, splashing through the mud and water. Will found it easier to leave the paved surface and take to the fields where his horse could pick its own footsteps. He moved in the middle of a vast mass of men and animals, surrounded by muted noise. It was nearly five now and the darkness of the night was fading into the white mist of dawn. To his left he could see the ground beginning to rise, the grass beginning to thin as it became rock and outcrop. It disappeared into the mist.

Away to the right, beyond the road and the marching army, even through the gloom he could see the glare of the great fire. It had been lit by the Western patrols to guide their army on its retreat. All night they had withdrawn, as Iyeyasu had prophesied, despite their success of the afternoon. Now, perhaps, they rested on their arms, in position. But yet they would have had no sleep.

Thus, was he confident of victory? The signs were good. But his life depended upon the ultimate loyalties of a man with the unlikely name of Kobayakawa, whom he had never seen, and the handle of the short sword bit into his belly as he rode. He had taken the sword from its scabbard last night, and tested the blade. It would have taken the shortest hair from his chin and left not a mark upon the flesh. Imagine what it would do to his belly. Supposing he had the courage ever to use it.

Well then, was he afraid of defeat? Strangely, he felt no emotion at all, knew only that there could be no thinking of tomorrow until this day was done, and this day had too long to go.

The hills loomed in front of him as well, now. He turned his horse, rode towards the road, and plunged into the midst of the marching soldiers. They halted without comment to let him through; the sun had risen, although the mist limited visibility to under a hundred yards, and they could see the white scabbard of his long sword just as he could see theirs. To further assist their identification, each section carried a white flag, drooping in the rain.

His progress was slowed to a walk by the mass of men. As yet he had seen nothing to convince him he could use his guns at all. The road was clogged, and would remain so; the ground to either side was too soft. Ahead of him, to complete the artillerist's nightmare, there were suddenly houses lining the road, disappearing into the slopes on either side. Sekigahara. A name to remember.

The men thronged the narrow street, their armour clanging, their feet squelching in the mud. More men than even upon the road outside, pressing forward, calling to each other, commanders looming through the rain on horseback, shouting orders and disappearing again. Will kicked his horse to drive the animal into the crowd, was hailed by several of the men. But these no longer wore white scabbards. And a banner, clinging damply to its staff a few feet in front of him, lacked the golden fan.

The Western army. His heart gave a lurch, and he turned his mount again. Someone was shouting, very close. A white scabbard. But not close enough. Two men reached up for his bridle, and one had drawn his weapon. Desperately Will tugged his own sword from its sheath, kicked his horse forward, struck down with the blade, right and left, realised he too was bellowing with ferocity. Or was it fear?

The horse reared and he nearly slipped from its back. The man in front of him was gone, and he was swinging his sword again. The blade was wet, dull in the steady drizzle and the half-light; but the wetness was blood. Christ in Heaven, he thought; I have killed a man.

There was a gigantic hiss, and something whistled past his ear. Instinctively he twisted to one side, and lost his seat. He slid from the saddle, but his horse seemed to be sliding beside him and for a terrifying moment he thought he was going to be pinned. Then he was seized by the arm and jerked clear, and he realised that he was in the midst of a crowd of Tokugawa spearmen, and the air was filled with the arrow hiss, and loud with the wailing of the conch shells and the blasts of trumpets.

'Stop the advance,' an officer shouted, riding his horse into the midst of the mêlée. 'Stop the advance.'

An arrow struck the Japanese in the shoulder and he tumbled out of his saddle. Instantly four men lifted him and carried him into the nearest house. Will discovered that he had dropped his sword, but a fresh one was quickly pressed into his hand, and he found himself facing up the suddenly empty street. Having fired a volley of arrows, the Westerners had withdrawn into the mist, melted through the cluster of houses which fringed the road.

There were half a dozen dead men lying in the street, most with arrows sticking into them, but one lying on his face with his left arm almost severed at the shoulder and blood spreading in a vast pool around him. The man he had killed. He looked down at his hand; there was blood on his knuckles. Japanese blood, as red as his own. He had the strangest temptation to raise the fist and smell it, but he knew this would make him vomit.

'Will Adams. Will Adams.'

Several horsemen came out of a side street, shouting orders to the soldiers, bullying them into line. And one called his name. He turned and recognised the bristling moustache and brilliant silver-painted armour of the lord Hosokawa. 'What do you wish here, Englishman?'

'I was sent by my lord Iyeyasu to discover a suitable place for my cannon.'

'It cannot be here. And you were nearly killed. The prince would not have been pleased. Take this horse and return. And tell my lord Iyeyasu that we urgently await his commands.'

'And what shall I tell him of this skirmish, my lord Hosokawa?'

The daimyo closed his nosepiece to hide the better part of his face. 'We advanced too quickly, Will Adams, and they retreated too slowly; thus the two armies became mingled before either realised it. But the ground beyond the village rises steeply. We shall wait here until our orders arrive.'

Will mounted, and bowed from the saddle. 'I wish you fortune, my lord Hosokawa.'

'And to the prince. But look, it is already ours.' The mist was suddenly tinged with crimson, as the sun rose.

By eight o'clock the rain had stopped, and the mist only clung in patches to the valleys, occasionally shrouded a peak. But most of the peaks were brilliant, dominated by the banners, and the morning sun glinted from endless lines of spearheads, towering above the massed iron helmets. The ranks of the Western army formed an unbroken chain, from mountain top down into valley, and back up to mountain top again, barring the road to Kyoto. Eighty thousand men.

Below them the Eastern army—almost equal in number now that the Kato and Asano clans had come up—splashed across the waterlogged lower slopes streaming into the positions chosen for them by Iyeyasu. Gentle slopes, certainly, but still slopes, and the slope was upwards. Will drove his horse to and fro, round and round the twelve cannon, now no longer dependent upon their oxen alone, but pushed and hauled by teams of sweating men. Every time he looked up, those silent ranks of spears and helmets stared down at him. Were he in command of that army he would be very tempted to launch an all-out assault at this moment. But apparently that would be dishonourable. And the chaos which had left the road and straggled on to the slopes was gradually assuming order, each detachment forming their lines, drawing their arrows from the quivers on their backs, making sure their bowstrings were dry. Yet the difference between the two armies was more marked than ever because of the endless din which arose from the Easterners, the shouts of command merging one into the other, the whistling of the conch shells, the blare of the trumpets, even the ceaseless clash of weapons, as spears were tested and swords unsheathed. He felt like a spectator at some gigantic play, or a bird, winging over the scene, as near two hundred thousand men prepared to destroy each other. Wishful thinking; he would at this moment far rather be a bird, high above the spears, watching, and perhaps laughing, at these foolish mortals.

Kosuke no-Suke's mount splashed towards him. 'My lord Iyeyasu commands you, Anjin Sama, to establish your cannon here. That banner on the hill belongs to Ikeda of Bizen, general commander of the Western army. Bring that down, Anjin Sama, and the day is ours.'

Will glanced to his right. Morale apart, the ground was as well chosen as possible in these circumstances; Ikeda had taken his position where the hills receded into the west, and the ground was reasonably level. 'But you must tell the prince that the ball will have little effect on this soft earth.'

Suke nodded. 'Nonetheless, form up your men. You will be supported by the arquebusiers, and the prince himself is at your rear.'

'There's good news.' Will dismounted, sank up to his knees in the mud. 'Halt those beasts, Master Kimura,' he told his gunner. 'And we'll get these cannon into line.'

'Yes, Anjin Sama,' Kimura said, for the name had spread, and scurried around the toiling men, bringing them to a halt with a series of commands. Will looked to the left, where the regiment of arquebusiers was also halting, the men unloading their firepieces and placing their staffs. They were no better trained than his own, were here mainly for the suggestion that this was an irresistible force. And what of the prince?

There was a rustle amongst the men behind him and he turned to watch the group of horsemen riding towards him, led and dominated by the short, plump figure with the white handkerchief round his head, and carrying the lacquered paper baton which denoted the general in chief. Hastily he bowed from the waist.

'The guns are good, Anjin Sama,' Iyeyasu said. 'Soon we shall be ready to commence our battle.'

'I can promise no great execution, my lord.'

'You will give me noise, and noise is more frightening than blood, if it is loud enough,' Iyeyasu said.

'Yes, my lord Iyeyasu. May I wish you every fortune on this day?'

Iyeyasu smiled. 'I have made my own fortune, Anjin Sama, and yours, and all of these men's. I did this yesterday and the day before, last week and the week before that, last month and the month before that. Now I can do little more. We are in the hands of the gods. Wait for the signal.'

Will bowed once more, and the horses splashed by. Behind him the rustle told him that his men were straightening, and indeed at that moment a silence descended over the entire Tokugawa army. The moment had come. God, how he sweated, and trembled as well. With cold. But it was not cold, now, with the sun high in the sky. Then with damp. It was certainly damp.

And perhaps with discomfort. The hilt of the short sword kept biting into his stomach as he moved. The hilt.

A conch shell wailed, and from the Tokugawa ranks to the right a solitary horseman rode forth. He wore gold painted armour and his nose-piece was lifted to reveal his face, young, eager, intense. His lance remained in its socket, immediately behind his left arm, and his swords were still in their sheaths. The faint breeze coming down from the mountains rippled the pennant which rose above his helmet, extending it into long streams of lacquered paper. His horse moved at a walk, and then slowly increased to a trot as he urged it forward, up the slight slope, until he was midway between the armies, when he brought it to a halt. There, for several seconds, he remained still, staring at the Western army; his position was chosen so as to be overlooked by almost everyone on the field.

Then, with great deliberateness, he took the lance from its socket, held it in his right hand, and raised it high in the air. 'Listen to me, men of Osaka and men of Nara, men of Satsuma and men of Bizen, men of Tosa and men of Hizen. Listen to me, Ikeda of Bizen. I am Kato Kenshin of Kumamoto. My uncles are amongst the greatest of living generals. My father accompanied lord Hideyoshi to Korea and earned fame there. My ancestors fought against the Mongols, and greatly distinguished themselves. Now I have come to do battle with you, Ikeda of Bizen, in the name of the great prince, Tokugawa Iyeyasu. Prepare yourself to die.'

A trumpet blast echoed behind him, and the young man kicked his horse and galloped up the hill, straight at the opposing line. The entire army uttered a shout, which seemed to hit the hills surrounding the battlefield and come bouncing back, and with a screaming of conch shells Kato Kenshin's followers ran behind their commander, up the hill and at the enemy. Kenshin himself had already reached the bristling pikes; but these were opened for him and he plunged into their midst. Will attempted to lick his lips and found they were dry.

'Why did he do that?' he asked Kimura.

'It was his duty this day, Anjin Sama. This is traditional. Now the battle will become general.'

His duty. God in Heaven, Will thought, to have such courage, such recognition of duty. He looked up as an officer splashed towards him.

'Greetings, Anjin Sama. My lord Iyeyasu commands you to begin firing at the enemy.'

The sun, so slow to rise and take its proper place in the sky, now yielded to nothing. The last of the mist and the rain had disappeared; the blue was unending, shrouding the hilltops, forming a canopy to the mayhem below. It was noon.

Will wiped sweat from his forehead; the heat of the day, the heat of tension. Not the heat of battle, for him. His cannon had long ceased their roaring, after only an hour's bombardment. It had made sense, tactically, because the balls were doing no more than churn up the earth, and strategically, because although the rumble of fire had certainly been loud enough, to have continued so ineffectively would have encouraged the enemy to lose their fear of the guns. And so, since about nine of the morning, he had waited, and watched, and listened, and wondered.

The battle had ground to one of its temporary halts. The Tokugawa and their allies, licking their wounds, had withdrawn from yet another tumultuous assault up the hill. Not all of them; there were mounds of dead up the slope. This at least was of some value; it marked the original Western line. For Ikeda of Bizen had withdrawn his men, but only about two hundred yards. They still lined the hills, still blocked the road to the capital city of Kyoto, still had the best of the field. Whereas the Tokugawa, wearily re-forming their lines after six charges, *steamed*. The damp which had accumulated in their clothing during the rain of the dawn now rose into the still air like smoke, sucked from them by the heat. Horses stamped and neighed, men chattered, where they could find the necessary saliva, the wounded screamed as they died. No doubt similar scenes were being enacted in the Western army. But he could not hear those.

And he could not smell them, either. Here the smell of battle, of fear, and of death, seemed to clog his nostrils. He smelt the tang of sweat-dampened leather, of sweat-shrouded bodies; he smelt the unhealthy fart of fear-released belly air; he smelt, above all, the heavy stench of blood. There was blood everywhere, trickling through the mud, staining the brown slopes above him, clinging to every sword blade, every pikehead.

Kimura gave him a cup of saké, only slightly warmed; he had lit a fire behind the battery. Will sipped, and only felt more thirsty. 'We do no good here, Kimura. I have a mind to ask the prince for permission to take part in the next charge.'

'Then do so, Anjin Sama, and for me as well,' Kimura agreed. 'The prince comes.'

Iyeyasu had dismounted, and plodded through the drying mud with his officers, pausing to talk with men here, to exhort them there. His handkerchief still clung to his head, soaked with sweat. His sword remained in its scabbard, and he looked every bit as cheerful as usual, despite the lack of success which had attended the previous four hours. 'Well, Anjin Sama? How goes it?'

Will bowed. 'I am not sufficiently experienced in these affairs to judge, my lord Iyeyasu.'

'I am of a mind that the time has come to make an end,' the prince said. 'I should think my lord Ikeda will shortly be calling upon his right wing to enter the battle, and I would prefer to use it for myself. You observe my lord Kobayakawa's division?'

Will followed the direction of the pointing baton, at the mass of men on the hillside away to the Tokugawa left, hitherto having taken no part in the battle. 'I do, my lord Iyeyasu.'

'When he starts to move, not against us, but against those Western troops beside him, I wish you to recommence firing. The ground is drying and your cannon will be more effective. More important, they will occupy the minds of the enemy in front of you.'

Will bowed.

Iyeyasu turned to one of his aides. 'Now fire the arrow.'

The samurai took the fire arrow from his quiver, set it in place, and drew back the string. Another samurai thrust the torch into Kimura's fire, saw it catch alight, and touched it to the bundle of bitumen-soaked cloth and reed which had replaced the barb. The archer released the string, and the flaming dart shot into the air, high above the Tokugawa army, and arched through the sky towards the Western ranks, where it was greeted with shouts of derision.

'Load,' Will told his gunners. 'Quickly, now, Master Kimura.'

Iyeyasu gazed to the south. 'Patience.'

'But he should act immediately,' said Kosuke no-Suke.

Iyeyasu continued to watch Kobayakawa's division for some seconds and the humour gradually left his face. 'What, does the wretch seek to betray me in turn?' he asked, half of himself, and in a strangely youthful gesture he raised his right hand and bit the end of his index finger. 'Anjin Sama, will your cannon fetch that distance?'

'I think so, my lord Iyeyasu. But to fire into my lord Kobayakawa, will that not drive him from our support?'

'He must either act for us, or against us, *now*,' Iyeyasu said. 'Fire into him, Anjin Sama.'

Will gave the command, and two of the cannon were turned to the south. The matches were applied, and the guns roared, sending their iron balls bounding over the slopes towards the Kobayakawa standard.

'Look, my lord,' Kosuke no-Suke shouted.

For the banners were moving, not forward, as Will had feared, but down the hill immediately on their left, and up the farther slope, their spears levelled as they charged the Western troops beside them.

'Now,' Iyeyasu said. 'Now, my Tokugawa. Command your men, my lords. The day is ours.' He slapped Will on the shoulder. 'Set your cannon straight again, Anjin Sama. Fire into that mass for a space of a thousand seconds, and then cease, and join in the advance.' He called for his horse, and a moment later the staff moved away, slivers of hardening mud flying from their hooves.

'Fire,' Will commanded. 'Fire as fast as you can load.'

Kimura gave a high-pitched scream, and the cannon roared; and again and again. The morning exploded with noise, and the very sun seemed to fade from the heavens. Will moved some distance away and regained his mount, to stare up the hill. The men opposed to them had seemed to surge forward, only to be met by the flying ball. He watched in horror as the first singing iron crashed through the ranks of spearmen. Even at this distance he could see the blood flying, the spears and swords and shattered heads and limbs thudding to the ground on every side. Yet all the while he counted, slowly and rhythmically, until he reached the thousand.

'Cease firing,' he shouted. The order was repeated by the gun captains down the line, and the cannon fell silent. Iyeyasu's timing had been perfect. The iron balls had ploughed great holes in the ranks of the forces opposing them, and this had been until now the only force with the slightest semblance of order about it. On the right the Kato clan's impetuous assault had more than avenged the death of their prince which had opened the battle. And the troops on the hill, whom they had assaulted time and again without success in the morning, now that they could hear the sounds of conflict coming from beside and even behind them had wavered and broken, to go streaming through the valleys, seeking mercy where there was none to be had. And now that the cannon had done their work, the centre too was fading away.

Will drew his long sword. 'Come, Kimura. Call your men and let us complete this rout.'

The gunners gave the victory cry of 'Banzai' and ran forward behind Will's horse. But there was no more fighting to be done. They arrived on the upper slopes to a scene of desolation, accentuated by the return of the heavy clouds, gathering low over the field of death, and as the air chilled the first drops began to fall. The rain could no longer affect the dead; it could not even clean their sweat-stained blood-soaked features, for these no longer existed. The warriors lay in headless clusters, their great swords useless, their spears broken, their bows flaccid, while the blood dripped silently from their empty necks.

The victors were busy, quiet now, the shouts of challenge and triumph only a soreness in their throats, their sword arms wearying as they went about their dreadful work. The heads were accumulated, a score to each net, and carried away to set before their generals. Heads were more than merely a means of estimating the slain; they were a source of reward as well. The head of an enemy lord would bring glory and fortune to the samurai who could lay it at the foot of his prince.

Will left Kimura and his men to continue the ghastly task, and turned his horse away. To go, where? There were still sounds of combat from the village to the north. No doubt the battle still raged, for there Ishida Mitsunari himself was in command, and the policeman would not give up until all was irretrievably lost.

He rode back down the hillside, head bowed. But even in the Tokugawa position there was too much blood, too many dead and dying, too many wounded, gritting their teeth against the pain as their comrades tore out the barbed arrowheads from their thighs and shoulders. And he remained unhurt. There was the most remarkable thing of all. Not a scratch, from the guns of the Armada, from the Portuguese at Annabon, from those vile beings in South America, and now not a scratch from the swords of the Western army. Yodogimi's army. The thought made him check his mount. For what would happen to the princess now, and her women?

'Anjin Sama.'

He turned. Tokugawa Iyeyasu rode towards him, his staff at his back. Their armour still glittered, their pennants still flew in the breeze. They too were unhurt. They were the victors.

'My lord Iyeyasu.' He bowed.

'Come with me, Anjin Sama. To your triumph.' Iyeyasu led him back up the hill. 'As I prophesied, the enemy flee in disorder. The policeman has left the field without his weapons, coward that he is, but the act will avail him naught. Of the Western generals, only Shimadzu of Satsuma has escaped; surrounded, with seventy of his kinsmen, by Kobayakawa's men, and called upon to perform seppuku, he laughed, and with a single charge cut his way clear and rode for the sea.'

Will's heart leapt. 'For that I am grateful, my lord Iyeyasu.

The Shimadzu, and especially Shimadzu no-Tadatune, welcomed me upon my arrival in Japan. They will not be dishonoured by their action?'

'On the contrary; they will take their place in Japanese history. To be forced to surrender, and not commit seppuku, is the height of dishonour. To be called upon to surrender, and yet fight your way to freedom with your sword in your hand, is a passport to immortality. And I am pleased to know that you feel gratitude towards them, Anjin Sama. I understand that Shimadzu no-Tadatune has accompanied his kinsman. I will make peace with the men of Satsuma. They are too brave to be opposed to me. But now, Anjin Sama, we complete our victory.' He reined his horse at the top of the hill, and pointed with his baton. 'Your prayers, my lord, for an honourable enemy.'

Below them, on the reverse slope, some fifty yards away, there was a cluster of Tokugawa samurai, in a circle around the defeated general. Only one soldier stood close to the kneeling man; the one who had claimed his surrender. He held his long sword in both hands, the back of the blade resting on his left shoulder, and breathed slowly and evenly, sweating with tension, for if this day's work should prove his making, he could undo much of it by carelessness now.

As there was no temple close by, five mats had been laid upon the earth, and on these the lord knelt. At last he sighed, and reached behind himself to unfasten his breastplate, and allow it to fall to the earth before his knees. Another quick movement released the garment beneath, so that he was suddenly naked from the waist, while the drizzle pattered on his shaved head and on his sweat-wet flesh, sufficiently cool to start a shiver, quickly suppressed.

Still gazing at the ground, the lord drew his short sword, and reflectively stroked blade and point with his forefinger. The samurai, the watching generals, were motionless; to disturb him now would be the depths of dishonour.

Once again he sighed. The short sword, held in his right hand, was carried away from his body to the full extent of his arm, and brought back, suddenly and violently; the razor-sharp blade bit into the pulsing brown belly, and in the same movement was carried to the right, opening a wound several inches across, from which the blood seeped like water penetrating a dam. Still the lord stared at the earth, and still the blade moved, now turning downwards to extend the wound into a right angle.

The only sound was the hiss of breath escaping the dying man's nostrils, but in the same movement as he had started the belly cut he had thrown his left arm away from his body, fingers spread. At this signal the man standing above him had commenced the sweep of the long sword, bringing it down on the lord's neck with tremendous force and consummate accuracy. The head seemed to leap, the eyes driven upwards by the impact so as to appear to give their enemies a last stare. The executioner seized the top-knot while it was still in mid-air, and held it there, while the neck spurted blood and the headless trunk fell forward, the legs unfolding from their kneeling position and slowly extending.

The samurai raised the head, panting, but smiling now. He had played his part to perfection. The men surrounding him gave a shout, which was echoed by their comrades elsewhere on the field. From his belt the executioner took his foodsticks, made of finely carved wood and engraved with his clan crest. These he thrust through his victim's top-knot, while the men around him formed a corridor to allow him to pass.

The executioner walked between the cheering soldiers, carrying the dripping head in front of him, until he reached the horsemen. Here he stopped, and bowed from the waist. When he straightened, he raised his head. 'Behold, my lord Iyeyasu,' he said. 'The head of Ikeda of Bizen.'

Iyeyasu smiled. 'A notable victory. What is your name?'

The executioner bowed again. 'Keiko, my lord Iyeyasu.'

'None other?'

'None other, my lord Iyeyasu.'

'There will be another, Keiko. Now leave the head of lord Ikeda, and be certain of my reward.'

Keiko bowed a third time and rejoined his comrades.

'A notable victory,' Iyeyasu said again, and glanced at Will. 'I give it to you, Anjin Sama.'

'It was my fortune to be here, my lord Iyeyasu.' Will stared at Ikeda's head, the eyes still open and returning the gaze, the features freezing into eternity.

'*My* fortune, Will,' Iyeyasu said softly. 'All my life I have waited for a triumph such as this. And thus all my life I have waited, for you. Therefore it must be that all your life you have been coming towards me, whether you knew of it or not. From the other side of the earth, Will, you have been seeking me, without even knowing I existed. We must investigate this, you and I. We must learn about the workings of Fate, for never was there a day more fateful to Japan than the morning you dropped your anchor off the coast of Bungo. And together we must plan the great deeds that surely lie ahead, for us to perform, together.' The round face, so unusually serious, once again broke up into a happy smile. 'But that is for our leisure. Suke, bring me my helmet.'

Kosuke no-Suke bowed as he held out the helmet. 'You have fought this day with but a handkerchief on your head, my lord Iyeyasu. Where is the need for a helmet now?'

Iyeyasu smiled at them all. 'Because now, it is necessary to work. *After* victory, knot the cords of your helmet. Come, my lords. The road to Kyoto is open.'

———————

The wind was off Lake Biwa, whistling down from the mountain passes which surrounded the water before it reached Kyoto. It was cold. It was the time of the Fall of Hoar Frost, and tomorrow would be the Beginning of Winter. A good moment to die.

'It is time,' said the guard.

Ishida Mitsunari struggled to his feet, tried to straighten, and was bent double by the sudden pain in his belly. He dropped to his knees, sucking air into his lungs, while the guards watched him, without pity. He was here, alive, their prisoner, and he should be dead. They did not understand.

'Allow me to assist you.' Konishi of Udo took his arm. Konishi's face was serene. He was an old friend. He had confidence, still, in himself and in his future. He was a Christian. As a Christian, he had spurned seppuku, because it was against the teaching of the priests, and the guards respected that. Ishida Mitsunari they regarded as a coward, and he could not tell them of his oath to Toyotomi Hideyoshi, not without betraying those who still lived, and prospered.

He shook his head, and his arm free of Konishi's grasp. The

pain was subsiding. And yet, it might well come again, before he reached the Sanjo. 'I would like some water,' he said. 'Warm water, to drink.'

'My lord Mitsunari wishes warm water,' Konishi said.

'There is none,' said the guard. 'And we have not the time to boil any. Let the policeman eat this.'

He held out a persimmon. Mitsunari gazed at it for a moment, and then shook his head.

'It will aggravate the pain.'

'The pain is fear,' the guard said. 'You are a coward, Ishida Mitsunari. You should be made to crawl to the Sanjo.'

Mitsunari stood straight. 'You are a fool. Worse than that, you are a little thing. A sparrow. How can the sparrow understand the way of the eagle?'

But he was no eagle. Hideyoshi had told him that, two years before. He had ignored the words of his master and attempted to fly with the eagles, and here he was, an old man at forty-two. And even that was all the life he would live.

'Then come,' said the guard, and signalled the man who would march in front. This man carried the spear on which was the head of Nagatsuka Masaiye of Minakuchi. Another old friend. Masaiye had been Hideyoshi's Minister of Finance, and he and the Minister of Police had worked closely together on many things. They had worked closely together, after Hideyoshi's death. Now, for the last time, they worked closely together. Masaiye had performed seppuku, but yet it had not preserved his honour from the vengeance of the Tokugawa. Even in death he would share the humiliation of the policeman.

'You next,' said the guard, and Ankokuji came forward, head bowed. Was Ankokuji afraid? He appeared to tremble, but this might be because of the wind, so cold.

The guard hung the placard around Ankokuji's neck, denouncing him as a common criminal who had disturbed the public peace. Two more guards fell into place behind him, their pikeheads resting on his shoulders. Then it was the turn of Konishi.

Mitsunari breathed, slowly and deeply, as the placard was hung around his own neck. The others were out on the street now, and he could hear the jeering of the people. These effete nobles, these hastily gathered peasants, had little enough to cheer about normally. The life of Kyoto was the life of the cloister. The public execution of three daimyo was an event they would savour, and talk about for years. And make the most of, while it lasted.

He squared his shoulders as the pikeheads rested on his bones. How heavy. But he was used to ridicule and contumely. For a week he had sat in his own filth, chained in the doorway of the Tokugawa's palace, here in Kyoto, while his enemies, and those of his friends who had made their peace with the victors, came to look at him, and spit upon him. He had answered them with spirit, had caused Kobayakawa to hang his head in shame. It could not be said that Ishida Mitsunari died with shame, even if he had refused seppuku, had been taken like an escaped convict, dressed in woodsmen's clothes. They did not understand.

He stepped through the gate of the fortress, checked as the blast of noise and excitement surged at him. The people of Kyoto, come to jeer. And it was still a long way to the Sanjo. But his stomach had settled since that early attack. He smiled. Iyeyasu himself had given him medicine for his aching belly, while arranging his execution.

The pikehead on his shoulder moved, a gentle reminder. He began to walk, staring at Konishi's back, fifty paces in front of him. The roar of the crowd rose around him. 'The policeman,' they chanted. They hated him, for that. But had he sat in the stand farther down the road, and Prince Iyeyasu walked here, they would have loved him. Or at least, pretended to do so. As they pretended to love the Tokugawa?

Who was in the stand? It was coming closer now. He raised his head but the wind was blowing straight down the street, and the cold filled his eyes with tears. The Mikado himself would be there, on the high dais. He would not be visible, of course, but would be inside his gold-encrusted box: No common eyes could ever be permitted to look upon his countenance. But he would be able to see out, and he would be surrounded by his nobles and his ladies. A pleasing treat for the viceregent of the gods, a change from the endless round of flower arranging and poetry competitions which filled his days. A chance to bring Kyoto to life again. For this was a dead city, and thus a suitable place to die. Most of the buildings were still in ruins, relics of the last civil war, fought by Nobunaga, so many years ago. Hideyoshi had never bothered to come here at all. Even the Imperial Palace was sadly neglected. But not the new, gleaming white palace of the Tokugawa, only a few streets away.

Below the emperor sat the conquerors. He would not deign them a glance. He knew them all, the lords who had marched behind the golden fan, the Tokugawa princes, even the Tokugawa women were present to witness the end of the policeman. And then, Iyeyasu himself. And at his shoulder, the man Anjin Sama, clearly visible because of his great height, his pale skin, his thick beard. Anjin Sama. The man with the guns. Some said that without Anjin Sama the Tokugawa would not have won this war. And more said that without Anjin Sama the Tokugawa would not even have begun this war.

His feet slapped the earth, his toe kicked a stone, and he winced. The wince became a shiver, and the crowd, watching keenly, gave a roar of contempt. Yet they were no doubt shivering as well. The wind was cold.

Was Asai Yodogimi shivering? *She* was not here. And neither was Ono Harunaga nor his brother. They remained behind the unbreachable bastions of Osaka Castle where they were safe. Only Oda Nobunaga had ever taken Osaka Castle, and since then Hideyoshi had doubled the strength of the place to make it absolutely impregnable. So the princess could afford to ignore the soft words of the Tokugawa, his claim to have undertaken this entire campaign just for her son, and remain in safety. With her lover, and her women. And her women's lovers. For Norihasa was not here, either, to watch his father die. Norihasa lived, as he had to do, as he must continue to do, for the sake of their oath to Hideyoshi. While Norihasa lived, the cause of the Toyotomi still lived. While Norihasa lived, and remembered, the day of reckoning loomed ahead for the Tokugawa. And Norihasa would remember.

The Sanjo. The crowd pressed close around the square, and were kept back by the pikes of the Tokugawa soldiery. Nagatsuka Masaiye's head was already isolated, the spear thrust hard into the dust. And Ankokuji was kneeling, his head thrust forward. How he must wish he had cut his belly on the field of Sekigahara. Or joined the Satsuma in their wild, gallant, and successful dash for freedom. Perhaps, had *he* joined the Satsuma, he might still be alive and powerful. The Satsuma still held the south island and would continue to do so.

Ankokuji's head rolled in the dust. Mitsunari watched the blood pumping from his empty neck. Ankokuji had been a strong man. Would there be as much blood pumping from his own neck?

It was time. How quickly it had come. For Konishi was also dead. As he knelt he had made the sign of the cross, the Christian mystery which he apparently believed would in some miraculous way reunite his head with his body and waft him away to paradise. So Ishida Mitsunari, in what do you believe?

How quickly, and yet how slowly. The dust of the square was eating into his knees, even through the skirt of his kimono. The wind was whistling around his head. His head. And the noise bubbled in and out of his ears, an indistinct mumble, like distant thunder.

Something touched his neck; the merest sliver of steel, and was withdrawn again. Now. Now. Now. *Now.*

PART THREE

The Samurai

Chapter 1

THE HORSEMEN followed the road down from the hills, towards the beach. The group behind were clearly servants, undistinguished alike in dress and mounts, laden with boxes and an assortment of arms. The two in front each rode a black stallion, each wore a pale green silk kimono, and each, like their servants, resisted the summer heat with a dish-shaped peasant's hat. The similarity did not reach beyond their clothes. Kosuke no-Suke's beard was as thin as his body, no more than a few strands of greying black on his chin; Will Adams' entire face was shrouded in the dark hair, clipped close as he had always worn it, and even in the saddle he towered above his companion.

Suke reined as the ground levelled. 'This is the peninsula of Miura.'

Will estimated that they had ridden some twenty miles south from Edo, following always the curve of the shore, with the endless swamps on their left, and beyond the swamps, the calm water of the bay itself. They had passed the ancient township of Kamakura, where the Minamoto had first created the Shogunate five hundred years before, and where the great bronze Buddha still stared impassively at the world he dominated. Now the sea remained on their left, but it had appeared on their right as well, and in front of them. And this was the ocean, at least immediately ahead. To his right, in the distance, he could make out mountains, and even a town nestling at their feet. Another twenty miles, perhaps. Another bay.

'That town is Ito,' Suke said. 'It is where my lord Iyeyasu would have you build your ship. But he would prefer you to live here. This is closer to Edo, and you will be able to visit him the more easily. As for Ito, there will be a galley stationed here for you to cross the bay whenever you choose.'

There was one waiting on the beach now, hardly larger than a big rowing boat, close to the house. The house stood by itself; they had passed the nearest village nearly an hour previously. But this was no ordinary house. The outer wall was composed of timbers set on end in the earth to form a stockade, and was entered by a gatehouse, while inside he could see the roofs of several dwellings.

'This is a fortress,' he remarked.

Suke kicked his horse, and they continued along the road. 'It is a suitable residence for a hatamoto. You will have a retinue of forty people. Here you see some of them at work.'

'These people?' Will asked in amazement, for they were riding between the inevitable rice paddies, filled with men and women, their cotton kimonos tucked up above their knees and into their girdles as they worked at harvesting the grain, but now all hastening to the paths that ran between the small fields to perform the kowtow to their new master. 'Forty of them? I am but a shipmaster, as you well know, Suke. Where will I find the money to maintain such a host?'

'Not penniless any longer, Will.' Suke treasured this privilege of addressing Anjin Sama by his European given name. 'Did you not know what it meant when my lord Iyeyasu gave you his favour? Apart from the rank of samurai to which you will soon become entitled, he grants you this estate, with an annual income of eighty koku of rice.'

'Has this a money value?'

'A koku, Will, is the amount of rice that is required to feed one man for one year. The value of each estate in the land as represented by koku, is decided by the lord to whom you owe fealty, and so on up to the Mikado, who decides the daimyos' portions. Although in practice this has always been done by the Shoguns, and since their abolition, by lord Hideyoshi. And of course, this last redistribution of land was made by the prince himself.'

'So, let me understand,' Will said. 'I am now worth eighty kokus of rice a year, but I employ only forty people.'

'You may employ more, if you wish, of course,' Suke said.

'But if I do not, then I have forty spare yearly incomes. Which I would say makes me a wealthy man.'

'Oh, indeed, Will. You may barter your excess for money, which is worthless, or for goods and services, which are often very valuable. Or you could gather around you a force of samurai, sworn to do your will. Twenty such men would guarantee your home perpetual protection. And they are easy to come by, especially now. The land is filled with ronin.'

'And what is a ronin?'

'A leaderless man. All the many samurai who fought for the

policeman at Sekigahara are now without a leader, and roam the country. If they do not find employment soon they will become brigands. A hundred years ago, before the coming of Oda Nobunaga, Japan was infested with robbers.'

'And they would be faithful to me, if I offered some of these men employment?'

Suke smiled. 'They would swear it, Will. As to the future, no man can foresee that.'

'And it is part of Japanese ethics to practise treachery.'

'Subterfuge is a prettier word. Is there none in your country?'

'A great deal. But it is generally frowned upon.'

'Yet you have just admitted that it is practised. Here in Japan it is encouraged openly, so that every daimyo, every hatamoto, every gokenin, expects it from his followers and is on his guard against it. It occurs to me that your Europe is a nest of hypocrisy. I do not think I would care for it.'

'No doubt you are right, Suke. But as this house is in the heart of the Tokugawa land, I'll not require soldiers except perhaps one or two for show. In any event, would it not displease my lord prince were I to start raising private armies?'

Suke made a noise which was the nearest he had ever come to a laugh. 'Oh, it would, Will. Prince Iyeyasu would be indeed disturbed about this force suddenly arisen on his southern flank. Your income is eighty koku. Do you know my lord Iyeyasu's youngest son, the lord Tokugawa no-Yoshinao?'

'I have seen the babe,' Will said. 'A promising child.'

'He is but two years old, Will. Yet as daimyo of Owari his income is six hundred and ten thousand koku a year.'

'Six hundred and ten *thousand*?' Will reined his horse before the gate. 'By God. Then what, may I ask, Suke, is the income of the prince himself?'

Suke smiled. 'My lord Iyeyasu is valued at two million, five hundred and fifty-seven thousand koku.'

Will did some calculation. If each koku was indeed the equivalent of one man's living for a year, then the prince was just about equal to the King of Scotland, in wealth and power. 'You have convinced me of my place.'

'The prince,' Suke said gravely, 'is the most powerful man in all Japan, not excluding the Mikado, although that is an opinion one should keep to oneself. Before Sekigahara, Mori Terumoto and Uyesugi Tenshin were both valued at more than a million, although even they were less than half as powerful as the prince.

But since the reassignment of wealth and land, there is no one save my lord Iyeyasu with a million koku.'

'And yet our prince pretends only to modesty, and to a complete lack of ambition? I had thought to see his flag flying over Osaka by now.'

Suke laid one finger beside his nose. 'Our prince pursues his path, steadfastly, as a man walking through mud must choose his steps carefully, Will. The power is his, now, because there is no single rival big enough to take it from him. And yet nearly all the daimyo in Japan still look back on Hideyoshi as their leader, and thus feel a reverence for his name, and for his son. Many of them, I have no doubt, look forward to seeing the prince abdicate, when the boy is a reasonable age, and hand over the power.'

'And will he do this?'

'Never, Will. Never. The power will go to his own sons. Oh, no, Hideyori must be destroyed, and before he is a man. But my lord, and yours, must prepare the ground with care. Now come. You may not be worth a million koku, but you will find being lord of eighty koku sufficiently pleasant, I assure you.'

The doors were already swinging open, and four armoured samurai were bending low to the ground.

'What's this?' Will demanded

'Your army,' Suke said. 'These men have been appointed by the prince to serve you, and are happy to do so.'

Will dismounted, and signalled the soldiers to ride. The men straightened with some reverence. For who in all Japan had not heard of Anjin Sama, who had come from across the great sea to command the guns at Sekigahara? Just to have been at the battle, on the side of the Tokugawa, was sufficient for immortality.

'It might, indeed, be wise to add to their numbers, Will,' Suke suggested. 'At least by half a dozen. You live in an isolated place here, open to assault from the sea.'

'Were there ships upon that sea.' Will strolled to the wall, gazed at the collection of weapons hanging there. 'Now these things I have not seen before.'

'It is part of your house's defence, when a stranger of unknown quality comes to call, Will. You see, here is the grappling iron. Notice how the hooks on the end make a sort of ball, and face in every direction.'

'By God, what a fearsome toy,' Will said. 'It reminds me of an iron hedgehog.'

'Indeed. Well, you see, mounted on this ten-foot staff, it can be thrust into your enemy's kimono and with a twist, he is helpless, and can be kept at bay. But should he manage to avoid this, then your second guard will thrust this long, double-ended stick between his legs, to trip him up. Either way, he will be brought to the ground before he can do any damage. Then here is a pitchfork to hold him down, and should he continue to prove stubborn, your men will beat him about the head with these quarterstaves.'

Will removed his hat to scratch his head. 'And the house of every samurai is equipped with these things?'

'Every gokenin, certainly. The knowledge of this is a great inducement to peace. Now I, you see, being, I hope, an old and trusted friend, I remove my long sword, here and now, and give it into the keeping of your guards.' He did so; the samurai accepted the weapon with a reverent bow. 'And am in turn invested with this robe, which is the sign that I am welcome.' One of the samurai held the crimson gown for him to step into.

'I see that I have a lot to learn,' Will said. 'It will be like going back to school. But seriously, Suke, I think my first task must be to devise some kind of uniform for my retainers, for to say truth I doubt I would recognise any of these four fellows were he to come knocking at my door. As for the other thirty-odd . . . '

'A problem to every hatamoto, Will. And taken care of. Here,' Suke pointed to another hook in the wall, on which hung a collection of wooden tags, 'you see these? Before leaving this gate, every one of your retainers must possess himself or herself of one of these tickets, and he will only be readmitted upon presentation of the pass.'

'And this is also common to every house of importance?'

'Naturally.'

'If I have a fault to find with this country of yours, Suke, it is that everything is too well organised, too carefully thought out. Do you never feel the need for some disorder?'

Suke smiled. 'We shall investigate that aspect of life at a more suitable occasion. Now come, shall we go in?'

He opened the inner doorway, but Will's attention was taken by the immense conch shell which waited there on a shelf. 'And this, no doubt, is to sound dinner.'

'No, no, Will. This shell must always be available, in every house of the empire. It must only be sounded for one of four reasons, but for each of those reasons it *must* be sounded. It will be blown once for tumult, twice for fire, three times for thieves, and four times for treason. Anyone hearing one of those signals must immediately repeat it, and then hurry with all aid to the scene of the original call.'

'I must remember that.' Will stepped through the doorway and into the courtyard. Here there were gathered a group of people, four men and some eight women, as well as several children. All immediately dropped to their knees and inclined their heads towards the dirt. Hastily Will summoned them upright again.

'Your domestics,' Suke said. 'You remember Kimura?'

'Kimura,' Will cried, extending both arms for a European embrace, and then recalling himself to his dignity. 'Well met.'

'And for me, Anjin Sama.'

'He begged especially to be released from the service of the prince to enter yours. An unusual request, to be sure, but one the prince was happy to grant,' Suke said. 'He will be your steward, and will assist us in making you into a samurai. But come to the house. I think you will find it most satisfactory. It is a matter of some forty-eight tatami, which is a goodly size.'

'You'll have to explain that to me, Suke. This word tatami has me utterly confused.'

'It is really very simple, Will. A tatami is the mat which we use to cover the floor. It is made from rice straw, and to a fixed size, roughly the amount of space which would permit a man to lie comfortably without encroaching upon his neighbour. So, you see, when we speak of a room, we say that it is so many tatami, and everyone immediately knows the exact size, as the mats cover every inch of every floor.' He glanced at Will with a smile. 'The measurement is based upon a Japanese man, of course. I think you would just fit upon a single tatami mat, but as for not encroaching on your neighbour, now there I am not sure.'

Kimura hurried ahead of them to see that every screen was open. They mounted three steps, and came into a porch very like the one that the lord Takanawa and his son had sat in to judge the Hollanders, a year previously. By God, Will realised, I am now the same rank, a hatamoto.

The door was open, and waiting to take their sandals and

replace them with slippers were two young girls. 'These will be your personal servants,' Suke said.

'This is another thing about which we must speak,' Will said. 'I am by no means sure where the duties of a personal servant like this begin and where they end.'

Suke smiled, and switched to Portuguese. 'A man's personal servants should be regarded in the light of an extra pair of hands Will. You may interpret that as you will. These girls will not complain; they seek only to serve you.'

He led Will through the inner screen into what was obviously the main chamber of the house. Here there were twelve tatami mats upon the floor, and the paper-framed window looked out upon a delightful garden, apparently in the formal Japanese style, for it resembled Magome Kageyu's garden in Bungo, with the bath house and the house of office standing together at the end of the path. And here, too, there waited Shimadzu no-Tadatune. 'Tadatune,' Will cried, and embraced the young nobleman. 'Well met, indeed. I had supposed you dead.'

'I was one of the seventy samurai who joined the standard of my uncle and cut our way through the forces of the traitor Kobayakawa,' Tadatune said. 'We rode at a gallop, all the way to Osaka, and there took ship. The Tokagawa came after us, but we engaged them in battle, galley against galley, and so made our way back to Bungo.'

'I heard tell of that battle,' Will said. 'A famous encounter. It was there I supposed you lost your life, as I heard that you were wounded.'

'Nothing of any importance, and now you see me as well as ever in my life. And happy to be welcomed into your house, Anjin Sama, as the last time we met it was my unpleasant duty to condemn you to death.'

'It *was* your duty,' Will agreed. 'And your uncle has made his peace with the prince?'

'From henceforth we march behind the golden fan. And in this regard you will be pleased to learn that your two betrayers, the man de Conning and the man van Owater have been beheaded for bearing false witness.'

'Beheaded? By God.' Will found his hand stroking the back of his neck.

'It is what they deserved, Will,' Suke said. 'To lie, as I told you when first we met, is lower than to play the coward. Now, come, this is an occasion for celebration, not for brooding upon the fate of two utter scoundrels.'

Kimura, who had remained in the doorway, clapped his hands, and the two girls hurried forward with cups of boiling green tea.

Suke sat down, sipped his drink with great relish. 'I invited lord Tadatune here to act as your sponsor, Will. When it was decided to make you into a samurai, my lord Iyeyasu was of a mind himself to be your sponsor, but it was pointed out that this was without precedent, and besides, as it is a lengthy business, he would not be able to devote himself to it with the necessary single-mindedness. Being asked to name a substitute, I could think of none better than your oldest Japanese friend.'

'And I am grateful to both of you,' Will said. 'But tell me of this induction as a samurai. I must confess it leaves me somewhat uneasy. Is it then so very lengthy?'

'To a Japanese boy, it is a matter of some years,' Tadatune explained. 'But not of course to the exclusion of all else. In your case, we must endeavour to cover all the ground that would have elapsed between your third and your fifteenth birthdays, in a matter of months.'

'A matter of weeks,' Suke said. 'Our lord prince is anxious to have the keel of his first ocean-going ship laid, and this is in Anjin Sama's care. I may say that he will himself visit Ito in the not too distant future, and expect to find you there.'

'Then we should begin immediately,' Tadatune said.

Suke smiled. 'At least give Anjin Sama time to appreciate his new surroundings. I have arranged for some women to come in tonight, to entertain us.'

'Women?' Will asked, frowning.

'Geisha. Do not confuse them with prostitutes, Will. You asked me just now if we never felt the need to shed our dignity. Certainly, it is not something that a samurai may do in public, or even in private, where members of his own family are involved. Thus the geisha. They are trained, almost from birth, to entertain. That, at the end of the evening, they may be good enough to satisfy one's desire is a matter of chance to many. But not to Kosuke no-Suke. Or to Anjin Sama, I may promise you that. Tonight we shall celebrate the new lord of Miura.'

'And so I drink to you, my friend, Anjin Sama.' Tadatune raised his cup. 'May your fame never grow less, may your ships radiate across the waters of the earth, and may they never, never sink.'

'To the unsinkable ships of Anjin Sama,' Suke said, also drinking.

Will's glass was empty. But the girl, her name was Kita, was already refilling it, kneeling beside him as she poured from his pitcher. Kita. A pretty name for a pretty thing. A geisha. She had served him throughout the meal, like any other serving girl, and yet there had been more. She had anticipated what would follow, expected that he would be doing the same. There was not a hint of lewdness in her behaviour, in anything she said or did; but there was a special air of intimacy, with which she attended to him. A practised intimacy, there was the rub. He could not get it out of his mind that it was all practised, here. In all Japan. All practised.

'I thank you, my friends,' he said. 'The man who can invent the unsinkable ship, should there be such a thing, will be immortal indeed. I suspect it is beyond my powers.'

'Nonsense,' declared Tadatune. 'Nothing is beyond the powers of Anjin Sama.'

Incredibly, the young hatamoto was drunk. So was Suke. He had never seen them drunk before. They had not struck him as belonging to a nation which believed in drunkenness, unlike the English, and he found it difficult to believe that it was possible to *get* drunk on a few cups of saké topped by a goblet of thin wine.

Or perhaps they were merely drunk with anticipation. 'Let us have dancing,' Suke said. 'Dance for our lord of Miura.'

The girls giggled, very gently, and seized their fans. They rose together, fluttering the fans in front of their faces. Three gaily coloured butterflies. Kita wore a crimson kimono, the other two wore a pale blue and a dark green. Unlike ordinary women, their hair was bound on the tops of their heads, like a samurai's topknot, although of course they retained all their hair. And now they danced, if such was the word, standing in front of the three men and swaying their bodies, moving their hands and fingers, extending and closing their fans, while from beyond the screens someone, no doubt instructed by Kimura, who had taken a great interest in this feast, plucked the strings of some lute-like instrument.

And the girls also knew their parts. Each had eyes only for her lord of the night. Kita never failed to gaze at Will, never ceased to smile, her lips a wide red gash in the white of her paint. So what did he feel? By now, no doubt, his rod should be hard as iron, his body sweating with anticipation. He had known no woman since the Princess Asai Yodogimi. No man, either. In this utterly free sexual community it was necessary to remind himself of this. Life had been too full, too exciting. At times, too dreadful. He remembered the execution of the three daimyo at Kyoto as clearly as he remembered his disappointment with the imperial city itself. Suke, sitting ever at his elbow, had pointed out that, as Kyoto had been for some centuries the goal of every ambitious adventurer, whether he sought to be Shogun, Naidaijin, or Kwambaku, it had suffered time and again, and the Mikados, for all their spiritual powers, were really not very rich men, able to rebuild at will. Suke, for all his apparent reverence, was somewhat contemptuous of the Mikado. In many ways he was a Japanese Marlowe, although anyone less like that gay hellhound than this dignified, moustachioed secretary would be hard to find. But this night Suke was revealing a new side to his character. His eyes gleamed as he gazed at the girl, the one in blue, and there could be no doubt about the hardness of his weapon. And yet, he was married to a most comely woman; Will had met her in Edo. So then, did Japanese marriages also sour?

As for the executions, Suke had dismissed them with even greater contempt. 'They had their chance for seppuku,' he had said. 'Once neglected, that chance is not returned. They have forfeited their rights as human beings, and more important, as samurai. They are lower than the eta. And they fought against the prince.'

There was the truly unforgivable crime. In this country defeat was final. But victory was the gift of the gods, and suitably rewarded.

The music stopped, and the girls also stopped, lowering their fans and bowing from the waist. For a few seconds the room was quite still, disturbed only by a belch from Suke. And then the minister gave a sudden bellow, and scrambled to his feet. The girl in blue uttered a shriek and ran for the door. Suke reached for her, and she ducked under his arms, uttered another cry, or was it really a giggle, and darted into the doorway. There she hesitated, but as Suke reached for her again, she laughed once more, and ran through, the secretary behind her.

The other two girls had remained still, watching Tadatune and Will.

'What in the name of God brought that on?' Will cried. 'I

have never seen one of your women behave like that before. Nor one of your men.'

Tadatune smiled and drank some more plum wine. 'This is the way of the geisha. Their reason for existence, indeed. For what pleasure would there be in approaching one of these sweet creatures were she to submit to your every requirement, like a good wife?'

'Christ in Heaven,' Will said. 'What a backwards world we live in, to be sure, Tadatune. In my country, it is the wife who resists, and when we seek a whore it is just to achieve submission.'

Tadatune put down his goblet. 'I must be frank, Anjin Sama, and say to you that I do not think I would like to live in your country. But I pray you not to take offence at my words.'

'How could I?' Will asked. 'When I so thoroughly agree with you.'

'Good. Then I will say farewell. For a while, anyway.' He put down his cup and got to his feet and the girl in green gave a squeal of pleasure and simulated alarm, and hurried for the doorway.

Kita remained, standing still, her face smiling prettily, her eyes apparently quiescent, although they moved from time to time. No doubt she felt a certain anxiety, for fear this strange man from across the sea might wish something out of the ordinary. So then, what could he wish, that was out of the ordinary? He wanted her, now. Oh, yes, she was in no danger of being left standing there the night. And yet, he was reluctant to get up and chase her about the house like a schoolboy. Perhaps that *would*, after all, heighten passion. But it was not what he *wanted*, and here, in his own house, at last, was he able to take what he wanted. A frightening thought.

He beckoned, with his finger. Kita hesitated for a moment, and then came round the little table which remained in front of him, and knelt on the mat beside him. Her eyes were wide, her face now anxious.

'My ways are strange ways, Kita,' he said. 'Because I come from a strange land, from across the ocean.'

She nodded, still gazing at him. 'You are Anjin Sama, the the friend of Prince Iyeyasu. I know that, my lord.'

'So you must be patient with me, Kita.'

'Yes, my lord. I will be patient.'

He reached for her girdle, slowly released it so that it fell on each side of her knees, allowing her kimono to open as well.

She hesitated, and then did the same for him. Slowly he parted the blouse of the kimono; she wore nothing underneath, as he had seen when she was dancing. He wondered how old she was. Older than the girls who had been appointed to serve him, the girls who had bathed him in Bungo. Older than Magome Shikibu? Her breasts filled his hand and the nipples were hard. And large, like small pebbles, caressing his palm. And now, after another brief hesitation, she was doing the same to him. But his were insufficiently hard to please her. She glanced at him and then leaned forward, still kneeling, to lick each one into erection.

He looked down on the head of glossy black hair. God in Heaven, he thought. My own whore, in my own house. For how many years had he dreamed of this, of being thus, of owning, so much. But equally, God in Heaven, did this not require more? To live, in such a house, with just such a whore to come in from the village whenever he felt the need?

Her head rested on his chest, for a moment, and was then raised again to look at him. Her mouth was only inches away. But to touch the white cheeks, to let his tongue brush against those blackened teeth—which seemed part of the geisha uniform, married or not—seemed obscene. Besides, he could still see those teeth, picking at the raw fish during their tempora dinner. The fish that had still been gasping for breath, while Tadatune had sliced the flesh from its ribs, and the girls had giggled, and reached for food. Did the Princess Asai Yodogimi and Pinto Magdalena ever tear a living creature apart, and laugh, and chatter, as they did so? Strange. All strange. He did not belong here. Or if he did, then Mary belonged here too. Mary and Deliverance.

Kita parted his kimono entirely, took it back over his shoulders, and her fingers released his waistband. Her own gown was open as she leaned forward. If not her lips, her body was there for the kissing. Would her love forest smell as sweet as Asai Yodogimi's?

God in Heaven, Yodogimi. And beyond her, always, Pinto Magdalena. The unattainable? Because they were locked away in Osaka Castle. Virtually in a prison, although everything was done with the utmost politeness and decorum, and there was no suggestion of force involved, beyond the mere fact that the castle was garrisoned by twenty thousand men, equipped for a siege, and commanded by such men as the Ono brothers and Ishida Norihasa, son of the executed policeman. But unattainable for him, in any event. Because he was married. Because his life belonged across the ocean, in that land which Tadatune and Suke, through him, had come to despise. Which he himself despised? Now, there was the truth. He lay on his back, and Kita had absorbed him into her being, without his being aware of it. Not dead. Not reborn. No more than a stranger, wandering the paths of paradise.

Chapter 2

'OUR FIRST responsibility,' Tadatune explained, 'must be to make you *look* like a samurai, at the least.'

Will allowed Kimura to remove his kimono. He then sat on the extra mat placed in the centre of the room, back straight, arms folded, and waited. One of the girls knelt on his left hand, holding a tray on which were the various accessories necessary to the coming ceremony. The other was absent, although he gathered that she too had an important part to play. Kimura remained discreetly at the back of the room, but Suke and Tadatune were both seated in front of him, each having beside him a large lacquered box.

'It will be difficult,' Suke said. 'You see, Will, while we shave a child's head up to the third year, from the fifteenth day of the eleventh month of that year his hair is permitted to grow. Whereas yours would seem to have been shaved within these past three years.'

'We do not shave our hair at all,' Will explained. 'But we keep it cut short. At least our menfolk.'

'Why?' asked Tadatune.

'For cleanliness. Else it becomes a mess of nits and ticks. We do not practise washing to quite such an extent as do you. Indeed there is a body of opinion in Europe which claims too much bathing is bad for the health.'

'And do you, then, consider us to be unhealthy?' Suke demanded.

'Quite the contrary.'

'Besides,' Tadatune said. 'You say only the men in Europe keep their hair short. Do not these nits nest in the hair of your womenfolk?'

'Why, yes, I suppose they do.'

Tadatune shook his head, slowly. 'Let us proceed. I have chosen your position carefully, you understand, Anjin Sama, for it is important that you face the most auspicious point of the heavens for this ceremony.'

'Which is that?'

'I have consulted the various tables, and have decided that

north-east is the most appropriate. This will bring you fortune. Now.' He took a pair of scissors from the tray, knelt in front of Will, reached forward, and gave three snips of his scissors at the hair on Will's left temple, then three snips on the right, and then three snips in the centre. Next he replaced the scissors, and took instead a large piece of cloth, which he placed on Will's head, like a wig, arranging it to begin on Will's forehead, and carrying it back so it hung down behind. He then took a piece of fish and seven rice straws, and attached them to the bottom of the cloth, tying them into two loops with a length of string. 'There,' he said. 'Your hair is now suitable for acceptance by the gods. Now we must drink to your fortune. You will come and sit on my left hand, Anjin Sama.'

Suke smiled. 'You should sit on his knee, Anjin Sama, but I am afraid you would press him to the floor. Remember you are but three years old.'

Will obeyed, sitting on Tadatune's left-hand side, while the other girl brought in a small lacquered table which she placed in front of the hatamoto; Kimura came forward with a bowl of rice.

'This has been offered to the gods,' Tadatune explained, and carefully took some of the rice from the bowl and placed it on the table, in the corner nearest Will. He now took the food sticks from his waistband, and placed three grains of rice, one after the other, in Will's mouth. While this was going on the girl returned with five cakes of rice meal, and with these Tadatune also pretended to feed Will, without actually placing any of the food in his mouth. 'Now you may resume your seat.'

Will returned to face them, while Kimura brought in a tray on which were three winecups, each hardly larger than a thimble. Tadatune drank from each of the cups in turn, and then presented the first one to Will. There was not enough liquid left to wet his lips. The second cup was also presented, and then Tadatune took another pair of food sticks from his sash. 'These I give to you, Anjin Sama, for your use in the future.'

Will examined the sticks in wonder. They were quite exquisitely made, and on the top of each one was carved a tiny replica of a cannon, small, and yet perfect in detail. 'Why, Tadatune, I don't know how to thank you.'

Suke placed his finger on his lips, and shook his head.

'Of course, I forget, I am but three years old.'

Tadatune now gravely presented the third cup, and Will

again drank. Kimura was hovering with a fresh tray, on which were three more cups and a small dish of dried fish.

'Three times,' Suke whispered. 'But only pretend to drink.'

Will nodded, sipped from each of the cups, and passed them to Tadatune, who drank in turn. Each man then broke off a piece of fish and ate it.

'And now, Shimadzu no-Tadatune, on behalf of this child,' Suke said, 'I present you with this robe of white silk.'

'But I should have procured that,' Will said in dismay. It was clearly a most expensive garment.

'It is my responsibility,' Suke explained. 'I am acting as your godfather. We have now completed the first ceremony. Shall we take a little walk while the room is prepared?'

Will removed the cloth from his head, put on his kimono, and accompanied the two samurai on to the porch, to gaze at his assembled retainers, all waiting in the yard, even the children, and all bowing as he appeared.

'They do no work today,' Tadatune explained. 'Because of the honour being done to their lord. Even the children do not go to school.'

'But they must attend school, normally?' Will asked.

'Every child must go to school, to learn how to read and write, that he may study the history of his country.'

'Is history, then, so important?'

'Can there be a more important subject than a thorough knowledge of the deeds of one's ancestors, of the great occasions in the nation's past? I think Kimura is again ready for us.'

They returned inside. Now a chequerboard had been placed on Will's mat, and on this he took his seat. Tadatune delved once again into his box.

'It would now be, in normal circumstances, the fifth day of the eleventh month of the fourth year,' Suke explained. 'You have aged a year.'

'And I present you with this.' Tadatune held out, across both his arms, a most splendid outer dress, in pale green, on which were embroidered storks and tortoises, fir trees and bamboos.

'What a marvellous piece of work,' Will remarked. 'No doubt the emblems are symbolic?'

'Oh, indeed,' Tadatune agreed. 'The stork and the tortoise are emblems of longevity; it is said the stork lives for a thousand years, and the tortoise for ten thousand; we pray that you may be similarly blessed. The fir trees, being evergreen, are symbols of an unchanging virtuous heart. And the bamboo is symbolic of an upright and straight mind. These things we already know you possess, Anjin Sama.'

'I thank you, Shimadzu no-Tadatune,' Will said.

'And with these,' Tadatune said, once more opening his box, 'I give you the hayama.' He produced a pair of loose, baggy trousers which the samurai wore when not in armour, to distinguish them from the bare-legged peasants. 'And also with this sword and dirk, made of wood.'

Will accepted the gifts, while Kimura hurried forward with the two girls, to resume the wine ceremony. This time, Suke's gift to Tadatune was a piece of gold embroidery for a girdle, another vast piece of expense, Will supposed.

'Truly, Suke, this business seems costly,' he remarked, as they once again strolled on the porch.

'Because it is an occasion of great importance in a man's life, Will. Indeed, there are only two more important; the day of his marriage and the day of his death. But do not suppose you will escape the expense; you will have to provide all this for your own sons.'

For my own sons, Will thought. Had I any. Should I ever have any. Or at least, any I can call my own.

Tadatune had observed the expression on his face. 'But that is for the distant future, Anjin Sama. Come, let us now make you a samurai.'

The actual shaving of his head was performed by Kimura, assisted by the two girls. They worked with great care, and equal skill, removing all the hair except for three patches, one on each temple and one in the centre, and leaving also a long lock of hair attached to his forehead, and then combing out the tress which extended from the crown of his head.

'It is now time for me to give you your final name, Anjin Sama,' Tadatune said.

'You mean I am to have another?'

'The adult name is usually bestowed at the age of fifteen, the time when this final ceremony of cutting the forelock is performed, and is related to a young man's gifts or ambitions. But as my lord Prince Iyeyasu has already called you Anjin Sama, Master Pilot, he has decided to bestow upon you a most special privilege, and call you by the name of your estate, which is usually reserved only for great lords. Henceforth you will be known as Anjin Miura. Now then, let us drink to your fame as a samurai.'

This time the girl had only a single earthenware cup on her tray, but it was a large one. Tadatune drank three times, and passed the cup to Will, who also took three sips.

'Now come and kneel over here,' Tadatune instructed. Will obeyed, and Tadatune moved behind him, for all the world like a hairdresser attending to my lady's toilet, and gathered the long hair falling from Will's crown to tie it on top in a r asonable facsimile of a true topknot. 'Now bend forward, from the waist,' he commanded. Will obeyed, so that his head all but touched a willow board, held out by Kimura. He watched Tadatune out of the corner of his eye, with some apprehension, as the young hatamoto drew his short sword with his right hand, while with his left hand he gathered the forelock and pulled it forward so that it lay on the board. There was a quick movement of Tadatune's arm, and the sword struck the board, and indeed bit into the wood. Will jerked upright, and watched his hair lying in front of him.

'By God,' he said. 'I had almost thought my head was on the block.'

Tadatune was carefully folding the forelock into a piece of paper decorated with black and white paintings of cannon. 'You will keep this in a safe place for ever, Anjin Miura,' he said gravely. 'So that it may bring eternal good fortune upon you and your family. And when you die, let it be buried in your coffin, to protect you through the after life.'

Will took the folded paper with due deference. It seemed to have quite as much significance as any of the ritual undergone in the Christian Church, with the difference that a man was his own god, bound to observe his honour and courage at all times, bound to create his own fortune, not only in this life but in the after life. Two different ways of expressing the doctrine of free will, perhaps.

The girls were back with goblets of wine, and he and Tadatune exchanged sips, while Suke was looking into his box, to present Tadatune with another large bale of silk, decorated with a lozenge pattern.

'And now,' Tadatune said, 'all that remains, Anjin Miura, is for us to teach you the code of the samurai. But first, let us eat.'

Will put his hands, cautiously, to stroke first of all his shaven scalp, and then his topknot, balanced precariously on the top of his head. 'No doubt this hairstyle has a special significance?'

'It has two,' Suke said. 'In the first place, it is designed to prevent the hair from falling into the eyes in battle, and hence is the mark of the warrior.'

'That makes sense enough. And the other?'

'The other, Anjin Miura, is for the convenience of your conqueror,' Tadatune said. 'Should you ever come to such a grievous state of affairs. For he will thrust his food sticks into your topknot, and thereby carry your head with the greater ease.'

'Your equipment,' Suke said proudly. 'I had them made especially for you, Will. There is none like it in all Japan.'

'But these must have cost a fortune.'

'They are a gift from the prince.'

There was a shield, round and thick, and an iron helmet, lined with buckskin, with a flap of articulated iron rings which would droop below his shoulders. The visor was made of thin, lacquered iron, with a removable nose- and mouth-piece, while his eyes would be partially protected by the projecting front piece. There was also a false moustache, to add to the terror of his appearance. And skilfully worked on the centre of the front piece was once again the replica of the cannon. The mark of Anjin Miura. The thought made his blood tingle.

The helmet itself was very tall, not less than three feet, he estimated, and in the top there was a hole, into which fitted an ornament like a pear.

'That is what your enemies will aim for, when they swing at your head,' Tadatune explained.

'Aye,' Will said thoughtfully. But the armour itself was tough enough. The breastplate was composed of thin scales of iron, over which he would wear a chain-mail surcoat. His arms, legs, abdomen and thighs would be protected by plates joined with woven chains, and there were great loose brassarts to be worn on his shoulders. There were also greaves for his legs, but apparently he would wear his normal sandals below them. Perhaps a samurai thought it dishonourable to thrust at an opponent's feet. The entire suit, which was painted green, was laced and bound with iron clamps and cords of silk, decorated with gilt tassels and glittering insignia, principally the golden fan of Iyeyasu, to leave an enemy in no doubt as to whom he served. 'Truly, a spectacular piece of equipment.'

'Now for what you will always carry into battle,' Suke said, and produced a satchel which contained several layers of thick paper, with an adhesive side, which meant that each layer had to be peeled off from the next.

'For binding up your wounds,' Tadatune explained. 'Every samurai carries this. The paper will be laid over the wound, to which it will immediately stick. It is then wrapped around the limb, or left flat should the wound be on a flat part of the body. If it is desired to wet the wound, then the water can be added without disturbing the paper, for it will soak through.'

'And will the paper not aggravate the injury?'

'On the contrary,' Suke said. 'It has healing powers of its own.'

'Next,' Tadatune said. 'Here is your bow.'

Will took the weapon. It was made of oak of the most perfect quality. On either side it was encased in a semi-cylinder of split bamboo, black where it had been toughened by fire. The three pieces had been bound into a whole with withes of rattan, and the result was a weapon of remarkable lightness, and with even more remarkable elasticity. He began to understand how, with a bow certainly smaller in every way than the old English yew, the Japanese could yet hurl an arrow nearly as far, and with equal accuracy. The string was hemp.

'And the arrows.' Suke produced the quiver. 'We have given you a selection of the most deadly. They all have their names. This one, for instance, is called the turnip head, from its shape.'

'I doubt it could pierce this armour,' Will remarked.

'It is not intended to, Anjin Miura,' Tadatune pointed out. 'Its purpose is to make a singing noise as it passes through the air. A volley of these arrows is decidedly alarming to the enemy, as a warning of what will follow. No doubt this one is more to your liking.' He showed Will a bolt with a two-edged head, but a nearly blunt point. 'This is called the willow leaf, and is intended to knock a man from his horse.'

'This,' Suke said, handling a similarly shaped arrow, but with sharply serrated edges, 'is known as the bowel raker.'

'Very apt,' Will agreed. 'And this?' From the quiver he drew the plainest of bolts.

'The armour piercer,' Tadatune said. '*That* will puncture your breastplate, Anjin Miura, if properly aimed.'

Will examined the arrow; the barb was made of steel, and the shaft of cane bamboo. The string piece was horn, whipped on with silk, and the arrows were contained in a leather quiver, as usual splendidly decorated with the golden fan of the Tokugawa.

'I must confess, my friends, that I am pleased to make the acquaintance of these fearsome things *after* the campaign has ended.'

'That may be so, Anjin Miura,' Tadatune said. 'And if you are unfortunate, you may never have the opportunity to fire one of these arrows in anger. And yet, certainly you will use the sword.'

'This too is presented by the Prince Iyeyasu,' Suke said, and with great reverence laid the weapon, the reverse towards Will, across his left forearm. It was very like the sword of Tadatune, which he had first examined in Bungo, except that here he was able actually to touch the weapon, and half draw it from its white scabbard. Once again, both haft, long enough to take the grip of about four hands, he estimated, and scabbard were worked with the golden fan design, together with the occasional cannon. And set into the blade, near the guard, was the name Masamune.

'The maker,' Tadatune said. 'There is none finer in Japan.'

'In the world,' Suke said reverently.

The more closely he looked at the sword, the more was Will prepared to grant that opinion.

'It would be good for you to give your sword a name,' Tadatune said. 'Mine is called Beard-Cutter, because it is so sharp it will slice through a man's beard on its way to his body.'

'Then mine had best be called Air-Splitter,' Will said. 'For I doubt it will ever meet with anything more substantial.'

'Do not count on that,' Suke said. 'That weapon is the guardian of everything a man should hold sacred. It took Masamune sixty days of labour and prayer to forge.'

'And prayer?'

'He had to pray for guidance with every inch of the blade, every design on the hilt. That is not just a weapon, Anjin Miura. It is your soul, as of this moment.'

'Is it not said,' Tadatune remarked, 'that one's fate is in the hands of heaven, but a skilful fighter does not meet with death?'

'And also,' Suke said, 'that in the last days, one's sword is the wealth of one's posterity.'

There was no suggestion of humour in either man's face. Here, Will realised, he *was* in the presence of a religion.

'But it is necessary to know how to behave with a sword,' Tadatune said. 'More than just the use of it. For example, you must always leave your long sword with the servant on the gate, as Suke and I have done, before entering the house of a friend. If there is no servant, you must lay your sword on a mat in the vestibule; then at a later moment the servants of your host will fold the sword in a napkin, and place it in the weapon rack. When you are in the house of an inferior or a stranger, you do not discard your weapon, but lay it on the floor beside you when you sit.'

'As you did in the inn in Bungo,' Will said.

'That is correct. The short sword, of course, is never discarded, except when on long visits to a friend. It should be kept in the belt beside the ko-kotana.'

He gave Will a short sword, with a blade perhaps a foot long, and a little knife, obviously for entirely personal use. On both, the sheath and the hilt were worked in the same designs as the long sword. Will tucked them into his girdle beside their brother; as he did so, the two swords scraped against each other.

'Careful,' Suke said. 'That is a deadly insult. Were we not your friends we should regard the clashing of your two swords as a challenge.'

'To turn the sheath in the belt as if about to draw also constitutes a challenge,' Tadatune said. 'Also to lay your weapon on the floor and kick the guard towards another, or to touch another's sword.'

'And you must never, ever, draw your weapon unless you have begged pardon in advance,' Suke added. 'You should never even ask to see another's sword.'

'But if it is done, then it must be held in the silk napkin, as I showed you in Bungo,' Tadatune said. 'You should always carry such a napkin on your person.'

'You will have to have patience with me, my friends. And the little sword? The dirk?'

'That is for the performance of seppuku, nothing else,' Tadatune said. 'It can never be used in combat.'

'I would know about this seppuku,' Will said.

'It is not a light matter, Will,' Suke said. 'The reasoning is very simply this. Should you engage in battle with another samurai, and be beaten into surrender, or even more, should you commit a crime, and be adjudged guilty by law, in either event your life, your property, and the lives and property of your family and all your serfs, belong to the victor, in the first instance, or the daimyo who has judged you, in the second. The common man of course has no alternative. But the samurai has been granted this special privilege, that by the performance of seppuku, thus forfeiting his life, he confines the punishment to himself, and himself alone. His property, his wife, his family and his tenants are left unharmed and unaffected, which means that his eldest son may inherit his rights and wealth.'

'Correctly speaking,' Tadatune said, 'seppuku should be performed in a temple, but it is more often carried out on the field of battle.'

'In the case of a daimyo,' Suke said, 'it may be performed in the garden of his house, or in a room especially set aside and purefied for the purpose.'

'And on the field of battle, for instance,' Will said, 'will no man, perhaps the daimyo who has just conquered another, prevent the performance, in order to gain his victim's land and property?'

'Never,' Tadatune declared. 'That were the height of dishonour. Once a man prepares for seppuku, his person is inviolate, until he himself gives the signal. As you must have seen, there were several thousand seppuku on the field of Sekigahara.'

'But of course the Shimadzu were exempt,' Suke said. 'Because they regained their home lands with their swords still in their hands. Seppuku is the consequence of surrender, not merely defeat.'

'I understand that,' Will said. 'But I do not understand what Tadatune meant just now, about giving the signal. You mean the principal does not actually kill himself?'

'He does kill himself, Anjin Miura, but as you know, it is not our custom to prolong the suffering that leads to death. Let us suppose I have been condemned by my lord of Satsuma for some crime. My lord will send to my house two of his most trusted secretaries, who will come to me in ceremonial dress, as we are wearing now, and will solemnly read the sentence to me, after which I am allowed to take leave of my wife and family and friends, while the room is prepared for me. If it is to be performed in the garden, screens must be erected around the mats to keep out the vulgar gaze. Once this has been done, and the place or the room has been purefied, the secretaries and various other witnesses take their places, together with the man I have appointed to be my second.'

'The position of second is a most honoured one,' Suke pointed out. 'And indeed, the second's honour is equally at stake, with that of the principal.'

'Having been informed that all is ready,' Tadatune said, 'I make my entry and take my seat upon the mat, opposite the two secretaries. My second, his long sword already drawn and tested, stands immediately behind my right shoulder. I may make my last prayer, if I wish, and then I release my girdle so that my gown falls from my shoulders, and I am naked to the waist. Now I take my short sword in my right hand, thrust it into my belly, on the left side, thus, and draw it across to the right. When I have reached the right-hand side of my belly, I must turn the blade downwards, to make an angle.'

'And you will have the strength of mind to do this?' Will asked.

'If I do not, Anjin Miura, then I am no true samurai, and thus worthy of disgrace.'

'And when does the second intervene?'

'At the moment of the downward cut,' Tadatune said. 'Once the knife turns downwards, the principal throws his left hand away from his body and at this signal the second must strike off his head.'

'There are men,' Suke said drily, 'who have been known to throw out their left arm the moment the dagger enters their body at all. In which case the disgrace is not the second's, as he *must* obey the signal, and instantly.'

'But it *is* a disgrace.'

'The matter is still in debate,' Tadatune said. 'The problem is that there is no written code of conduct for the samurai. It has grown up over the centuries. It is time for some great daimyo to codify the law, and make it plain once and for all what is right and what is wrong. At this moment it rests too much upon the attitudes of the two official witnesses.'

'But for the second,' Suke said, 'there is no doubt at all. He must decapitate his principal, on the signal, and it must be done with a single blow. Else is *he* disgraced.'

'But in Bungo,' Will said, 'you told me that no samurai may take life, except in battle?'

'Seppuku is a different matter,' Tadatune said. 'For the principal, it is an honourable way to die. The only honourable way, except in battle.'

'But the second must necessarily go to a temple and be purefied after the incident,' Suke said. 'Besides, I think you must have misunderstood what Tadatune told you. A samurai may not kill another *samurai* except in battle or during a blood feud. He may take the life of a common person, provided it is necessary, and he can justify his action to his lord.'

'Tell me of this blood feud.'

'Why,' Tadatune said, 'it is merely a private conflict between two samurai, over a point of law or honour, which is recognised *by* the law to exist. But as every samurai is alone responsible for his wife, his children, and his retainers, the feud is extended to cover all of them, and can, in fact, only be ended by the total extinction of one side, or by the performance of seppuku on the part of one of the principals.'

'The commencement of the feud is usually announced by the killing of one of the offending samurai's servants,' Suke said. 'His head will then be cut off and left outside his master's house, with the ko-kotana of his murderer thrust through his ear, so that there can be no doubt as to who claims responsibility.'

Will eased the short sword from its scabbard, tested the edge. Once again, as sharp as a razor . . . And now he was a samurai. It was no longer a matter of choice, but of duty.

'Now all that remains for me to do,' Tadatune said, 'is to give you a course of instruction in the proper use of the long sword, for without such knowledge you are too vulnerable to insult.'

'And there is no one better qualified to be your teacher than Tadatune,' Suke said. 'He is one of the most famous swordsmen in Japan.'

Will shook his head. 'Time enough for that, Tadatune, if the prince should ever find it necessary to go to war again. I am a man of peace, however often I may have been thrown into the cauldron of battle. I doubt my long sword will ever be drawn in anger, and besides, I am in haste to visit Ito, and see what can be done about building the prince a ship.'

The man panted; his half-naked body glistened with sweat. He fell to his knees at Will's feet, scarce spared a glance for the gigantic mystery rising behind the white man. 'The prince comes,' he said. 'Here, to Ito.'

The various shipwrights laid down their tools, to listen. The noise of labour died away in the huge workshop, and there was no sound above the faint soughing of the breeze coming in the open north end of the building, where the restless waters of Sagami Wan lapped at the slipway. Outside, too, the noises of life in the town were dying. It was as if, in the middle of the day, Ito had been plunged into the middle of the night. For several seconds there was no noise at all, above the wind. And then they heard the gigantic whisper of several hundred people, marching. Nothing else. The Tokugawa, but this time on a peaceful mission.

Will ran outside, Kimura at his elbow. He gazed up the street, now filled with onlookers, passersby, checking on their way, artisans and merchants, neglecting their wares for this unique occasion, even the beggars, desisting from their eternal supplication. All knelt, by the side of the road, heads bowed as the procession approached, in the most complete silence save for that whisper of feet.

Kimura glanced at Will, and then himself dropped to his knees, as did the workmen, leaving Will alone standing in the doorway of the workshop, gazing up the road.

He watched five horses, leading the procession. These were magnificent black mounts, and were riderless, each led by two grooms, one on each side, and followed by two footmen, carrying the banner of the golden fan. They came up to the workshop, and passed on, to halt at a predetermined distance farther down the road. Behind them came six porters, each clad in the richest of kimonos above their loin-cloths, walking one by one, carrying lacquered chests and japanned trunks and baskets upon their shoulders; the prince's daily necessaries.

Behind the porters came ten soldiers, also walking one by one, carrying, apart from their own weapons, a selection of swords, pikes, firearms, bows and quivers, all decorated in the most costly and exotic designs. Even weighed down as they were, they yet performed the step peculiar to marching soldiers when entering a township: they lifted one foot behind them until it almost touched their backs, at the same time stretching out the opposite arm as far as they could, as if about to start swimming through the air; then the leg came down and was thrust forward as the arm was brought in, and the whole wearying business was repeated with the other pair of limbs. Thus had they marched all the way from Edo, resting only when their lord had decided to rest.

Behind the soldiers there came another file of chest-bearers, and six more led horses, this time each of pure white. These were followed by three more soldiers, each carrying the prince's pike of state, held high above their heads, the ends decorated with bunches of cock's feathers. After these there walked a lone samurai, accompanied by two footmen; he carried, on a cushion held in front of him, the prince's hat, beneath a covering of black velvet.

Now once again, six men carrying trunks, all of a likeness, this time, made out of varnished leather and marked with the Tokugawa crest. Each of these was accompanied by two footmen. Then another samurai, again accompanied by two footmen, carrying an instrument Will had never seen before, a thick stick covered with waterproofed cloth, which expanded to keep out the rain, or indeed, the worst of the sun, when the prince was walking. This also was covered in black velvet.

The prince himself was now approaching. He was preceded by sixteen more samurai, each accompanied by a page, each dressed in the richest of clothing, positively gleaming, in a kaleidoscope of reds and greens, blacks and silvers, golds and blues as they made their way through the dusty, sun-bathed streets. And behind this was the norimono of the Tokugawa, hung with brilliantly decorated trappings, emblazoned with the golden fan, and carried by eight men, each dressed in a shining green livery, and followed by another sixteen, waiting to take their turns at carrying their lord. Walking behind these there were another four samurai, whose duty it was to assist Iyeyasu in and out of his chair, and behind them were the three black horses of state, one of which the prince would mount should the occasion arise. Their saddles were covered with the inevitable black velvet, and each was attended by two grooms.

Behind the norimono the procession continued in an apparently endless stream, the bearers of the twelve empty baskets, symbolic of the prince's right to tribute, and then more gentlemen of his court, and then an immense crowd of lesser courtiers, domestics, pages, this group headed by Kosuke no-Suke.

But the norimono itself had stopped at the entrance to the workshop and the gentlemen were hurrying forward to part the curtains. Now Will dropped to his knees like all those around him, laid his palms on the ground, and lowered his head.

'Rise, Anjin Miura,' Iyeyasu said, speaking as softly as ever. 'The kowtow does not become a giant.'

Will stood up, gazed at the small, green-clad figure, and the smiling face. Was it superstition? Or was it more than that, which attracted so much greatness to so simple a human being? Iyeyasu's physical interest in him had remained frighteningly obvious, during all the winter, as they had spent every evening together while he had laboured to teach the prince what he knew of mathematics and astronomy, gunnery and navigation. And yet, as he had promised the night before Sekigahara, Iyeyasu had never sought to force the issue. Did he, then, wait with the remarkable patience which was his chief characteristic, for Will himself to make the first advance? Or, far more frightening, did he know it would, eventually, be a matter of force, and thus waited until the Englishman was of no more value to him?

'We had heard of your approach, my lord prince,' he said.

Iyeyasu tapped him on the shoulder with his fan. 'And yet you did not prepare yourselves?'

'We considered it best for us to work the harder, my lord prince, and forget the ceremony.'

Iyeyasu gazed at him for a moment. 'You always amaze me, Will. Tell me, are all Englishmen as blunt, as arrogant, and yet as unerringly right, as yourself?'

'My lord prince is a flatterer,' Will said. 'And as he once said to me, that is not good, for a man.'

'One day, Will,' Iyeyasu said. 'One day I shall lose patience with you. Let me see what you have done.'

Will brushed aside the gentlemen who darted forward, and himself opened the door to the converted warehouse. The prince stepped inside.

'Close the door,' he said. 'On everyone except yourself.'

Will obeyed, his heart pounding like a young girl's. Whenever he was alone with this man, he felt like a virgin approaching her marriage bed. In a sense, no doubt, he was. He had hitherto considered nothing more than the physical relationship between them; any other was beyond his experience. But was it not at least possible that the prince actually felt love for him? For now, after their six months' separation, Iyeyasu was drawing his finger down Will's shoulder, and arm, to feel the bicep as he might have sought a woman's breast.

And then turning away, to gaze at the ship. 'It makes me think of a whale. A dead whale, stranded on a beach.'

The vessel was nearly seventy feet long on the keel, and from the immense wooden base there arose the first of the ribs, to which were already connected the stringers and even the first of the planking.

'When will she be ready?'

'I shall dismantle the roof of this building shortly, my lord, in order to commence work on the upper decks.'

'And the masts?'

'The masts will not be stepped until she is launched, my lord.'

'How many masts?'

'She will have three, my lord.'

'And guns, of course?'

'Providing we can procure them, my lord prince.'

Iyeyasu stepped past him and walked to the open end of the building, gazed at the sunshine sparkling from the waters of the bay. 'We will procure them, Will,' he said. 'There is so much to be done. So much. Have you seen your friends, the Dutchmen?'

'No, my lord prince. I invited them to visit me, but they have not yet done so.'

'They have been importuning Suke, for permission to leave,' Iyeyasu said, without turning his head. 'That is, your friends Quaeckernaeck and Zandvoort. The others have become mere charges upon my charity. Which but makes me the more amazed that you are the man you are, Will.'

Will stood at his shoulder. 'And you would grant them such permission, my lord prince?'

'When first we met, what is it, two years ago now, Will? Then you told me your purpose in coming to Japan was to open trade between your countries of England and Holland and my own. I have thought about this matter, and now I would see such a trade. The reason why I have chosen to consider it for so long is that I am sure it will lead to recrimination, and possibly worse, from the Portuguese, and I wished to discover more about these people who claim to be so powerful before I would risk exposing the coasts of Japan to their wrath. But now, having learned from you that they are no more than one nation amongst many in this Europe of yours, and more, that they have been defeated by your country, which you say is less populous than my own, why, I am prepared to risk their anger. The Portuguese will not give us what we wish. They deal in baubles, trinkets, as if we were savages. I wish cannon, Will. And arquebuses. Will your people send us these?'

'I know not, my lord prince. They may well be reluctant. It would be better . . . ' He bit off the end of his words.

Iyeyasu gazed at him, frowning. 'What would you have said?'

'I have no wish to offend you, my lord.'

'You, Will? You can never offend me. I give you my word on this.'

'You say you will permit the *Liefde* to leave Edo when she is fitted out, my lord prince? Who will man her?'

'Not the *Liefde*, Will. I will send a Japanese ship, but I will permit Zandvoort and Quaeckernaeck to sail in her, as far as Siam. I am informed that there is a Dutch trading post there. From there, your friends will obtain a passage back to Holland. I will give them letters to their rulers, and perhaps to yours as well. You can assist me in this, Will.'

'I would assist you more, my lord prince, were I to be allowed to accompany them.'

Iyeyasu had been watching the waves. Now his head turned, slowly.

'I would return, my lord prince,' Will said. 'This I swear.'

'On your voyage here, Will, you told me that twenty-four men survived, out of five hundred. I do not like those odds, on your return. At the best you would be away for three years.'

'A short time, my lord, when set against the span of a man's life.'

'A long time, to me, Will, because my life's span is already nearly run. My supporters wish me to take the rank and title of Sei-i-tai Shogun. Had you heard this?'

'No, my lord. But it is no more than fitting.'

'Agreed. It is my due, both by virtue of my heritage and by the feats of my sword. It will be a great occasion, Will. There has been no Shogun installed in Japan for a generation. More than a generation. Kyoto will live again for a season. I will have you there.' He smiled. 'I have much to show you. My Nijo Palace is nearly completed. I too have been playing the carpenter, Will. Often must I have told you of the continuing problem we have here, with our thin walls and screen doors, over the eavesdroppers and spies who haunt our great houses. I have solved that problem, Will. I have caused the various galleries which surround the rooms at Nijo to be made of planks of wood with a certain spring in them. Where each beam joins the supporting timbers there is an iron nail; so aimed as to touch the joist. The slightest movement of the floor, which is to say, the slightest step upon that floor, causes the plank to move, merely the smallest fraction, and this in turn causes the nail to scratch, and give forth a shrill sound. The floor *sings*, Will, and no man may stop it doing so, should he move on its surface. I call it my nightingale floor.'

'A most ingenious plan, my lord prince. I look forward to hearing the notes of this new bird. But after you are Shogun, when you are truly ruler of this land, then you will no longer have need of your lucky pilot.'

'Truly ruler of this land.' The humour left Iyeyasu's face, and he turned away to look at the bay once again. 'It is a fair land, Will.'

'The fairest I have ever seen, my lord prince, and I have travelled over half the globe.'

'It has a stormy history, as you will have gathered by now. My people are warriors, at heart, even the priests amongst them. They need strength, they need continuity of strength, from one rule to the next, to develop their own strength and increase it, else will it be dissipated in internicine wars, as has happened so often in the past. My generals, and those daimyo who march behind the golden fan, agree that this is necessary, and already there are rumblings of quarrels between the daimyo in the north island, and those in the south. Thus I am to become Shogun, to give my authority, my strength, to the land. And yet, and I speak now to you, Will, as I would speak to no other man, saving perhaps only Suke, they regard this as a mere necessity, and say that, of course, I will still only be acting as regent for the boy Hideyori, who will become Shogun in his turn when he is of a suitable age. Or if that is impossible, at least assume the full prerogatives of the Kwambaku.'

'But you say the boy is a half-wit, my lord prince.'

'I have heard that. I believe that. But I do not *know* it. I have not seen the child since he was five years old. The Princess Yodogimi will not leave Osaka Castle, and I am not permitted to enter. Yet there are those who do enter, and leave again, and come to me and say that every year, nay, every month, Osaka's strength is increased, more rice is stored, more arrows are cut, more swords are forged.'

'You mean to take the field again?'

'Not this season, Will. Nor even next. The way must be prepared with great care. I will tell you this, however. Once the Shogunate has been resumed by my family, it shall not leave us again. The Tokugawa Shogunate will be no thing of a few short years. I see in it the creation of a new Japan. I will let no boy, whoever may have been his father, and I will let no woman, however beautiful, stand in my way. So you see, Will, your presence here is needed. And not only because you are my fortune. Because, too, part of my plans for that future rest in the ships you will build for me.'

'Yes, my lord prince.'

'And yet your face is sad. You are unhappy here?'

Will sucked air into his lungs. Did he *dare*, in view of the relationship he shared with this man? But would there ever be a better opportunity? 'I have grown to love Japan, these last two years, my lord prince.'

'Then what ails you? You have but to ask, and you shall receive. Within reason.'

'Look there, my lord prince.' Will pointed across the bay. It was a fine day, and the peninsula of Miura was clearly visible. 'If you look closely, you may even see my house.'

'Once, perhaps,' Iyeyasu agreed. 'My eyes are no longer young. Do you not like your house, Will?'

'I am prouder of that house than of anything I have ever possessed, my lord. No doubt because I have never possessed before, anything of such value. Or indeed, of value at all. And yet, my lord prince, I assure you I can see the house from here, and it stands alone. So very much alone.'

'You wish to live in the centre of a town? You have but to say so. Although I would have supposed Miura would suit you best, with its nearness to the sea.'

'I would live nowhere else, my lord. But the loneliness of my house on that spit of land is but the same as my own loneliness within it.'

'Ah.' Iyeyasu turned away from the sea, looked at the ship once again. 'You have servants,' he said pensively. 'Boys as well as girls. You have your faithful Kimura. You lack a wife. And a family. Yes, Will. A man should have a wife and a family.'

'I already have a wife and a family, my lord prince.'

'And for them you would sail around the world? To regain that woman, and that child? An honourable sentiment, Will, could I believe it were true. For have you not yourself told me your marriage is unhappy? Indeed, when you spoke to me of the man Marlowe, of your dreams, planted by his words, which made Cathay and Cipangu so exciting to you, I sensed it was a dream of our women as much as our wealth or our glory which conquered your mind.'

'Yet no man can exist only on dreams, my lord. As husband, I owe my wife a duty. It is my misfortune to come from a different civilisation, where women perhaps know less of *their* duties.'

'And you imagine that by transporting her here, you would somehow accomplish a transformation? Not if my knowledge of the priests and what they say is accurate. Besides, how old is this woman?'

Will calculated. 'She will be thirty-six years old, my lord.'

'Thirty-eight before you see her again, were you to leave this afternoon. Forty before you could return her here. A woman who knows how to love, Will, is but approaching perfection, at forty. A woman who does not know how to love by then, will never learn. As for your daughter, be sure that during these last five years she will have become like her mother.'

'Yet they are mine, my lord. My wife, and my daughter.'

'You are mouthing words given to you by your priests, Anjin Miura. Forget them. Divorce them, in your mind. Take a wife, here, in Japan. I will give her to you.' He turned to face Will. 'I cannot offer you a princess, the sister or daughter of a daimyo. These things are beyond even my power to grant. But you have only to choose any woman of your own station.'

'Forget my wife?' Will whispered. Forget Mary, and Deliverance? There was a cruel joke. He had already forgotten them, the substance. If he retained the dream, it was merely to add to his other dreams. And forgetting Mary, of whom could he then start to dream, adding reality to his hopes?

'Nor can I permit you to hope for Pinto Magdalena,' Iyeyasu said. 'She is the favourite concubine of Ishida Norihasa.'

'Ishida Norihasa,' Will said.

'He is the son of the traitor Mitsunari, and thus is disgraced by his father's dishonour. As a ronin he has taken service with the Toyotomi, and indeed, commands the Princess Yodogimi's guard. I cannot obtain the girl, and even if I could, for me to do so would be to cause a blood feud, in which I would be in the wrong. When I march on Osaka, there must be no doubt in any man's mind that I am in the right. And *when* I march on Osaka, if Norihasa is still there, then you may begin to dream again, for you will enter the castle as conqueror. But that is some years away, as yet, and I would not have you pine for the lack of a woman. In any event, Will, only a fool would take as wife someone who dominates his every thought. Keep her for your dreams. Write poetry about her, if you wish. Who knows, it will be submitted to the Mikado for his judgement and may even bring you more fame and fortune than you already possess. For a wife, choose a girl who you know loves *you* to such distraction, and who you further know to be good, and kind, and eager to please, and above all, healthy. It is your comfort, your happiness, that we seek. For be sure that if you are happy in your marriage, then so will be your wife. Whereas if she is the cause of unhappiness in you, no love will stand the strain. These are the words of a man who has lived a long time, not your prince. Think of them, Will.'

Will gazed at him. To have a wife in the house by the bay. To have a girl, always by his side, always to be there, to share, with her alone, as she would share with him alone, instead of turning on her charm for the evening's entertainment.

'In your two years in Japan, Will, have you met no such girl?'

Will blinked; for a moment the prince's face had disappeared. 'In my religion, my culture, my lord, a man may not put aside his wife, once they have been granted the sanction of the Church.'

'But now you are living in *my* culture, Will. And here in Japan, a man *may* put aside his wife, should he desire another more. For where may a man find happiness, be it not in his own home? Now come. You are thinking of one girl in particular.'

One girl. The softest hands, the sweetest smile, he had ever known.

Chapter 3

WHEN THE time came, he took with him Keiko, the leader of the six ronin who had taken service under the cannon flag of Anjin Miura. A famous warrior, Keiko, who had struck off the head of Ikeda of Bizen at Sekigahara, and presented it to the prince. But his lord had been Kato Kenshin, who had also died that day, and he had elected to fight for the man with the guns. There was a compliment.

When the time came. Will would have taken horse within an hour of obtaining Iyeyasu's blessing. But things were not done in that fashion, in Japan. No wild romantics, in this warrior world. A man's marriage, as Suke had told him, fitted neatly in importance between his induction as a samurai and his death. Everything had to be arranged according to etiquette and tradition. At least the matter had been placed in the hands of the Shimadzu. He could trust in Tadatune.

They followed the road known as the Tokkaido, whence the Tokugawa army had marched two years before, clinging to the coast as far as the town of Nagoya, where they turned inland, just as the army had done, for Ogaki and the Moor of the Barrier.

How long ago that seemed, and now, how empty the road. It was not, of course. There were endless columns of travellers, on their way to Kyoto, on a pilgrimage to the great Buddhist shrine of Ise, or heading for the old imperial capital of Nara, still sacred ground. Most of them were religious processions, varying from virtual armies of men and women clad all in white, marching with stately tread, to groups of men naked except for pieces of straw tied round their waists, running along the road as if possessed of endless energy.

Rivalling the devotees in numbers were the beggars; it was often difficult to tell which was which, and indeed Keiko told him that one large group of rough looking men they encountered were actually mountain priests, known as yamabushi. Accompanying the mendicants was a crowd of remarkably handsome young people of both sexes, who had shaved their heads and wore but a single robe. According to Keiko most of the girls had been trained as geisha but had forsworn their profession and placed themselves under the protection of the nunneries at Kamakura and Miyako, to which they contributed a portion of whatever alms they obtained.

Not that they were fastidious about the means they employed to raise money. Seeing Will's interest, Keiko hired one of the girls for a performance. She came that night to the inn where they lodged, and there removed her garment, replacing it instead with a wooden contraption which fitted over her head and rested on her shoulders, like wings. From various holes in this machine there were suspended eight strings, each with a bell on the end of it. The girl now commenced to whirl round and round, at ever greater speeds, until all the strings were extended horizontally from her body, while at the same time she hit the bells with two small hammers, one in each hand, playing a peculiarly haunting melody.

She kept this up for some minutes, until her body was a glistening mass of sweat, and then she stopped, panting, and bowed towards Will.

'Now she is in a state of ecstasy,' Keiko promised. 'For a further small fee she will be yours, Anjin Miura. And be sure that with her body so anointed with her own dew, she will be delightful to hold, and to know.'

Will shook his head. 'I do not doubt that for one moment, Keiko. But I will have none of her, or any woman, this night. Pay her and send her back to her companions.'

Keiko sighed, and did as he had been commanded. The girl gazed at Will for several seconds, and then shrugged, removed her harness, regained her robe, and went out of the room.

'Truly you are a strange man, Anjin Miura,' Keiko remarked. 'For how may a man live, without love? Yet you have knowledge of no one, not even your servants. And the geisha tell me that your disinterest is insulting to them. I had thought, then, that you might prefer boys, and perhaps I even hoped myself to be honoured with your affection. But truly, it is said in Miura that the lord is a man without love.'

How casually he spoke of fornication and sodomy. How casually he spoke of love. Because there was no such thing in Japan? Then what of Hosokawa's wife, who had destroyed her own children and herself, rather than become the prisoner of Mitsunari? Or was that not love, but just respect for her husband's honour?

So then, love, for these people, was a matter of pleasing one another in the flesh. A sound enough basis, where marriages were arranged by others, and the wife became the property of her husband. As she did, in the eyes of the law, in Europe. But here, there was more than law involved. A man should be pleased, endlessly, else were he distracted, and not fit for the duties of manhood. An admirable philosophy ... So was *he*, then, not fitted for the duties of manhood? He had no idea. He did not know whether he possessed the courage, the stoicism, of the Japanese, the ability to take his own life when all was lost save honour. He was sure that the ship he built had not suffered for lack of physical love. Only physical love, because he *loved*. He dreamed of Magdalena, morning and night, and preferred that dream to any other substance. The prince had seemed to recognise that, well enough. Although he had dismissed it as an emotion worthy only of the poetry competition.

No doubt it was, after all, the European in him. He could not accustom himself to the manners of this country, even now. To be waited on at table by two young women, in England, was to feel no affinity for them. In Japan, to be bathed by two young women, was of no greater importance, even to him, now. But to sleep with them, to take from them what Yodogimi had given to him, and still regard them as no more than his servants, this was impossible. He saw them every day, all day. To take them must be to love them.

So now he sought love. A substitute for the love he could not have. But a love which would become real. Perhaps.

Or perhaps he still wished to remember Yodogimi, would have no other woman until he was sure she could be matched. Then indeed was he doomed to a lifetime of disappointment. And in that he was a fool. For surely a priestess who had been trained as a geisha, who was aroused by her dancing and covered, as Keiko so beautifully put it, in her own dew, would be as capable of matching Yodogimi as anyone in Japan.

But then, perhaps, he had been disturbed by the constant presence of the yamabushi themselves; these husky fellows reminded him more of soldiers than priests; they did not shave *their* heads, and every one of them was armed, with either a sword or a stout staff.

But they were, after all, priests. Peace had come to Japan, or at least to the greater part of Honshu. The peace Iyeyasu was determined to protect, providing it did not interfere with his own plans. And the peace which in turn protected all those who travelled under the banner of the golden fan.

They skirted Kyoto and made their way west, past Osaka and Fukuyama, to Hiroshima, and thence down to the narrow Strait of Shimonoseki which gave access to the Inland Sea, always on their left. They crossed the Strait in a rowing boat, and now they were in Kyushu, with Bungo only a few miles farther on.

'A strange distance to travel for a wife, Anjin Miura,' Keiko remarked, as they once again approached the ocean. 'When I think of all the beautiful women in Edo.'

'This is the shore where I first landed, with my companions.'

'The land of the Satsuma,' Keiko grumbled, looking around him with some apprehension.

'They made their peace with the Tokugawa,' Will reminded him.

'That may be so, Anjin Miura. But they are warriors by nature, who seek only to fight. And there will be sufficient of their samurai who will remain unhappy about the defeat at Seki-gahara.'

'They will not attack us,' Will said. 'I travel under the protection of Shimadzu no-Tadatune.'

And so it proved. Whenever they stopped at inns, there was always a crowd to watch them dismount, and invariably two or three samurai, to stare at them, and make hissing noises through their teeth, and swagger past them as they stood on the street. But none ever allowed his two swords to touch. For all knew of Anjin Miura, even if they had not previously seen the cannon insignia on his sword and on his cloak, and on the pennant Keiko carried. What more could a man wish of life, save a loving, and willing wife?

Magome Shikibu.

'Anjin Miura.' Magome Kageyu performed the kowtow, and then himself removed the sandals from Will's feet, and replaced them with slippers, while a young woman performed the service for Keiko. 'We had heard of your approach, and have anxiously awaited you. Welcome to my humble inn.'

'It is I who must thank you, Kageyu, for receiving me into your home,' Will said. 'And rise, I beg of you, my friend. There is no need for you to kneel to me.'

Nothing had changed. In two years, nothing had changed. The sea breeze still blew across the beach and through the houses; were he to strain his eyes he had no doubt that he would still see the *Liefde* nodding to her anchor.

Kageyu bowed. 'My lord Shimadzu no-Tadatune awaits within, my lord Miura. If you will accompany me, I would have you renew your acquaintance with my wife.'

Magome Suoko was on her knees, her forehead hovering above the floor.

'Rise, madam, I beg of you,' Will said. 'As I told your husband, I come as supplicant.'

When she smiled, she was the mother of Shikibu. In repose her face was uncommonly serious. But then, all Japanese women seemed to possess this dual personality.

'It is we who are flattered, my lord Miura,' she protested. 'For the honour that you do us.'

Behind her, Tadatune waited with suitably grave features, as befitted the arranger.

'Then it is your wish that I may pay court to Miss Shikibu?' Will asked.

'But of course, my lord Miura. Have we not accepted your presents?'

Will glanced at Tadatune.

'They are here, Anjin Miura,' the hatamoto said. 'To your future father-in-law you have presented this fine sword, worked with the most exquisite art. And to Magome Suoko, this silk robe, together with five barrels of wine and three boxes of condiments.'

'For which, my lord Miura, we are eternally grateful,' Kageyu said. 'And in return, we beg of you to accept from us ten barrels of wine and five boxes of condiments, humbly apologising for the poorness of our gifts, but we are insignificant people, my lord, and unable to match your lordship in splendour.'

'Ten barrels of wine?' Will whispered to Tadatune. 'When I gave but five?'

'Ssssh,' Tadatune said. 'You will have to bear all the expense of the wedding itself.'

'And now,' Magome Suoko said, 'let Shikibu be brought in, Kageyu.'

Her husband bowed and went to the door.

'Do I not get to see her alone?' Will whispered to Tadatune.

'But of course not,' Tadatune said. 'Do not fear. I have seen to everything.'

'Yes, but supposing the girl does not wish to be my wife?'

'Not wish to be your wife? Not wish to be the wife of Anjin Miura lord of the cannon? There would be an impossibility. Below the rank of daimyo, there is not a girl in Japan but would be honoured to come into your house. My own sisters would not have refused such distinction.'

'Yes but . . . ' He swallowed the words. For Tadatune would not understand. Even Iyeyasu had but half understood, and he doubted there was a wiser man in all Japan. Besides, the door was opening. Magome Kageyu had returned.

And with him, Shikibu. She walked with bowed head, sank to her knees without looking at Will, inclined forward to bring her forehead to the floor. Will would have stopped her, but Tadatune warned him with a glance, and so he allowed the full kowtow before summoning her to her knees once again.

'Behold, the betrothal gifts of Anjin Miura,' Tadatune said, and clapped his hands.

One of the Satsuma retainers entered bearing a large tray, which he set on the floor. Tadatune proceeded to lift the gifts, one after the other, like some diminutive St Nicholas; they consisted mainly of silk, and embroidered stuffs for girdles, much as had been the presents exchanged between Suke and Tadatune himself at Will's induction into the ranks of the samurai. But on this occasion the silk robe was the piece of honour, apparently, for it had been laid on the tray without folding, and was lifted with great reverence by Tadatune, again making sure that there was no fold or crease in the garment.

All these were passed before Shikibu, while she never raised her head or acknowledged them in the slightest way, and were then given to her mother.

'And without,' Tadatune said, 'there await ten barrels of wine, and seven boxes of condiments. It is hoped by the lord Anjin Miura, that these gifts please you, Magome Shikibu.'

'I am pleased, my lord Tadatune,' Shikibu promised in a low voice. At last her head came up, and for the shortest second her gaze met Will's, and then the eyes were gone again. Beneath the caked white paint there was no hint of emotion, of pleasure or displeasure. She had sent him the wooden booklet containing the flower. But that had been nearly two years ago. How his heart pounded. How he longed to reach for her, to take her hand and properly pledge his troth. Why, he had not spoken to her for all of those two years. He had merely decided to have her as his wife and it was done. Without a word. He glanced at

Tadatune, almost begging with his eyes. But the young nobleman was rising to his feet, and bowing to the Magomes, one after the other. It was time to leave.

The courtyard of the house of Shimadzu no-Tadatune was lit by flaring torches, to form an avenue of light from the gate to the porch. On either side, this night, there had also been lit fires, to make the courtyard as bright as day. And now that the hour approached, the blenders of the rice meal had taken their places; two men and two women, one pair sitting on each side of the path, their mortars ready.

The whole household waited. The women from the household of Magome Kageyu had come up the hill yesterday, with the bride's effects, and her presents. These had been carried on a long tray, and presented to Will before Shimadzu no-Takanawa, his wife, and his son. On the tray had been two silken robes, stitched together; one of them was the same robe Will had given to Shikibu, a week before. Then there was a dress of ceremony, with epaulettes of hempen cloth; an upper girdle and an under girdle; a fan; five pocket books, and a sword. All that Magome Kageyu could afford, for the honour of his daughter. These had been placed in the bridal chamber, which was composed of three rooms converted into one by the removal of the inner screen walls, and newly decorated, by order of Shimadzu no-Takanawa. The presents, Shikibu's to Will, and his to her, were set out, in their two trays. Beside the trays, Will's clothes were draped on a clothes rack. The bedclothes were already laid out, and Shikibu's clothes and effects had been arranged next to Will's. Now all was ready; even the lacquer basin for washing the hands and face had been placed on the raised floor, and the books had been arranged on the shelf. The shrine containing the image of the family god of the Shimadzu, here acting as Will's parents, had been placed above the bed.

And in front of the bed, in the position of honour, waited the towel rack, with its full complement of warmed cloths.

All was ready. And Will sweated as he waited with Shimadzu no-Takanawa for the arrival of the litter. He tried to recall everything about her, standing next to the tub, smiling at him; he could remember almost nothing of the day last week when he had had his troth plighted for him by Tadatune.

Takanawa smiled at him. 'You are anxious, Anjin Miura.

This is good. An anxious husband is a fruitful one. Be sure that your bride will also be anxious.'

The old samurai was as excited as anyone. But when last *they* had met, this man had condemned him to death. He could not help but wonder, sometimes, is this all a dream, from which I will one day awaken, to discover myself still lying on the deck of the *Liefde*, tossing to and fro on the Great Sea? And then he would remember the Princess Yodogimi, and know it could be no dream. But perhaps, this night, even she would fade into the back of his mind.

'She comes,' Takanawa said. They did not go outside, but the outer door was open, and they could see the litter approaching, through the main gate. Tadatune came first, with Magome Ako, Shikibu's cousin. They walked together up the path between the flaring torches, both dressed in their finest garments, and paused at the steps to the porch to congratulate each other.

Behind them walked two of Magome Kageyu's manservants, carrying the huge bowl of broth, made from the clams Will had sent down the hill the previous day. This was solemnly presented at the doorway of the house, and received by Shimadzu no-Tamatane, Tadatune's brother.

Now the men and women on each side of the path commenced pounding the rice in their mortars, moving with careful emphasis, each stroke a timed function. For the litter was coming through the gate. And now, too, in the porch, two of the Shimadzu women each lit a candle, one standing on the left and one on the right of the corridor leading to the bridal chamber.

Slowly the litter, borne by four of the Magome male relatives, and completely enclosed in its decorated drapes, came across the courtyard. As it passed between the rice blenders, those on the left of the path handed their bowls to the blenders on the right, and the contents of the two bowls were mixed together.

The litter reached the steps to the porch, and here it was laid on the ground. The curtains were parted, and Magome Shikibu stepped out. She wore a white silk robe with a lozenge pattern, made from the bolt of cloth Tadatune had given her as a betrothal present, over an under robe, also of white silk. A veil of white silk hung from her head, so that only the crown of her black hair was visible as she slowly came up the steps, between the bowing women, who as she reached them, passed the left-hand candle over the right-hand candle, when the two wicks were brought together to be extinguished.

Will and Shimadzu no-Takanawa, together with all the assembled Shimadzu relations, and also the Magome family, bowed low as Shikibu came down the corridor towards them. For this occasion she was the most noble person present; to her both the deference and the place due to her rank. She swept past them, her face hidden beneath the veil, and was escorted into the room and beyond, into a small chamber set aside as a dressing room, by two of the Shimadzu women. When she had straightened her gown, and renewed her paint, she re-entered the room, and mounted the steps to the dais, where she took her place upon the embroidered mat.

Tadatune touched Will's elbow, and he started forward. How his heart pounded. Suppose . . . suppose . . . suppose she was undergoing this unwillingly? Suppose she had not the ability to love, as he wanted? Was this the only reason he married her? Of course. No hypocrisy in Japan. He wanted her body. He wanted her body to possess his, as Yodogimi's had done. He *accepted* her body, because Magdalena was beyond his reach, and Yodogimi as well. What condescension.

He reached the dais, and took his seat immediately below Shikibu. As instructed by Tadatune, he did not glance at her, but turned to face the room as the assembled relations came in and took their places before them, and the ladies prepared for the ceremony.

Two covered trays had already been laid upon the dais. Between them was a lacquered table, on which were fowls, fish, and two saké bottles, together with three cups and two kettles for warming the wine. The ladies now knelt before the couple, and handed them dried fish and seaweed to eat, accompanying each dish with a short speech in which they praised the beauty, industry, and virtue of Shikibu, and the manhood, valour, and fame of Anjin Miura, and promised the assembly that here was a union which would be honoured so long as Japan itself endured.

While they knelt thus, two married females, one a Shimadzu and one a Magome, each took one of the wine bottles to the lower part of the room. Two handmaids also took down the kettles, to be heated. The ladies attached a paper model of a female butterfly to one bottle, and a male butterfly to the other. The female butterfly was then removed and laid on its back, and wine poured from that bottle into the kettle. The male butterfly was now placed on top of the female, and wine poured

from the male bottle into the same kettle, after which the mixed
wine was poured into the second kettle, which was then placed
on the floor.

The handmaids were arranging small lacquered tables before
each person in the room, before Shikibu and before Will, and
before the two ladies who were acting as her bridesmaids. Now
at last Shikibu moved the veil from her face. But she never
looked at Will, remained gazing in front of her at the table;
beneath the white paint it was impossible to decide on her
expression.

One of the handmaids placed the three cups, each inside the
other, in front of Will. He sipped twice from the first cup, and
then poured some wine from the full kettle into the empty
kettle. He next poured wine into the cup, filling it rather fuller
than before, and drank half of it. The handmaid took the cup
up to Shikibu, who finished what remained of the wine, and then
in turn poured some from the full kettle into the empty one.

Condiments were then served, and the wine ceremony repeated, this time starting with Shikibu, and using the second
cup. Then a third cup was served, beginning with Will. This
done, he saw Tadatune giving him the signal, and rose and left
the room for the porch, where he wiped his brow. 'By God,
Tadatune, but this is serious work. The most serious work I
have ever undertaken.'

'Oh, indeed it is, Anjin Miura. As I told you when you
became a samurai, there is only one more serious event in a man's
life than his marriage, and that is his death.'

'Where is she going?' Will asked, as he saw Shikibu, escorted
by the two married ladies, also leaving the room.

'To change her gown,' Tadatune said. 'So come, you must
do the same.' He escorted Will into another dressing room. 'It
is more of an excuse to permit the families and the ladies to eat,
as they are not sustained by the emotion of the moment. They
will be given special soup, made of fish's fins, and a cup of
wine to drink, to give them strength for the rest of the
ceremony.'

'To give *them* strength,' Will muttered, accepting a change of
dress from Keiko.

The samurai closed one eye. 'Truly, my lord Miura, it is
enough to make a man wonder if marriage is worth it, when
there is a geisha house in every town.'

Once again he sat, on the mat below Shikibu, this time drinking clam soup and eating a preparation of rice, while the women placed two earthenware cups, one gilded and the other silvered, on a tray. Inscribed on the tray was a map of the island of Yakasago, in the province of Harima, on which there was a pine tree known as the pine of mutual old age. At the root, apparently, the tree was single, but towards the centre it split into two stems, and this twin-stemmed tree was a symbol that the happy pair would reach mutual old age together, while the evergreen leaves denoted the unchanging constancy of their hearts. Drawn under the two stems of the tree were the figures of an old man and an old woman, to represent the spirits of the pine.

Another wine ceremony, and then the wedding feast itself, beginning with soup made from the carp—according to Tadatune the most expensive fish in all Japan, but indispensable to a banquet—followed by twelve plates of sweetmeats, and then three courses, the first of seven dishes, the second of five, and the third of three dishes. During the meal Shikibu and Will were each taken out twice to change their garments, and at the end Shikibu put on the second of the silk robes he had given her as a betrothal present.

But at last he found himself sipping the cup of green tea, while the guests murmured discreetly amongst themselves, and Tadatune smiled at him from across the room. It was time. Nearly. He watched Magome Kageyu and his wife rise, and bow towards their daughter, and then low towards Shimadzu no-Takanawa and his wife, before going to the door to take their leave.

Once again the tea, sipped decorously. The room was nearly quiet. How far from the boisterous drunkenness of his first wedding. His first wedding. Christ in Heaven, there was a mistake, to allow such a thought at this moment. For did this not forever damn him, in the eyes of ... who, or what? Or anything?

He could feel her, close to him, could almost hear her breathing. They were married, now. It was only a matter of patience. Once before he had told himself that. Once before.

Tadatune was rising, and bowing, and smiling, and beckoning Will. He got up in turn, bowed to his wife, and to his foster father for this occasion, and to the handmaids and guests, before joining Tadatune outside. 'I had thought Shikibu would leave first,' he whispered.

'Not so, Anjin Miura, for we now have our duty to perform.'
He led the way to the porch.

'You mean I cannot stay in the same house as my bride?' Will demanded.

'In due time, Anjin Miura. In due time. First we must pay a visit to your mother and father-in-law, for no doubt this is the last time you will ever see them.'

'What nonsense, Tadatune. I like them both. And I have no intention of cutting Shikibu off from her own people.'

'As of now, they are not her people,' Tadatune said, gravely. 'Now she is your wife, she has become part of you, and is the lady of your house. Think well on this, Anjin Miura. It is a great step for a young woman to take, to abandon entirely one set of relatives in favour of another. A great step in any circumstances. But in normal circumstances she is at least assured of a large new family, who will protect her honour and guard her children. But you, Anjin Miura, have no family. You are the favourite of the Tokugawa himself, and this is the greatest single honour that can fall to anyone in the land, and yet, the Tokugawa is but a single man. Lacking the support of clansmen, a man may yet find himself alone, no matter whence his favour. Shikibu has taken a deep and grave step, for now she too is alone in the world, saving her lord.'

What have I done, Will thought. That aspect of things had not occurred to him. To be alone with Shikibu in this world of war and honour, of blood and courage. There was a responsibility. One he was capable of sustaining?

He watched the Shimadzu servants at work. The two trays used at the feast had been brought to the porch, and were now being loaded with fowl and fish and condiments, before being placed in a long box for transportation down the hill. Five hundred and eighty cakes of rice had also been prepared, and these were placed in lacquered boxes, to follow the rest of the food. Behind these there came the presents Will personally had to present to his parents-in-law, amounting to seven men's loads, as representing Will's wealth and status in the community. There were a sword and a silk robe for Magome Kageyu, and a silk robe for Suoko, and also presents to his new cousins-in-law, all chosen with great care by Tadatune.

'Truly, my heads spins,' Will said, as he started down the hill behind the porters. 'And what happens now, Tadatune?'

'Why, you will go through the wine-drinking ceremony with

Magome and his wife. Do not fret; Shikibu must at this moment be going through the same ceremony and exchange of presents with my father and mother.'

'And how long will this take?'

Tadatune shrugged. 'Perhaps an hour, perhaps more.'

'And then I return here?'

Tadatune smiled. 'Indeed, you will, Anjin Miura. But not to retire. For you must then await a return visit from Magome Kageyu, and his wife.'

'For another wine ceremony?'

'That is correct.'

'By Christ, Tadatune, do I get to see my wife, alone, at all?'

'You have all of your life left, to see her, alone, Anjin Miura. But do not be impatient. There will even be time for that, tonight.'

All his life, for Shikibu, alone. How vast was the room, on a sudden, for the dais was at the farthest end away from the doorway, through two opened walls, and seemed even farther than had been Iyeyasu on the occasion of their first meeting at Osaka.

But Osaka was not to be thought of, tonight.

She knelt, her body arched forward, her forehead close to the floor. Her brief enjoyment of power was over; now she was alone with her lord.

'Do not kneel, Shikibu,' he said. 'Not to me.'

Her body slowly raised itself. She wore, so far as he could see, a single robe of white silk, and knelt beside the mat on which they would sleep. On which they would consummate this night's work. Beside her was a tray, bearing a cup of saké. She gazed at him, her eyes black pinpoints in the whiteness of her face. Her face itself was expressionless.

He crossed the floor, slowly. Incredibly, at this moment he had no desire. He was old enough to be her father, and he felt like a father. Tadatune's words hung in his brain.

She watched him approach. 'May I serve my lord?' she whispered. Her voice trembled. The composure was, after all, only the depths of her paint.

He halted at the dais. 'I will serve you, Shikibu.'

He reached for the cup, lifted it to her lips. Her hand came up, and closed on his, and was as quickly withdrawn. She sipped the wine, watching him all the while.

'My lord has but to command,' she whispered.

Only command. Whatsoever I wish, from the sublime to the obscene; Shikibu will perform it on the instant. My child bride.

He shook his head. 'I have commanded, without intending to. I had no wish to make this happen, this way, Shikibu.'

She gazed at him.

He chewed his lip, took the cup, drank some wine. If ever he needed wine, it was now.

'Do I then, not please you, my lord?'

'Please me? You are like a gift from the gods, Shikibu. I meant that in my country, a man is at least granted permission to plight his own troth.'

'For what reason, my lord?'

'Why, because, if he is a man of any sensibility, he will be able to discern whether or not his future wife would have it so.'

'And he would be concerned with her wishes, my lord?'

'With common folk, yes. Where property or station is involved, no.'

'And I bring you nothing, my lord. I am a desolate creature.'

'No,' he said, and knelt beside her. 'You bring me yourself. Willingly, Shikibu?'

'Willingly, my lord.'

He took her hands, drawing them from the sleeves of the kimono. So small, so delicately formed. And now indeed his heart was pounding. Because, after all, there was mystery here. Her hands, and nothing more, all this while. 'I have dreamed of you, Shikibu.' A lie? No, not entirely. He *had* dreamed of her, from time to time.

'And I of you, my lord.'

'But I am a stranger to Japanese customs, Shikibu. Even after two years, I am a stranger. I would wish my wife to share in my customs as I am prepared to share in hers.'

'You have but to command, my lord.' But her gaze was watchful. What new and strange, and perhaps terrible fate was he about to inflict upon her? The bodice of her robe rose and fell more quickly. What lay beneath that? What beauty. What treasure. And he had done no more than touch her hand.

He stroked her chin, and her eyes flickered. He gripped the chin, and heard the intake of her breath. Perhaps she expected to be throttled. Still holding her chin, he brought her face forward. Her eyes widened, the pupils dilated. But she would submit

Submit, to whatever he wished, because she had been trained, for that.

His lips touched hers. Her eyes were an inch away, gazing at him, wider than ever. He moved his lips against hers, inhaled her breath as it came from her nostrils, felt the lips parting as he touched them with his tongue, and withdrew it in haste; her teeth were black.

Shikibu gazed at him, a faint line creasing the white paint between her eyes. 'My lord?' she whispered.

'Why do you blacken your teeth?'

'Because I am married, my lord. It is to signify my fidelity. Tomorrow I will shave my eyebrows.'

'Shave your . . . what I have just done, does that please you?'

'I am here to please *you*, my lord.'

'No,' he said. 'I would have it so for both of us. Shikibu, I would have you wash your face, remove your paint, take the blackness from your teeth. Will you do that for me?'

Still the unblinking gaze. 'I will do whatever you wish, my lord. But the teeth . . . I cannot cleanse them absolutely.'

'Nonetheless, do what you can. Now, Shikibu. I ask it of you.'

'Yes, my lord.' She knelt over the basin of water. Her back was turned to him, her body a wisp of life in the huge empty room. His. The thought came to him with increasing force. His. Absolutely. The realisation, the understanding, reached down from his mind into his belly, dragged up the dream-obscenities which had always lurked there. His.

He placed his hands on her thighs, moved them upwards and forwards. Beneath the silk, there were small, hand filling, hard pointed mounds of flesh. Beneath the silk.

His fingers released her girdle, parted the kimono while he knelt against her. Her hands scooped water to her face. Did she shiver? Was the water cold, or was it the touch of his fingers as they slid inside, to reach the firmness of the belly, stroke down to thigh and groin, move inwards, to jungle and gateway, prison and paradise.

'My face is clean, my lord,' she whispered.

And wet. His hands moved backwards, bringing the robe with it. He knelt, away from her, the robe in his hands. She rose to her feet, her back still to him, went down the steps to reach the towel rack, dried her face with careful pats, hesitated, and turned to face him. Perhaps consciously, she inhaled, to swell her chest, sucking her belly flat. Her midnight hair drifted forward over her left shoulder, lay in strands around her nipple. And below the lurking forest of love the legs were delicate stems, neither long nor strong, but entrancingly youthful. Here was no beauty, compared with Yodogimi; no breathtaking femininity, compared with Magdalena; but here was an eternal sweetness, a gentleness, such as he had never known. And she was his wife.

'Come,' he said.

She knelt beside him. And looked beyond him, to the shrine. Now she bent from the waist, and gave two quick claps with her hands.

'Why do you do that, Shikibu?'

'To summon the kami of the shrine, my lord. That I may pray to him for his protection.'

'Do you fear me, Shikibu?'

'No, my lord. Not if it is my power to make you happy.'

'And have you prayed?'

'Yes, my lord.'

'Then give me your tongue.'

She hesitated again, opened her mouth, waited, and thrust her tongue forward to be kissed and sucked, caressed with his own. Now she did tremble, but she did not move.

'In Japan,' he said, 'men and women do not kiss each other's mouths. Why is that?'

She gazed at him.

'Is it not stimulating, Shikibu?'

'Yes, my lord.'

He sighed. She would not resist him, even his thoughts. And so, he felt frustrated. Christ, was this manhood? Or was there, after all, a devil, lurking in the pit of his belly? She *was* beautiful. No question about that. An utterly beautiful child, and he was of an age to appreciate youth, and innocence. And yet he could not accept what she would so willingly give, without fear or without anger, without haste and without reluctance.

'Does my lord wish, again?' she asked. She was bewildered. He had chosen her as his bride, travelled nearly the length of Japan, to take possession of her, and now she could see the conflicting emotions in his eyes, perhaps feel the anger emanating from his body.

'No,' he said. 'Not now. Lie down, Shikibu. On your back. Stretch your arms above your head, and spread your legs as wide as you may.'

Prostrate yourself. But she obeyed, without question. Before him, then, was all he had ever wanted. Surrendered womanhood. Surrendered girlhood. Girl into woman, before him, at his feet. His, to do with as he wished.

Gazing at him, with anxious, watchful eyes, wishing only to anticipate his desires. To please.

Christ in Heaven, he thought, what is happening to me? Why do I sweat? Why do I dream? Why do I wish to slap her, kick her, scratch her, bite her? Can there be no love, without mastery? Where then are the sweet words of love, the soft caresses, the gentle touches, if this is the truth? Is then, a religious cloak, a religious barrier, essential for the protection of health and strength?

He knelt, between her legs, to take possession of his bride.

Chapter 4

THE GALLEY grounded on the beach, the rowers leapt over the side to run it up, away from the waves. Will Adams put his own shoulder to the stern, lent his own strength to the efforts of the others, while Keiko, in the bows, urged them on with high-pitched cries. They were a happy crew. They worked well together. And they trusted their lord, Anjin Miura. To lead them, and to work with them. Besides, on the water there was none like him.

It was hot. The sun hung over the house, brought shafts of brilliant light from the waters of the bay. Behind him, he could see the houses of Ito, so clear was the day, and there too, riding at anchor, was his ship, the *Endeavour*. A proud little vessel, to be sure, but nothing compared with the one rising in the workshop at this moment. Built by these men, conceived by this brain. Like his men, he wore only his loin-cloth; his kimono was slung over his shoulder as he started up the beach. He was tired, but it was the exhaustion of satisfaction.

'My lord.' Kimura performed the kowtow. He took his duties as steward seriously, and was dressed in his best robe, despite the heat. 'Welcome to Miura.'

'Rise, Kimura.' Will slapped him on the shoulder as he passed. Japanese formality was something he could not maintain for any great period of time. He made for the house. Did his heart beat faster, now? Yes. He looked forward, with pleasure, to regaining his possessions. All of his possessions.

The gate swung open, the samurai bowed. 'Welcome to Miura, my lord.' Inside, the many children, those of Kimura and Keiko, of the other samurai, of the workers in the fields, waited in the kowtow. They had watched the galley crossing the bay. And here, too, was the serving girl, Asoka. She was naked, her small body arched across a bar which was supported by two forked sticks, to leave her buttocks uppermost. Her wrists and ankles were secured to stakes in the ground, and although her skin was unmarked, her face, half shrouded in the drooping black hair, was suffused with blood and misery as it turned towards her lord.

'By God,' Will said. 'Who is responsible for this?'

'The girl is there by the command of my lady Shikibu, my lord,' Kimura said. 'But her punishment was to await your coming.'

'By God,' Will said again, and ran for the steps.

Kimura hurried at his elbow. 'There are visitors, my lord Miura. From Edo. The Dutchmen Melchior Zandvoort and Jacob Quaeckernaeck.'

'Jacob? And Melchior? Where?' They had promised to come, so often. But at what a time.

'They are waiting for you, my lord Miura,' Kimura said.

Will went up the steps, kicked off his sandals, allowed the girl to fit the slippers on his feet. Behind her, bowing low, was Shikibu. Shikibu the beautiful. Shikibu the compliant. When he looked on her, he felt pleasure. As a man might draw a beautiful sword from its sheath, or take the poop of a fine ship and know it would do his bidding, sail wherever he directed, at a speed he elected, granted a fair wind. How young she was, how fragile. And yet, how strong. He knew this, now. She had needed to reveal her strength to him.

But no longer Shikibu the laughing. That had ended with her marriage. Now she was serious, watchful. Not only for his whims, his desire to touch her tongue with his own, occasionally to lower his weight on to hers, as well as to sample the more Japanese, and reasonable, ways of lovemaking. But also because she was intelligent enough to know that theirs was not yet a marriage. They were lovers, but too often his mind was elsewhere. And yet, now she bore his child. Not visibly as yet, for her belly was tightly banded beneath her kimono as was the Japanese custom, but knowingly. And as willingly happy, for his sake, as she was in everything else that touched their lives together.

So, did he feel shame, when he looked upon her? Or had he slaked all that had been pent up inside of him for forty years? He had used her as an extension of himself, searching first of all for some spark of womanhood, as divorced from the wife, and then wondering at her eager submission, her subsequent solemnity. Truly, to be married to Shikibu was to live in hell. But he was the devil.

He took her hands, raised her up. She gazed into his eyes, her head thrust forward, her lips parted. The servants waited, heads bowed. They did not understand this European greeting. Perhaps they did not wish to understand it. They counted it obscene, where a European would count the bathing obscene. Did Shikibu count it obscene, still? His tongue brushed hers, his hand squeezed her arm. No Japanese formality here.

'Your bath awaits you, my lord,' she whispered.

'Kimura says my friends are here.'

'Yes, my lord. They wait for you.'

'Then I must go to them.'

'But my lord . . . ' Her hands were on his naked shoulders. Now she drew them down his arms before standing away from him, looked at the sweat on her palms.

'They are old friends, Shikibu. They have seen me dirtier than this. Where are they?'

'In the inner room, my lord.' She glanced down at the low table on which waited the cup and the small bottle of saké. Always, when he returned across the bay, they shared a cup of saké.

'In a moment, Shikibu,' he said. 'I would know about the girl.'

'She stole, my lord. A brooch of mine.'

'How long has she been tied thus?'

'Since daybreak, my lord.'

'Six hours? By Christ, surely she has suffered enough.'

'She has not suffered at all, as yet, my lord. She awaits your will.'

'Then have her released.'

'I told her she must suffer the cane, my lord.' Shikibu the compliant. The bending reed, with the stem of steel. Her face remained calm, her eyes watchful. But the implication was there. She would be mistress in her new home. He must see to it.

How little he really knew, of these people. He sighed. 'Very well, Shikibu. Six strokes of the cane.'

'I told her fifty, my lord.'

'Fifty? Christ in Heaven, Shikibu.'

'Were she taken before the magistrate, my lord, she would lose her head.'

Will hesitated. How serene the face, how delicate the body, how willing the limbs. And how determined the mind. 'Very well,' he said. 'Now.'

'Of course, my lord. You will attend me?'

'I must see to my friends.' He hurried past her, into the inner room, paused in surprise. Jacob and Melchior wore European clothes, looked as awkward as he remembered, seated on the floor, drinking saké. Now they scrambled to their feet.

'Will,' Jacob cried. 'By God, but you look a perfect Samson.'

'Aye,' Melchior said. 'Being a Japanese suits you, Will. Or should I say, Anjin Miura.'

Will embraced them both, one in each arm. 'I suspect jealousy, dear friends.'

'Oh, indeed,' Jacob agreed. 'We were shown in here by your wife. A truly beautiful young woman.'

'I thank you. And you will dine with us, of course. And stay for a season, I hope. I have much to tell you. And even more to show you. You will come across the bay and see the ship I am building. It is all but ready for launching.'

From the yard there came the first stroke of the cane, followed immediately by another. The men's heads turned, and then straightened again.

'We had heard of your venture,' Jacob said. 'And wish you well of it. And gladly shall we dine with you, Will. But we must continue our journey tomorrow morning. We sail from Nagasaki in a week.'

'Sail?' Will stared at them, frowning, and then sat down. The saké bottle was empty. He clapped his hands, and a serving girl hurried in with two fresh bottles and some more cups. 'You must explain.'

A thin wail of agony drifted across the regular rhythm of the cane. By Christ, Will thought. I am sweating, and my rod is made of iron. And Shikibu? Her face would be as expressionless as ever.

The two Hollanders also sat down; Will poured for Melchior, Melchior for Jacob, and Jacob for Will. In this, they were all Japanese. 'Why, simply it is this, Will,' Jacob said. 'The prince has given us permission to leave Japan. More, he has insisted that we do so.'

'He spoke of this, more than a year ago. I thought the project had been put aside.'

Melchior shook his head. 'The prince would have us deliver letters to Holland. He is distressed with the Portuguese. They have sent no ships here for some years now, and their priests preach against him. Worse, it is said that they are being made welcome at Osaka, by the boy Hideyori.'

'And this has angered the prince,' Jacob explained. 'Yet he knows that trade with Europe is for the good of his people. And thus he turns to us. It is what we came here to achieve, Will.'

Will nodded, slowly. 'He has sent no message for me?'

'None. You are too dear to him, Will. And too important. This fact is well known in Edo. We are not the only jealous ones. I would have you know this, Will. But it occurs to me that you might like to send a letter to England.'

'Aye,' Will said. 'Yes. Certainly I shall do so. To Master Diggines at the least. There is trade here for English ships, as well.'

The two Dutchmen exchanged glances. 'We had thought of Mistress Adams.'

Will poured saké. Christ in Heaven, he thought; have I, then, so thoroughly forgotten my wife, and child? But I have a wife, waiting without. The sweetest child in all the world. Was not Mary once the sweetest child in all the world, to him? And was not Deliverance still the sweetest child in all the world? Deliverance would be a young woman, now, in her middle teens, with the height of her father and the will, no doubt, of her mother.

In the yard the blows had ceased. The only noise was the sobbing of the girl.

'Of course, I will write to Mary as well,' he said.

Of what do you write, to a wife who no longer exists? You write 'Dear wife,' because this is how she would expect you to write. And then you sit and suck the end of your pen. Because it is so very long since you have written in English and the words, the very letters, seem strange to you.

Of what do you write, to the mother of your child, when there is another child waiting but a thin screen away? A child, not of your loins, but holding within her the fruit of your loins? Holding within her, too, a strength he had never suspected. To write now was to re-enter that world of sin which he had left behind. That world of innuendo and fear, that world of crime and punishment. So, was there nothing to fear, in this world? Nothing, for a samurai who followed the golden fan. Not even the vengeance of the Toyotomi could touch him here.

A soft sound caused him to raise his head. Melchior Zandvoort stood there, draped in his sleeping kimono.

'Come in, Melchior. Come in. This is no easy matter.'

'I did not suppose it would be.' Melchior sat beside him. 'Would you have me explain?'

'No,' Will said. 'There is nothing to explain. Nothing that she would understand. I had counted her gone, forever. I still count her gone, forever. This will be a communication from beyond the grave. No doubt, as no doubt we are supposed dead, she will have married again. Perhaps I should not write at all. And yet . . . I would have her, and my friends in England, and even more, my enemies, know that I have not ended my life in failure.'

'I will tell them that, Will,' Melchior promised.

'I am sure you will, Melchior. And will they understand? Know they anything of Japan in Limehouse? In Whitehall, even? Wish they to know anything of something they could never understand?' He began to write, quickly and vigorously.

'So, what do you say?'

'I write of our voyage,' Will said. 'That were best, I think. It may even be of some value to those who would come behind.' Now the pen raced over the paper. Perhaps he had always wanted to recall the voyage, the last events of that other life, which had been so long ago. The death of Will Adams, and all his companions. The events which had led to the birth of Anjin Miura, hatamoto of the Tokugawa Shogunate.

And after that birth? He wrote of Japan itself, of the wonders he had seen, of the wonders of which he had heard. But not of the people. The people were of no interest to Mary Adams.

And to finish? Why, he would say how he wished to come back, how he dreamed of them, every night, but how his return was prevented by the Japanese themselves. For what was a lie, from beyond the grave? It was the duty of the dead to provide comfort for the living. And at least Iyeyasu would *not* let him go, at this time.

'It comes easier, now?' Melchior asked.

'We are all hypocrites at heart.' Will signed his name. 'There, it is done. I wish you joy of your journey, Melchior. I try to convince myself that I wished I was accompanying you.'

'But this place has entered your blood,' Melchior agreed. 'I am no more sure than you that I wish to go. Jacob alone is happy at the prospect. Perhaps he alone has preserved his integrity.'

'Perhaps. But you are happy in Edo?'

'I have a woman, and an income, provided to me by the prince. I am more comfortable here than ever I was in Rotterdam, or at sea. Edo seems to grow, and thrive, every day. It hums with life, in a way no city has ever done, in my experience. It has become the wonder of the country. People visit Edo as they visit Nara. The old and the new. Your prince is very much the monarch since he took the title of Shogun.' Melchior watched Will folding the dried paper. 'He is even visited by daimyo from Osaka. Why, they say that Ishida Norihasa, the son of his bitterest enemy, is in residence in Edo for this summer.'

Will raised his head. 'Norihasa is in Edo?'

Melchior nodded. 'He has been given a palace in the south of the city.'

'You came here to tell me this?' God, how his heart leapt about inside his chest. Yodogimi's creature. Norihasa's concubine. Pinto Magdalena.

'No. I came here *not* to tell you this. God knows what came over me. But I can see that you are not happy, for all the wealth and beauty with which you are surrounded; your mind is elsewhere. I think you are wrong, Will. I think you will find happiness here, and nowhere else in all the world. I think that little girl, sleeping in your bed, will love you as no woman has ever loved a man before, but given the opportunity. And so I thought, watching you write a journal to your wife, that perhaps it were best for you to get it out of your blood. If that is possible.'

Pinto Magdalena. The girl with the long legs and the high tilted breasts with the shafts of red in her hair and the utterly beautiful face. The girl who looked at him with cool self-possession and yet, he was sure, bubbled beneath the surface like so many of the volcanoes which studded this land. Yodogimi's creature. Norihasa's woman.

'No doubt you understand how dangerous it would be,' Melchior said.

Will's head turned, slowly.

'Or perhaps it matters not to you, as you are yourself a samurai, now.'

Will got up, handed him the letter. 'That is for Mary, and I will write another to Master Diggines in the morning.'

He watched them out of sight, remained standing at his gate until the horsemen were nothing more than a group of spots dancing before his eyes.

'My lord is sad.' Kimura stood beside him, hands tucked into the sleeves of his kimono. 'He would like to be accompanying his friends.'

Will glanced at him. He often wondered just how much Kimura knew of what went on inside his master's mind; or more correctly, just how little he did *not* know. 'Not I, Kimura. I am happier here than in England.'

He turned, walked slowly back across the courtyard. Behind him, the gate closed with a soft click. And to his right the trestle remained, unoccupied now. But too full of memory.

'The girl expected it, my lord,' Kimura said.

He climbed the steps to the porch. Aya was there, bowing low. Asoka had this day been excused her duties. So then, what did she do, this day? She would lie on her belly and try to forget her aching back. And she would not hate her mistress or her master. They had done what she expected, what had been demanded of them by custom and convention.

'Keiko has the galley waiting, my lord,' Kimura said.

'Tell him to drag it up the beach, Kimura. I shall not go to Ito today.' He went inside, before the steward could remonstrate. Shikibu waited kneeling. This morning she wore the pale blue kimono he liked so much, and her hair lay on her shoulders and down her back. There was no visible alteration to the body beneath the kimono, either. She would still accommodate him; indeed, she had clearly been upset by his disinterest the previous night. She still fascinated him. Perhaps even more so since she had revealed to him the stronger side of her character. What had Melchior said? 'That little girl will love you as no woman has ever loved a man before, but given the opportunity.'

But suddenly she was no longer a little girl. There was the point.

'My lord does not go to Ito, this day?' Her tone, and her eyes, were watchful. Always watchful.

'Not this day.'

Then should she not have gained in attractiveness, to him? A girl, a daughter, can only ever be pleasing in body. A woman, while retaining that physical attraction, can match a man in the mind. If she chooses. And if he can understand *her* mind.

'Then my lord has made this day into a holiday?'

She was puzzled. With reason. This was not in the character he had revealed to her during the months they had been married. He had been utterly Japanese in his devotion to his duty. Perhaps, even when he had held her in his arms it had been a duty. Not entirely. She could excite him, and she could satisfy him. And she would love him. Given the chance. To make theirs a complete marriage, all that was required was that he should also love her. And that she should know he loved her.

He *would* love her, given time. Of that he had no doubt at all
Time for what? To forget, or properly to appreciate, the character
she had revealed in the punishment of Asoka? Time to reconcile
that with her complete subservience to *his* every wish? Certainly
he needed no more time to love her body.

He held her shoulders, raised her to her feet. 'Yes, sweetheart
Today shall be a holiday. A holiday for you and for me
Would you like that?'

She smiled. When she smiled, she was a different personality
How strange, he thought; I knew this, long ago, and had forgotten it. Because she has smiled so seldom these past months
But here again was the laughing girl of Bungo, who had made
the terrors of the Great Sea into nothing more substantial than
a nightmare. 'That will make me truly happy, my lord,' she
said. 'Let us walk into the hills, my lord. You and I. We will take
our food, and we will gather flowers, and arrange them in
beautiful designs. It is a beautiful day, my lord.'

Or time to forget all other women? How perceptive Melchior
was. And yet, was he doing anything more than dream? They
were enemies, now. Magdalena would know that he had chosen
his side at Sekigahara. There could be nothing but hatred
between them, at least on her part.

But just to look at her once more. Pinto Magdalena.

'My lord?' The smile was gone, the faint frown of concentration was back.

'Shikibu . . . ' He grasped her hands. 'I love you, Shikibu.'

The frown deepened. 'You do me much honour, my
lord.'

His turn to frown. 'Did you not know that?'

'I pray for your love, my lord. I pray to the lord Buddha, each
night.'

He could hear the quick clap of her hands as she knelt beside
their couch.

'Then pray no more, my sweet. I love you. Every day, I love
you more and more. To walk amongst the flowers with you is to
grasp at heaven itself. But this day . . . ' He hesitated, chewing
at his lip. He had small experience of lying, and lying to Shikibu
was something he had never contemplated. But there might
never be an opportunity like this again.

And as Melchior had suggested, might it not be for the best
to clear all obstacles between them?

'I must go to Edo,' he said. 'I must report to the Shogun

It was wrong of me to think of a holiday, when there is a duty to be performed.'

Shikibu bowed.

With every month, as Melchior had said, Edo grew. It reached outwards, streets and houses and people, swarming over the islands of the delta, and inwards towards the wall which protected it on the landward side. From a forest of hovels it had become a wood of palaces, thrusting their upcurving roofs towards the clear blue of the sky, dominated by its many-tiered pagodas.

And in the centre of them all, the Tokugawa palace was now close to completion. Indeed, it needed a skilled eye to decide that it was not already completed. The moat was wide and deep, the walls beyond were thick and steep, and inside the walls was the huge, complicated machinery of the Tokugawa bakufu, or military government, the inner bastions and fortifications, the villages which housed the troops and their families, the trees which shaded the houses, and in the heart of the defences, the citadel, where the Shogun held his court. Here were guards and courtiers, daimyo and samurai, brushing shoulders in the outer galleries, all seeking audience with the Shogun. Here was the panoply of empire.

And here there was welcome for Anjin Miura. No careful scrutiny for him, no minute examination of his belongings. He left his long sword and Keiko at the gate to the inner keep, was immediately taken along the covered outside galleries, past audience chambers filled with seated dignitaries, and through a small sliding screen into a room of six tatami. Here he sat, but for only a few moments, and then Kosuke no-Suke hurried in.

'Will. Here is sunshine after a month of rain. But what brings you to Edo, unannounced?'

'The ship is all but ready. I thought to inform the Shogun.'

'Splendid news. Splendid news. The prince will be pleased. You must go to him immediately.'

'I had thought my arrival too late in the day. He does not usually grant an audience in the evening.'

'For you, Will, he is there at any hour of the day or night. Those are his instructions. Now come.'

Suke led him through a labyrinth of galleries and small chambers, while Will selected his words with great care.

'Edo thrives.'

'And grows. We are on the threshold of great things, here.'

'I am told it attracts all the world. Even other daimyo.'

'Oh, indeed,' Suke said. 'They leave their wives and families here, as hostages. It is the oldest of customs, in Japan. And a wise one.'

'Including some from Osaka?'

'But of course,' Suke said, without turning his head He had paused before another low screen door. 'You will enter here.'

The screen slid aside and Tokugawa no-Hidetada came out, pausing before the men. 'Anjin Miura,' he said, contemptuously.

Will bowed from the waist.

'You are the star of the Edo sky,' Hidetada said. 'And so I should welcome you. Why, the Shogun commands *me* from his presence, in order to admit his teacher.'

'It is my good fortune to be of some value to the prince, my lord Hidetada.'

'Good fortune, Anjin Miura. Recognise it, for what it is. Fortune comes, and goes again, leaving those it has visited poorer than before.'

The prince stepped past them, and Will glanced at Suke. The secretary shrugged. 'He who would share the light of the Sun must beware the chill of the Moon. Now enter. The prince awaits you.'

Will stooped and dropped to his knees on the mats inside the screen. The room was large, and shaped like an L; in this portion of it there were only two serving girls, also kneeling, waiting for their summons, but unable to see the Shogun himself, or to hear his voice. Farther off, in the corner of the L, two kimono-clad ladies sat, one plucking at a musical instrument which allowed a gentle lament to seep through the chamber, and the other busy at her needlework, her head bowed close to the pattern, although she had a glowing candle beside her. They both half inclined their heads to glance at the intruder, and then hastily looked away again.

Hands clapped from beyond the corner. Will rose, and went forward. He passed the two princesses and turned to perform the kowtow before the dais where Iyeyasu sat drinking green tea. His cushion was specially made with an armrest for his right side, and on this he leaned.

'Will. Rise and come forward. Ladies, you may leave us.'

The princesses bowed and rose, bowed again, and moved

round the corner. Will sank to his knees at the edge of the dais.

Iyeyasu gazed at him. 'From the moment you entered the city walls four hours ago, Will, I felt a lightening of the spirit.'

'Has your spirit cause to feel heavy, my lord?'

'My spirit, Will? My spirit maintains this entire building. Nay this entire nation. So, sometimes, it feels weary. Do you know what I shall do, Will? I shall abdicate. That is what I have decided.'

'Abdicate the Shogunate, my lord?' Will gasped.

'Why not? It is an old custom, here in Japan. The Mikados resign their power, such as it is, with great regularity. Of course, in the old days, it was a device forced upon them by the Shoguns, to ensure a continuity of minority rule, which was simpler to manage. But in my case, why, my son Hidetada is well able to perform my duties. The country is at peace. What have I to do any more with ruling, or responsibility? I shall retire to Shidzuoka and there build myself a castle, and then, do you know what I shall do? I shall write down the code of the bushido, the law of the samurai, to give my soldiers a tangible guide to the proper living of their lives.'

'You are making merry at my expense, my lord.'

Iyeyasu clapped his hands. One of the serving girls brought in the tray of saké. The prince poured, and held out the cup. 'Drink. And then tell me why you have hurried to Edo. Is your wife not well?'

'She is, my lord.'

'And preparing to be a mother?'

'Soon, my lord.'

'I congratulate you, Will. So, then?'

'The new ship is all but ready, my lord. You may prepare for the launching.'

Iyeyasu drained the cup, held it out to be refilled. 'The new ship. It will be a great occasion. And then there will be others. Larger ships, eh, Will?'

'If you wish them, my lord. Of if your successor as Shogun wishes them.'

Iyeyasu smiled. 'Hidetada will wish what I wish, Will. Be sure of that. Ships are the future of our country. I told you this, some years ago. But the thought of having Hidetada as ruler disturbs you?'

'Who am I, my lord, to be disturbed by my rulers? To be ruled is sufficient.'

Iyeyasu gazed at him. 'It does not become you to appear like a Japanese, to *try* to appear like a Japanese, to ape our manners and our speech. I love you for what you are, for your roughness, for your honesty. Hidetada does not care for you as I do. Perhaps he is jealous of you. There are many who are jealous of you. But they are harmless, because I love you.'

'And after you die, my lord?'

'They will still be harmless, Will. I promise you that. In Japan we honour our ancestors, and their wishes. And when an ancestor is the greatest of his line, as I shall be, then even more honour is given to them. Now you are here, let me speak with you. To speak with you, Will, is to open my window and allow a breath of fresh air into my room. See that it remains always so. As you have guessed, I am not tired of ruling. I shall never tire of ruling. But there are many problems. Osaka. Yodogimi. The boy Hideyori. He will soon be a man. Have you thought of these things, Will?'

'Everyone in Japan thinks of these things, my lord.'

'That is true. It concerns us all. So, must everything we fought for at Sekigahara, all the blood that was shed that day, be wasted? Do you know what I hear? How the priests spend more time in Osaka Castle than in their churches. How there are two hundred thousand kokus of rice always stored within their granaries, to enable them to withstand a siege. And now, how there is much buying of powder and firearms. Perhaps even of cannon, if they can obtain them.'

'Can you not prevent these things, my lord?'

'Not openly. I can do nothing. The daimyo follow me because there is none other. But they fear me, not love me. They say to themselves, there will soon be another to follow. When Hideyori is a man.'

'But he is dim-witted, my lord.'

'So they say, Will. So they say. Did I *know* that, then would I sleep easy in my bed. But do I know that? I have not seen the boy since the age of five. I invited him to Kyoto for the marriage of my grand-daughter. He would not come. Yodogimi would not come. She said she would kill herself rather than leave Osaka. I invited them again, when I was created Shogun. I gave them public assurance of safety. But they would not come.'

'And so you withdraw from the Shogunate, my lord. I begin to understand.'

'Let us hope they do not. Nor do you, even. I retire, to wait.

All my life, I have waited for the correct moment. But I have endeavoured to make the correct moment arrive. As I have no reason to undertake the reduction of Osaka, with all the expense and bloodshed that would entail—no reason that the daimyo would accept, at any rate—I must force the overt act from Hideyori himself. His advisers, the Ono brothers, are hot-headed men. I seek to squeeze them, Will. On the one hand, with the old tiger sleeping at Shidzuoka, might not this be the best time to assert the name of the Toyotomi, before Hidetada establishes himself as Shogun? And on the other hand, having resigned the Shogunate in favour of my son, am I not establishing a Tokugawa succession, which, if not challenged, might well become permanent? There are great things afoot. So I will need you, Will, and not only to build me ships. But I need the strength too. And if the Portuguese will support the Toyotomi, then the Dutch must support the Tokugawa.'

'And the English, my lord.'

'I would hope so, Will. You have written letters?'

'I have, my lord. You will yet see an English ship at anchor in Edo Bay.'

'If it contains but half a dozen more like you, Will, then shall I be happy. Now I have been honest with you, so do you be honest with me. You told me the ship would be ready, next month, six months ago. So now you must hurry to Edo, to tell me again? Return to your home, to your wife, Will, and wait for my summons. There is naught here in Edo for you.' Iyeyasu turned his head. 'That is a command.'

'My lord . . . '

'Ishida Norihasa is here as my guest. I destroyed his father, now I pretend to make friends with the son. Nothing, Will, must in any way suggest to those in Osaka that I bear them enmity. Any of them. Besides, if they hate me, Will, think how greatly they hate you. They will seek to destroy you, and that would distress me. Now go to your couch, Will, and come to me again tomorrow, before you leave.'

How hard the floor, how hot the night. He should be back in Miura, sleeping beside Shikibu, feeling her turn, the softness of her shoulder, inhaling the sweet scent of her body. Knowing that she bore his child.

But for the moment he could not bring himself to touch her, even with the affection rather than the passion her pregnancy demanded. The girl Asoka remained a constant spur to his conscience, for all that *she* appeared to bear no ill will to her master, or her mistress.

So, how wasted, how criminal, this journey. And how gentle Iyeyasu's rebuke. Truly was he the most fortunate of men, and yet cursed with that waywardness which constantly threatened to bring him to disaster. But it was this very waywardness which had brought him to Japan. There was a riddle. All life was a riddle. But there were certain facts which were inescapable. The Toyotomi and the Tokugawa were preparing for the second and no doubt final round of their conflict, and he had chosen his side. Five years ago he had chosen his side. There could be no going back now.

How hard the floor. How high the ceiling. He lay on his back, and stared at the darkness. He would not sleep this night. Or perhaps he was already asleep. The room was strange to him, and it moved. For a long, dreadful moment, it moved, from left to right, and back again. He watched the ceiling separate into two pieces, and a strip of lacquered wood struck him across the face. He sat up, and was thrown sideways. He reached the outer wall, his ears singing in a gigantic rumble, crouched there, as the rest of the ceiling fell, and other ceilings above it, tumbling down through the tower in which he had been sleeping.

There was no floor, and he was crashing downwards. He jarred his shoulder, and heard the rip of his kimono. He was standing, in a suddenly clouded darkness. Dust obliterated his face, clogged his nostrils, stung his eyes. And there was silence. For a moment longer than the shock there was absolute silence, in the palace, in all Edo, perhaps in all Japan. And then the noise started again, but still muted. The rumble of a collapsing wall, a sudden thin shriek from close at hand in the darkness, as suddenly cut off. And now that he could breathe, he smelt the scorching scent of flame.

He panted, like a wild beast, clawed at rubble, fought his way through the darkness. He fell over dislodged beams, and into an unsuspected pit. For an eternity he slid, down, down, into hell itself, his mind screaming fear that this might be a crack in the earth which would close again and entomb him forever. But the earth was no longer moving. Only man, and man's creation moved. Where it could.

He landed in water, and the water was hot. Above and around him were tumbled boulders, carefully chosen stones. The inner moat. He had somehow stumbled out of the tower and fallen down the parapet. He waded forward and encountered an object. Something soft, floating, its kimono floating around it. Man or woman? Suke, or Keiko? The Shogun himself? Was not the entire country destroyed, in but a few unforgettable seconds?

He thrust the body aside, driven now by the cloud of smoke. He found himself on the other side of the moat, and for the first time looked upwards. There was the sky, clear and bright, already tinged with the rosy glow of dawn. But he did not wish for daylight. Daylight was too terrible to contemplate.

He climbed over the boulders. He fell into pits. He left the water behind and wandered, followed by the smoke, by the crackle of flames. Driven too by the screams and the wails, the begs for pity, the angry shouts of despair and dismay. He had no use for humanity now. The earthquake had cut across all that, had left his mind isolated, as he was himself isolated.

He ran down a suddenly clear pathway, a bridge between two chasms. The outer moat? Or a street? He did not know. But now it was light enough to see. To see what? A gigantic rubbish heap. Mile upon mile of stacked refuse, bits of wood standing on end, pieces of lacquered paper, floating in the wind, the occasional wall still erect, like some grotesque and prehistoric ruin. Were it clear, he would be able to see across the city to the sea. But it was not clear. Wave after wave of smoke clouded the morning sky, blotted the blue, seemed to pluck at his nostrils.

And now there was sound, as well. A low, but yet gigantic wail rose above the stricken city, compounded of a million throats uttering their cry of desperation at the catastrophe which had befallen them. A million, but yet not all the inhabitants of the city. Will picked his way through the rubble, stepping across giant cracks in the road, avoiding ensnaring timbers, stricken trees, and avoiding, too, the dead. For they were legion, and too many of the cracks were welling blood. Not since the field of Sekigahara had he seen such slaughter, and smelled such slaughter, too, for all that the true stench had not yet arisen from this carnage pile. And at Sekigahara they had all been men, in armour, determined to kill or be killed. Here there were children, pitiful bundles in tiny, pretty, sleeping kimonos, an arm here, a naked leg there, and too many women, motionless mounds of scattered black hair, sightless eyes peering towards the still rising sun.

Edo had been, and Edo was no more. All of Edo? He staggered onwards, dragged by his instincts, reaching out for the one thing he desired above all else. For where were Mikados and Shoguns, kings and emperors, armies and ambitions, the past and the future, on a day like this? Only man remained, and woman. And the present. And to imagine that timeless beauty lying a crumpled, broken mass beneath some collapsing palace was unthinkable. She had to be seen, to be known. To be rescued? He remained the romantic. The guilty romantic. For perhaps, while leaving Magdalena untouched, the tremor might have destroyed those around her. Ishida Norihasa?

He walked, and climbed, and staggered, and crawled, his sailor's instincts keeping the sun on his left hand, maintaining an unconscious tally of distance deep in his mind. He ignored appeals for help from those trapped beneath burning rubble, cries of anguish, cries of despair. He was struck across the forehead by a falling wall, and brushed it aside as if it were no more than paper, which indeed it was. Sweat tumbled down his body like a rushing river, and he discarded his kimono, retaining only his loin-cloth, and hurrying through the morning, weaponless, like some eta on a subhuman errand.

And in time he reached the distant suburb of Shiba, and could pause and look around him. Here the destruction seemed even more complete. His heart seemed to swell until it filled his chest, and left no more room for his lungs, or for air. Only thus could he prevent the tears.

A man stood by the roadside, gazing perhaps at the ruin of his house, his head slowly shaking from side to side. Will grasped him by the shoulder. 'The palace of my lord Ishida Norihasa. Tell me. Where.'

The man stared at him.

'My lord Norihasa,' Will shouted, shaking him to and fro. 'His palace was here, in Shiba. Show me.'

The man pointed, his hand trembling. Pointed, at what? There was nothing beyond there, save the still seething waters of the bay. But at least it was a direction.

He resumed his staggering march, and found the remains of an outer wall, of better quality than the tumbled rubbish surrounding it. He climbed over this, entered a courtyard which had surprisingly survived the worst of the shock. Here there was a group of women, seated on the grass, shaking and wailing. His heart tumbled and a fresh rush of sweat broke out on his shoulders as he ran forward. But they were all unmistakably Japanese.

'The lady Pinto Magdalena,' he shouted. 'Where is she?'

Heads turned, and they looked at him.

'I must find the lady Magdalena,' he begged. 'It is important. Where in the building was she?'

A finger pointed. There had been a tower, which was now no more. The roof had come down and the walls had fallen. But a tower supposed more than lacquered paper. There was hope. He had been sleeping in a tower.

He ran across the grass, was checked by another wall, this one eight feet high. He sucked air into his lungs, reached for the cementless crevasses which made climbing relatively easy. Eight feet up the stone ended and the wood began. The stone *had* ended and the wood *had* begun, once. But the wood had fallen inwards, lay littered in the well of the tower, together with tatami mats and small tables, backed cushions, clothes, and weapons.

And people. Three people. One was Pinto Magdalena.

Chapter 5

HE CARRIED her, where? He had very little sense of time, none of direction, any more. She lived, and her limbs seemed whole. That was enough.

It was not very far. Perhaps the garden. Here were tumbled rocks and disordered shrubs, and two fallen trees; the trunks had inclined towards one another, and met half way, to form an arbour, over a patch of untroubled grass. An oasis, in the wreckage that was Edo. Here there was even water, welling out of the spring in the garden, perhaps as yet uncontaminated.

Here he could explore. For this was necessary. She seemed to be no more than stunned, but who could say for sure? Her sleeping kimono was in any event torn to shreds. He removed it, as gently as a mother might disrobe her babe, held her for a moment cradled in his arms, an angel of pale brown, slow-breathing beauty, her face washed clean of paint for the night, her eyelids almost fluttering, her breasts swelling against his naked chest, and what breasts, grotesque by Japanese standards, larger even than those of Mary on her wedding night, breasts into which a man might sink his head and sleep, and have no more use for dreams. And then, her legs, long, as he had suspected and hoped, and strong. No doubt he had the best of her, now. Five years ago she had been still a girl, now she was a woman. For between legs and breasts there was a treasure house indeed, of wide thighs, curving buttocks, and in front a wealth of curling hair, surprisingly pale when he could remember only the blackness of Yodogimi and Shikibu, and the geisha. She was a creature from another world. His world. His dream, come back to life.

'Am I, then, dead?' she whispered.

He did not even blush, for having been so discovered. There could be no blushes, between them.

'No,' he said. 'Not dead, Magdalena. Not even harmed.'

She gazed at him, her eyes wide. 'They told me you had come to Edo,' she said. 'They said the lord Anjin Miura comes. My lord Norihasa . . . ' Her head turned wildly, to and fro.

'He is not here, Magdalena. No one is here. Saving you, and me.'

'The tower,' she said. 'It moved.'

'It fell. Was your lord with you, last night?'

She shook her head, and her hands came up, against his chest.

He tightened his arms around her shoulders. 'I came across the city to find you. I came to Edo to see you again, Magdalena.'

'You are married, Anjin Miura. And you refused the ring.'

He sighed. 'With a heavy heart, sweet child. But I had already made my choice, and I do not betray my master.'

'Yet you accepted the love of my lady Yodogimi.'

'I accepted her body. I could do no more, then. And I wished it could have been you. I said as much.'

Her tongue came out, and circled her lips. A dry tongue, issuing from a dry throat. Did he dare release her, even for an instant?

His hands slipped down her back, and he went to the spring, cupped his hands for the water, offered it to her. She gazed at him for some seconds, and then crawled across the grass towards him, knelt at his side, lowered her mouth to his hands. Again, and again. Her hair fell on either side of her face, clouded his arms. He looked down the long curve of her back to the twin mounds he longed to possess. Christ, that the world could end, now. That time could cease, forever. That this patch of grass might become Eternity.

'I have dreamed of you, every night, Magdalena.'

Her head remained bowed, but her tongue stroked his palms.

'Against my will, I have dreamed of you, Magdalena. Even while I took another for my wife, I have dreamed of you. When I have held her in my arms, I have dreamed of you.'

She raised her head. 'The gods will not forgive you for this, Anjin Miura.'

'My name is Will, Magdalena. And these gods are not my gods. I foreswore my gods too long ago. Now I only know my instincts as a man, and they have brought me here.'

God in Heaven, was this really Will Adams speaking? Uttering such blasphemy? And yet, every word of it was the truth.

Her hand came out, and touched his cheek, for a moment, before falling to her side. She seemed unaware of her nakedness. Unaware? Or uncaring?

'No man has ever spoken so, to me,' she said.

'Then say that you are not angry with me.'

'Angry with you, Will? How could I be, when you have risked so much for me? You may even have saved my life. But I fear for you. What you have done this day cannot be undone.'

'Why, Magdalena?' He seized her hand. 'Edo is wrecked. Utterly. Look around you. What you see here is but a tiny part of the whole. The city has disappeared. Perhaps all civilisation in Japan has disappeared. Now is no time for worrying about others. There are no others. There are only ourselves.'

She shook her head. 'There have been earthquakes before, Will. And there will be again. Here in Japan we merely rebuild our cities. Why do you suppose our houses are of so flimsy a construction? Within a year, Edo will stand again.'

Her hand was limp in his. She would submit of course. He could stretch her on her back and rape her until exhausted, nor, perhaps, would she even call it rape. But did he want that? Had not Shikibu submitted and thereby only raised his frustration to a higher pitch?

'Then let us turn our backs on Edo, Magdalena. Let us turn our backs upon Japan. We do not belong here. We are of different blood, different heritage, to these people. Even you, Magdalena. Your European forefathers are too strong within you. Come with me. I will find a ship, and we will put to sea. You and I, Magdalena. Together we can challenge the world. With you at my side, I will fear no man, respect no whim of nature. I will sail us back across the ocean, if need be.'

'Will,' she said. 'Will. We would perish.'

'And are you, then, so afraid of death?'

She shook her head. 'But before we died, you would hate me. Oh, you are filled with passion for me. I told you once, I am flattered. I have never met a man like you. No one in all Japan has met a man like you. To have you wish my body is the greatest honour that could befall me. But it is no more than a wish for my body. You would hate me, for destroying everything you hold dear. And for me to come with you would be to do that.'

'No,' he said. 'No. Can you not understand? Oh, I wish your body. I am a man. But love such as I bear for you cannot be assuaged by a mere physical consummation. This I swear, Magdalena.'

'And your wife? Your family? Your retainers? What would become of them?'

Christ in Heaven, my unborn child. What madness have I suffered, this day?

His fingers opened, and her hand fell to her side. And still she knelt, naked, in front of him, every fold of flesh in her timeless body beckoning him to her.

'What would you have me do?'

She sighed. Her breasts filled and swelled, and sagged again. 'No man may turn his back upon his duty, Will. Least of all a samurai.'

'God curse the samurai,' he said. 'God curse every code of honour. Where is honour, where love is concerned?'

'Men must live by honour,' she said. 'Else love is itself dishonourable.'

He nodded, slowly. She too was young enough to be his daughter, and yet old enough to be his teacher. He stood up, looked down at her red-streaked hair. 'At least, I have held you for a moment in my arms.'

Her head went back, and she gazed at him. Then suddenly she threw both arms around his legs to press her face into his thighs. 'May the gods forgive me,' she whispered. 'But I too, have dreamed. Too much.'

The sun scorched from a cloudless sky. It was as if the gods, having taken the earth and shaken it with vast humour, now wished to examine, closely, body by body, what they had achieved. Perhaps they gloated, over the still seething waters of Edo Bay, over the junks and sampans thrown helter-skelter on the beach, over the bridges which had disappeared and the rivers which had changed their courses, over the villages which had sunk and the hills which had risen. Over the clustered dead and the frantic living. Over Edo the rubbish dump. But Edo was not easily to be examined. The city was shrouded in a vast pall. Much of it was dust, swirling in the still air. But much of it, also, was smoke. Edo burned.

Edo burned, but was that of importance? Smoke drifted across the garden, titillated their nostrils, and then was dispelled again by the gentle breeze off the sea. Was that of importance?

Edo also stirred, as people realised that the shock was behind them, and they lived, while their friends and wives and children were dead. But in the garden this was least important of all. Beneath the clustering branches of the fallen trees there was solitude, and damp green grass, and an awareness only of self, and extension of self. What happened beyond the whispering green leaves, who might be calling their names, with fear or with hate in their hearts, was as irrelevant as the drifting smoke.

There was no food in the garden, but there was water, seeping from the shattered spring. Water was useful, for a great many purposes. For drinking, certainly. They had sucked each other dry. When first he had wanted her lips she had gazed at him with eyes as wide as Shikibu's, but her grandmother had told her that this was how her grandfather had wanted to love as well, and she had submitted, anxiously. Then she had used her tongue to better and more Japanese purpose, to explore his body, his armpits, his back, his belly, his thighs, torturing him by her circumvention of his genitals, by the speed of her movements, which constantly brought her own limbs, her own belly, her own buttocks within reach of his mouth as she turned and twisted, but always withdrawing them again before he could gain the possession he wanted. Truly, water was useful, for drinking.

It was needed, too, for washing. Possession of Pinto Magdalena was to be no small matter of making an entry. Where Asai Yodogimi had sought only to dominate, where Magome Shikibu had wished only to be dominated, Pinto Magdalena had wanted to share, to make his journey into her womb merely the pinnacle of a long sexual ascent. Far from restraining him, she had brought him to ejaculation within seconds, bathed her hands in his semen, lain away from him while performing a similar duty upon herself, with his own seed as lubricant, her eyes laughing, her hair scattered about her, her mouth beckoning even as her shaking head kept him away. So, water was necessary, for bathing. Because she had done this too, for both of them, before again calling him to even more anxious manhood with lip and tongue, gleaming white tooth and soft stroking fingers.

This time she had wanted his penetration, but again not in the simple sense that she would close her muscles upon his organ and massage him to orgasm. She wanted to feel his penis in her belly itself, had crouched on hands and knees, and urged him forward. Sinful? Oh, indeed, by all the teaching of his youth. But where was sin, when man and woman were coupled? Where was sin, where Pinto Magdalena was concerned? Where was sin, when all the world was scattered, and they might be the only two human beings left in the universe, a new Adam, a new Eve, with all of life yet to be explored.

And water was useful, for resuscitation. For that last bout, bearing as she had done most of his weight upon her forward sloping spine, had left her exhausted. She lay on her back on the warmed grass, pillowed on her hair, her eyes only half open.

'Truly, Will, truly,' she whispered, 'have you reached the fount of motherhood itself. For to enter the body, how small a thing. Woman is like the greatest of shrines, and so many men seek to possess only the torii, the outer gate. But you have passed beyond. Surely then I felt your tip wriggling within my very womb. There is the truest delight. The true sublimation.'

Had she achieved that? With Norihasa? Christ, what a thought, at such a time. It was not to be considered. Instead, for all the lifeless exhaustion of his own loins, he must fall to again, cupping little handfuls of water from the spring and allowing the liquid to drip through his fingers on to her breasts, to watch the nipples slowly lose their dimples and grow, reaching upwards for his tongue. To watch her eyes lose their lazy somnolence and widen. To watch her own tongue regain its power.

'Can you not be sated?' she whispered.

'I am sated,' he said. 'But to leave you, Magdalena, even for a moment, is not possible for me.'

She put her arms round his neck, pulled him down to rest his head on her breasts, to listen to the soft flutter of her heart. 'Then do not leave me, Will,' she whispered. 'Here, in this garden, have we known everything that life has to offer. There is nothing left for us to discover, about life, about love, about each other. Kill me now, Will. And then yourself, if you choose. That way, there will be no time for regrets. For consequences.'

How softly her heart beat beneath its sweet mound of flesh. How insistently the nipple stroked his cheek. And how tensed were the fingers on his back, suddenly.

'Are you, then, still too much of a Christian?'

'As are you, Magdalena.'

'I do not know. I do not know what I am, except a woman.'

He raised his head, leaned on his elbow to look into her face. 'As I only know that I am a man, and being a man I could not destroy you, Magdalena. No matter what might follow.'

She sighed. 'Then you must go now, and quickly. We have been fortunate indeed to have enjoyed this blessed day. But look, the sun is past its zenith. People will soon come looking for me. Indeed, they already do so. Can you not hear them?'

For there were voices all around them, beyond the leaves, calling, issuing orders, screams of pain, shrieks of dismay. The business of reviving Edo was gathering pace, while they had shared eternity.

'Come with me, Magdalena.'

She shook her head. 'There is nowhere in all Japan that you could escape the vengeance of my lord Norihasa.'

'And do you think that I could risk leaving *you* to face his vengeance! The serving girls saw me come, knew that I searched for you. When you are discovered alive, they will know that I found you.'

'My lord will have no vengeance for me, Will. Only anger. He has known anger towards me before, and I have survived.'

'He has beaten you?'

'Is that not the privilege of a man towards his woman?'

He saw the serving girl, once again strapped across the bar, waiting for the rod. But this was no serving girl.

'And you will submit, to be beaten again, by him?'

She sat up. 'Is he, then, so much lower than you, Will? Ishida Norihasa is a samurai, famous for his deeds of courage on the field of battle, for his loyalty to the Toyotomi. There my loyalty lies as well. Now, and always. The Toyotomi sought you, Will Adams, and you refused them. Your loyalty is to the Tokugawa. And believe me, we in Osaka well know that the day of reckoning must come; it is merely a matter of having it come at our choosing, and not that of the prince. That I love you is my misfortune, nothing more. I have surrendered to my passion, and it would be right that I am now punished for it.'

'Magdalena . . . '

'Go,' she whispered. 'Please. I beg this of you, Will. If you love me, if you pity me, go now.'

He stood up, tied his cloth.

'And remember only this morning,' she said.

Christ in Heaven, to leave so much beauty, sitting naked at his feet. To turn away, knowing that were he once again to kneel, she once again would submit. So would he, then, be found lying on her body, to be taken thus? Better then, to do as she had first wanted, and wrap his fingers round her neck.

But better still, perhaps, to wait.

'Then *you* remember, Magdalena,' he said. 'One day I shall come to Osaka.'

'I know that,' she said. 'With all the millions of the Tokugawa at your back. And that day, Will Adams, will I defy you.'

He gazed at her, his hands opening and shutting in impotence. How European she looked, how European she seemed, how

European she was. And yet, how Japanese her honour. Betray her master, yes. Betray her mistress, never.

'Go,' she begged. 'Please. The voices come closer.'

It had to be now. He turned, ducked beneath the fallen tree trunk, emerged on to the tumbled stone of the garden, looked up, and gazed at four men, standing on the ruined wall. They were fully dressed, unlike himself, and wore swords. And one stood a little in advance of the rest. A thin man, taller than average for a Japanese, with unusually crisp features and a drooping black moustache. Ishida Norihasa.

A quick glance to left and right convinced Will that there was no escaping, even had he wished. Progress through the wreckage would be too slow, and there would be other of Norihasa's retainers around, if only they were women, to give chase and perhaps bring him down. He was sufficient of a samurai not to wish to die, running away.

'Where is Pinto Magdalena, Englishman?' Norihasa asked, his voice low.

'She is unharmed, my lord Norihasa,' Will said.

And now she stood behind him. 'Anjin Miura saved my life, my lord,' she said. 'He pulled me from that fallen tower, brought me to the garden and revived me with water from the spring.'

She stood, half sheltered by the fallen tree, but yet clearly naked.

'And with the seed of his loins as well, no doubt,' Norihasa said.

'I have loved Magdalena since I first saw her, in Osaka Castle, five years ago,' Will said. 'I would ask you this; let her come with me. She is but one woman amongst many, to you. To me she is all the woman in the world.'

Norihasa's face never changed expression. But he slowly climbed down the tumbled wall, his three samurai behind him. 'Anjin Miura,' he said. 'This is what they call you. I call you English dog, creature of the Tokugawa.'

Will licked his lips. Did Norihasa refuse to recognise him as a samurai then he might very well be cut down on the instant. 'My lord Norihasa would do well to remember that he stands in the city of the Tokugawa.'

'The city,' Norihasa said contemptuously. 'The dung heap. But did it stand until its towers touched the clouds, English dog, no Tokugawa could help you now. You have entered my house, to rape my woman. You have forfeited your life to me.'

Sweat trickled down Will's back; how hot the afternoon, on a sudden. And how silent, Magdalena. She stood by the tree, watching the men, but saying nothing. She had nothing to say, now, no words of defence to offer. For should she attempt to save his life, then was he dishonoured as a man. He remained the guilty one. But to die, like a trapped pig.

'I am a samurai,' he said.

'This day you have betrayed your class.'

'Yet I have the right to die with a sword in my hand, my lord.'

'The short one,' Norihasa said. 'I give you the right of seppuku, now.' He took the short sword from his own belt, and tossed it forward. It struck the earth with a gentle thump.

Will listened to the slow hiss as Magdalena drew her breath.

'The long sword, my lord Norihasa,' he said.

'You seek to defy me?'

'My lord, mistake me not,' Will said, speaking slowly and with great care. 'I am no Japanese. I am an Englishman, and my life is not to be talked away. To defend it, I would defy the gods themselves. Give me a long sword, or prepare to die yourself, for murder.'

Norihasa hesitated, frowning. One of his samurai whispered something in his ear, thrusting his chin in Will's direction. For how could a mere Englishman hope to fight a daimyo, whose sole upbringing from the day of his birth had been in the way of the sword? And how true that was. How bitterly did Will regret not having received instruction from Tadatune. How much would he give, to have Tadatune at his side now. Or would Tadatune stand aside, from a dishonoured samurai?

Norihasa smiled and replied to his aide. The man drew the long sword from his girdle, handed it to his master; the challenge had to come from Norihasa himself. The daimyo slowly took the sword, in both hands, turned it over, and stepped over the last of the stones on to the grass. Out of the corner of his eye Will saw Magdalena withdrawing under the tree trunk to the safety of the farther side.

Norihasa stopped, placed the sword upon the grass, and kicked the hilt towards Will. His own weapon remained in its sheath. But still, he could draw and cut long before Will could pick the weapon up. That was no part of the code of the samurai, but Will remained uncertain as to how much of the code was being used here. Or was the mere fact that he had been offered a sword proving that he was being accorded the honour due to his rank?

Slowly he moved towards the weapon, watching Norihasa, being watched in turn by him, by the three samurai, and no doubt by Magdalena as well as by several other female servants who had appeared amidst the rubble. Had they been there all the time, all morning, watching and listening sending their messages forth to the world? The world he had supposed no longer to exist.

His right hand closed on the hilt, his left on the sheath. Slowly he rose to his full height at the same time once again stepping back. What to do now? He had only ever handled a cutlass, except for that brief moment at Sekigahara. This sword in many ways resembled a cutlass, except that it was longer and heavier, and required both hands for its proper use. And always there was the certainty that Norihasa would be as expert with this weapon as with his foodsticks.

The daimyo continued to smile, and now he nodded, at the same time drawing his own weapon, and removing the sheath as well from his girdle, to toss it to one side. Will did likewise, without haste; above all else, now, he must keep his wits.

Norihasa grasped the sword in both hands, the right in advance of the left, the blade thrust straight out from his body, the hilt itself held immediately in front of his belly. He advanced the right leg as well, and made a peculiar hissing sound, through nose and mouth. Will followed his example, at least as regards stance. He could only wait, and hope to defend; at the least he outreached his assailant by several inches.

Norihasa moved in a semicircle to his left, still keeping his distance, still hissing, pawing at the earth with his right foot, testing the quality of the hold. Will circled to *his* left, trying to remember where there were broken stones protruding through the grass, or where the branches of the fallen tree might possibly wrap themselves around his ankles.

The hiss became a sudden gasp, and three feet of flailing steel carved towards him, whipping to and fro, leaving the air vibrant in its wake. Will reacted instinctively, put up his own sword, listened to the clang, and suffered a jar which all but tore the weapon from his hands, and was then away, moving fast to his right, cannoning into the tree trunk and hearing a stifled gasp from Magdalena as he struggled to regain his balance.

Norihasa turned, his smile wider as he saw Will pant. His

own breathing had altered not at all. And he knew how close he had come to victory in that first assault. Now he commenced his preamble again, accompanied by the hissing breaths which apparently gave him such control over his lungs. Will found his own breathing still painfully uneven, seeming to drain his muscles of power as it emptied his lungs of air. Think, he told himself. Be calm, and think. You know now what he will do. Avoid the next charge, and instead of losing your balance by the momentum of your escape, turn on the spot, and you will be in a position to strike while *he* is still off balance. You will kill him, surely, with a single stroke from your sword. He remembered the man at Sekigahara, the blood on his hand. Would he feel sick, this time? Did he hate Norihasa? He had not hated the man at Sekigahara. But he hated Norihasa, with a wild, un-reasoning hate. An animal hate.

Norihasa moved forward, the blade flicking the air. Will's sword came up, but Norihasa had checked, midway across the grass. His sword went flat, and scythed the air as Will's still whirled over his head. A stab of agonising pain ran right across his belly.

And yet he stood, and instinctively brought his sword down to parry the next scything blow. The two weapons met with another tremendous clang, and Norihasa stepped away, smiling, even pausing to say something over his shoulder to his three companions. Will leaned on his sword and looked down, watched the blood welling from the slash across his belly, soaking his cloth, dripping down his legs to form a small pool at his feet. Nothing more than a skin-deep cut, but nothing more had been intended. Next time his gut would be opened, because next time Norihasa would again try something different, and Will would be progressively weaker.

He sighed, drew the back of his hand across his forehead, and raised his sword once again. How weary he was, on a sudden. Still, now it would soon be over. One more clash of blades, and then the end. He hoped it would be instantaneous, but he doubted this. Norihasa was too skilful, and would wish to watch his adversary bleed to death at his feet. At Magdalena's feet, also.

Norihasa moved forward, slowly, right leg extended, blade held in front of him, waving to and fro. Will began to circle to his right, was checked by a shout from the wall beyond the samurai.

'Throw down your sword, my lord Norihasa. And you, Anjin Miura.'

Norihasa's head half turned, while Will gazed in amazement at the short, plump figure in the green kimono; the prince was accompanied by twenty bowmen, who surrounded the garden, their arrows already against their strings. The prince? Iyeyasu himself, patrolling the stricken city like a common officer?

'Obey me, my lord Norihasa.'

Norihasa's sword point slowly drooped to the grass. 'This is a duel between samurai, my lord Iyeyasu. There is no law which permits you to interfere.'

'There is only one law in Edo, my lord Norihasa,' Iyeyasu said. 'The law of the Tokugawa.'

Norihasa continued to gaze at Will. 'Then, my lord, I wish to charge this man with rape. I will provide witnesses. That is the law of the *land*, my lord Iyeyasu.'

'Only one person here can accuse Anjin Miura of rape, my lord Norihasa,' Iyeyasu said.

The garden was silent, while Will waited for his life to be decided, and his blood ran down his legs. But to save his life would cost her, what?

'Anjin Miura saved my life,' Magdalena said in a low voice. 'And when he would have gone again, I begged him to remain.'

Breath whistled through Norihasa's nostrils, and his sword moved almost without control.

'I must offer you my most humble apologies, my lord,' Iyeyasu said. 'But if you raise your weapon again I shall send a bolt through your heart.'

Norihasa hesitated, and then stooped, and picked up his discarded scabbard. 'You are dishonoured, Anjin Miura.'

Will looked down at the sword in his hand, at the blood still trickling down his belly. He did not look over his shoulder at Magdalena. He reversed the sword, held the haft towards the daimyo. 'You shall have your opportunity, my lord Norihasa. I give you my word.'

Norihasa took the blade, allowed the point to touch the grass. 'Be sure of it, Anjin Miura. We of Osaka, of the Toyotomi, have much in our minds concerning you. Your betrayal of the Princess Yodogimi is equalled only by your assault upon my woman. Be sure that we shall find you out.'

Will stepped past him, the entire stricken garden now commencing to whirl about his head. Above him, Iyeyasu waited, the adhesive paper bandages already in his hand, while his soldiers kept their bows ready for any overt move on the part of the Ishida. But the prince would not come down to help him. He was sufficiently dishonoured by this day's events, as Norihasa had said. He must make this climb on his own.

He clambered over the stones, reached the wall. 'You should have let him kill me, my lord. I have dishonoured the Tokugawa.'

'And I also, Anjin Miura,' Iyeyasu said. 'To interfere in a duel between samurai . . . that will not easily be forgotten.'

'My lord . . . '

'So what, then, do I say to myself, Will?' Iyeyasu's face was grim. 'When I realised I lived, this morning, what did I do? Did I command my officers to see to my people? Did I pray to the gods? Did I tear my hair in distress for the fate of my city? I summoned what remained of my guard and I searched for you, Will. Because you will build me ships? What use have I for ships? Because you are my fortune? What use have I for superstition? Because I love you? What right has a ruling prince to love one human being more than all the rest?'

Will sighed. 'My lord, your words reduce me to nothing. If you could but understand . . . as with you, when I woke to that trembling of the earth, when I saw the horror that had been Edo, I conceived the world to be coming to an end, and so thought of nothing save my love for that woman. I love her still. I shall love her, always. I make no excuses, beg for no mercy. I would only have you understand.'

'To understand, Will, is simple for any man of intelligence. To forgive, that is different.' His gaze seemed to hold Will's face in a vice. 'I do not wish to look upon you again, Anjin Miura. I will prefer to remember, for the future. For you, there remains only your duty. That lies at Miura, with your family, and at Ito, with your ship. This earthquake will have travelled the length of Honshu. Should the ship be wrecked, then expect my vengeance. My men will bind your wound, and then you will make haste to the south, and remain there the rest of your days.' From his girdle he took Will's Air Splitter. 'And wear this. A samurai who walks the street without his sword forfeits his place in the world of men.'

Miura was unchanged, its wooden palisades as firm as ever, its beach untroubled by the shock waves to the north. And its inhabitants?

The gates swung open for the lord, and his escort of Tokugawa bowmen. The samurai within waited to perform the kowtow, their wives and families behind them in the courtyard. With Kimura.

'Welcome home, my lord,' Kimura said. 'These have been sad times.'

'You will prepare me a galley, immediately, Kimura. I must go to Ito, to make sure the ship is unharmed.'

'If my words can bring you solace, my lord,' Kimura said. 'I have myself been to Ito, and indeed, only returned last night. There too the shock was not severe. The ship is unharmed.'

'Thank God for that, at least. And my wife?'

'Awaits you in the house, my lord.' Kimura's gaze flickered over the bowmen. 'Keiko has not returned?'

For the two men had become close friends.

'Alas, Kimura, he has not been found since the shock. But there is no cause for despair; the quarters in which he slept were not badly damaged, and those who were there with him say he wandered off, no doubt in search of me. He will be found, as soon as order is returned to the city, you may be sure of that. Or, indeed, learning of my departure, he could well be on his way here now. I would have stayed and searched for him myself, had not the prince wanted me to see to the ship.'

He went up the steps, past the kneeling girls, and into the house. Shikibu also knelt, beside the small table on which waited the bottle of saké, and the cup. Shikibu the faithful, the trusting.

'Welcome home, my lord.'

Her mouth opened, waiting. But this day he could not bring himself to kiss her. He knelt, slowly, because of the pain in his belly, and poured himself a cup of saké. He drank, quickly, refilled the cup, and handed it to her. What to say? What to do? Better, perhaps, to say and do nothing, to allow time to play its part, rely upon her ignorance of what had happened. She could also be Shikibu the determined, Shikibu the angry.

Shikibu sipped, placed the cup on the table. She reached forward to unfasten his girdle, and part his kimono. He listened to the sucking in of her breath as she gazed at the extent of his wound. Her ignorance of what had happened? This was Japan, where news travelled faster than the birds themselves.

'You must lie down, my lord,' she said. 'And allow me to bathe your cut, and dress it for you. I have an ointment which will help to prevent it festering.'

253

'Shikibu . . . '

She clapped her hands and the girl entered. 'Prepare my lord of Miura's bath,' she said. 'And quickly.'

The girl bowed, and withdrew.

'Shikibu,' he said.

She herself bowed, her forehead close to the floor. 'I will fetch the ointment, my lord.'

He caught her arms as she straightened her body, preparatory to standing. 'Wait,' he said.

She gazed at him, her face as watchful as ever. Or was it more so today?

'What I did was wrong,' he said. 'But I would have you know of it, Shikibu.'

She waited, because he was her lord. But there was no forgiveness in her eyes.

'I thought the end of the world had come,' he said. 'I have no experience of earthquakes. I could not imagine survival, after such a shock. And this girl . . . I loved her, before you, Shikibu. Believe me, I love you, now. I could not imagine life without you, now. But she was in Edo, and Edo was destroyed. And so I sought her, and found her. Tell me that you understand that, Shikibu.'

'If the world was destroyed, my lord, than so was Miura.'

How dark her eyes. How little he knew of her. As he had known so little of Magdalena herself. What thoughts, what emotions, were locked away inside that marvellous little head, shielded by those splendid eyes?

'I ask your forgiveness, Shikibu. I need your forgiveness. By my foolish act I have forfeited many friends. Even the respect of the prince himself. I stand as alone in Japan now as the day I landed here, five years ago. And on that day, Shikibu, I thought *you* were my friend. I beg you to forgive me, to grant me that friendship, again.'

'Who am I to forgive my lord? I am but your wife. I stand here, ready to do your bidding, whatever that might be, now and always. I bear your child in my belly. You should not so demean yourself by asking forgiveness from your wife.'

What had Magdalena said? Is it not the privilege of a man to beat his woman? He had truly never considered lifting his hand to Shikibu, nor would ever do so, he was sure. But Magdalena had meant more than that, as Shikibu had just tried to tell him. This was a man's world, and women could only submit.

But it was not the world he wanted *them* to share. More than ever, now.

'Shikibu . . .'

She rose to her feet. 'I must get the ointment, my lord, else will your wound fester.'

He breakfasted on fruit, a bowl of rice, two cups of steaming green tea. He was served by Shikibu herself, on her knees beside him. Earlier she had supervised his bath, had herself changed the dressing on his wound. She had done these things, every day since his return, as she had supervised his bath and served his breakfast, every day since their marriage.

Now she bowed. 'I would withdraw, my lord. The carpenter comes.'

'I will see this contraption,' he said.

She bowed again, and remained bowing, until he had risen and walked past her. In the next room the workmen were already busy. They constructed a piece of furniture shaped like an armchair, but without legs. In this Shikibu would kneel to be delivered, and here she would remain kneeling for twenty-one days after the birth of the child. The physician said this was best, for it would prevent any risk of blood rushing to her head. And yet, to kneel, for upwards of three weeks, with support only for her arms? Her face was as impassive as ever, as she gazed at the chair. It was as impassive as ever when she gazed at him, as well. Childbirth was part of her duty, as a woman, as a wife. She had been taught this when still a young girl, and she was not likely to be afraid of it, now. Her life had been designed by her lord; she would live it, according to custom and duty and responsibility, until she died.

So must her lord, then, live his life, according to custom, and duty, and responsibility. He was all but fully recovered from his wound, thanks to her ointments and the care of her soft hands. Six days a week he rowed across the bay to Ito, to return exhausted in the late evening. The ship was ready for launching; pending instructions from Edo he had already laid the keel of a yet larger vessel. The foundations of the Japanese navy, were Iyeyasu ever to use them.

But today he would remain at home, both to rest and to attend to his duties as lord of Miura. So, within the hour Kimura would bring the horses to the steps, and he would mount and go out to inspect his fields, and his crops, now close to harvesting. His tenants would prostrate themselves as he passed, with honest reverence. His relationship to his wife, to his lord in Edo, was none of their concern, any more than the daily passage of the sun from the ocean in the east to the mountains in the west was their concern.

He would return, at noon, for his meal. It would be fish, perhaps still breathing, its flesh stripped from its bones by Shikibu's own soft hands, while the bowls of rice and condiments, of green tea and saké, were placed beside his plate, and Shikibu watched him, with impassive respect.

After his meal, this one day in the week, he would be at leisure. He would retire to the room set aside for his pleasure, and there he would read, slowly and painfully, for he still laboured at Japanese literature. He had recently finished the *Genji Monogatari*, a long and somewhat tedious tale, which he had enjoyed entirely because it had been written by a lady, Murasaki Shikibu. Now he would commence the *Makura no Soshi*, contemptuously known as the Pillow Book, also written by a court lady, Sei Shonagon. Certainly, in its serious discussions and descriptions of relations between man and woman, Japanese literature was different to anything he had ever read as a boy.

When the heat had left the sun, Kimura would attend him again, for discussion of the business of Miura, and perhaps for a tour of inspection of some part of the outer wall, or some outbuilding, which required attention. Then it would be dusk, and the evening meal, with Shikibu. Perhaps a mitsusaki, with the tender slices of young chicken broiled beside him, and the bottles of saké constantly refilled. They lived well, at Miura. And after supper, why, perhaps she would sing to him, in that high, clear voice of hers, before retiring. Separately, now; her belly was too swollen for him to play the lover. But would they not have retired separately, anyway, now? Was she not grateful for the physical condition which protected her from a part of her duty, at the least?

There was hubbub, from the gate, a shouting and a wailing. And there was Kimura, standing in the doorway, forgetting even to bow.

'My lord . . . ' he stammered. 'Keiko . . . '

Will ran from the room, regardless of the pain in his gut. He burst across the porch and down the steps. In the courtyard the Miura samurai stood in a circle with their women, already commencing the wail of doom.

'It was left outside the gate, my lord,' Kimura panted. 'We did not see the bearer. But he rode a horse.'

The men parted to allow Will through. On the dust, in front of them, was Keiko's head with foodsticks thrust through its topknot. The face was expressionless, almost careless. But he had seen death coming towards him, and he had known that he died, for his lord. Slowly Will reached out and drew the kokotana from the blood-dried ear. An unnecessary gesture. He handed it to Kimura, still gazing at the frozen features.

'The mark of Ishida Norihasa, my lord.'

The little knife was replaced in Will's hand, for him to look at, and remember. How little we know, of our actions, at the time.

'Kimura,' he said. 'I have a task for you. I wish you to ride south to Kyushu, to the home of Shimadzu no-Tadatune. Tell the lord Tadatune from me, that if he does not find it in his heart to hate me for what I have done then I have a request to make of him. Once he offered to teach me the ways of the sword and I refused him. Now I would learn the ways of the sword from a master. Tell him this, and beg him to spend a season at Miura.'

'Yes, my lord.' Kimura's eyes gleamed. 'Keiko will be avenged.'

The samurai uttered a howl of pleasure. 'Keiko will be avenged.'

A hand touched Will's arm. 'Thus will you restore your manhood, my lord,' Shikibu said. 'And thus will I give you a son to keep the name of Anjin ever famous.'

The hand was soft, and so were the eyes. Christ in Heaven, he thought; she was angry, not because of Pinto Magdalena, but because I had to be rescued from the duel.

Magome Shikibu.

The lilting music filled the huge room, and the geisha, seventy in number, gently moved their bodies to and fro, fluttered fans and hands, and bowed low, a kaleidoscope of grace and colour, before hurrying behind the screens.

The men gave a murmur of approval, and the serving girls hurried in with the cups of green tea which signalled the end of the banquet. The grumble of conversation grew. It seemed all Japan was present, this evening, in the Nijo Palace in the centre of Kyoto. The blaze of light which told that the Tokugawa were on a ceremonial visit to the capital could be seen for miles; it bathed the rest of the city, lit up even the great wooden structure supporting the temple of Kiyomizu on the hills shrouding Lake Biwa. No doubt the light, and the hubbub, even disturbed the Mikado, forbidden by his imperial seclusion from attending a function given by a subject, no matter how exalted.

For this night it was the turn of the men who *ruled* Japan, of the Asano and the Kato, of the Mori and the Satsuma. They had fought against each other at Sekigahara. This night, they assembled in homage to their masters.

Because here too were the six Tokugawa princes, grouped about the new Shogun, Prince Hidetada. An assembly of such wealth and power had not been seen within Kyoto in living memory, and the great chamber, no less than sixty tatami in size, glittered with the many coloured lanterns and the splendidly variegated kimonos and girdles of the distinguished guests, with the gleaming silver spearheads of the Tokugawa guards, with the scintillating shafts of light from the jewelled hafts of the short swords in dozens of belts, for every samurai wore his ceremonial weapons this night.

The heart of Japan, assembled within a single room, each man a king within his own province, an absolute ruler over ten thousand lesser samurai, a million serfs, and uncounted numbers of subhumans. And yet every ear, and occasionally every head, was directed towards the two smallest figures in the room. They sat together, at the right-hand corner of the huge U formed by the myriad lacquered tables, smiling at the assembled guests, occasionally turning towards each other for a scrap of small talk. The prince suggested a good-humoured ball, a ball who enjoyed good living, who had eaten a hearty meal, laughed at all the jokes, answered a fair number of the riddles, and eyed the geisha with proper appreciation. He looked, and perhaps he saw himself, as the father of all the great men present, not merely their acknowledged leader. For if every man in the room followed the Tokugawa, no man in the room doubted whom the Tokugawa followed.

No man, except perhaps the boy seated beside him. Toyotomi no-Hideyori was eighteen years of age, a tiny figure strangely reminiscent of *his* father at least to those, like Iyeyasu himself, who could remember the youthful Hideyoshi. He had eaten sparingly, drunk little, watched the girls with less than full attention. He had leaned away from the Tokugawa throughout the meal, except when actually engaged in conversation, and his gaze drifted, time and again, perhaps looking for reassurance, to the men who had accompanied him from Osaka, to Ishida Norihasa and Ono Harufusa.

But now the tea was served, and the end was in sight. Iyeyasu sipped, and gazed at the boy over the rim of his red lacquered bowl. 'This has been the most memorable night of my life, Toyotomi no-Hideyori. I had truly thought that I would go to my grave without ever again seeing the son of my oldest, my dearest friend. Had only your charming mother been able to make the journey to Kyoto with you, then would my happiness have been complete.'

'I can but repeat my mother's apologies, my lord Iyeyasu,' Hideyori said.

'Of course. Yet is much of her indisposition caused by her mistrust of me.'

'My lord . . . '

'And so I would have you tell her, Toyotomi no-Hideyori, that her fears are groundless. Have you been shown the slightest discourtesy here, the slightest cause for suspicion?'

'You have treated my lords and myself with the utmost courtesy, my lord Iyeyasu.'

'Have I not caused your father to be deified? Is not his monument the most splendid in Japan?'

'I am grateful, my lord Iyeyasu. I would have you know that. Perhaps my mother feels too old to undertake such a journey.'

'What journey? It is scarce thirty miles from Osaka Castle to Kyoto. And old? The Princess Asai Yodogimi? Now that I cannot believe.'

Hideyori smiled. 'And you would be right, my lord Iyeyasu. My mother is ageless, and so is her beauty.'

'Such beauty.' Iyeyasu sighed. 'She has been turned against me by the Portuguese priests.'

'My lord?'

'Oh, I am aware, Toyotomi no-Hideyori, of how the priests regard Osaka as even more of a refuge for them than Nagasaki.'

'Indeed they are welcome there, my lord. Not only because they are subject to so much abuse, and indeed, persecution, throughout the empire, since you withdrew your protection over them, but because I seek knowledge of the West, because they have much to teach us, about literature and art, about politics, and of course about religion.'

'And about warfare, and the use of firearms,' Iyeyasu remarked.

Hideyori inclined his head. 'That too, my lord Iyeyasu. Warfare, and the use of firearms, is but another aspect of politics, is it not?'

Iyeyasu glanced at the boy. 'You would wish to increase the trade with Portugal?'

'I would wish to have the trade with Portugal continue, my lord, for the benefit of us all. As you would have us trade with Holland.'

Again the quick glance. 'You are as well informed as I, Toyotomi no-Hideyori. I but sought Holland as a nation with whom we could trade, because although your father came to an agreement with the Portuguese, no ship from Lisbon has visited our shores for five years.'

'They have domestic problems, my lord. So the priests tell me. But is Holland any more anxious to deal with Japan? Is it not some five years since you sent the Dutchmen Quaeckernaeck and Zandvoort to Siam?'

Iyeyasu nodded. 'And Zandvoort brought me back assurances.'

Hideyori permitted himself another smile. 'But no ships. And no guns, my lord Iyeyasu. The Europeans are careless when it comes to matters of their word. But there is no cause for us to despair of their contact. The priests tell me, with some misgivings, that the greatest of European nations is now extending its activities into our waters. Or at least those close to the south.'

Iyeyasu frowned. 'I had not heard of this.'

'Nonetheless, my lord, it will soon be so. The priests have explained it to me at great length. For it seems that Spain and Portugal were each promulgators of expeditions to discover new lands for trade, a century ago, and for fear that their navies would meet and fight, they appealed to the Mikado of all Europe, the one known as the Pope, for a judgment in the matter, and he in turn divided the world between them, the Spaniards to have the place known as America, and the Portuguese to have the nations they call of the East, which is to say, Cathay and the

Spice Islands, and Japan.'

'How arrogant, these people, and their Pope,' Iyeyasu remarked.

'Indeed, my lord, but yet useful.'

'And now you say the Spaniards are entering these waters? How can this be so?'

'Why, my lord, a new Pope and a new appeal has cancelled the other. As you will know, they have in any event long been established in the Ladrones. The Spaniards, my lord, are feared by all. Even, I would say, by your Englishman. They are the Chinese of Europe.' He smiled at Iyeyasu's frown. 'They are wealthiest of all, my lord. And they have the most firearms.'

Iyeyasu nodded. 'Perhaps, with the Spaniards, we had best be cautious, Toyotomi no-Hideyori. Perhaps they will approach our shores not as supplicants, but as conquerors.'

'And will we not throw them back into the ocean as we did the Mongols?'

'Undoubtedly,' Iyeyasu agreed. 'Yet would it be best for all the many factions in our country to bury their differences, and compose themselves to look outwards. I have thought long on this matter, Toyotomi no-Hideyori. I loved your father like a brother. His sister was my wife for the greater part of my life. And I have always loved you as a son. Is not your own sister married to the Shogun? Our families should be as one, Toyotomi no-Hideyori. Not in opposition to each other.'

'Your words are to my spirit as the first cherry blossoms in the spring, my lord Iyeyasu.'

'I am pleased that you feel so. There is but one stumbling block between us; the mistrust your mother feels for me.'

'My lord, I do assure you . . . '

'Assurances count for nothing, Prince Hideyori, beside deeds. Fortunately, I have hit upon a way for us truly to end our differences. Forever.'

Hideyori waited, his face politely composed.

'My dear wife,' Iyeyasu said. 'Your own aunt, for so many years the comfort of my bed, has rejoined her ancestors.'

'I had heard, my lord, and grieved.' But the boy's eyes were watchful.

'And so you see me, Prince Hideyori, a lonely old man, beset with the problems of empire, with the intrigues and hatreds that always surround one who rules. Of which the largest is the difference between our two factions. Were that resolved, were the Princess Asai Yodogimi to consent to come to my bed . . . '

'My lord?'

'As wife, Hideyori. I would pay her the greatest honour possible to any woman.'

'You see my mother as your wife, Prince Iyeyasu?'

Iyeyasu's head came up. 'You find this amusing?'

The young man smiled. 'My lord, I find the thought of my mother's reaction to your proposal, amusing. Asai Yodogimi, wed to Tokugawa no-Iyeyasu? Forgive me, my lord.' He began to laugh.

The room fell silent, and within a few seconds even the boy's high-pitched, slightly nervous giggle subsided. Every man present gazed at Iyeyasu.

The prince smiled. 'As you say, Prince Hideyori; an amusing suggestion. At least, while we laugh together, we shall not fight. I must think of other, and better ways, to keep us amused.'

The two boys undressed the prince, slowly and carefully. They themselves wore only their kimonos, with their girdles already loosed. It was their business to be ready for whatever their master might require of them. But this night he was preoccupied, wrapped himself in his sleeping kimono, and himself tied his girdle, and waved them away as the screen slid aside and Hidetada entered, accompanied by Kosuke no-Suke. 'A successful evening, my lord father,' the Shogun remarked, taking his seat on the dais.

'Yet my lord does not look pleased.' Suke knelt on the lower level.

Iyeyasu clapped his hands, and the two youths served green tea. 'This boy has all these years been represented to me as a buffoon. His mind is as sharp as my own.'

'Yet he is but a boy, my lord,' Hidetada said.

'And that concerns me more than anything. He is eighteen years of age. When I was eighteen I fought on the field of Okehazama, with Oda Nobunaga and Toyotomi Hideyoshi, and none of us doubted then that we had set our feet on the path to Kyoto. But because I was eighteen and they were each some ten years older, they feared me most, even then. I had the youth, the energy . . . and I had the time.'

'Then, my lord,' Suke began.

Iyeyasu waved his hand, and the two boys performed the kowtow and left the room. 'There can be no alternative to war.

And this is *your* war, Hidetada. The fate of you and your children will depend upon it.'

'I know that, my lord father. Could we but lure the Toyotomi from their stronghold . . .'

'That we shall never do, except under solemn assurances of faith.'

'But to besiege Osaka, my lord,' Suke said. 'That is an immense project.'

'For which we must prepare. And for more than that. We must prepare a pretext, so that when the siege takes months, or perhaps even years, the daimyo who ride with us will have no weakening of resolve. The Toyotomi must be in the wrong.'

'Yes, my lord,' Suke said, frowning.

'And we must arm ourselves as well as they. They seek cannon.'

'The Portuguese will give them nothing,' Hidetada said contemptuously.

'Do not be sure of that, my son. The priests well know your hatred for them, and they would prefer to see Hideyori as ruler of Japan. In any event, the boy's mind roams elsewhere. We must beat him to the Spaniards. Suke, I wish you to visit Anjin Miura.'

'My lord?'

'He has been in retirement long enough. He is trustworthy, and he knows these Europeans.'

'He is also proud, as are all Europeans. The man Kimura reports to me that he spends much time brooding and smiles only when with his children.'

'He is angry because I have withdrawn my favour, in his eyes. Remind him that as he still lives, and prospers, that too is by my favour. And tell him that now I would see him climb back into my affection. You will require him to undertake a mission for me, to the Ladrone Islands, to see these Spaniards.'

'You would send Anjin Miura from Japan, my lord?'

'He will come back,' Iyeyasu said. 'He smiles in the presence of his wife as well as his children, Kimura tells *me*, and he will leave them behind him. Besides, there is nothing for him in the West any longer.'

'You would trust him with a diplomatic mission?' Hidetada asked. 'A man who has already failed you, by virtue of his impetuosity and romantic desires? Those are not the qualities of a diplomat. And now even his courage is in question.'

'Not to me, my son. And now he will be older, and wiser,

and who knows, he may even be able to persuade the Dutch to come as well.'

'The Dutch,' Hidetada said angrily. 'The Spaniards. The Portuguese. It grieves me, my lord father, to hear you suggest that we are dependent upon the goodwill of such foreigners, such barbarians, upon their insidious doctrines and their haughty demeanours. I say cast them out. Destroy all foreign influence here in Japan. Execute the priests. Let us turn our back on the West. Osaka is not that impregnable. Oda Nobunaga took it.'

'Forty years ago Osaka was a monastery,' Iyeyasu said. 'Ishida Norihasa and the Ono brothers are not monks; they are professional soldiers. And do not forget that Hideyoshi increased the defences of the castle, and made it into the strongest fortress in the empire. And once we call our allies to the field, my son, we cannot afford to fail. Suke, you will leave for Miura at daybreak.'

PART FOUR

The Shogun

Chapter 1

THE SUN, rising slowly out of the east, flooded first of all the outer walls of the house on the headland, and then cascaded into the yard, across the porch and through the windows. It filled the bedrooms, glinted from the tatami mats, bathed the small, pale face. It was a welcome sun, after more than a week of storms and rains; there had been damage enough without. But now the skies were clear and the sun could shine. On Shikibu the magnificent.

Will sat up, his heart pounding. And today the sun itself was exciting. Because it promised to be an exciting day. The most exciting day for a long time. More exciting even than the sudden reappearance of Suke at the gate, two years ago now. That had been the signal that his crimes were forgiven. Almost. Providing he was still the man he had been, to the prince. The man of fortune. *That* day had been exciting enough. For five long years he had rowed across the bay, firstly to finish and then merely to inspect, the two ships which were his gifts to Japan. Unwanted gifts, because the man himself had been unwanted. Ships which had ridden to their moorings, and done nothing more than that, nor ever would, it seemed. Until that day, when he had been told to select a crew, and sail south, for Manila. On that day, he had come alive again. And Shikibu had wept.

He threw aside the covers, got up, walked on to the porch. Around him the mountains seemed to stretch forever, shrouded in cloud above the green of their lower slopes. So clear was the day he almost thought he could see Mount Aso. Aso rumbled continuously. And no man could tell when it would again erupt, just as no man could tell when the earth would again shake and the streets open. This was Japan, a way of life and a community with death, which pervaded all levels of society, was perhaps responsible for the aggression of the samurai no less than for the resignation of the eta. A way of living next to the grave, which gave life itself purpose, and made reflections upon what one might encounter in the afterworld so much wasted anticipation. A way of life to be admired, by Anjin Miura, at any rate.

A way of life symbolised by the perfect cone of Mount Fuji,

the guardian Fujiyama, rising behind the house, above the hills of Hakone. A mountain which meant as much to him as any Japanese, now, because it was the mountain he looked for, when returning. His mountain. How strange that this should be so. He had made two voyages south to Manila, and Siam, and the Spice Islands. On either of those voyages he could easily have replaced his Japanese crews with Europeans and continued on his way, across the Indian Ocean and round the Cape of Storms. Perhaps, on the first occasion, he had been tempted. While sailing south. Not after reaching Siam, to meet a disillusioned Melchior, to listen to the Dutch prattling about their political and religious problems, to learn how even Jacob had never returned to Europe, but instead had taken service in the Indies, and died within the year, fighting the Spaniards in the Ladrones. What a waste of time. What a waste of a man. No such waste for Will Adams. More than seven years ago he had written letters to be delivered in England, and Melchior assured him that they had, at the least, been forwarded from Siam. But never an answer, from his own folk. So, Will Adams was dead.

Of all those five hundred men, not one still lived, as a European. Even Melchior had returned to Japan, taken as wife a charming girl from Edo and accepted an income from the prince, as Will's assistant. But not, remarkably, a Japanese name.

What *had* brought the lad back? Not the quest for a fortune certainly. But there was a mystical greatness about the place, or, to be more precise, an absence of littleness, which reached out and touched the chords of a man's heart. When nature felt unkind, in Japan, it destroyed, utterly. When men fought, in Japan, it was to the death. And when women loved, in Japan, it was with the last quivering fibres of their bodies. He could no longer consider it heaven, because of the innate savagery which lay just beneath the surface. He could never think of it as hell, because of the sheer excitement of belonging to such a community. Purgatory? But purgatory was a grey pleasureless place. Japan was unique. What had Tadatune said to him, that first day in Bungo? 'With a sword in his hand and a knowledge of how to use it, there is nothing a man may not achieve.'

Then he had made the mistake of smiling to himself at such an unChristian principle. A mistake. The world had been laid at his feet, and he had sought to grasp it, without the sword being in his hand. Even on that dreadful day of the earthquake, had he had the knowledge of how to use a sword, and killed Norihasa, all would have been forgiven. He no longer doubted this. To the samurai, his disobedience of Iyeyasu's command counted as nothing beside the fact that the prince had had to hurry himself to extricate him from a perilous situation, as one might hasten to save a woman or a child. There was the true cause of his banishment from the court. And of what use to say, afterwards, now I can fight the man with every chance of success? Now I have been trained in the art of swordsmanship by Shimadzu no-Tadatune, himself the greatest duellist in the empire. For what purpose? Norihasa was again securely locked away within the walls of Osaka Castle, and Anjin Miura had been banished to his home and Sagami Wan. The blood feud remained unassuaged but it was Keiko who was dead, not one of Norihasa's servants.

And Magdalena? She had saved his life, to the destruction of her honour, and to some physical risk as well. Had that been love? He would never know. He had adopted the Japanese way and put her from his mind. The only way. For one crowded morning she had been his, the most beautiful object he had ever seen. He had worshipped at her body. Had *he* loved *her*? What was love, then? A purely physical desire, an eruption of the penis? Surely there had to be more to it than that. He had married Mary Hine to satisfy his penis. He had ruined his career to satisfy his body's demand for Magdalena. But there was no love in that. Love lay behind him on the mat. Still a girl, small, neat, utterly beautiful, utterly loyal, utterly willing. A girl, although a mother twice over. The love also came from Joseph and Susanna. How could he ever leave *them*? And the love came, not only from his family, but from Melchior and his wife, and from Kimura and Asoka and all the inhabitants of Miura.

But it was a love which carried a responsibility. Not only never to betray them again, but yet to avenge Keiko's death. This was the only cloud upon his horizon. Until that was done, there could be no peace for Anjin Miura, and now that he had at last been summoned to Shidzuoka, the fulfilment of that duty loomed so much closer. But to do that, what might it not involve? He did not think that to see Magdalena again would affect him. His own death?

His own death. There was the point. Was he, then, a coward? He did not think so. He was a man of peace. In Japan the two words were synonymous. There was the Christian in him. He had been happy, being once more at sea, standing on the poop deck of a ship he not only captained but had actually built with his own hands. He had felt her hull move through the waves to his bidding; the wind might fill the sails, but he had commanded how those sails should be set, and he had plotted the course they took through the water. And now, somewhere across the ocean, in Acapulco or even beyond, was his other ship. What a strange business that had been, in every way. Strange that Will Adams, shipmaster, of Gillingham, Kent, should have undertaken a peaceful voyage to the Ladrones, to call upon the Spaniards. Strange that they should have accepted him, rather than handed him straight over to the Inquisition. But then, they had accepted him, not as Will Adams, but as Anjin Miura, hatamoto in the service of the great prince, Tokugawa Minamoto no-Iyeyasu.

Accepted him, and yet ignored him. Polite words, polite interest, in Japan. At the time. He had imagined then that the Adams' star was in decline. That that fortune which had so intrigued Iyeyasu had fled, and so left him nothing more than an ordinary man. And at that time he had been unconcerned. He had had Miura to return to, and he had had his own business interests, now that he had gained access to the rich markets of the south, to occupy his time.

And he had been wrong. The Spaniards might indeed have been disinterested, at that time. But then had come the business of the Acapulco galleon, driven from her course by a succession of storms and at last wrecked off the coast of Bungo. Thirty-odd men of her crew had drowned, but more than three hundred had been saved. And amongst them had been the viceroy himself, retiring to Spain, Don Rodrigo Vivero y Velasco.

What fortune. A busy time for Anjin Miura, travelling first of all south to meet and renew his acquaintance with the viceroy, and then escorting him north to Edo, for a meeting with the Shogun. Out of that had come something close to friendship, as the great Don had discovered in Japan much of the fascination that the English seaman had always felt. And the result? Promises of ambassadors, and the loan of the larger of Anjin Miura's two ships, renamed the *Santa Buenaventura* for the occasion. Where was she now, he wondered?

Even then he had not been allowed into Iyeyasu's presence. The prince had preserved his mark of disfavour, and Will had been treated like any other dignitary. But the fortune that Iyeyasu wanted, having once again shown its face, had then clustered thick and fast. Another year, and the Dutch ship they had awaited for so long had entered Nagasaki Harbour. The goods the Hollanders had brought had been worthless, to be sure, but they had come and they would come again. They had left an embassy as a token of *their* interest, had delivered letters from their stadholder to the prince, promising a regular trading vessel, even though they had brought nothing for Will Adams.

Forgotten in England. But not in Japan, now. For the waiting was over . . . Yesterday had come the summons to Shidzuoka. So then, he was again grasping at the pinnacle of worldly success. What business had he with blood feuds? What business had he with taking life?

Shikibu's eyes were open, and her hands closed on the empty bedclothes. He knelt beside her. 'I did not mean to wake you.'

'I have scarcely slept,' she said. 'I have lain here, feeling you against me, knowing you were there, my lord. For a last time.'

'Do you suppose I will not return?'

How serious her eyes. They seemed to stretch forever into her mind. A timeless mind, the inside of which he had never even glimpsed, much less possessed. Perhaps he had never tried hard enough. Perhaps now was the time.

'Supposing one could tame an eagle,' she said. 'But then, no one can tame an eagle. So perhaps the eagle comes to one, lamed and wishing shelter, because he is handsome, and strong, and capable of flying through the air. But there comes a moment, my lord, when the eagle is again well, and must be released.'

'I am no eagle, Shikibu.' His fingers slid down her back, so deep curved, so strong for all its slimness. She had all the strength of Pinto Magdalena, as she had proved often enough in satisfying his desires.

His desires. How senseless to dream, when here in his hand was all the reality any man could ever wish, all the passion, all the acquiescence, all the humility and yet all the pride, all the submission and yet all of the power, as well. And none of the danger. But there was the truth of the matter.

'But you will sail again, my lord,' she said. 'Now that you have regained the favour of the prince, there will be other missions for you. You will be away from your home for many long periods.'

'I know not, Shikibu. I know not. I know not whether I *have* yet regained the favour of the prince.' His hands curved on her buttocks, brought her body against his. Last night they had sated themselves, and yet he hungered. Her crotch worked against his, her mouth sagged open in the latent desire he had come to know so well, and the screen door at the foot of the room began to edge back.

Will sat up, and Shikibu rolled away from him. 'I shall beat them and send them away, my lord.'

'No. I have seen too little of them as well.' The screen was wide and the two children stood there. Joseph was seven, strangely European in feature, with streaks of lightness in his hair, like Magdalena, and yet utterly Japanese in the smallness of his frame. Susanna was but five, already possessing the diminutive grace of her mother. And the endless loveliness of her features, as well. Shikibu had named them both; although a believer in the Shinto way, with the strange ambivalence which seemed not to bother these people in the slightest, she had listened to the priests, and these names she thought would please her lord. As they did. Joseph and Susanna. Joseph's hair was already shaved, for he also would be a samurai. For that ceremony, too, Tadatune had come to Miura, where Suke had not. But Suke was above all else the creature of the prince. Shimadzu no-Tadatune was a Satsuma, and the Satsuma followed their own bidding. And Tadatune was his friend. Now and always. In a way not even Melchior could equal.

Intrigue, deceit, gossip, confusion, there was as much of it in Japan as ever in England. Only in Japan he was a part of it. Anjin Miura. The man with the guns. The man who had gained the victory of Sekigahara. So some said. Who had fought against Ishida Norihasa, but not to the death. The man at once loved and despised, it was said, by the prince. All true. All true. And because of it, even now the future must remain clouded.

'Come in,' he said. 'Do not spend the day skulking there.'

The two children crossed the floor, slowly, timidly. They could see their mother's anger. Shikibu had also sat up, and now formed a small black-haired ball, her arms clasped around her knees. This was European custom, not Japanese. The children should not be allowed in their parents' bedchamber, except on a ceremonial occasion.

Will folded one in each arm, hugged them to his chest, kissed them on the cheeks. Shikibu gazed at the trio.

'What will you be when you grow up?' he asked Joseph.

'A pilot, father. Like you.'

'And will you sail across the oceans?'

'Of course, father. Like you. I too will sail to Siam.'

'Siam,' Susanna said. Now, where had she heard that word? Or had it been mentioned so often during his absence? He glanced at Shikibu, and she turned her head away.

'Tell me about Siam, father,' Joseph begged.

'I shall. In time. Truly it is a wondrous place. There is more gold there than you could possibly imagine. And elephants.'

'I have seen a picture of an elephant,' Joseph said.

'Mythical beasts,' Shikibu muttered.

'Real beasts, Shikibu. I have seen them. Oh, there are many wonders in Siam. Perhaps one day I shall take you there, Joseph. All of you,' he hastily added.

Shikibu knelt, began to fold the bedclothes. 'Travel, seafaring, is man's work, my lord.'

'In Japan. In my country, women also travel. If I would have it so, then it shall be so.'

'Providing the prince also will have it so, my lord.'

She was still angry, and in her own way poking fun at him. So he would poke fun back at her.

'All things, Shikibu, are in the lap of the gods. Are they not?'

She gave him another of her fathomless stares, for a very long minute, and then clapped her hands above the children. 'It is time for your food. Hurry now. And then to school. Asoka will take you. Hurry now.'

They gave squeals of feigned terror and rushed from the room.

'They are sweet children, Shikibu,' Will said. 'As we say in my country, they will be the comfort of my old age.'

Shikibu, her own bedding stored in the wall cupboard, knelt beside him in turn. His hands closed on her arms, slipped up to her shoulders.

'The time is past, my lord,' she said. 'The day is upon us.'

'Can I not spend at least this morning upon my couch? With my wife? I can still reach Shidzuoka by night.'

'There is a time for all things, my lord. The day is for work. Have you not known me a thousand, perhaps a million times? Can a few hours be so desperate a time?'

'Yes,' he said. 'Yes, when I am consumed with passion for you.'

She looked over his shoulder. 'Kimura comes.'

'Oh, God damn Kimura into hell.' But he turned, for he had

spoken in English and could now smile at his faithful steward.
'Good day to you, Kimura.'

'It is a good day, my lord.' Kimura bowed. 'And Melchior
Zandvoort awaits you outside. The horses are ready.'

Will turned. Shikibu stood in the doorway. She had not tied
her girdle and held her sleeping kimono closed with her hands.
'Fortune ride with you, my lord,' she said. 'Return soon. And
bring me good news of the prince.'

By which she meant, bring her news that you are restored to
favour, and thus to the full rights of a samurai. And to the
responsibilities, as well? Eight years, and Shikibu had not
forgotten, or forgiven, the wrong she conceived done to her lord.
Faithful Shikibu.

Eight years. How long a time. Edo had no scars left to show.
The city had been rebuilt. The towers and pagodas once again
reached for the sky; the rivers flowed as sluggishly as ever
towards the bay; the air smelt sweet and the people were as
busily concerned as ever with the matter of living.

Shidzuoka lay to the south, even farther south than Miura,
and had been unaffected by the shock. Here the building had
gone on unabated since the day Iyeyasu had chosen it for his
summer resort. Now the great fortress loomed above the town
like a protective mother goddess.

And here, too, was all the hustle and bustle of an imperial
court, even if the prince had now officially been in retirement
for seven years. Suke met them almost as soon as they entered
the inner court. 'Will. Welcome to Shidzuoka. It has been too
long. And Melchior. Well met, friend. A great day, Will. A
great day. There is an ambassaor from the famous King Philip
himself. A man called Sotomayor. He seeks a formal treaty of
friendship with our people. Is not that great news, Will?'

'Indeed, it is, Suke. And the prince?'

Suke smiled. 'Waits for you, Will. After all these years. But
then I do not think he was ever truly angry with you. He but
wished to appear so. And now that the time has come to deal
with these Spaniards, he wishes you by his side. Come.'

He led the two Europeans along the gallery. Here there waited
dozens of courtiers, hoping for an audience with the prince, or
perhaps having followed the Shogun from Edo. And here too
were the Hollanders, all the way from Nagasaki.

'Captain Adams.' Meinheer Specx was a short, anxious man,

perpetually wringing his hands. 'This is sad news. Sad news.'

'Sad news, meinheer? And good day to you, Meinheer Segerszoon.'

The other Dutchman, taller than his companion, with a long, thin face, nodded. 'And to you, Captain. Meinheer Zandvoort, well met. What are we to do about this Don?'

'Do, gentlemen?' Will inquired. 'Why, sirs, it is in Japan's interest to trade with Spain. I imagine the Don will be welcomed.'

'And is it in *our* interest, Captain?'

'If you suffer, it will be at your own door that you must lay the blame. Time and again I have told you what it is the prince wishes from Europe, but you persist in bringing him your glass mirrors and your timepieces, your bales of worthless cloth and your knick-knacks. When will you learn, meinheer, that Japan is no Africa, but a civilisation in many ways in advance of your own.'

'By God, sir, your words amaze me,' Specx declared. 'Are you not of the reformed faith? This Sotomayor is a Papist. More, he represents all the evil power of Spain, against which our two peoples have fought for too long.'

'Your people, Meinheer Specx. *My* people have not yet fought the Spaniards, nor need they ever do so, at this distance.'

'By God,' Specx declared. 'By God.'

'And yet,' Segerszoon remarked, with a glance at Suke, 'your own prince seems to prefer the Protestant to the Roman view of Christianity. Is it true that he commanded the daimyo of Arima to attack the Portuguese great ship?'

'That is so, Master Segerszoon. With small profit to anyone. But you would be in error to suppose he acted on religious grounds. Unlike you in Europe, those are the very least of the prince's motivations. He acted to prevent the Portuguese cargo, which was reported to be firearms and powder, from reaching the Toyotomi faction in Osaka.'

'And that the report was accurate, honourable gentlemen,' Suke pointed out, 'was proved when the galleon caught fire and blew up. They say the noise was louder than that made by a volcano.'

'Ah, bah,' Specx said. 'These petty princelings and their eternal quarrels.'

'You would do well to watch your tongue, sir,' Will reminded him. 'Seeing that you stand in the palace of one of these petty princelings, as you call him, and remembering that the prince, with a wave of his hand, can summon armies greater than those of Spain and Austria put together. Now, sirs, you will excuse us. My master is waiting.'

'But you will do your best for us, Captain Adams,' Segerszoon said anxiously. 'Meinheer Zandvoort, we implore you in the name of our common heritage.'

'Be sure, Meinheer Segerszoon,' Melchior said, 'that Captain Adams and myself will do what is best for Japan, and in that you may repose your confidence.'

The council chamber, a room of forty tatami, was crowded with kneeling dignitaries, amongst whom were to be seen several Spanish gentlemen, resplendent in brilliant velvet doublets and satin hose, glancing around them with a strange mixture of interest and apprehension. The prince sat on the dais at the end of the room, with the Shogun at his elbow, and immediately in front of him stood the tall figure of Don Nuno de Sotomayor.

Will sighed, for clearly difficult times were ahead. He had found the viceroy, Vivero y Velasco, a surprisingly easy man to know and to like, a man eager to learn about Japan and to fall in with local custom. But Sotomayor not only remained standing, utterly incongruous in a room filled with kneeling men, but he had insisted upon retaining his sword, and rested his hand upon the hilt in a most ostentatious manner.

Iyeyasu's face however, remained as blandly contented as ever, although Hidetada wore a frown. Now the prince clapped his hands, and Will and Suke went forward, leaving Melchior to take his place amongst the nobles.

Will performed the kowtow, Suke at his elbow. How painfully his heart pounded. How many times had he done this, and felt like this? And for how long had he waited to do this again? Suke might suppose the prince used his anger as a tool. But not for eight years, and not where his Anjin Miura was concerned. Iyeyasu *had* been angry. Too angry for a mere indiscretion. There was jealousy here. For a man to take a wife, this was good, in order to make his home a happy one, and to provide children to bear his name into the future. For a man to take a lover, when the greatest in the land had offered him that favour and been rejected . . . in many ways it was a miracle that he had not been invited to perform seppuku.

'Anjin Miura,' Iyeyasu said. 'Anjin Miura is my adviser on foreign affairs, my lord Sotomayor.'

The Spaniard looked down, his features contemptuous. 'The Englishman.' he said. 'I have heard much of you, Englishman.'

'I am flattered, my lord.'

'And do you not feel it demeaning for a European and a Christian, of whatever apostasised faith, to kneel before a heathen potentate?'

'No, my lord. Nor would I think it detrimental to your own dignity were you to do so. I would also advise it, if I am to be of much service here.'

Sotomayor gazed at him for a moment, and then turned back to Iyeyasu. 'If we may now proceed to business, Prince Iyeyasu,' he said in halting Japanese. 'I have the text of the document you agreed with Don Rodrigo y Velasco.'

Iyeyasu inclined his head.

'This sets out a joint declaration between the viceroy and yourself to protect all Christian priests in Japan, and secondly to work for an alliance between Spain and Japan, and thirdly to suppress all Dutch pirates.'

Iyeyasu inclined his head.

'Nothing was said at that time, Prince Iyeyasu, regarding the destruction of the Portuguese, here in Japan. And yet I learn that a Portuguese ship was attacked and sunk in Japanese waters, only recently.'

'A sad affair,' Iyeyasu remarked. 'A combination of several errors, my lord Sotomayor. It was so long since the Portuguese last sent a ship to our shores that we assumed *her* to be the pirate. In any event, we understood the Spanish to be the rivals of the Portuguese in these waters.'

'Rivals, Prince Iyeyasu, but not to the point of bloodshed,' Sotomayor said seriously. 'Both of our peoples are far more certain where our true enemies lie, in the countries of England, and Holland.'

Iyeyasu nodded. 'I have heard this. Now I would hear your viceroy's proposals for making a definitive treaty with my country.'

Sotomayor unfolded another length of parchment. 'The clauses are but four in number, Prince Iyeyasu, that they be more clearly understood by us all. Clause One: That as friends, and allies, of the Mikado, and people of Japan, the Spanish shall be allowed to build as many and such vessels in Japan as are needed.'

Iyeyasu glanced at Will.

'I shall be happy to assist the Spanish in this matter, my lord prince,' Will said. 'The more ships that are built, the more trade can we expect with Spain.'

'It is so,' Iyeyasu said.

Sotomayor glanced at Will in turn, and now half addressed him. 'Clause Two: Spanish pilots are to be permitted to survey Japanese harbours, with a view to the preparation of proper charts of these waters, to prevent further shipwrecks.'

'This is also greatly to our advantage, my lord prince,' Will said. 'Proper charts of Japanese waters, providing they are made available to our seamen as well, will be of great benefit to our sailors.'

'They shall be made available to the Japanese,' Sotomayor agreed.

'Then it shall be so,' Iyeyasu said.

'Clause Three: The Shogun . . . ' he gave a glance to Hidetada, 'will forbid the Dutch to trade or enter into these waters, and the Spanish navy will seek out and destroy all Dutch ships discovered within reach of Japanese harbours.'

Iyeyasu gazed at Will, and Will returned his gaze without speaking.

'You mentioned four clauses, honourable sir,' Iyeyasu said.

'You have not yet signified your agreement to the Third Clause, Prince Iyeyasu.'

'You mentioned four clauses, honourable sir.'

Sotomayor hesitated, looked at Will, and then down at his parchment once again. 'Clause Four: Spanish ships are to be exempt from the search we understand is now carried out upon Dutch and Portuguese vessels when calling at Japanese ports.'

'I have agreed to the first two clauses in your paper,' Iyeyasu said. 'This is reason for great satisfaction, on both sides. Now I think we should celebrate. You will wish to withdraw, and . . . ' he gazed pointedly at the Spaniard's legs, 'rest yourself after standing for so long. But I should be honoured if you would attend a banquet with me this evening, my lord Sotomayor.'

'There are four clauses in the treaty, Prince Iyeyasu.'

'Of which I have agreed to two,' Iyeyasu said. 'My mathematics teacher will agree with me, I am sure, that that represents half of what has been asked for.'

'Half, my lord prince,' Will said.

'Which is a considerable achievement, my lord Sotomayor. Now, if you will excuse me . . . '

'I must insist, Prince Iyeyasu, that the other two matters are dealt with, immediately.'

Iyeyasu gazed at him for a moment, his face as impassive as ever. 'I shall excuse you from my presence, honourable sir,' he said. 'We shall meet again this evening, and then, no doubt, we shall discuss what goods your ships will bring to Japan in exchange for the privileges I grant them.'

Sotomayor glared at the prince, then at Hidetada, then at Will. Then he turned and left the chamber.

'Leave us,' Iyeyasu said. 'Except you, Anjin Miura.'

The room emptied, slowly. How had the clock turned back, Will thought, to the evening before Sekigahara. To the dawn of great things, then.

'You also, my son,' Iyeyasu said, gently, as Hidetada had not moved. 'I would have private words with my pilot.'

Hidetada rose to his feet and bowed to his father before leaving the room. He did not look at Will.

Iyeyasu clapped his hands, and a boy brought in a tray of saké. 'You handled yourself well,' he remarked. 'And I. We might have been speaking with each other every day for the last eight years.'

'I have, my lord, in my thoughts.'

Iyeyasu poured saké and held out the cup.

'I have waited many years for this, my lord prince,' Will said, and drank.

'Then embrace me, Will. Give me your arms.'

Will hesitated, and then mounted the dais itself, to kneel beside the prince. How small he was, he realised. And frail. He had never known how frail, before. As his arms went round the green silk kimono he might have been taking Joseph to his breast.

'Now sit beside me,' Iyeyasu said. 'There is still stiffness in your manner. In your body.'

'The stiffness, my lord, is in my heritage, not my affection for you.' He poured saké in turn, and the prince drank, gazing at him.

'And yet, you would be Japanese, Will. You have twice taken a ship from these waters. Each time you have returned, where each time I had thought to see you fly away.'

The same simile that Shikibu had used. Was it coincidence? Will stared into the small dark eyes. 'You expected me to, my lord?'

Iyeyasu's shoulders moved. 'I waited, certainly, to see what you would do, Will. And I will confess that you continue to surprise me. But perhaps that is why I love you. What thought you of Sotomayor?'

'My lord . . . '

'He conceives himself to be greater than he is. But I saw the same symptoms in their viceroy. Are all Spaniards cast in this mould?'

'In the main, my lord prince. They have better than a century of conquest and glory behind them.'

Iyeyasu nodded. 'One day, perhaps, Japan will enjoy such a period of success. And no doubt our people will become similarly arrogant.'

'My lord would be unwise to permit the Spaniards to have undisputed and unlimited access to Japanese harbours.'

'That I shall never do,' Iyeyasu said. 'You are sure your interest in this is not on behalf of your Dutch friends?'

'My interest is on behalf of Japan, my lord prince. But if I may make this point, Holland is a tiny country, hardly larger than one of your feudal fiefs, interested only in obtaining the best exchange they may for their goods. Spain is an empire already, and thrives on empire. She lays claim to an entire continent, not to mention untold lands in Europe itself. To her, Japan is but one more treasure to be added to her king's crown.'

Iyeyasu nodded. 'The years have not dimmed the force of your tongue, Will, nor the wisdom it utters. How I have managed without you at my side these last eight years amazes me.'

'My lord prince . . . '

Iyeyasu held out the filled cup. 'What is done is done, and is not a matter for discussion. Only the future concerns men who are still alive, Will. And our future now *is* alive, with hope, and endeavour. What thought you of that attack upon the Portuguese galleon?'

'I have no doubt my lord had a very good reason for his action,' Will said cautiously.

'It was an act of war, Will. You know the Portuguese governor of Macao put to death several Japanese sailors, but two years ago.'

'I had heard this, my lord, and was sorely grieved.'

'For the men, Will. They sailed my ship, and flew the banner of the golden fan beneath that of the rising sun. So they were

considered enemies of the Portuguese. So far have things pro-
gressed while you domesticated at Miura. Why, but a year gone
I was privileged to receive a visit from Father Paez, the one they
call the Vice-Provincial; we discussed many matters and agreed
on many matters, and I made the mistake of assuming that I
could deal with the man as I have so often dealt with you. And
what do you think he did? He left Shidzuoka and straightaway
made his way to Osaka, no doubt to report on everything that
was said to Hideyori and that whore of a mother of his. More,
it came to light that he was the founder of a plot to bring Portuguese armies to Japan, and impose Christianity upon my people
by force of arms. A wild, fanciful, impossible scheme, Will, but
nonetheless indicative of their thinking in Osaka. They prepare
for war, Will. I told you this would happen, eight years ago.
And all that time they have prepared for war.'

'And yet, my lord prince . . . '

'You have been in retirement for too long, Will. I know what
you would say, that Hideyori is a fool. Will, I will tell you this;
that boy has a brain as sharp as Hidetada's. I finally persuaded
him out of Osaka, three years ago. Why else do you think I sent
for you, then? I had Hideyori as my guest, in the Nijo Palace,
for a week, and we talked of many things. And that boy is no
fool. And now he prepares to fight for what he considers his
rights. And yet he is sufficiently intelligent to know that war
between the Toyotomi and the Tokugawa can only destroy
Japan. He would come to terms with me, I am sure. But his
mother drives him on. She is the great evil spirit of our time,
Will. She is dedicated to only one thing. Not the glory of her son.
Not the rule of the Toyotomi. Only my destruction. She hates
me with a consuming passion, Will. Why, in order to bring
some end to this faction, I even offered her my bed as my wife,
now that I am a widower. She, a widow of past forty, with the
instincts of a common urchin, as every man in Japan knows.
I offered her my bed, Will. And do you know what reply she
sent?'

'No, my lord.' Will gazed at the old man. By Christ, he thought.
Can it be?

'She replied that she would sooner spend the rest of her life
tied to a dog. Aye, Will; she said that. And so it shall be. When
Osaka falls, she shall spend the rest of her life, tied to a dog in
front of my house.'

An old man, consumed with passion for the one thing he had

never been able to possess. A terrifying thought, when the man held so much power, an entire nation, in his grasp. 'Once you said to me, my lord, that no woman was worth so much of a man's mind.'

Iyeyasu glanced at him. 'One woman, Will? Were she only that I would have forgotten her long ago. Oh, I will not deny the desire I feel for her, to you. You, of all people, Will, must know how capable she is of raising desire.'

'It is one of the events of my life that I most regret, my lord.'

'And why? Was it not one of the most memorable? But even then she was seeking only to use you. A woman like Yodogimi uses her body as a man might use his sword. So I shall make her surrender that body as a man might surrender his sword. Only thus can I break the power of the Toyotomi, Will. By breaking that woman.'

How strange, Will thought, that this man, so wise, so all seeing, so dominant, cannot understand his own nature. Cannot, or will not? Because, where his physical desires are concerned, only two people have ever dared to resist him. And so, he loves both of us, to distraction. 'I wonder at your patience in waiting so long, my lord prince.'

'Patience is my watchword, Will. Try as I might, these many years, I could not persuade the daimyo who supported the fan at Sekigahara to march behind me on Osaka. They remember Hideyoshi, too well, consider only that Hideyori will be his son, his true son. To fight them and Hideyori would be impossible. And so, I waited. I have waited all my life, for the right moment, for everything. And so, I have seen Asano Nagomasa into the grave, and Kato Kiyomasa, too. And this last month both Ikeda Terumasa and Asano Yukinaga have died. I have outlived them all, Will. Now I have only their sons, to whom Hideyoshi is no more than a name in a history book, to command. So now we may look upon Osaka with new eyes, Will. And do not forget that you have a personal interest in Osaka.'

'An affair I have spent these eight years trying to forget, my lord, as it brought me so much disgrace.'

'All the more reason for remembering, Will. Oh, the woman can be nothing, now. But Norihasa you must never forget, or the death of your servant. But still we shall not be hasty. I still need an excuse to go to war, finally. This is in hand. In your hands I place the necessaries of war. Cannon, Will. Bigger and better than even those carried by the *Liefde*. We will get them,

Will, whether from Holland or Spain or elsewhere, we will get them.'

Will bowed.

'You say nothing?'

'That I am, once again, speaking privily with my prince is all I ask.'

Iyeyasu nodded. 'Aye. I trust you, Will. I pray the years have given you discretion. Your wife is well?'

'Never better, my lord prince, nor more beautiful.'

'Now that is what I had hoped to hear. And your children?'

'They thrive, my lord.'

'You lack for nothing, down in Miura?'

'Now you have given me permission to voyage, my lord prince, I lack for nothing.'

'Aye. I have heard how you have set up in business for your own account. You would be both a merchant and a samurai. You, Will. No Japanese could do that, or indeed, would. And yet . . . have you no regrets? Do you never dream of your homeland?'

'Every man dreams, my lord prince.'

'You are piqued, perhaps, because you have never had a reply to your letters. Aye. I wonder if the Dutch may not have had a hand in that. Do you know the English have been trading with the Spice Islands these last two years?'

Will gazed at him, his heart leaping about his chest. 'I did not, my lord prince.'

'They have. And you have been acting on the Dutch behalf, here in Japan, for all those two years, with never a word of it to you. They are cunning people, the Dutch.'

'Indeed, they must be, my lord,' Will said thoughtfully. 'Perhaps . . . perhaps my lord prince would grant me permission to make another voyage.'

'Now why, Will, why?' Iyeyasu said. 'Why should the sun visit the stars, when assuredly the stars must eventually come to the sun?' He smiled, and almost laughed as he poured a cup of saké and held it out. 'There is an English ship in Nagasaki at this moment, Will. Go to them, in my name.'

Chapter 2

H OW CLEAR the sky, how brilliant the day. And how clouded his own vision. Will stood on the waterfront in Hirado and gazed at the ship, at the longboat approaching him with unmistakable sweeps of the oars. Unmistakably English, even had he been unable to see the red cross of St George drooping from her stern. Unmistakably English after fifteen years. God curse the tears which constantly welled into his eyes.

And what would *they* see? A tall figure in a blue kimono, his head shaved save for his topknot, and two magnificent swords in his girdle. Unmistakably Japanese?

'Five weeks she has been here, Anjin Miura,' said the daimyo at his elbow. 'Five weeks, and that wretched man I sent to find you lingered on the way.'

'I was with the prince at Shidzuoka, my lord Matsura,' Will explained. 'It is scarcely your messenger's fault that he first chose to search for me at Miura, and then at Edo.'

'Nonetheless, I have told the wretch that should he ever show his head in Hirado again, I will see it on a stick over my gateway,' Matsura promised. He puffed, and expanded his chest. In the last few years Hirado had blossomed from a tiny island on the remotest southern coast of Kyushu into the entry port for all Japan, because it was the nearest good harbour on the voyage from the south. Here was a Dutch factory and also a Portuguese one. And here, no doubt, the Spaniards would in time erect a factory as well. And the English?

The boat was coming alongside. 'You'll accompany me, my lord Matsura?'

The daimyo bowed. 'No, Anjin Miura. This is a European occasion. I shall be happy to entertain you at my home, when you have completed your business. The prince is well?'

'In excellent health, my lord Matsura.'

'The wonder of the age,' Matsura said reverently. 'Is he not past seventy years?'

'And ripe for another seventy, my lord. Now if you will excuse us . . . '

'My lord Matsura is right, Will,' Melchior said. 'This is not even a European affair, but an English one. Kimura and I will remain here. You are entitled to make this journey by yourself.'

Had they seen how close he was to tears, to being overwhelmed by the emotion bubbling in his belly?

'I thank you, dear friend,' Will said, and walked down the wooden dock.

There were eight sailors in the longboat, and a coxswain in the stern. 'No, no,' he said. 'We were told to look for an English gentleman.'

Will gathered the skirt of his kimono to step into the boat. 'You have found him.'

'Begging your pardon, sir,' the coxswain said hastily. 'I had not expected so strange a dress. Give way, lads. Give way.'

Will sat beside him, gave Melchior and Kimura a wave, and then turned to gaze at the ship as they approached. Unmistakably English. As they came closer, he saw her name was the *Clove*. Only the English, again, would choose such a prosaic title, and yet, so apt for a vessel trading in spices.

But what were they at now? For as he watched the decks he saw a great deal of activity, and a moment later a gun was run out.

'What, do they mean to fire into us?' he demanded.

The coxswain allowed himself a smile. 'Why, sir, you are to be greeted with the ceremony due to your rank.'

The cannon exploded, and then another, and then another. A three-gun salute, for William Adams, pilot major of Gillingham, Kent. Now he had to pretend the wind was too strong, and wipe it from his eyes. For now the boat was coming alongside, and above him was the ladder leading to the deck. Up which he must mount, hand over hand, to be assisted over the gunwale and face the assembled crew in the waist.

'By God, sir, but for your size I would suppose we had made a mistake. I am Captain John Saris, Master Adams, and I welcome you to the *Clove*.'

A tall, thin man, with a pointed beard, carefully clipped in the Elizabethan fashion, and cold blue eyes.

'My pleasure, Captain Saris.' Will held out his hand. 'I have waited overlong for this moment, sir.'

'I imagine you have,' Saris agreed. 'And this is my factor, Master Richard Cocks.'

Cocks was a smaller and altogether friendlier-looking man,

285

with a merry face and soft brown eyes. 'My pleasure, also, Master Adams, or should we call you captain?'

'My name, sirs, is Anjin Miura,' Will said.

'By God, sir,' Saris said. 'We had heard you were more Japanese than English. What might those words signify?'

'Why, the pilot from Miura, where I have my estate.'

'Your estate, sir? You'll take a glass?'

'Willingly, sir.'

Saris led him into the great cabin, followed by Cocks; the ship's boy was already setting out tankards of beer.

'Now there's a drink I have not tasted for too long,' Will said.

'We make our own,' Saris explained. 'Yet these are the last of the hops, and I fear they have done badly during the weeks we have sat here waiting for your coming.'

'It was unfortunate that I was with the prince on matters of importance,' Will said.

'Oh, no matter, no matter, Master Adams,' Saris said. 'I am well aware that you are a man of distinction in these parts.'

Sarcasm? Undoubtedly. The two men gazed at each other, and Will raised his mug. 'I give you a toast, sirs. The Queen.'

Saris stared at him for a moment, and then uttered a short laugh. 'Indeed, sir, you have been away from England for too long. The Queen has been dead these ten years. Our King is James, of Scotland.'

'You mean the Scots have conquered England?'

'By no means. We are become a dual monarchy. But the King has his throne in Whitehall. You'll drink to him?'

'Willingly.' Will took a long suck at the beer. How foul it tasted when compared with saké. 'I should be pleased if you in turn would toast the prince, Tokugawa Minamoto no-Iyeyasu.'

Saris glanced at Cocks, and shrugged.

'With pleasure, Master Adams,' Cocks said. 'Tokugawa Minamoto no-Iyeyasu. Difficult words, sir. But no doubt we shall find much that is strange here. And it is to you that we look for assistance in this matter, sir. You may imagine how overjoyed we were to learn that there was an Englishman living in this heathen land, and more, enjoying the favour of the king.'

Will sighed. 'As you say, Master Cocks, you have a great deal to learn. But I would know firstly how you came to hear of me. You have no letters for me?'

'Why, no,' Saris said. 'Should we have?'

'I had written . . . but no matter.' How heavy his heart, on a sudden. 'Then I must ask you for some information, regarding my wife and daughter.'

The two Englishmen exchanged glances. 'Why, Master Adams, we were unaware that you had close family in England,' Cocks said.

'Unaware? Then what of Master Nicholas Diggines of Limehouse? The merchant and shipbuilder.'

'Now, I have heard of Master Diggines,' Saris said. 'But I am afraid he also is dead these twelve years.'

'By Christ,' Will said. 'Then, sir, what of Thomas Best, or Nicholas Isaac? He had a brother, as I recall, by name of William.'

'I'm afraid, sir, that these names are strange to us,' Saris said.

'By Christ,' Will said again, and sat down. 'Indeed, sir, as you say, I have been away too long.' Too long. Too long. All gone. Not a face or a name left, and his own so unknown in England that they were not even aware he had a wife and family.

The two Englishmen were gazing at him. He squared his shoulders. 'You must forgive me, sirs. For the moment I was lost in considering the past. Now I must offer you my services.'

'For which we thank you, sir,' Saris said. 'The mayor of this place, the man Matsura, has very kindly rented me a house on shore for the transaction of business. My suggestion is that we should remove ourselves there, where perhaps we may enjoy a meal while we talk.'

'Willingly,' Will agreed, and got up.

'You'll order the boat, Master Cocks,' Saris said. 'Master Adams, I have heard you described as admiral to the ... Shogun?'

'That is so, Captain Saris.'

Saris smiled, coldly. 'No doubt in due course you'll permit us to inspect this gentleman's fleet. But we'll pay you the respect due to an admiral, by God. Instruct the gunner to fire a nine-gun salute, if you please, Master Cocks, as we leave. We'll let these people hear the sound of English cannon.'

All contempt? Now, why should that be so? Was it not just his own discontented spirit rising up from his belly? The salutes, the deference with which Saris and Cocks had treated him as they had landed had been patently false, but nonetheless surely intended to impress the crowd of onlookers no less than Matsura himself. And now this feast, at which the English sat so awkwardly on the floor, and regarded their saké and raw fish with all the suspicion that he himself, and Melchior, had shown at Bungo, so long ago? Now Melchior drank and talked with his hosts on the other side of the room, and the Japanese guests also looked at ease . . . but so did Saris. There was the difference. This man was no humble shipmaster.

As no doubt he meant to make clear. 'Adams, Adams,' he said. 'I must confess the name intrigued me when I heard tell of it, in Siam. I knew a Sir Joshua Adams, once. He was a friend of my father's. A Somerset man, as I recall.'

'I am not related to anyone from that county,' Will said.

'Ah. True, you have no trace of a West Country accent, and I would have supposed that would linger over even fifteen years in this place. Well, then, as I thought, you are one of the Adams from Essex. I know them well, by repute. Good farming stock, who will, it is said, be ennobled before long. Who knows, you may be of assistance to them in that achievement.'

'I know of no relations of mine in Essex,' Will said.

'No? Then indeed, sir, you are a man of mystery. Where does your family hold its estates?'

'My family has no estates, sir,' Will said. 'My father was a seaman, who lived in Gillingham, Kent. He died of the plague, as did my mother. I was apprenticed as a shipwright when I was but a lad, and my brother with me. He also is dead.'

'A shipwright, you say. By God, sir, you have done well for yourself.' Saris finished his cup of wine, poured himself another, and drank that too. 'Thin stuff. Thin stuff. Not the drink to warm a man's blood.'

'Excellent stuff, sir, as you call it,' Will said. 'To be savoured rather than swilled.'

Saris' head came up, and the two men gazed at each other. Then the captain smiled. 'No doubt I have a lot to learn, Master Adams. And I will be honest with you, sir, and say that I am impatient to be doing it. Five months is a long time to sit in this heat. I would talk with your king.'

'There is no king in Japan, Captain Saris.'

'Well, then, whatever his title. Shogun, eh? I would have words with the fellow. I bear him a letter from King James himself.'

'Then, sir, should you give me the letter, I will be pleased to convey it to him.'

'Give it to you, Master Adams? Give it to you? Why, by God, sir, my instructions were not to let it from my hand until I could place it in the hands of the King of Japan himself.'

'Then, sir,' Will said, 'you will wait here for a great deal longer than five months. No man may see the Shogun merely for the asking of it.'

'Sir, I would have you know that I am an ambassador, for England, your own country, and I will be put off by no upstart savage.'

'Upstart savage?' Will demanded. 'The prince, Captain Saris, is more of a monarch, more of an emperor, and more of a man, than any puling creature who ever sat upon the throne of England.'

'Treason,' Saris shouted. 'You speak treason, sir.' He struggled to his feet.

Will also got up. 'Sit down, man, or I'll carve you into steaks. Would you match that toothpick against this blade, these arms? As for treason, sir, I make no claim on England as my country. This is my country and right proud I am of it.'

The room was silent, as Japanese and Englishmen alike stared at the men.

'Come, Melchior, we shall take our leave of these gentlemen,' Will said. 'And perhaps tomorrow, when this *thin* wine has somewhat left their veins, we may discuss our business.'

Melchior also got up. 'But what ails you, man?' he asked in Japanese.

'Perchance I had forgotten,' Will muttered, 'how stiff-necked are my own people. How concerned they are with the doings of father and grandfather, rather than with man himself. How small and self-centred their outlook upon the world. How limited their horizons.'

Cocks had been whispering in Saris' ear, and now the captain was attempting to arrange his features in a smile, although he remained flushed with a combination of wine and passion.

'Come, come, Master Adams,' he said. 'I was hasty. By God, sir, I admire a man who stands up for the people who have treated him well. As for your remarks concerning King James, well, when you left England he was all but an enemy, and to be sure, there are many at home who experience difficulty in reconciling his head with the crown. Come, sir, I did not sail halfway around the globe to quarrel with a fellow countryman, and there's my hand on it.'

Will hesitated.

'Do not quarrel, Will, I beg of you,' Melchior whispered. 'The prince is himself in favour of this trade.'

'Very well, sir.' Will clasped the proffered hand. 'I shall be pleased to assist you in any way I may.'

'I expected nothing less, sir, and neither did my masters. To which end they have commanded me to present you with these small tokens of their esteem. And mine, to be sure.'

Cocks had left the room while they had been speaking, together with another of the factors. Now they returned with a tray of goods.

'For you, Master Adams, here are three rolls of good English cloth, a hat, a shirt, stockings, leather slippers, just in case you ever feel the urge to don a more Christian garb than your own, and even here, for your fireside, a Turkey carpet.'

'The man seeks to insult me,' Will muttered in Japanese.

'Yet you must acknowledge them,' Melchior said.

He nodded. 'Your generosity overwhelms me, Captain Saris. I regret that I have so little to offer in exchange. Perhaps . . . ' He felt in his girdle. 'This small box which contains a healing ointment of great benefit to cuts or abrasions which you may from time to time suffer.' It was a medicine Shikibu had insisted that he carry, always, for the sword cut on his belly had been slow to heal, although now no more than a mark on his flesh.

Saris took the box, slowly, glancing from it to the pile of goods on the floor, obviously comparing the respective monetary values of the gifts. 'I thank you, Master Adams,' he said at last. 'And now, may we offer you some more wine?'

'I must take my leave,' Will said. 'The hour is late.'

'But . . . I had anticipated you would spend the evening here. The night as well. And your servants.'

'Melchior Zandvoort is my friend, not my servant,' Will pointed out. 'As for Kimura, if you feel the need of an interpreter, he will be happy to remain and assist you. But I have already arranged to spend the night with my lord of Matsura. So I must beg you to excuse me.'

'But we'll meet again tomorrow?'

'No, sir,' Will said. 'Tomorrow I must pay a call upon the Portuguese factor here, to discuss certain matters of importance.'

'And the day after? Will you be free then?'

'The day after, sir, I must spend with the Dutch.'

'By God, sir, are you aware that the English and the Dutch are virtually in a state of war in these waters?'

'Not in *these* waters, Captain Saris. And it would be unwise for you to pursue the matter to that extremity while subject to Japanese law.'

'But we *will* talk with you again, Master Adams?' Cocks asked.

'Indeed, sir, I will be at your disposal in two days' time. And in the meanwhile I shall make the necessary arrangements for our journey to Edo and Shidzuoka, in order to introduce you to the prince. I will bid you good night, sirs.'

'By God, sir,' Saris declared. 'By God.'

The audience chamber was crowded, the air was hushed with expectancy. It had all happened before. Portuguese sea captains, Jesuit priests, Dutch shipmasters and Spanish dons had all stood or knelt where John Saris and Richard Cocks now knelt, discontentedly, to be sure, but obeying Will's instructions, as they perforce had had to obey his instructions regarding the actual delivery of the letter, and submit to the interpretations of Suke. But that was behind them now, and today they were to hear the Shogun's reply.

Will knelt immediately beside the dais on which Iyeyasu and Hidetada sat, Suke at his side. The prince had already clapped his hands for silence, and the dignitaries, amongst them more than one of the lesser daimyo from Osaka, hostages for the good conduct of their lord Hideyori, waited expectantly.

Will unfolded the parchment on which he had made the translation of the king's letter. '"James, by the Grace of Almighty God, King of Great Britain, France and Ireland, Defender of the Christian Faith, etc., etc., to the High and Mighty Prince, the Emperor of Japan, etc., Greetings.

'"Most High and Mighty Prince.

'"As there is nothing which increaseth more the Glory and Dignity of Sovereign Princes upon Earth than to extend their renown into far distant Nations; so having understood of late Years from some of our living subjects that had traded into divers Countries near adjoining unto Yours of the reputation and Greatness of your Power and Dominion, we have encouraged our said Subjects to undertake a Voyage into your Country, as well to solicit your Friendship and Amity with us, as to interchange such commodities of each others Countries as may be most of use one to the other; being nothing doubtful but such will be your Princely Magnanimity and Disposition as to be ready to embrace this our Desire, and not only to receive our People with your accustomed Benignity and Favour, but for their better Encouragement to afford them your royal protection for the settling of a factory there, with such security and Liberty of Commerce as shall be most convenient for the Advancement of the mutual Profit and Commodity of each others Subjects; wherein, for our Part, we do willingly offer ourselves and the liberty of our Kingdoms and Countries whensoever any of your subjects shall undertake to have communication with us. And so we pray to Almighty God to bless and prosper You and to make you victorious against your enemies. From our palace at Westminster this day of January, in the Eighth Year of our Reign over Great Britain, France and Ireland."'

Will paused, and the dignitaries nodded in assent and politely clapped their hands.

Suke handed him the second parchment.

'"Minamoto no-Iyeyasu of Japan replies to his Honour the Lord of England. By the naval envoy who had borne the fatigue of a long journey we have for the first time received a letter, from which we have seen that the Government of your honoured country as described on the paper preserves the right way. In particular I have received numerous presents of your productions, in which I esteem myself very fortunate. I will follow your proposals in respect of cultivating neighbourly feelings with my country, and maintaining mutual intercourse by merchant vessels. Though separated by ten thousand leagues of clouds and waves, our territories are, as it were, close to each other. I send some poor specimens of what this country affords, as enumerated in the accompanying list, as a slight token of respect. Spare yourself as the weather changes."'

Will paused and glanced at Iyeyasu, the list in his hand, but the prince gave a brief shake of his head.

The audience once again applauded, and Hidetada nodded. 'It is done. The audience is at an end, Suke.'

The secretary gave the signal, and the dignitaries performed the kowtow and withdrew. The two Englishmen remained by the screen door.

'Bid them come forward, Will,' Iyeyasu said.

'You may approach the dais, gentlemen,' Will said.

Saris and Cocks came closer.

'Ask them if they are satisfied with our arrangements,' Iyeyasu said.

Will translated.

'Very satisfied with his reply, Master Adams,' Saris said. 'There remains but the details to be completed.'

Will translated.

Iyeyasu nodded. 'This I leave with you, Will. Take these men down to your estate at Miura, and entertain them there for a season. And make all arrangements.'

'I have already invited them to visit my home, my lord prince.'

'This is good,' Iyeyasu said. 'A profitable day, eh, my son?'

'It is to be hoped so, my lord father,' Hidetada stared at Will.

'Then ask your friends to withdraw, Will.'

'The prince is satisfied, gentlemen, and requests you to withdraw. He will see you again, I am sure, and I will shortly be with you.'

Saris and Cocks exchanged glances, and then bowed and left the chamber with Suke.

'They are, indeed, men like you, Will,' Iyeyasu said, thoughtfully. 'And yet, only in certain ways. This king of yours, do you know him?'

'No, my lord prince. When I left England there was no king upon our throne, but rather a queen. And I would be dishonest were I to pretend I ever approached her palace, or would have been permitted to do so.'

'We in Japan have not been ruled by a queen for close on a thousand years,' Hidetada said.

'Because queens cannot command armies, and because they hand over the power to their lovers,' Iyeyasu remarked. 'Now, Will, I had thought to see you this day the happiest of men. Surely it is for this reason alone that you came to Japan? How long is it now? Thirteen years since your ship dropped its anchor off the coast of Bungo, and then you promised me that one day I should see an English vessel riding to its anchor in my bay. And here it is. Yet your eyes are clouded.'

'Your compatriots will bring us firearms?' Hidetada inquired.

'I shall ask them to do so, my lord prince. I can guarantee nothing.'

'They have reminded you of your past, Will,' Iyeyasu said. 'Of your youth. Of your other wife, perhaps. What news of her?'

'None, my lord prince. These men do not know she exists.'

'And your parents are long dead. Yet you would like to return to your homeland.'

'A man must always dream of his birthplace, my lord prince. As he grows older his youth means more to him.'

Iyeyasu nodded. 'You have my permission to sail with the *Clove*.'

Will stared at him. 'To sail . . . to leave Japan, my lord prince?'

'If this is what you desire above all else, Will. I ask you to sacrifice nothing. Take your Japanese wife, and your children, if you think they will be happy in this England of yours. Leave them here, if you do not. Be sure that I shall care for them. In addition, your estate will remain here for you, when you choose to return to Japan. But as of this moment you are a free agent, and I wish you Godspeed.'

'But . . . my lord prince . . . ' What a dazzling prospect sang before his eyes. 'What of your plans? Osaka . . . '

Iyeyasu's head half turned. 'If you will excuse us, my son.'

Hidetada bowed, glanced at Will, who performed the kowtow, and left the room.

'My lord Prince Hidetada is strangely affable this morning, my lord prince,' Will observed.

'Oh, indeed. Our plans are moving forward with some prospects of success. You will forgive me, Will, if I do not tell even you what they are. However, it is you we are discussing. My son does not love the Europeans as you know.'

'Yes, my lord prince.'

'He regards my interest in European trade as being to the detriment of our country. In many ways he is right. Your European notions of honour and dealing between men are not ours. Their personal habits are not ours. This way they have of inhaling smoke into their lungs is not ours. And now, indeed, they seek my permission to plant this weed in which they find so much solace, to the exclusion of rice. Yet these are but trifling matters compared with their religious doctrines, which substitute a system of bribery for our way of duty and honour. Your Christians do what they do for fear of eternal punishment should they break a law of God, and in the hopes of eternal life should they faithfully carry out the instructions of their priests, whereas we in Japan perform our duty solely because it *is* our duty, ordained by our parents and grandparents, without hope of reward except within ourselves, without fear of punishment should our actions not meet with general approval, so long as we ourselves are convinced they are right actions. In all these things, my son sees a worm, gnawing at the very intestines of Japanese life. As do I. And yet, when I look at the Europeans, when I think of the future, I fear for my people. Yours, who have turned the destructive powder of gunpowder to such terrible effect, who can construct ships which carry them round the world, in ever and more numbers . . . I think this Europe of yours seeks the domination of the earth, Will, and how else may we ever combat them, save we deal with them, and know what they are about? When I married my grand-daughter to Hideyori it was less to cement our friendship than to have my agents within the walls of Osaka Castle. Thus I would have my merchants and my traders, my sea captains and my ambassadors, within the courts of Europe to understand their ways, and their intentions.'

'This is wise, my lord prince.'

'Hidetada would not have it so. He speaks to me for long periods about the iniquities of my policy, and would have us turn our backs on all Europe, on all the world, and live as our fathers have done for so many years, by the rules of duty and respect for those who have gone before. Duty, Will. This is hard, even for you, because you are European. Here is what you must choose. I say your estate will wait here for you. But I would advise, should you leave, then do not return to Japan. For within a short span now I will be dead.'

'You, my lord prince? I cannot imagine Japan without the prince seeing to its affairs.'

'Nonetheless, you will soon see such a Japan. I am past seventy, and no man may look upon such an age with equanimity. Think well on this, Will.'

'And on my other duties, my lord? My feud with Ishida Norihasa?'

Iyeyasu sighed. 'On that, too, Will. It is not in your blood, to pursue such an affair. This is clear to all, and to me most of all. They call you a coward.'

'I, my lord prince?'

'For not pursuing vengeance.'

'I was banished to my estate, my lord prince, by your order, and under pain of death.'

'Oh, indeed, Will. But where is death, where duty is involved?'

'You mean I should have disobeyed you, once again?'

'Only duty is important in this life, Will. Duty to one's master, certainly. But duty to oneself, first and always. They laugh at you in Osaka and spit upon your memory. For eight years the death of your servant has lain across your reputation like a cloud. Now, I know you are not a coward. I not only love you, Will. I admire you. It is the great regret of my life that you have never found it in your heart to love me.'

'My lord? I . . .'

'You know of what I speak. Yet for that too, I admire you. And I know that the reason you have not yet sought out Norihasa is not that you fear the man, but that perhaps you fear to see the Portuguese woman again, and even more because, as I said just now, it is not in your blood to carry affairs of honour to such a pitch. But if you would be Japanese, Will, you must *be* Japanese. If not, go. Leave now, while the sun still shines upon you.'

'My lord, much of what you say is true. Yet do I still have an awareness of my duty, to you and to the Tokugawa, who have given me all I possess. Am I not your good fortune? Should I desert your side now, as you approach your greatest trial?'

Iyeyasu smiled. 'Certainly you have brought me much fortune in the past, Will. And I have no doubt that you will bring me even more in the future. But there is nothing supernatural in fortune, as I have told you often enough. It is a matter of recognising what may be put to use, and what must be discarded. I speak now to *you*, Will, and not some ill-educated soldier. I love you, Will. It is because I love you that I tell you to think well on your future. I can no longer turn my back upon the certainty that the Toyotomi, everyone living inside Osaka, in fact, wait only for my death to destroy the Tokugawa. So I must destroy them, Will, before I die. Every man, woman and child in that fortress must perish. Only thus may I truly establish the rule of the Tokugawa, the rule of law, in this country of mine. If you would not see this happen, if you feel unable to watch this happen, then leave, now, while you may. And do not ever come back. Think well on this.'

Think well on this. On England, with all its beauty, all its peace; on ships, lazily breasting the Channel tide as they rounded the Foreland. On a ground which never shakes, on green hills which never smoke. On Shikibu, wearing a felt hat and a ruff around her neck, and picking roses in a garden by the Thames.

He watched her now, walking in the garden behind the house, with John Saris. She had a few words of Portuguese, and he had enough to carry on a conversation. They smiled, and discussed the beauty of the cherry blossoms. They could almost be in England already. And how tiny she was, beside the tall Englishman. Why, she must look even smaller when walking beside him, he realised, as he was taller than Saris. But only physically; certainly for them to take passage on the *Clove* was out of the question. From the moment they raised the anchor he would, once again, be nothing more than a sailing master.

He wondered what Shikibu was thinking, as she smiled so politely. What did she think all the time. They call you coward, Anjin Miura, for not again disobeying the prince. Did Shikibu, in her heart, feel she was married to a coward? She had never spoken of it, from that day to this. But she had, every day, watched him practise his swordsmanship with Tadatune. Dreaming of revenge? It was impossible to imagine someone so gentle, so peaceful by nature, holding thoughts of revenge. So then, did she dream of his never again being held up to ridicule?

Or did she dream of Magdalena, as Iyeyasu dreamed of Yodogimi; someone to love, in his case, and being spurned, to hate. When Osaka fell, man, woman and child must perish. There was anger. There was vengeance. There was determination. There was the stuff of empire. To which he had been invited. Because Iyeyasu's strictures had been less than just. He had asked Tadatune, and Tadatune had said that how a man conducted the feud was his affair, providing he did not die with his servant's death unavenged. But the prince had given him a choice. Because *all* in Osaka must perish. So, Will Adams, if you lack the stomach for that, leave now, while you may. Yodogimi, tied to a dog. And Pinto Magdalena?

'True peace.' Richard Cocks sat beside him. 'I envy you your home, Master Adams. Indeed, I envy much about you. Your wife and family. May I hope to enjoy surroundings this peaceful?'

'Should you come to the east, Master Cocks, certainly,' Will said. 'But as I have said, this is to your advantage on every count.'

'Then why do our rivals maintain their factories in the south?'

'I imagine because there are better harbours in Kyushu, and less liability to earthquake.'

'Sound reasons, would you not agree?'

'Not sufficiently sound, in my opinion, Master Cocks. Is not the voyage from England sufficiently perilous. Yet you willingly undertake it for the sake of the gain you hope for, in Japan. You will lose perhaps one ship, with its entire complement, every voyage, yet you think this worthwhile. Here in the east, close to Edo, is where you will do your best business, and be most likely to keep the friendship of the Shogun. So what do you risk? A slightly longer journey, and perhaps once in ten years an earthquake which will level your factory. Better odds than the voyage, I fancy.'

Cocks pulled his nose, watched Saris and Shikibu approaching. 'Master Adams again suggests that these waters will be best for our factory, John.'

'Say you so.' Saris sat beside them, while Shikibu bowed before leaving the porch. 'We must, of course, listen to the advice of so knowledgeable a man, Richard. In many ways. You have a charming house, Master Adams. And a charming wife, and charming children.'

'I thank you, Captain Saris.'

'I can see that you would not wish to leave it, to live in the south.'

'I fail to understand you, sir,' Will said. 'As there is no question of that. But in any event, my wife is from Kyushu, so you may be sure that I would be welcomed there should I ever choose to remove myself.'

'Why, sir, and would you not remove yourself, should we elect to build our factory in Hirado?'

Cocks smiled. 'I fancy Captain Saris is offering you employment, Master Adams.'

Will frowned. 'Are you, sir?'

'Why, yes, Master Adams. I would appreciate it if you would take service with the East India Company. We need you, sir. And I may say that you would not find us ungenerous. What say you, sir, to eighty English pounds per annum?'

'Eighty English pounds?' Will smiled.

'A princely sum,' Saris said. 'For . . .' He glanced at Cocks. 'For the service we would require.'

'You meant, sir, for one such as I, a shipwright-cum-pilot, without a single knight in my family tree, and not an acre of land to call my own in England.'

'Why, sir . . .'

'Let it pass. I shall not quarrel today, and never with my guests.' He clapped his hands, and Asoka hurried in with a small table and a bottle of saké. 'However, sir, be sure that eighty pounds will not tempt me from here.'

'Why, perhaps I mistook the situation,' Saris agreed. 'Indeed,

I must have done when I look around me. You have but to name your price, Master Adams. Ninety, a hundred . . .'

'You must add at least a hundred to your first offer, sir, even to make me consider the matter.'

'One hundred and eighty pounds a year?' Saris cried. his left hand dropping to the hilt of his sword. 'Why, sir, you take me for a fool. That is fifteen pound a month.'

'So it is. Now tell me, sir, is it still possible for a man to live, simply, to be sure, on twelve pound a year, in England?'

'Why certainly, sir, which but illustrates the absurdity of your claim."

Will poured saké for the two men, and gestured Asoka from the porch. 'In Japan, sir, there is little currency, and so we would call your twelve pound a year worth one koku. My income is eighty koku, so you will see that by your own reasoning my income is nine hundred and sixty pounds a year. Should I find eighty so very attractive?'

'Nine hundred and sixty pounds a year?' Saris gazed around him.

'We have been miserly, of course, Master Adams,' Cocks said. 'But then, we in England lack Japanese wealth. The real difficulty arises from the point that, as factor, I shall only be receiving one hundred and fifty pounds per annum, and the other employees of the company correspondingly less. You understand the situation which would exist if you were paid more than the factor himself.'

'Indeed I do, sir,' Will said. 'And I have no wish to be unreasonable. Offer me one hundred and twenty pounds a year, Captain Saris, and I am your man. But I shall continue to live in Miura.'

'One hundred and twenty pounds,' Saris muttered.

'A very reasonable attitude,' Cocks said. 'I'm sure you agree, John.'

Saris sighed. 'For which we should, of course, demand the exclusive use of your services, Master Adams.'

'Now that is impossible,' Will said. 'I serve the prince, as you well know, and in his interests I deal with the Dutch, and the Portuguese and the Spaniards. They also pay me a retaining sum to represent their interests at Edo. For you I would be willing to do the same.'

'By God, sir,' Saris shouted, scrambling to his feet. 'You are a rogue, sir. An unpatriotic rogue.'

'Captain, captain,' Cocks remonstrated. 'Master Adams is at least being honest with us.'

'Honest? Honest, sir? Having wheedled a hundred and twenty pounds from us, he now informs us that we are only entitled to a quarter, or less, of his interest? I will pay a hundred, sir, and not a penny more.'

'Well, then,' Will smiled. 'One hundred pounds per annum, Captain Saris, to prove that I am yet an Englishman.'

'An Englishman. I tell you, sir, you are a rogue. It seems to me that all Japanese are rogues. And since we are being *honest* with each other, Master Adams, let me tell you that I have here a serious complaint from my people in Hirado regarding the conduct of your servant. What's the fellow's name, Cocks?'

'Kimura,' Cocks said. 'But surely . . . '

'Oh, there is no doubt of it. This fellow has been cheating our people left, right and centre, Master Adams. And I shall have redress, be sure of that.'

Will reached over and refilled their cups. 'I suggest you sit down, Captain Saris, and in future mind your words more carefully.'

'What, sir, what?' Saris shouted.

'Words, Captain Saris, mean a great deal more in Japan than they do in England. To be convicted of theft, in Japan, is to lose your head. To be accused of theft is halfway there. As for Kimura, I have every confidence in him. I have already made an investigation into the matter of which you speak, and am certain it is nothing more than a misunderstanding. As I just explained to you, there is little currency used in Japan, whereas your people are accustomed to setting a monetary value upon everything. If you will leave the affair in my hands, I promise you that whatever is owed your people will be paid in full. But be sure, sir, that should you seek your remedy before the law, then will I make a reciprocal charge, and not only will an English head roll in the dust, but your hopes for a factory will accompany it.'

'By God,' Saris said. 'By God.' He sat down. 'The sooner I am away from this pestilential country the better, I say. I pity you, Richard, indeed I do.'

'No doubt I will learn to get along with these people,' Cocks remarked. 'As I observe Master Adams has managed to do.'

'Aye, by becoming one of them,' Saris grumbled.

Shikibu stood at the end of the porch, her hands lost in the sleeves of her kimono, anxiously watching the men.

'Come closer, Shikibu,' Will said. 'We but discussed a matter. There will be no blows.'

Shikibu advanced, and bowed. 'Truly, my lord, if this is how the English discuss, then a quarrel must be a loud affair. I but wished to say, my lord, that dinner is prepared.'

'Then shall we eat,' Will agreed. 'Gentlemen?' He led them into the inner room. 'You'll sit on my left hand, Master Cocks, and you on my right, if you please, Captain Saris.'

The Englishmen did as he asked, and Shikibu bowed to them from the doorway, before kneeling at the end of the room, not to eat with the men, but to supervise the serving girls; she raised her head to exchange a glance with her husband as Saris smiled triumphantly at his factor, in ignorance of the importance of the left hand.

Asoka and Aya now brought in the lacquered tables, one for each person, and then the bowls of rice, the cups of green tea, the coal-filled brazier on which they would cook the sukiyaki, the wooden platter of sliced fowl, the plates of bean curds and rice cakes, and lastly, the small bottles of heated saké, with their matching cups.

'My word, Master Adams, but this is a banquet,' Cocks declared.

'I am entertaining, Master Cocks. When my wife and I eat alone we are much more simply inclined. A bowl of rice, a piece of fish, a cup of tea, and we are well pleased.'

'Oh, indeed, I am sure you on occasion live as simply as the next man. And yet I will confess that I am intrigued, if I may be so bold. When I look around me, at your rice paddies, at your house, at the ships which ride to anchor in this bay, and the contents of your warehouse, when I listen to the tales told of you, of your wealth and power, and more, of your influence with the Shogun and his father, I find myself wondering how you accomplished all of this.'

Will smiled at him. 'Seeing that I am a humble seaman.'

'Sir, that matter seems to tax you, unduly.'

Will glanced at Saris, but the captain was concentrating on his foodsticks. 'Well, sir, I will admit that I have been fortunate. And yet I am not so powerful as I seem.'

'Indeed? I would describe you as almost a Minister of the Crown. Do you not handle all the prince's foreign affairs?'

'I handle nothing, Master Cocks. Nor am I the favourite of the Shogun, as you supposed. Indeed, I suspect Prince Hidetada most heartily dislikes me. It was my fortune to be of some service to the prince, many years ago. Out of that service there arose a common regard, one for the other. So now he takes my advice in matters on which he presumes I am knowledgeable, the sea, certain of the sciences, and of course, the European nations. But the advice is sought, and given, in a purely personal capacity.'

'Yet the Hollanders claim that without your favour they can accomplish nothing, and indeed, that they might well have been prosecuted as pirates before now, had you not defended them before the prince.'

'Indeed, sir, they claim to be grateful for my help. But to be sure the prince had already formed his own opinions on the matter, and I but confirmed him in that.'

'Your frankness does you credit, sir, yet you have just admitted that you accept their money to represent them, and more from the Spaniards. And now we have offered you remuneration to assist us. May I ask you, sir, what services we can truly expect to gain in return?'

'You will obtain an honest representation of your acts and, so far as I myself understand them, your intentions, at the court of the Shogun, Master Cocks.'

'But nothing more than that? Not even for your own countrymen?'

'I have endeavoured to make it clear to you, sir, that my country is now Japan.' He gazed at Shikibu; her eyes were sad. She understood enough of the conversation. And she understood, too, what temptations must be tugging at his heart. And so, what lies he was mouthing?

'By God, sir,' Saris said. 'It amazes me that with all this apparent wealth and prosperity you still deign to accept our few pounds of payment.'

But did she understand what conflicting emotions were battling in his mind? He could scarcely see these men without quarrelling. Why? Because they counted him so much lower than themselves? Or because he was, after all, so different to them, now? If the first, were they not right? They probed his wealth, and power, with reason. There was no reality in either. He was lord of some sixty people now, and even so his warehouse was filled with surplus rice. With that, as Suke had once so truly said, he could employ even more samurai, or obtain more and more services—here in Japan; the rice would be of no value in England. To the best of his ability he had traded with Siam, these past few years, but even there it had been mainly in barter. Perhaps he could take with him as much as a few hundred pounds in money when he left; what would *that* paltry sum purchase for him, in John Saris' society?

As for his apparent power, as he had admitted, that depended upon the goodwill of Iyeyasu, and would certainly end with the prince's death. After all these years, what *had* he achieved? Beyond a loving wife and faithful servants. And a duty.

Think well on this, Will Adams.

Chapter 3

THE BREEZE was fresh and cold. The *Sea Adventure* seemed to race between the islands, the whitecaps bursting into foam on her stem and clouding upwards over the bowsprit while the crew scrambled aloft with a will, eager to hand the sails, for ahead of them lay the island of Hirado, and home.

Home for them, certainly; they were Japanese. Home for Anjin Miura, equally certainly. But for Will Adams?

Was he even now preparing for his departure? He had not discussed the matter with Shikibu. This could only be to complicate matters. Whatever her true feelings, she would bow, slowly and gracefully, and agree with his decision. And could it be to her disadvantage? In all the world, she had only herself, and her two children. She would have them as well, in England. And she would have none of the pressures which lay heavy upon her, through her husband, in Japan. What was it Iyeyasu had said, many years ago, in the warehouse at Ito? So long as the husband is happy, then is the entire household happy. But when the lord is unhappy . . .

Yet happiness, in England, required wealth, as did happiness in Japan, for that matter. Only wealth in England was a matter of gold, preferably inherited, but essentially plentiful. To take Shikibu to England as the wife of a penniless seafarer would be a crime. Thus it had been easy to postpone the actual decision for one more voyage, to swell the goods in his warehouses one more time.

But this voyage had been a disaster. He had been forced to take along, as mate, Richard Wickham, one of the handful of English factors left in Japan by Saris to establish the English company. To Will's great relief he had found Cocks easy enough to work with, but this Wickham was at once quarrelsome and incompetent. They had run into a violent storm, and sprung several planks; the crew had all but mutinied, and finally he had run for shelter into the Ryuku Islands, there to remain for month after tedious month while he virtually rebuilt the ship. A far cry from Siam and the pepper of the Spice Islands.

But despite all, they had survived, *he* had survived, and now once again he was approaching Kyushu. Already the wind was dropping as the ship slipped behind the mountains, and some of the bite was leaving the air. Wickham would have remained in the islands for another three months; he had said it was madness to take to the ocean in winter. But the crew had elected to follow their Anjin Miura, and now they were home, only just after the turn of the year. The turn of the English year. 1615. Christ in Heaven, Will thought; I will soon be fifty-one years old. And Shikibu is thirty. And Joseph is twelve, and Susanna is ten. And Mary? And Deliverance? How *can* I go back?

'And yet, how can I not?' he asked of the wind, and Wickham turned his head.

'You called, Master Adams?'

'Aye. Hand your mainsail, Master Wickham, and make ready to anchor. It is good to be back, would you not say?'

'Good to be done with this infernal ocean for a season.' Wickham was very much the dandy; even after nearly a year's voyaging his velvet breeches sparkled red in the morning sun, and his stockings were new. He kept an apparently inexhaustible supply of stockings, donned a fresh pair whenever there was a port to be entered. 'You will be away north to Miura, once we have unloaded the ship's cargo?'

'And I have shipped a fresh crew, yes.' He watched the shore approaching. How blasé were the citizens of Hirado, now. Where once the entire city would have turned out to welcome a returning trading vessel, today there was only a handful of men on the dockside, and most of those were Europeans. Amongst them would be Cocks, anxious as ever to reckon up his profit, to peruse the log books and make copious notes in his diaries.

So, was he still angry because Saris had chosen to ignore his advice, and after all erect his factory here, close to the Portuguese and the Dutch and the Spaniards? No doubt there were sound reasons behind Saris' decision. In Hirado they were not only in the heart of Christian Japan, but were far removed from the immediate control of the Tokugawa. Quite the opposite reasoning to his own. But then, the other Europeans feared the Tokugawa, whenever the prince should die. And surely that could not now be long delayed. He wondered if *there* was the reason he postponed his decision. To leave this place, to say, I shall never see Iyeyasu again, never feel those eyes drinking me in, never share a cup of saké with that subtle, brilliant mind, that ageless, arrogant, demanding spirit . . . that was more than he could force himself to do. Better leave the decision with inexorable Nature.

And now, the time for brooding was past, for a while. As he had told Wickham, within a few days he would be on his way again, to Miura. And Shikibu. Thirty years old. Christ in Heaven. Thirteen years his wife. Christ in Heaven. So, of course she had aged. Those breasts had grown. Slightly. That flat belly had the smallest roll to it. And perhaps there was a wrinkle under that pointed chin. Nothing more. Compare that with the roll of fat around *his* thighs, with the speckles of grey which flecked his beard, with his slowness of recovery, when she had slipped her silky smooth, sweet-smelling body the length of his.

Thirteen years, and his heart beat as keenly as ever at the thought of once more regaining her. For her body, only? No. For the many little things which made up their life, for the cup of saké which would be waiting, for the touch of her hand, for the quick smile with which she greeted him, for the inspection of his property, ruled with iron discipline by herself and Kimura, for the walks in the garden, when she would slowly move from blossom to blossom, inspecting them with as much care as she bestowed on her children. For the way she tucked up her sleeves before settling down to arranging flowers. For the very art with which she handled the delicate stems. For the bow with which she presented to him his cup of tea.

Was he then, at last, in love? No more. But at last he *loved*. There was the difference. Perhaps, more than anything else, it was the thought of upsetting this so delicate balance of perfection which left him waiting upon events, rather than making the events follow his bidding.

And then, what of her? Did *she* love? She was his wife, and she claimed, and for how many years had he believed, that this duty transcended all else in her existence. Of course it was so. But what of *her*? What went on inside that glossy head? Christ, to know that, after thirteen years, to know that.

For *did* she, too, call him coward? Surely a wife could know her husband better than that. Yet, what did she know of *him*, save as the lord of Miura, the man who shared her couch? She had never sailed with him, had never, in fact, set foot on one of his ships. She knew nothing of the mastery he possessed over his profession, of the feeling of exultation he knew when the anchor left the mud and the wind filled the sails. She knew that he had once faced Norihasa, and been rescued. But no courage had there been revealed; he had had no other choice. She knew he had fought at Sekigahara but then so had almost every man in Japan able to bear arms.

'They wait, like vultures,' Wickham grumbled. 'Even the Dutchmen.'

Will turned his gaze on the group by the water's edge, at this moment clambering into a boat to pull out to the ship. 'Melchior?' He leaned over the gunwale. 'Well met, old friend.' He frowned, and his heart did a sudden lurch; there was none of the usual smiles. 'What news?'

'The saddest, Will,' Melchior called.

'The country is convulsed with war, Will,' Cocks shouted.

'What? What do you say?' He ran to the gangway to greet them as they climbed the ladder.

'Look around you, Will,' Melchior said. 'You will find no samurai in all Kyushu. My lord of Satsuma summoned his knights to accompany him north, at the call of the Tokugawa.'

'But how did this come about?'

'God knows,' Cocks said. 'These people are a mystery to me.'

'It was to do with the dedication of the great statue of the Buddha in Nara,' Melchior said. 'You know how important this was. First it was completed, and then fire destroyed half of it, and it had to be rebuilt. The bell was cast last year, and it was the prince's wish that the boy Hideyori should pronounce the dedication, as son of Hideyoshi. But relations between Osaka and Edo had deteriorated so far, as you will remember, that the Princess Yodogimi refused to let her son leave the fortress. Yet was she unwise enough to send a dedication to be spoken in Hideyori's name.'

'And this caused a war?'

'Indeed. For the speech contained words which were unacceptable to the Tokugawa. In fact, they so inflamed the population of Kyoto that there was a riot, and many buildings were destroyed.'

'What words?'

'I know little of this language, Will. But there were references to the sun which had risen in the east beginning to lose its power as it was forced to share the western sky with the brightness of the moon. These were taken to mean the end of the Tokugawa power.'

'By Christ,' Will said. 'And this speech was not approved by the prince beforehand?'

'Now there is a mystery, Will. It is said that Iyeyasu well knew what was to be said. And yet took offence. There was parleying and even apologies from the Toyotomi. But the prince claimed that there must be a plot against his power, and demanded hostages.'

'This is standard procedure.'

'Indeed it is. But not a hostage of this magnitude.'

'He demanded the Princess Yodogimi?'

'This is what is said.'

'By Christ,' Will said. 'He hinted to me that he had found a way to force the Toyotomi to war. The princess refused?'

'Indignantly, it is said, and put it about that it was a plot to force her into Iyeyasu's bed. And so your prince summoned his vassals to the field,' Cocks said.

'No doubt there was more to it than that, Will,' Melchior said.

'No doubt.' Although he wondered; by such personal enmities, by such personal desires, are decided so many of the destinies of men. 'When was this?'

'The quarrel took place last summer. But the armies did not take the field until the time of the Great Snow.'

Which would have been just before Christmas. What an absurd time to commence a campaign. Because he had been due back in November and would have been back, but for the unseaworthiness of his ship. Despite all, despite even his decision to permit Will to leave, Iyeyasu had still waited, for his good fortune, his master pilot, to return. But when he had not come, when perhaps the prince had decided that he never would return, the campaign had been commenced, anyway. There was a myth exploded.

He sighed. 'Well, then, you have been privileged to look upon the end of an era. For how long have the Toyotomi and the Tokugawa faced each other, at the least in spirit. Did Osaka burn?'

And with it, Pinto Magdalena and Ishida Norihasa? And Yodogimi herself? Did he feel a weight lifting from his shoulders? Or would he now carry that burden forever more? Because of his unfulfilled duties. Certainly, nothing now remained to hold him in Japan.

'Osaka?' Cocks asked. 'The Japanese claim that Osaka Castle is impregnable.'

Will, already turned to lead them into the cabin, checked, and looked over his shoulder. 'What do you mean? If Iyeyasu marched on Osaka, and the castle did not burn . . . what do you mean?'

'Why, simply this, Will,' Melchior said. 'The Tokugawa have been defeated. The news arrived yesterday.'

They sat around the cabin, and drank saké, while Melchior talked. How commonplace, to be sitting here, in such familiar surroundings, drinking such a familiar drink, while around them the world was crumbling.

'One hundred and eighty thousand men, they say, Will,' Melchior said. 'Behind the golden fan. And some eighty thousand within the walls. The city is surrounded. The Ikeda brothers seized the island of Nakajima, you remember where the old *Liefde* was moored when first she came to Osaka. And the southern daimyo occupied the north bank of the river. While the Tokugawa themselves with the main army encamped on the plain east of the city. No doubt your prince thought that the sight of such a mighty armament would strike fear into the hearts of the Toyotomi. So do you know what your defenders did? They came forth and defeated the Tokugawa in a pitched battle.'

'They drove Iyeyasu from the field?' Will asked in horror.

'Why, no. That they could not accomplish. Yet were the Tokugawa beaten, Will. They suffered immense casualties, it is said. And certain it is that the fortress remains as strong as ever.'

'Who did this?'

'A general called Sanada. Supported by the Ono brothers and Ishida Norihasa.'

Will nodded. 'And who commanded our cannon?'

'That I cannot say. Some say it was the prince himself. But it seems this was an unexpected sortie by the garrison, and there was little time for organised development.'

Will got up, head bowed to avoid the timbers of the deck above, leaned on the stern window, and looked at the sparkling waters of the bay. A defeat, which meant what? Iyeyasu's boast was that he had never lost a battle in eighty-eight engagements. Was this, then, the end, of how many years of careful planning, careful creating of just the right moment, the right circumstances? The Tokugawa; the Shogunate; the rule upon which Iyeyasu had staked his career; the continuity; come to an end at its first hurdle. Because the Toyotomi had this time acted with decision, forestalled Iyeyasu's normal course of bribery and betrayal. Now the bribery and betrayal might well come from the other side.

Or because the Toyotomi were, after all, the supreme party? Perhaps the party ordained by the gods eventually to rule Japan. Asai Yodogimi. How strange that this woman, whom he had only ever seen twice in his life, had so come to dominate that life. But she dominated all Japan, without ever daring to venture from the stronghold of her castle. And besides, what is *seeing*? Can a man not see more in a few minutes than in his entire life, if he should know how, and where, to look?

Or was the defeat because Iyeyasu had been forced to begin the siege without the support of his pilot? There was vanity.

He turned. 'Richard,' he said. 'Find me a horse, if you will.'

'But the ship . . . '

'Melchior will command the ship, to return to Miura. You have sailed these waters often enough, old friend, to do that?'

'Indeed I have, Will,' Melchior agreed. 'But you have been away nearly a year. And indeed, have been given up for lost. I visited Shikibu only a few weeks ago, and she was sorely distressed at your long absence.'

'Then you must tell her that I am alive and well, and desperate once again to hold her in my arms.'

'But your duty calls you to Osaka.'

'More than duty, Melchior. That were too simple an answer.'

Then what was the answer? Norihasa, and the blood of Keiko? Magdalena, and the love she had allowed him? Yodogimi, in all the flush of her greatest triumph? Or Iyeyasu, brought to his first defeat? He could put no name to it. He only knew that for him, no less than for any of the Tokugawa, or any of the Toyotomi, life was impossible while the issue at Osaka remained unresolved.

He travelled by the coast road, north from Hiroshima, keeping the snow-clad mountains always on his left; at sea level the air was damp and chill, but not cold enough for frost. He rode alone, using his known authority as the prince's admiral to obtain fresh horses at every posting house, riding all day and only reluctantly stopping for the night. And even while the Tokugawa authority was being challenged, he rode in perfect safety. Such was the iron grip of discipline in which Iyeyasu held this land.

On the heights above Osaka he checked his mount, to gaze down upon the city, and the fortress. How proudly the banners and the pennants rode the air, every one a mass of golden gourds, each gourd representing a victory gained by Hideyoshi. But then, how vast the besieging army; wherever he looked *their* tents and huts and banners spread into the distance, and the plain beyond the city was nothing more than a huge encampment.

He was on the wrong side of the river, and must make his way to the north, to the ford. He whipped his horse ever faster, but was forced to slow as he approached the water, for here again there was an army encamped, behind its wooden defensive walls. The samurai crowded their parapets to watch him ride by, at first with suspicion which brought a few conch shell wails of alarm, and even a fleeting arrow, and then with a cry of acclamation as they recognised him. As he now recognised their pennants: the ring-enclosed cross of the Satsuma.

A body of horsemen debouched from the gate of the camp, and a moment later he was surrounded.

'Anjin Miura,' Tadatune called. Beside him was his brother Tamatane and others of his kinsmen; they wore furs over their armour and, as ever, bristled with weapons. 'We had heard you were dead.'

'Now you see that I am not,' Will told him. 'And I have heard that you have lost a battle.'

Tadatune laughed. 'Not the Satsuma, Will. You should know better than that. But the main army, certainly. Yet it can have been no more than a check. We await the prince's orders to resume the onslaught.'

'Aye,' Will said. 'I must hurry to his side, Tadatune, and see what task he has for me.'

'I will ride with you to the bridge.' Tadatune waved his brothers to the camp. Now his face was serious. 'That you are here may be fortune enough, Will. But I pray you to ask the prince for haste in his decisions. My brothers begin to wonder if we have chosen the right side in this conflict. And my father and uncle. You will remember that we fought for the Toyotomi at Sekigahara.'

'I am not likely to forget that,' Will said.

Tadatune reined his mount. 'Part of the terms of peace between my people and the Tokugawa was this pledge to ride behind the golden fan when the occasion arose. We have honoured this pledge, Will, and *we* have not been defeated. This west bank of the river the Toyotomi held in force. But we drove them into the water. We piled their heads as high as your horse and over a great area. *We* gained a victory. Now men come to us from Prince Hideyori, and ask us why we fight for the Tokugawa, when, were the Toyotomi to rule Japan, our lands would be doubled. Say these things to the prince, Will.'

'You may be sure of that,' Will agreed. 'But I would first know, dear friend, what are *your* feelings in the matter?'

Tadatune hesitated. 'I will be frank with you, Will, because I think I speak for all my people. We wish to see an end to this conflict. Nothing more. A victory, one way or the other. Winter is no time to be campaigning. But for me, I still incline to the side of the Tokugawa, because that is your side, Will. And Ishida Norihasa still lives.'

'Aye,' Will said. 'I am constantly reminded of my duty.' He thrust out his hand. 'I shall arrange your victory for you, Shimadzu no-Tadatune.'

The hatamoto hesitated, and then grasped Will's fingers. 'It will be a great occasion, Anjin Miura, when I enter Osaka Castle at your side. The gods ride with you.'

'And with you,' Will said, and kicked his horse into a gallop.

It was evening before he had crossed the bridge and entered the Tokugawa encampment. Here he again faced protecting walls of thick wood, at a distance of some two miles from the fortress. Although the sun was low in the sky, he wondered if anyone on the watchtowers of Osaka had seen him approach, had heard the acclamation with which he had been greeted as he rode past the encampments of the Mori and the Asano, north of the city. Certainly there had been noise enough.

'Hold there,' shouted the guard. 'Who comes?'

'Anjin Miura.'

'Anjin Miura.' The wooden gate swung inwards, the officer came forward to peer at him. 'Anjin Miura? May the gods be praised.'

' Is the prince well?'

'Aye, Anjin Miura. And will be better to hear of your coming. We had thought you dead.'

'Then let me pass, man.' Will dismounted, and strode through the gate. 'And see to my horse; the poor creature is broken.'

The officer ran behind him. 'Anjin Miura comes. Sound the shell.'

The wail struck out across the enclosure, to be picked up and repeated by the next post. Men came out of their huts to form a crowd of onlookers.

'Anjin Miura comes.' It sounded like a paean. 'Anjin Miura comes.'

They bowed to him, the guards and the spectators. Will stood at the gateway to the prince's private camp, and bowed in response. Anjin Miura comes. To what?

He crossed the bridge, beneath its twin guardians, the open-mouthed monster signifying the beginning of all things, and the tight-lipped giant, the end of all things, and faced Kosuke no-Suke.

'Anjin Miura?' the secretary whispered. 'Can it really be you? Will? News came, last year, of a shipwreck . . . '

'We beached, Suke, to mend a leak. I but needed time. Believe me, I am no ghost.'

'No ghost, Will.' Suke ran forward and seized his hands. 'This will make the prince smile. And it has been a long time since he did that.'

'And during that time much has happened,' Will said.

'Much indeed, Will. And too much of it is sad.'

'This I have heard. But not enough.'

Suke hurried ahead of him, waving a corridor through the crowd of spectators. 'The prince will tell you what he wishes you to know.'

The screens slid aside as they entered the antechamber of the prince's house. Here the crowd was thicker. But he recognised few of the faces. These were generals, not courtiers.

They stood at the rear of the council chamber, next to the guards, behind kneeling rows of perhaps thirty daimyo who faced the dais on which the Shogun sat, alone. Hidetada looked tired, and somewhat irritable, as the heads were already beginning to turn.

'What means this disturbance?' he demanded. 'What news, Suke?'

'I bring Anjin Miura, my lord Shogun.'

Hidetada's head came up, and he peered into the gloom. 'Anjin Miura?' he asked. 'I heard the shells and supposed there was another sortie. Anjin Miura? Come forward.'

Will advanced, performed the kowtow before the dais. His mouth trembled with questions he dared not ask.

'I had not supposed you would return, Anjin Miura,' Hidetada said. 'Not now. How long have you been in Japan?'

'Three days, my lord Shogun. I came here with all haste.'

'Indeed, you must have done so. Come.'

Hidetada rose, and with him the entire room, to bend forward in obeisance as their ruler turned and led Will through the screen at the rear of the dais, and into the inner, smaller, darker room where Iyeyasu lay on his bed, attended by two young women, and his Chinese scribe, Hayashi Nobukatsu. The scholar was reading from a scroll, in a low voice, but as the screen slid aside the prince's head seemed to jerk, and he attempted to raise himself on his elbow. How old he looked, and how tired. The victor in eighty-eight battles, brought to his first defeat.

'Anjin Miura,' he said, his voice hardly more than a whisper. 'Anjin Miura? Can it really be?'

'Go forward. Quickly,' Hidetada commanded.

Will stepped on to the dais, dropped to his knees beside the bedclothes.

'Anjin Miura,' Iyeyasu said. 'Leave us. Leave us alone. You also my son.'

Will remained in the kowtow, his head close to the floor, while the women and the scribe withdrew. Hidetada waited for them, before he too bowed, and left the room.

'Anjin Miura,' Iyeyasu said. 'Will. Rise, man, rise. And come closer. I cannot touch you, there.'

Will leaned forward, his heart pounding, his eyes moist. By Christ, he thought, I love this old man. Perhaps I have loved him for fifteen years. Perhaps, had I recognised that earlier, much might have been different.

Iyeyasu's arms went round his neck, hugged his body down against his chest, stroked his hair as a father might stroke his son.

'May the lord Buddha be thanked,' he said softly. 'I had thought . . . but no matter. They told me you were dead, Will. Drowned.'

'We sprang a leak in a gale, my lord. Nothing more. But it was necessary to beach the ship and make repairs, and still the weather remained bad. I sent a message.'

'And they told me you were drowned. Toyotomi work. Look at me, Will.'

Will raised his head, gazed into the small, round face. The plumpness had dissolved into empty skin, hanging from the high cheekbones. The moustache was white. And now he looked closer he could see that the shoulders were hunched, the hands suddenly thin.

'My lord . . . '

'You have heard of the battle?'

'Indeed, my lord. I could not believe my ears.'

'Yet it is true. A premature assault by the boy Mayeda, which was repulsed, involved my forces in a general action before my dispositions were complete. Yet we nearly carried the day. Do you know what finally cost us the victory?'

'I have heard so many things, my lord.'

'But nothing approaching the truth. Give me your hand.'

Will obeyed, and Iyeyasu's fingers closed on his wrist, and then took his hand up the front of his kimono and inside.

'Reach for yourself.'

Will's hand slid round the suddenly rib-filled torso, caressing the soft silk, and arrived at the ridges of paper bandage. His head rested on Iyeyasu's shoulder. 'My lord?'

'A lance thrust; I was forced to ride into the mêlée to restore some order to our forces. They say it is of no import, and requires only rest. But the fact of it has been kept from the army at large, and must remain a secret. At seventy-two, even a scratch on the finger is important.'

'Yet you remain here, my lord, when you should be returned to Shidzuoka to rest.'

The arms, so weak, were round his shoulders, holding him close. 'No one knows of this, Will, save my immediate family. And Suke, of course. No one must know.' The arms tightened. 'No, Will, do not rise. Holding you thus the pain is no longer of concern. My weakness is no longer of concern. I can feel the strength coming from your body. What strength, Will.'

'I, too, am no longer a young man, my lord.'

'You, Will? You have preserved your strength. All your strength. How I need that now. How I needed you at my side, last week, Will.'

'If you had but waited, my lord. And for a better season, as well.'

'Waited, Will? They told me you were dead. The Toyotomi told me they had heard it from a Portuguese, how your ship had been lost and you with it. And I believed them, fool that I was.'

'Yet will you still triumph, my lord Iyeyasu.'

The fingers tightened. 'Aye. I will still triumph. With you here, Will, it is assured. Tomorrow we will order a general assault.'

Slowly Will pushed himself up. 'You will attempt to carry Osaka Castle by storm, my lord?'

'Fortune will be on our side, Will. I know this. Fortune will ride with us, now.'

'My lord, fifteen years ago, before Sekigahara, you told me that fortune was but another word for preparedness.'

The small figure seemed to slump. 'I have raised an army of one hundred and eighty thousand men, Will. I have no choice over ground. I have introduced my agents into the castle and I have sought to sow discord amongst my enemies as well as to bribe the best of their generals. These things have not succeeded. This has become no longer a war for personal wealth and power, Will. For too long there has been no other basis for war, in Japan. But here we are fighting something different, something intangible, something more dangerous. We are fighting an idea, Will. The daimyo inside Osaka *believe* in the Toyotomi. Perhaps their minds have been addled by the princess. Perhaps they see in the prince a reincarnation of their beloved Hideyoshi. Perhaps by deifying him I made an error. Perhaps they now do see him as a god, and his son also. Whatever the reason, they will fight, and to the death. So it must be a bloody day. Yet will it be ours, eventually.'

Will gazed at the small face, the tight mouth, which could smile so beguilingly, the eyes which had dominated so many men, so many millions, so many decisions. At seventy-two, a lance thrust is a serious business. And all these hundred and eighty thousand samurai were here only because the prince was here. He wondered if Hidetada understood that, understood that the moment his father died his armies would melt away, and with them his power. Because certainly the Princess Yodogimi and her followers knew that. Whether they knew the prince was wounded or not, they would know that the entire will opposed to them was contained inside the brain of a man who had already passed the allotted span. There was the spur to their determination, just to stand, and hold, and wait.

So perhaps for him, too, this was a time for choice. For the final choice. Iyeyasu had never doubted that this would be the decisive confrontation. Within the next few days the entire future of this nation would be decided. Sooner than that. For if Iyeyasu did mean to order a general assault on the morrow, and it failed, as it most certainly would, against *those* endless bastions, endlessly defended, the decision would come even sooner than he had supposed possible. One more defeat must mean the end of the Tokugawa legend of invincibility.

So, what was the choice? Between Toyotomi and Tokugawa? Both sought absolute power. Between Hideyori and Hidetada? He had never met Hideyori, but he most certainly disliked the Shogun, and was disliked in turn. Between a romantic conception of the greatness of Japan, as envisaged by Hideyoshi, and a disciplined order, involving every human being in the empire, from Shogun to honin, as evolved by Iyeyasu? Between, perhaps, a return to endless internicine war or an advance into endless peace?

What other choice could he make, when he thought of his wife and his children and his friends? And his children's children. And his home. And his people. *His* people.

And yet, to destroy Asai Yodogimi. And Pinto Magdalena.

'Why so serious, Will?' Iyeyasu asked.

'My lord, I fear that such an assault as you plan must fail, should the defenders be determined, and you have sufficient evidence of their determination.'

'I have no other course now, Will. Already the daimyo mutter amongst themselves.'

'In Europe, my lord, few barons can any longer risk defending their castles against their rightful rulers, because of the cannon.'

Iyeyasu sighed. 'And do you not think I tried bombardment, Will? All day yesterday our guns spoke. And the balls merely bounced off the walls. Oh, one or two stones may have been dislodged. At this rate it would take us a year to breach the outer wall. And then there is the inner wall, and then the keep. Three years, Will?'

'My lord, if once again I may recall your words to me on the eve of Sekigahara, cannon do damage out of all proportion to their actual destruction.'

'Then they were less well known in our country. Now there are as many cannon within the fortress as out here. Thanks to the Portuguese.'

'And yet, my lord, their shot, flying into an open plain, are doing as little damage as yours, hurling themselves against solid stone. They have no alternative.'

'And we have?'

'Give me a day, my lord, to direct your shot.'

Iyeyasu's head turned. 'One day, Will?'

'I have an idea, my lord, which may well bring the Toyo

out to face you in the field, again. Only this time you will be ready for them.'

'In one day? Why were you not here last week, Will? You have your day. Tomorrow. And you have but to command any man, any daimyo, in the army to assist you.'

'My gunners will suffice, my lord, although I would wish the cannon themselves transported as close to the walls as possible. In which case they will need a suitable force to resist a sortie.'

'You shall be protected by the entire army, Will. What else?'

Will stroked his beard. 'I need nothing else, my lord Iyeyasu. I would but beg a favour of you.'

Iyeyasu's head turned.

'You spoke of the utter destruction of the Toyotomi, my lord.'

'This must be, Will. For they are dedicated to the total destruction of the Tokugawa. And do not forget they include Anjin Miura in that holocaust.'

'Nonetheless, my lord, while I do not beg for the men, I would ask clemency in advance for the women and children.'

'Because once you knew her body?'

'Because once she was kind to me, my lord.'

'Kind? She but sought to use you, Will.'

'Nonetheless, my lord prince. I ask this favour. Shut her up, banish her and her women, but do not put them to death.'

Iyeyasu smiled. 'It was never my intention to execute the women, Will. Not even Asai Yodogimi. Take me that castle, and she may, if she chooses, live to a ripe old age.'

The gunners worked with a will, but it had sleeted in the night, and the ground was soft. It took them several hours to drag the cannon from the Tokugawa encampment and on to a reasonably firm patch of ground. Several hours in which they attracted endless attention not only from their own army but from the Toyotomi as well; the ramparts were crowded, and one or two shots were fired in their direction, but the garrison seemed more curious than alarmed by the manoeuvre.

As were the daimyo who rode beside Will. 'What do you hope to achieve, Anjin Miura, by approaching another few hundred yards?' Tokugawa no-Yoshinobu demanded.

'It is not the distance we seek, my lord Yoshinobu,' Will said. 'But ground sufficiently firm to take an elevation. This will do.'

He called a halt, and the cannon were brought into line. Will dismounted and himself tested the earth under the four huge culverins. 'Aye, this will do very well. Now, lads, you'll build a parapet. Here in front. It must be solid.'

The gunners fell to work, while the daimyo's horses stamped and neighed, and the lords exchanged muttered comments. By mid-morning the earth had been piled to a height of some three feet in front of each cannon, and packed firm.

'So now we may repel an assault, perhaps, Anjin Miura,' Hidetada said.

'And your entire army will receive it,' Will agreed.

For the whole Tokugawa strength had also marched forth, to take its position in battle array just to the right of the guns.

'Aye, so we shall, Anjin Miura. But I doubt a few cannon shot will bring them out to risk another day.'

'We can but hope, my lord Shogun. Now, lads,' he told his gunners. 'We must get these cannon forward, and up, until their front wheels rest on the parapets. Only their front wheels, mind; their rear wheels must stay on the lower level, and must be most firmly wedged.'

This time the gunners exchanged glances, but there were sufficient of them to do the task, although it was heavy work.

Hidetada pulled his nose. 'I begin to see your strategy, Anjin Miura. Truly, you are a man of genius.'

'Of study, my lord. From time immemorial the knocking down of stout walls has posed insuperable problems to the besiegers. But in Europe, even before the invention of gun-powder, it was learned that equally disconcerting for the defenders is to have shot lobbed into their midst, as dropping from above, it is impossible to tell where the missiles may fall. Indeed, we have certain cannon, made with a short barrel but capable of withstanding a very powerful charge of powder, designed for this purpose and nothing else.'

'Then I think our armourers, suitably directed by yourself, Anjin Miura, had best fall to making us some of these weapons.'

'Certainly if you intend to besiege many more castles, my lord Shogun. But for now, these culverins should be enough, providing we can obtain a sufficient elevation.'

He moved forward to the guns, estimated the distance, and the direction as best he might, and gave the command to load. He himself held the match over the touchhole of the first of the cannon, gave another glance at the waiting fortress, and indeed, the entire morning was suddenly silent, as if both armies were holding their breaths, and then lowered the match. The culverin roared, and rode backwards on to its restraining chocks, displacing them and falling on its side, so that Will had to jump out of the way. But the ball was arcing through the sky, to disappear amongst the houses of the garrison town, and by chance, on its way dislodging one of the waving banners. A tremendous shout of acclamation went up from the Tokugawa ranks, accompanied by a screaming of conch shells, while from the castle there arose firstly a human wail of dismay, which was rapidly turned into a shout of defiance.

'Of course,' Will panted, 'had we specially constructed bombards, there would be no risk of these cannon destroying themselves. Haste, now, lads, set that fellow on his wheels again.' He moved to the second cannon. This one also rode back over its chocks, but remained standing. And once again the ball plummeted into the inner defences of the castle.

'Tell your captains to stand by their arms,' Hidetada told his brother. 'If they intend to come forth, it will be soon.'

Yoshinobu nodded, and galloped off to where the army commanders sat, their horses in a cluster.

But the defenders made no move, even after all four cannon had been fired, and reloaded, and remounted.

'What now, Anjin Miura?' Hidetada demanded.

'Why, my lord Shogun, we continue firing. I will endeavour to shorten the range, by reducing the charge, so as to assail the defending army itself, as I imagine it is gathered immediately behind the outer gate.'

'Your plan is excellent, Anjin Miura, and no doubt, if we had some means of causing an explosion where the shot pitches, we should soon force the Toyotomi into action. But I fear that these dropping balls, while undoubtedly difficult for them, will soon lose their terror. We must use them to greater effect.'

'Willingly, my lord Shogun, did I know any better way.'

'You are too discreet, Anjin Miura. I would suggest that you *increase* your charges, so as to send the ball beyond the inner defences, and so assail the keep itself. For be sure that it is from there that Asai Yodogimi watches this conflict.' He glanced at Will. 'Do not pretend to me, Anjin Miura. I know as much about your life as you do yourself. The princess has so far succeeded in keeping a distance between herself and the reality of war. But if we sent one ball through the wall of that tower . . . '

'My lord. To fire upon women . . . '

'Women? The great whore herself, and all the lesser whores?

In any event, Anjin Miura, we shall not be firing upon them in the sense that they are standing in a line before us. We are merely going to frighten them.'

'But to increase the charges, my lord, also involves a risk to the cannon themselves.'

'There are another dozen in the camp. I would have you direct your fire at the tower, Anjin Miura.'

Will hesitated. But the Shogun was in nominal command of the army. 'Very well, my lord Shogun.' He went to the first gun, squinted along the barrel. 'We shall want to alter the trajectory somewhat to the left.'

'Then do so, and quickly,' Hidetada said.

Will gave the order, and the guns were slowly redirected to bring their fire upon the great, square tower of Osaka, palace of the Kwambaku.

'You understand, my lord Shogun, that most of the shot will now fall harmlessly into the moat, on one side or the other.'

'It will require only one to strike home, Anjin Miura. Commence firing.'

Will raised his head, and the first ball curved through the air. The smoke cleared, and they watched it plummet into the moat beside the tower with a gigantic splash. The garrison gave a yell of derision, and the Tokugawa conch shells were silent.

'And again,' Hidetada said.

The next cannon exploded. The ball struck the stone outer wall of the donjon, and bounced back into the courtyard below. But there were no men there, and once again there was a shout of contempt.

'And again,' Hidetada said.

The third ball seemed to hang in the air; the trajectory of this cannon had been higher. Then it plummeted downwards and crashed into the first roof of the palace, scattering wooden tiles in every direction, disappearing into the tower itself. The shout of derision changed into a cry of dismay.

Hidetada smiled. 'This day you have done us great service, Anjin Miura. Be sure of my reward. Keep your fire directed at the tower. I will inform my father.'

He turned his horse and rode away, towards the howl of the conch shells, for the Tokugawa had also seen the damage done by the shot. Will shaded his eyes. Certainly the roof had been struck a tremendous blow, but it had been an extraordinarily lucky aim. He gave the command to fire the next culverin, and this ball followed the example of the first and disappeared into the moat. But this time there were no cheers from the Toyotomi.

'Reload,' he commanded, and hurried to supervise the righting of the first cannon, which had again overturned. And done worse than that; as he had feared, there was a crack in the iron casing. Will pulled at his beard. 'Just these three, then,' he told his captain.

'But soon they also will burst, my lord Miura,' protested the gunner. 'And then, then the Toyotomi will cheer.'

'Nonetheless, we must obey the Shogun,' Will said. Would to God they would all burst, on the next round. Far better had he avoided this conflict and gone straight home to Miura. No man could blame him for that, after nearly a year away from his wife and family.

But the Tokugawa would have done so. For what was happening here transcended family and love. This was once again fundamental, like the storm in the Great Sea.

'The cannon are ready, Anjin Miura,' said the gunner.

Will turned towards the fortress. Each required to be slightly altered, to give them more chance of hitting the tower. Or to make sure they all missed? Here again it was a matter of his will, his decision. One had struck. Surely that was sufficient. And Hidetada could never blame him, could never know if the others had been deliberate misses or not. He bent over the first barrel, gazed along it as he tried once more to estimate range and bearing, and listened to a renewed wailing of conch shells, accompanied this time by a spreading cheer. From the Tokugawa ranks. And before the cannon had resumed firing.

'Anjin Miura,' cried the gunner. 'Anjin Miura. Look there.'

The gates of the fortress were swinging open, and a group of horsemen was emerging, riding behind a white flag.

The hut was ringed with Tokugawa guards, and there were other guards inside. Within, on the dais, the prince himself took the centre position, the Shogun on his right, and his remaining two sons on his left. Behind him knelt Kosuke no-Suke, three of his army commanders, and Will Adams. Facing them was a smaller group: the lord Shigenari on the left, and on the right, Asai Yodogimi's nephew, Kyugoku Tadataka. These were expected. It was the woman in the centre, the chief negotiator, who surprised them all, Asai Jokoin, Yodogimi's younger sister. How beautiful she was. How like her sister. Will had only seen her on one occasion before in his life, on that first night in Osaka, fifteen years ago. But that had also been his first sight of Pinto Magdalena, and Yodogimi herself. The third woman had seemed irrelevant. Now he wondered that a single family should have produced so much magnificent femininity. And so much composure. In their greetings to each other, the princess and Iyeyasu might have been attending a social function, so deep and profound were their bows, so gentle their words of pleasure, at once again seeing one another. But now the preliminaries were over, and Iyeyasu waited for the Princess Jokoin to speak.

'My sister, the Princess Asai Yodogimi, is dismayed, my lord Iyeyasu, to discover that the Tokugawa can discover no better way to wage war than upon the apartments of women.'

Iyeyasu glanced at Hidetada.

The Shogun bowed. 'You will extend to the princess our most profound apologies, my lady Jokoin. We but sought to assail the garrison to the best of our ability. That one of our shot struck the tower of the Asai is a tragedy that will ever haunt our dreams. Was much damage done?'

'The ball entered my sister's bedroom, my lord Shogun,' Jokoin said. 'And killed two of her maids.'

'Two of . . . ' Will said without thinking, and checked, while every head turned in his direction.

'My master gunner,' Iyeyasu said. 'Anjin Miura. It is possible that you will have heard of him, my lady Jokoin.'

Jokoin's nostrils spread as she inhaled. 'Who in all Japan has not heard of Anjin Miura,' she said. 'Besides, we have met. Once. Perhaps Anjin Miura has forgotten.'

'I remember our meeting, my lady,' Will said.

'Ah. And was it your hand guided the shot to the Asai Tower?'

Iyeyasu bowed. 'And none here regret the misfortune more than he, my lady Jokoin. You will say a prayer for us over the two dead ladies. I can but ask you to remember that when lightning strikes, it cuts down young and old, fair and foul, man and woman, without discrimination. Those who would go to war are deliberately placing themselves in the way of the thunderstorm.'

Jokoin gazed at Will for several seconds, her face expressionless beneath its white paint. Then she turned back to Iyeyasu. 'This war was not of our making, my lord Iyeyasu. My sister would have you know that. And she in turn would know what brings the host of the Tokugawa to the gates of Osaka, in this season when men were better in their beds.'

Iyeyasu sighed. 'My lady Yodogimi and I have talked on this matter, through intermediaries, before,' he said. 'I can but repeat what I have said on previous occasions. Far from this being a war of my choosing, I have done everything in my power to restrain my followers, my son the Shogun, my many vassals, from raising their standards on this plain before now. For what news comes to me out of Osaka? How the princess daily pronounces curses on my head and all my family? How she entertains the Portuguese and their priests, who have been found guilty of conspiring against the rule of my son? How the princess and her advisers spend vast sums on the purchase of weapons of war, including firearms and powder. How the castle of Osaka but a year ago threw open its gates to every ronin in the empire, and caused it to be announced throughout the land. These are not the deeds of people who wish to live at peace under the Tokugawa.'

'The Toyotomi live *under* no man, my lord Iyeyasu, saving only the Mikado,' Jokoin said. 'Yet they do, for the moment . . .' her gaze drifted to the left, to embrace Hidetada, 'concede the power of the Tokugawa, nor would they willingly divide the nation once again into civil war.'

'Then let them lay down their arms and trust to the mercy of the Tokugawa, which is well known,' the Shogun pointed out. 'For should they not do so, be sure that our cannon will resume firing at dawn tomorrow. And more. Our engineers are already commencing to dig mines beneath your fortress. Within a fortnight even your mighty walls will begin to crumble.'

Jokoin glanced to left and right at her two companions. 'Be sure, my lord, that it will take more than mines and cannonballs, more than any force the Tokugawa can raise or create, to force the surrender of the Toyotomi. Yet we seek only an honourable peace, my lord Shogun,' she added in a softer tone. 'I have here a paper . . .'

'Read it, my lady Jokoin,' Iyeyasu said. 'Read it.'

'It contains but few clauses, my lord Iyeyasu, and none that so mighty a soldier and statesman might not agree. Firstly, we wish your word that the ronin who have come to Osaka in support of the Toyotomi should suffer no punishment for this occasion.'

Iyeyasu nodded.

324

'Secondly, we ask that the Prince Hideyori's income shall remain as it has always been.'

'I will increase the Prince's income,' Iyeyasu said.

'Thirdly, my sister the Princess Yodogimi wishes your word that she shall never be required to live in Edo.'

'The Princess Yodogimi may live wherever in the empire she chooses.'

'Fourthly, we wish your word that should the Prince Hideyori decide to leave Osaka, he may select any province he chooses as a fief.'

Iyeyasu nodded.

'And fifthly, my lord Iyeyasu, the Prince Hideyori wishes your assurance that his person will remain always inviolate.'

'I wish the boy no harm,' Iyeyasu said. 'Nor have I ever done. I have said this. These things you ask do not seem to be impossible for us to grant, my lady Jokoin. I have but two things to say to you. Firstly, I would know why the Toyotomi have sent a woman to conduct their negotiations. Does this not mean that the Princess Yodogimi's decision to treat with us has not been accepted by her commanders?'

'Whatever is agreed here, will be agreed by all, my lord Iyeyasu. Certain of our military commanders merely doubted that it would be worth our whole in speaking with you at all.'

'And but a few scant years ago they would have been right,' Iyeyasu said, his voice sad. 'But now, now I am an old man, and seek only to see peace in Japan before I die. Yet, I would ask this of you, my lady Jokoin. Sad indeed would I be, to die with my last engagement having ended in so decisive a defeat. For be sure that the world will count this peace a victory for the Toyotomi.'

'It is a victory for reason, my lord Iyeyasu.'

'Ah, my lady, *you* are reasonable, and your sweet sister is reasonable, and perhaps my sons and I are reasonable. But the world at large is inhabited by unreasonable men, and women, who seek only to regard the fact and not the intention. I shall willingly agree to all of your terms, will you agree to give me the recognition of victory here.'

'Willingly, my lord Iyeyasu, in any way possible. We shall say this throughout the land.'

'They shall want facts, my lady Jokoin. Not words. And in this regard I ask very little. I am about to sign a document which guarantees the person, and the income, and the power and prestige of Prince Hideyori, his mother, his family, and his retainers forever more. There can never again be any cause of enmity between the Toyotomi and the Tokugawa. Thus I ask, on my own behalf, and that of my family, that my soldiers be allowed to fill in the outermost of the moats of this castle, and raze the outer wall to the ground.'

'Fill the moat?' Shigenari demanded.

'The *outer* moat, my lord Shigenari.'

'I am sure,' Jokoin said, 'that my lord Iyeyasu means only what he says, my lord Shigenari. The dismantling of the very outermost fortifications can in no way weaken the fortress itself, and yet will they be taken, as my lord wishes, to indicate a surrender on the part of the Toyotomi. This goes hard with you, my lord Shigenari, and yet it is a small price to pay for the safety of our lives and property. I shall agree to this request of yours, my lord Iyeyasu.'

'And will your generals also agree?'

'I have been granted the necessary power to treat, my lord.'

'Then let me put my signature to that document.'

Jokoin held it out, and hesitated, glancing at Hidetada. 'And will all of *your* generals, your family, my lord Iyeyasu, adhere to it after you are dead? Forgive me, my lord, but it is necessary to ask this.'

From his girdle Iyeyasu drew his ko-kotana, and with a quick gesture pricked the end of the little finger on his left hand. Then he took the parchment from Jokoin's hand, laid it on the mat in front of him, held his finger over it, and squeezed the blood from the tiny cut. In this blood he scrawled his name.

'That is signed for eternity, my lady Jokoin,' he said. 'No one will gainsay that. Hidetada, you too will sign.'

'But not in blood,' the Shogun muttered, and took the paper.

Iyeyasu smiled at Jokoin. 'This is a happy day. There but remains the agreeing of hostages, for the safety of my men while the work on the outer moat is carried out.'

'Of course, my lord. Who would you?'

'The sons of Ono Harunaga.'

Jokoin's head came up.

'Of course,' Iyeyasu said. 'I had forgotten that they are also the sons of the Princess Yodogimi, and thus your nephews as well, my lady. Be sure that their treatment shall be of the best.'

Still Jokoin stared at him, for several seconds. 'Agreed,' she said at last. 'And from your side, my lord Iyeyasu?'

'You have but to ask, my lady Jokoin. Providing he is not a ruling daimyo.'

Which excluded all of *his* sons.

'Of course,' Jokoin agreed. Her head lowered as if in thought, and then raised again. 'We should not aim so high, my lord Iyeyasu. As hostage for your part in this agreement, we ask nothing more than the person of Anjin Miura.'

Chapter 4

HOW SMALL the figure, how frail, and how sad the face. What effort must it have cost him to sit erect for so long. And had it been that effort, the pain of his wound, which had caused him to take so pessimistic a view, to allow the Toyotomi so much evidence of victory?

Now he sighed, and the slender fingers closed on Will's wrist. 'Fifteen years, Will. Since you first came to me. And now I must ask of you this greatest of tasks.'

'For only a short while, my lord. Surely. And to say truth, I am looking forward to entering Osaka again.' He smiled. 'And perhaps I am happy to be protected by the name of hostage.'

'Aye,' Iyeyasu said. 'You will be protected so long as there is peace between the Toyotomi and the Tokugawa. See that you protect yourself, Will. Commit no overt act. There are many enemies waiting for you, within the fortress. It is even possible . . . but no matter.'

'My lord, they would scarcely risk all that they have gained, and the Princess Yodogimi would certainly not risk her sons, to be avenged upon one such as me. I imagine they also have been fooled by the superstition that I bring you good fortune, and seek in this small way to lessen your power.'

'That I know,' Iyeyasu said. The eyes, almost shut, suddenly opened, and turned towards him. 'Yet, Will, I would say this to you. Sleep with your sword by your side, and should the time come, use it.'

Will frowned. 'I would I could understand you, my lord. I would I could understand much about this matter. I promised to bring the Toyotomi forth, to fight you, by means of my bombardment. Yet when they asked for a parley you readily granted their request. And when they asked for peace, on their terms, my lord, you granted that as well. I suppose the fact is that I shall never understand the ways of diplomacy.'

'You would have had us stay here for years, Will?'

'A further bombardment, my lord . . . '

'They asked for a parley because the Princess Yodogimi was terrified by the shot you put through her roof, Will. But I know the princess, too well. Soon enough she would have recovered her courage, and then her will would have been twice as strong. It was then, or never.'

'But what have we gained, my lord? If I could understand that . . .'

'Will, I allow no man, save the Shogun, into my innermost councils. Not even you, Will. Believe only that whatever I do, I do for Japan.' The thin lips half smiled. 'At least for my conception of Japan, which is a Tokugawa Japan. Believe this. And remember it. Which is why I ask you to be careful, and to be ready at all times. I may yet call upon you to die for me, Will.'

The eyes were steady, gazing at his face. By Christ, Will thought. He is asking me to do that, now. By Christ. And yet, with Yodogimi's sons in the Tokugawa camp, and the siege about to be lifted, how can I be in danger? No mother would sacrifice two of her sons, even for the sake of a third. Not even a Japanese mother, surely. Not even the Princess Asai Yodogimi. Surely.

'But be sure, Will,' Iyeyasu whispered, 'that you shall be avenged. No matter what happens, Will, be sure of that. And be sure too that your wife and children will be honoured, so long as there is a rising sun.'

'My lord, I . . .'

'Now go. I hear the shell.'

The conchs were wailing. Will performed the kowtow, rose, and went to the door. There he turned to bow again, and saw the prince staring at him. Were those eyes filled with tears? He was too far away to see.

Suke waited in the gallery, with Hidetada and a group of daimyo.

'So then, Anjin Miura,' Hidetada said. 'This day you take on your greatest duty for the Tokugawa. Be sure that your name will always be honoured by my family and my people. And be sure too, Anjin Miura, that although you will see this army melt away within the week, our thoughts will remain always with you.'

'My lord,' Will said. 'I am to be but hostage. You speak as if I were marching to my execution.'

Hidetada gazed at him for a moment. 'These are perilous times, Anjin Miura. For us all. I bid you goodbye.'

Will went outside, Suke at his elbow. 'Now tell me straight, Suke,' he whispered. 'As we are such old friends, what is afoot here?'

'Why, nothing, Will,' Suke said. 'At least, nothing that you do not already know. A peace has been agreed and the war is at an end. You are not afraid to enter Osaka as a hostage?'

By Christ, Will thought. He is lying to me. They are all lying to me. 'Why should I be afraid to enter Osaka, Suke? Because Ishida Norihasa is one of the garrison commanders? I am a hostage, and therefore inviolate. So long as the Tokugawa perform their side of the treaty.'

'Exactly what I meant, Will. Now, here is your horse. The finest that we could procure for you. It is a shame that you have no armour with you. We would send to Miura for it, except that, as you say, your stay in Osaka will be for such a short time.'

How his eyes shifted. 'Aye,' Will said. 'But will you send my love to my wife, Suke? I have not laid eyes upon her these nine months.'

Suke bowed. 'That shall be done, Will. And she shall be told how you are performing your duty as a Tokugawa.'

'To the death, eh, Suke?'

'Now there is a strange thing to say, Will.'

'Nonetheless, old friend. As all things in this life are necessarily uncertain, saving only the certainty of death, I shall bid you farewell as if I am never going to see you again.' He held out his hand. 'I wish you Godspeed. And the Tokugawa, Godspeed.'

Suke hesitated, and then grasped the proffered hand between both of his. 'And to you, Will.'

Will turned to the horse, where the page held his stirrup. And then checked. 'I leave Shikibu and my children in your charge, Suke. Be sure of that.'

'Of course, Will. But why speak of death? We shall take many a cup together in the years to come. I am sure of *that*.'

Their eyes met, for the shortest of seconds. For this, then, Will thought, I came to Japan. No. But for this, certainly, I elected to follow the golden fan. For this was I rewarded with a house and wealth, with serfs and position, with honour and a beautiful wife. To die, when the time came. As the young knight, Kato Kenshin, had died, on the field of Sekigahara, fifteen years before. Because it was his duty, that day.

He was in the saddle, and the page had stepped away. He touched the horse with his heels, and it walked out of the gateway and over the grass. It was cold. The sun was high, and yet it was cold. January was no time to be campaigning. The armies would be glad to go home. Indeed, they clearly felt the same. A tremendous wailing of conch shells and a storm of cheering arose from the wooden palisades, and from the camps of the Asano and the Mori away to the north. The sound would be heard, and echoed, by the Satsuma on the far side of the river. The war was over. And Anjin Miura? Anjin Miura performed his duty.

Were *his* eyes, then, full of tears? Or was it the cold. The wind came down from Lake Biwa, only thirty miles to the north, whistled over the fortress and the city before raising whitecaps on the Inland Sea. There had been whitecaps on the Inland Sea fifteen years ago, when he and Suke had first come here, to meet the Tokugawa. What had he hoped for then? How odd. Then, and now. Then he had been concerned with saving his life, and the lives of his companions, and had been uncertain as to what he would find, what he would experience, what was happening around him. Now again he must be concerned with his life, and again he was uncertain as to the future, and was aware that events were taking place of which he understood nothing.

But this time the certain factor was what he would find in Osaka Castle. What a painful combination of apprehension and anticipation filled his brain. Nothing else, now. Now he was past the age where his penis could also be filled with painful anticipation. Perhaps. Was man ever beyond that age, where Asai Yodogimi was concerned?

And Pinto Magdalena?

The gates of the castle stood open, and two horsemen were riding towards him. Slowly. They too would be aware that their lives hung upon the decisions of others. And they too were being seen upon their way to cheers and wailing conch shells, from the embrasured walls of the castle. They too performed their duty. What stupidity. When he reached those two boys, why did he not say, we are sacrificial lambs for the ambitions of others. Come. Ride with me. Let us gallop west to Miura. There my friend, Melchior Zandvoort, will soon make his appearance with a stout ship. Indeed, he may already have arrived. And there are my wife and family and my faithful Kimura. There we can kick the mud of this country from our feet, and sail and sail.

And they would stare at him in horror. As, were it to come to pass, Shikibu and Joseph and Susanna, and Kimura and Asoka and Aya would stare at him in horror. For where was a samurai, *what* was a samurai, without honour? Without duty? Where was a samurai who counted his life superior to the will, or the whim, of his lord?

The two young men approached. They were each in their early teens. But one was not less than fifteen. By Christ, Will thought. This boy may have lain in Yodogimi's womb when I made my entry there.

The horses checked, and they gazed at each other. 'My lords,' Will said. 'I bid you welcome to the camp of the Tokugawa, and I promise you that your treatment there shall be nothing less than your rank requires.'

'Anjin Miura,' said the eldest of the two boys. 'We bid you welcome to Osaka, and the ranks of the Toyotomi. My mother awaits you.' He kicked his horse, and they rode by.

Will's mount proceeded of itself, without bidding by him. Even the horses, raised by the Tokugawa, knew their duty. Above him the outer walls rose high, high, masses of undressed stone, huge blocks lowered into place, when, how? Gained from where? Beneath his horses' hooves was only mud. Above his head, now, was the wooden arch of the gateway, and the faces of the Toyotomi samurai, looking down upon him. Not a man there but would know there was a blood feud between the white man and Ishida Norihasa, would know that once again it must wait, upon other things. Not a man up there smiled.

There were samurai at the guardhouse, as well, waiting, their weapons at attention. How lonely he felt, as he rode beneath the huge gateway. How lonely he was. The wooden doors closed behind him, gently, with scarce a sound. His horse stood on cobbled stones, with an avenue of armed soldiers to his right, leading to the next bridge, the next moat, the next wall. To his left, at a greater distance, almost the entire Toyotomi army was assembled, rank upon rank upon rank, staring at him. Anjin Miura. The man with the guns. The man who had commanded the guns to fire into the castle. The man whose coming had, perhaps, made a decisive difference to the war.

He walked his horse down the ranks. The fortress showed little evidence of having been under siege for some weeks. Except for the crowds of armed men. And now there were women, as well, and children, as he crossed the second bridge. For now he was in the garrison town. And still they stared at him, silently, while the avenue of samurai continued to the next gate, this time diagonally to the left. Truly was he entering an endless chasm, here.

The gate swung open, and he gazed at the high stone walls of the keep, with even, to his right, the window of the cell in which he and Melchior had spent six weeks, so many years ago; at his feet was the inner moat, deepest of all. And beyond was the tower, its uppermost roof still revealing a gaping hole where his ball had hit. Two women had died there. Which two?

His horse crossed the bridge. In the courtyard there was drawn up a guard of honour, several hundred strong. And here too, wearing dark kimonos which contrasted with the brilliance of the armour-clad soldiers, were the principal generals of the Toyotomi. He recognised them at once, although only one was known to him by better than hearsay. The small, slight figure, strangely reminiscent of the young Iyeyasu, was Ono Harunaga, Yodogimi's lover, as was known throughout the empire. He had been Yodogimi's lover when first Will had come to Osaka, fifteen years ago. It was his own sons who were at this moment being welcomed to the Tokugawa encampment.

On his right stood Ono Harufusa, his brother, taller but with similarly open, almost youthful features. Two men to trust, and perhaps to like. Certainly they had proved sufficiently trustworthy, to the Toyotomi.

On Harunaga's left stood Oda Yuraku, the old man, cousin of the great Oda Nobunaga, and Princess Yodogimi's uncle. His moustaches were long and white, his shoulders bowed.

Behind the three leaders waited Sanada Yokimura, the great warrior who had gained the victory of the previous week, this day also dressed in full armour, with the golden horns of a triumphant general rising above his helmet. And beside him, Ishida Norihasa. A Norihasa who had perhaps not aged at all, and whose thin face registered nothing but satisfaction as he watched his enemy dismount.

Will stood before the five generals, and bowed from the waist, held the bow for three seconds, and straightened again. The generals bowed in turn.

Slowly, very slowly and carefully, Will drew his sheathed long sword from his belt, grasping it in both hands, and with the same great care held it towards Ono Harunaga.

Once again Harunaga bowed, and took the sword. 'A fine blade,' he said. 'A Masamune blade. There can be none better.'

'I yield it for the duration of my stay in Osaka, my lord Harunaga,' Will said.

Harunaga nodded. 'For the duration of your stay, Anjin Miura.' He raised the sword above his head, still held in both hands. 'Behold the sword of Anjin Miura,' he shouted. And now at last the samurai gave voice. The huge cry welled up around the tower, and Will allowed his gaze to drift to the windows. There were women there, watching the scene. Christ, how he sweated. But this man's own sons were outside.

Harunaga handed the sword to an aide. 'Your quarters await you, Anjin Miura,' he said. 'My lord Norihasa?'

Will's head turned, sharply.

Norihasa bowed in his direction. 'You will accompany me, Anjin Miura.'

Will bowed, and stepped behind the daimyo, who had already turned. Behind them came a file of six soldiers. So, he thought, I have surrendered myself to these people, and am now their prisoner. Norihasa's prisoner. There was a studied insult. And whose else? For a last time his gaze drifted up the tower to the fluttering bright kimonos of the women, and then he stepped beneath the huge doorway, and followed Norihasa along the polished wooden hall. How memory flooded back. And not only of this tower. Of the hell, deep below the courtyard outside. Of Iyeyasu's council chamber, away to his left. Of following Magdalena up narrow staircases and along narrow corridors. Fifteen years. Christ in Heaven. Fifteen years.

Norihasa mounted the main staircase, broad, polished, the bannisters carved into endless intricate designs, and guarded, on every fourth step, by an armoured warrior. He marched along the first-floor hall, always over polished floors, past armed guards, past walls hung with magnificent drapes, past chambers of twenty, thirty or more tatami, decorated with all the splendid pictures that Will remembered from the past. No one spoke. Their sandals made scarcely a sound as they passed over the floor.

But at last the daimyo paused before a pair of large wooden doors, situated at the rear of the tower, and decorated, as were all the doors in this castle, with the golden gourds of Hideyoshi. 'Your apartments, Anjin Miura.' He clapped his hands, and the doors opened. Inside, performing the kowtow, were four young women. 'And your attendants,' Norihasa added. He walked into the outer room, passed the girls, and went to the windows. Will waited while his sandals were changed for slippers, then signalled the girls to rise, and stood beside his captor.

'Your army prepares to leave,' Norihasa said. From this corner of the castle they could see the Tokugawa camp. This was already being dismantled, and columns of men were making their way over the plains to the east. But others, too, were commencing work on the outer moat, wheeling up huge loads of mud to be dumped into the water, as had been agreed between the Princess Jokoin and Iyeyasu.

'I thank you, my lord Norihasa,' Will said. 'For the comfort with which I see I am surrounded.'

Norihasa bowed.

Will sucked air into his lungs, slowly. 'There is much between us, my lord. Circumstances have not hitherto permitted me to return your ko-kotana. It is in my belt at this moment, however, and when these affairs of state have been settled, I shall be glad to offer it to you.'

Norihasa, straight again, stared at him for a moment. 'Words, Anjin Miura,' he said. 'You are good, with words. Tell me, does your belly still ache?'

'Aye, my lord Norihasa. When I look upon you, it smarts. And since our last meeting I have learnt to use other weapons than words.'

Norihasa smiled. 'I look forward to discovering, Anjin Miura, how much you have learned. But I doubt that it shall ever come to pass. You will die with dishonour thick upon your hands and your name, Anjin Miura. Be sure of that. Now I leave you. To the care of these women. But I have another attendant for you.' He turned to the door, and clapped his hands.

A boy came in. A very small boy, perhaps nine years old. But tall, for a Japanese, with peculiarly light coloured hair. And what features; at once large and aquiline. Large, for a *Japanese*?

Norihasa continued to smile. 'You will find him a very suitable companion, Anjin Miura. I have had him trained from birth, to do nothing but please men. And he is now just approaching perfection.' He went to the doorway, and bowed, from the waist. 'We wish you to be happy here, Anjin Miura.'

The room was silent. The women remained kneeling, awaiting his bidding. And the boy crossed the floor.

Oh, Christ, Will thought. Oh, Christ in Heaven; it cannot be. Yet there could be no doubt.

The boy stood before him, and bowed. 'I am told to bid you welcome, Anjin Miura,' he said, his voice high and clear.

Will seemed to awaken from a deep sleep. He clapped his hands, and the young women bowed. 'I am hungry,' he said. 'Is there no food in this castle?'

They giggled, and bowed again, and hurried from the room.

Will went into the sleeping apartment, which opened to the left, sat down on the mats, watched the boy approach.

'You do not like me, Anjin Miura?' His eyes filled with tears.

'I like you very much,' Will assured him.

The boy hurried forward, knelt beside him. What fair skin he had. What an entrancingly pretty child. Oh, Christ, Will thought. Oh, Christ. And he had been warned against an overt act. Had Iyeyasu known? He had his spies inside this fortress, as he had his spies inside every fortress, almost every house, in all Japan. Had he known?

'What are you called, boy?'

'My name is Philip, my lord. I do not know what it means.'

'And your mother's name?'

The boy frowned. 'I do not know, my lord.'

Will seized his shoulders. 'What do you mean? Is she dead? Is Magdalena dead?'

The boy's mouth flopped open. 'Magdalena, my lord? What has my lady Magdalena to do with me?'

Will's hands slipped down the brown cloth of the kimono. 'Do you see the lady Magdalena often?'

'Oh, yes, my lord. She is always kind to me.' The tears were back.

Oh, Christ, Will thought. There can be no doubt, now. Oh, indeed, Norihasa has no need of a sword with which to cut me. 'And others are not always kind to you?'

'Sometimes they beat me, my lord.'

'Who does this?'

'The men I go to, my lord.'

'The men . . . my lord Norihasa?'

'Oh, yes, my lord. My lord Norihasa always beats me. But that is his pleasure, as I am his. I do not mind being beaten, for pleasure. Will you beat me, my lord?'

'No,' Will said. 'No, I will not beat you, Philip.'

Yet again the tears. 'Because you do not like me, my lord.'

'On the contrary, Philip. I like you very much. I think I love you.'

'My lord,' Philip cried with pleasure. 'To be loved is all my joy.' His kimono was loosed, his hands seized Will's, brought them forward on to his thighs while he busied himself with Will's girdle. 'So big, my lord,' he panted. 'So big.' His hands were cold, but more insistent even than Shikibu's, and Will could feel the blood pumping down his body as his weapon swelled.

'Christ in Heaven,' he shouted, and swung his hand. The blow caught Philip above the ear, and sent him rolling across the mats.

The screens slid back, and two of the young women returned, bringing the lacquered table and the red lacquered bowls for the meal. Will scrambled to his feet. 'You,' he told the first one. 'On the floor. Quickly, now. Loose your girdle.'

The girl stared at him. Then she slowly bent and placed the table on the floor.

From beside her, Philip whimpered.

'I want *you*,' Will said. 'Now. I will have you, now. Tell your companion to go away.'

The girl's head turned, to gaze at Philip. 'You do not like the boy, Anjin Miura?'

'No . . . Not today. You . . . '

Slowly she straightened, and backed away from him at the same time. Her head shook. 'I cannot, my lord.'

'You cannot? By Christ . . . '

He reached for her, and she ran back to the doorway. The other girl hastily placed the cups on the table and ran behind her companion.

'Wait a moment,' Will shouted. 'I am not going to hurt you.'

The door opened to admit the other two girls, carrying the platters of food and the brazier for cooking. The first pair seemed glad to see them. Certainly he could not take one if all four were against it.

'Why can you not?' he asked.

One of the other girls spoke. 'It is the order of my lord Norihasa, Anjin Miura. You are to have the boy. My lord Norihasa said you would prefer that, and he said we were to permit no other.' Her gaze dropped to Will's genitals, for his kimono remained open. 'We shall withdraw, my lord. I can relight the brazier when it is time.'

'No,' Will tied his girdle. 'I will eat now. And afterwards you will prepare me a bath.'

The girls bowed. Philip slowly sat up, and then turned on to his knees. He was at least a year away from puberty. But he could respond. Could, and would.

'And I, my lord?' he whispered.

'I am not angry with you, Philip,' Will said. 'I would like to speak with you, again. But I have taken a vow of chastity. You know, like the priests?'

Philip gazed at him.

'So, while I would like you to stay here with me, you must keep your hands to yourself. You will see how you affected me, just now.'

'Yes, my lord.'

'Now come, and sit here beside me, and share my food.'

'I, my lord?'

'You.'

The boy hesitated, and then sat beside Will. The girls exchanged glances, and then set out the foodsticks for the boy as well.

'Saké,' Will said.

The girl bowed, and placed the little bottle beside the cup. He poured, and drank, and poured again. The girls stared at him.

'Have you known many men, Philip?' he asked.

'Oh, yes, my lord,' the boy said proudly. 'The daimyo, even, ask for me. And when they have banquets, I perform for them.'

Will drained another cup of saké. 'You perform for them?'

'With my friend Kokuji. It is strange that my lord Norihasa has not sent Kokuji here with me, to entertain you.'

'Yes,' Will said. 'No doubt it is strange.'

The girls knelt in front of him, smiling at him. Did they know? Of course. Or they were now guessing.

'Perhaps,' he said. 'Perhaps my lord Norihasa felt that you would be sufficient. No doubt he was aware of my vow.'

Philip gazed at him, his lower lip trembling. 'He did not tell me, my lord. He beat me, this morning, to make me better with you, because when I am beaten my prick stands very high and firm. My lord, why do you not beat me, and then, my lord, you will find me good to handle. The daimyo find me good to handle, my lord.'

Will discovered the saké bottle to be empty. He raised his hands to clap them, and lowered them again. Where would be the point in drunkenness? Indeed, that way lay positive danger, for Philip was certainly a most attractive boy, and the very air seemed cloyed with desire. He waved his hand again. 'Take it away.'

'My lord has eaten nothing,' protested the senior girl.

'I am not hungry,' Will said. 'Take it away. And spread the bedding. I would retire.'

They glanced at each other, and then at Philip, and giggled their pleasure.

'Anjin Miura is a lord of great strength,' said the senior girl, appreciatively. 'It is good. The nights are long, in January.'

He stood at the window, and watched the Tokugawa encampment. He had stood thus, every day now, for a fortnight, watching the clouds building over the mountains and drifting down to the plain as rain, and occasionally sleet. No snow here, so close to the sea, and now it was well into February: The Beginning of Spring.

He had also watched the Tokugawa workmen, so busy. They had filled in the outer moat, and demolished the outer wall, as agreed in the treaty of peace. But that had been several days ago, and still the Shogun's army remained in camp. And still they worked. At what, he could not tell, from this window. But every day the work force marched forth, with picks and shovels, and every day the Toyotomi samurai lined the wall of the fortress proper, to watch them, to blow conch shells and give derisory hoots.

How strange. He should have been released from here a week ago.

But what then? Ishida Norihasa had been given his chance for revenge, and had seized it. When Anjin Miura left Osaka, he must also leave his son. To a lifetime of sodomy and male prostitution. Nothing dishonourable in that, to a samurai. Ishida Norihasa had thought long on this matter, clearly, and come up with the answer to his desire for revenge. This way he treated Anjin Miura with the most perfect courtesy, with, indeed, more comfort and luxury than was required for a hostage who was not also of noble birth. To Japanese eyes. And this way he destroyed the man. For how could Anjin Miura ever again sleep easy in his bed, thinking of Philip entertaining the daimyo in Osaka?

This was hard enough. But harder yet was the consideration of Magdalena. To have her son taken from her side, surely within a few weeks of his birth. And had that been her only punishment? Or had she, perhaps, agreed to Norihasa's plan? She had, apparently, returned to her original position of honour, serving the Princess Yodogimi.

Could any woman agree to something like that, where her own son was involved? Who could tell? Who could tell what went on in any of their minds. Even inside the mind of Shikibu.

Christ, he was sweating. There was a careless thought. Shikibu would be beside herself with worry at the thought of her husband a hostage inside Osaka, and the news would have reached her by now.

Or would she be? He was doing his duty, to the Tokugawa. Did that permit of anxiety, for his fate?

The outer doors opened, and he turned. For fourteen days he had remained in these apartments, never allowed forth, served by the same four girls, and Philip. The girls had not come as yet, to serve his evening meal, but Philip, as usual, crouched in the far corner, drawing. The girls had brought paper and ink, and Will had sketched a ship, because Philip had asked about ships. 'You are Anjin Miura,' he had said. 'The great pilot. We have heard of you, my lord.'

'From your mother?' The question had slipped out before he had intended.

'Everyone speaks of Anjin Miura,' Philip had said. 'The man who can build ships better even than the Portuguese.'

So he had drawn Philip a ship. An English ship, riding proudly upon the waves. He had done more, and drawn the interior plans, and a cutaway section. His trade. He was a shipwright. Nothing more. A shipwright translated to hell. And working for the devil.

Philip had been delighted. He spent hours staring at the drawings, obviously playing a mental game in which he, perhaps, wandered the length and breadth of the vessel, or perhaps even commanded it. After all, the sea, and ships, were in his blood.

And so he talked, by the hour. It was the only thing to do, apart from the other. He had talked of his days at sea, told Philip of the fight with the Armada, of the floating ice off the North Cape, of the savage warriors of Cape Lopez, of the endless wastes of the South Atlantic, of the penguins and the snows of the Horn, and of the Great Sea. A father, talking to his son.

Perhaps, for fourteen days, he had even been happy . . . Not Philip, at first. Philip had been bewildered. And his instincts had been so carefully cultivated he clearly felt deprived. But these last few days even he had been happy, surely.

Slowly the doors swung open. Outside were the usual guards. How *had* the years rolled away. But this evening there were not the giggling girls bringing in the tables and the food, but, instead,

Oda Yuraku, dressed in a brilliant orange kimono, and alone.

'Anjin Miura,' Oda Yuraku said, and bowed. 'I very much regret that I have been unable to visit you sooner. You have been neglected.'

'My surroundings are pleasant enough,' Will said.

'And you have the boy,' Yuraku pointed out. 'He is to your taste, Anjin Miura?'

Will bowed. 'He is an intelligent lad, my lord Yuraku . . . He has done much to make my stay here pleasant.'

Yuraku stared at him for some seconds, a faint frown between his eyes. Then once more he bowed, and moved to the windows. 'I am the cousin of Oda Nobunaga. I rode at his right hand, for fifteen years.'

Will frowned. 'I know that, my lord.'

'When Nobunaga died, I had to make a decision, Anjin Miura. And Asai Yodogimi is my niece.'

'I know that, my lord.' But his heart was commencing to pound. Did he, after all, possess a friend, in this castle?

'These people,' Yuraku said. 'They are nothing. Common folk. I am of the greatest family in the land.'

'As great as the Minamoto, my lord?' Will asked.

Yuraku glanced at him, and then turned, towards the door. 'I would make amends for my earlier neglect of you, Anjin Miura. You will dine with me?'

'Willingly, my lord Yuraku. If you will permit me the time to bathe and change my clothing.'

Yuraku bowed, and half an hour later Will accompanied him along the broad wood-floored corridor, up interminable decorated staircases, along draped stone halls, and once more climbing. In these enclosed areas he had no sense of direction. And yet now they were most certainly high in the tower. Going where? To see whom? How he sweated. And how the haft of his short sword ate into his belly. But most of all, how surprising had been Yuraku's words.

Screens slid aside; no prison here. Yuraku entered a room of perhaps thirty tatami, where there were waiting half a dozen nobles. Here were the Ono brothers, and Sanada, and Ishida Norihasa, but these all remained on the lower level. For here too, seated on the dais, was the small, slight figure of a boy in his early twenties, wearing a sky blue kimono.

'The kowtow, Anjin Miura,' Yuraku whispered, and himself fell to his knees. Will did the same, and Hideyori rested his hands on his hips in the time-honoured manner before gesturing them up, and forward.

'The man Anjin Miura, my lord prince,' Yuraku said.

Will knelt beside the dais.

'The man with the guns,' Hideyori said. 'I have heard much of you, Anjin Miura. Your cannon balls all but killed my mother.'

'For which I would dearly like to apologise to the princess herself, my lord,' Will said.

Hideyori gazed at him for a moment. 'No doubt you will have the opportunity,' he remarked. 'Now come. We shall eat, my lord Harunaga.'

The daimyo bowed, and clapped his hands. The screens slid aside and the serving girls hurried in with the lacquered tables and the simmering braziers. And Will had the opportunity to look around him. A rich chamber, to be sure, with the newest and freshest of mats upon the floor, with vast bowls of flowers in every corner, with decorated drapes hung from the walls. And behind the drapes? For there was a subtle scent in the chamber. A scent he had not inhaled for fifteen years, and then he had been in this very tower. He was sure of that. The requirements of etiquette forbade even the Princess Yodogimi to dine with her menfolk; but to all intents and purposes he was now in her presence. And that of her maids?

Rice was served. Hideyori sipped his bowl of tea, and gazed at Will over the rim, in a gesture strangely reminiscent of Iyeyasu, from whom perhaps it was copied. 'You have enjoyed your stay in Osaka, Anjin Miura?'

'It has been interesting, my lord.'

'We had not supposed you would have remained this long,' Hideyori said. 'You have watched the Tokugawa at work, filling in the moat?'

'As agreed by the Princess Jokoin, my lord.'

'The outer moat was filled several days ago,' Oda Yuraku remarked. 'Yet the work continues.'

Will turned his head to look at the old man. 'I know nothing of this, my lord. I cannot see sufficiently from my window, nor have I been permitted to walk upon the battlements.'

Hideyori nodded. 'Yet it is so. But we shall learn of this, now.'

'The man comes, my lord prince,' Sanada said.

The girl kneeling beside Will gave him a cautious smile as she delicately placed fried slices of fowl upon his plate. The screens were again opening, to admit a samurai in full armour save only for his helmet. He slowly lowered himself to the floor, and was immediately brought upright again by a gesture from Hideyori.

'Speak, man. You have seen the Shogun?'

'The Shogun was otherwise occupied, my lord prince,' the samurai said. 'I was taken before my lord Honda Masazumi.'

'And presented him with our protest?'

'Indeed, my lord prince.'

'And what was my lord Masazumi's reply?'

'He has been unwell, my lord prince, and therefore confined to his house. Thus he has not been personally superintending the work. But he was dismayed to hear that his soldiers had exceeded their instructions. He promised to send immediately to my lord Itakura in Kyoto, to discover the truth of the matter.'

'The truth?' Norihasa demanded. 'Is not the work under the personal supervision of the Shogun? Who else can give orders to cease?'

'It would appear, my lord Norihasa, that this work was commanded by Prince Iyeyasu himself. Not even the Shogun dares interfere with orders given by the prince.'

'And the prince is in Kyoto?'

'No, my lord. He is thought to be in Shidzuoka. But this is not certain. It is understood by lord Masazumi, however, that the orders are in the keeping of the prince's resident in Kyoto, my lord Itakura, and thus he has sent there to learn what is to be done.'

'These are nothing but lies, my lord prince,' Sanada said.

Hideyori gazed at the general, his brows knitted, his jaw trembling with uncertainty.

'And meanwhile, the work goes on, my lord prince,' Norihasa said. 'The outer moat is filled, the outer wall is razed. Now they commence filling in the second moat. What, my lord, would you wait until they commence to pull down the second wall? This is a Tokugawa trick, my lord prince. Iyeyasu implements all his desires by treachery.'

'What would you have me do?' Hideyori muttered. 'Perhaps he means no harm. Perhaps . . . '

'Perhaps,' Norihasa said. 'Perhaps, my lord prince. It is well known that the Tokugawa seek only the extermination of the Toyotomi. It is well known, my lord prince, that the armies of the Mori, and the Asano, and the Satsuma, have not yet returned to their own provinces, but lie encamped in those hills, all around

343

us, waiting their opportunity. My lord, the days of your power, of your freedom, of your *life*, are slipping away from you, with every spadeful of dirt that is thrown into that second moat.'

'But my lord . . . ' Hideyori turned to Ono Harunaga. 'My lord Harunaga, your sons . . . '

'Are samurai, my lord prince,' Harunaga said. But his voice was sad, and when he spoke he gazed at Will. 'They will be prepared to die, for the Toyotomi.'

'What say you, my lord Sanada?' Hideyori asked. 'What can we do to prevent this treachery?'

'Why, nothing, my lord, save we fire upon the working parties. Which will bring an end to the truce.'

'And then sally forth and destroy the Shogun,' Norihasa said. 'Aye. It will be a great victory.'

'But not great enough, my lord Norihasa,' Sanada said. 'Hidetada is nothing while his father lives. There are too many Tokugawa princes. Be sure that if filling in the second moat, and perhaps levelling the second wall, is part of the Tokugawa's plan, then will it be his plan to carry the fortress by assault, when it is done. So will it be his plan to reassemble his armies here, and this will be done the moment we end the truce. I would wait for that occasion, my lord prince. In the meanwhile, renounce the truce, call back any of your followers who may have left the castle, buy munitions where you may, and drive away the working parties. This will bring the Tokugawa back. And the moment you see the golden fan flying above that encampment, my lord prince, *then* let us sally forth, with all the men we command, and settle this issue upon a single day. Can we but reach out, and seize the heart of the Tokugawa, their forces will melt away into nothing, and the day, the empire, will be yours, my lord prince.'

By God, Will thought, but this man has the nub of the matter. And in the meanwhile, it is my own life they are discussing. The girl at his elbow frowned. The piece of meat she would have conveyed to his mouth was cold. But he could no more chew meat at this moment than he could spit. His mouth was dry.

'But to renounce the truce,' Hideyori said, half to himself. 'That is to condemn my half-brothers to death.'

'And yourself, my lord,' Yuraku said. 'Should we not meet with success. Iyeyasu will honour no agreement should you fire upon his men.'

'To renounce the truce now, my lord,' Norihasa said, 'also means that we hold here Anjin Miura. Is he not spoken of as the

Tokugawa's fortune. Did we not gain a great victory while he was absent? Did not the cannon ball strike this tower the moment he returned?'

'Do you believe in such nonsense, my lord Norihasa?' Oda Yuraku asked.

'Not I, my lord Yuraku, but it is certain that the common folk believe in it. More to the point, it is whispered that the Tokugawa himself believes in it. He is an old man, my lord prince, and perhaps given to fantasies.'

Hideyori's gaze turned to Will. Now, he thought; the Englishman in him shouted get up and fight for your life. Draw your short sword, at the least, and perhaps hope to gain a long sword, and die, now. Before they can murder you in their own time.

But the Japanese in him demanded he remain seated, and regard them with dignified contempt. As he could not win this battle, against such odds, then must he submit with a cold indifference.

'I cannot,' Hideyori said. 'I cannot make such a decision.'

'You cannot make any decision, my lord prince,' Asai Yodogimi said, quietly. 'It is your great failing as a ruler.'

She stood behind Will, and he could feel the hairs rising on his neck. Hastily he followed the example of the daimyo, of the serving girls, of the samurai in the doorway, and dropped forward into the kowtow. The princess. How her scent clouded the room. Fifteen years. And was she alone?

'Oh, rise,' she said contemptuously 'Seat yourselves, my lords. Why bow you to a mere woman?'

Slowly they came upright. By Christ, Will thought; I can feel her gaze upon my skin.

'If I may remind my lady mother,' Hideyori said. 'It was her decision to treat with the Tokugawa, at all.'

'My decision,' Yodogimi said. 'I was afraid. I am but a woman, and when that ball came through the roof, plunged past my very bed, I was afraid. And I knew then who had sent that ball. Who must have sent that ball. That man is the devil himself, my lords. But no longer. My womanhood is behind me, now. If you would not be men, then shall I be the man for you. My lord Sanada, I place you in general command of the Toyotomi armies, responsible only to myself.'

'My lady princess,' Sanada said, bowing close to the floor. 'Be sure that I shall carry out my duties with all honour to the name I protect.'

'Be sure you shall,' Yodogimi said.

'And my brothers, my lady mother?' Hideyori demanded. 'Your sons?'

'Were given life to serve you, my lord prince. None other. I was pleased to bear them, to raise them, for that purpose. I had hoped, I had prayed, that we might reach a peace with the Tokugawa, for this season. The prince cannot live forever. Not even the prince. I had hoped to await that event, and deal only with his son. But if that cannot be, then we must fight, as my lord Sanada says, and to our best advantage. We hold here the devil himself, the evil spirit who stands at the prince's shoulders. He must be destroyed.'

Will turned, his kicking foot overturning the low table in front of him, his moving left hand tumbling the serving girl on to her back and scattering the platter of food. So much the Englishman. But yet he knelt, gazing at the four women. Four women. Asai Yodogimi, in a white kimono, unchanged in the slightest from when he had first beheld her, fifteen years before. At her right hand, Asai Jokoin, her face angry, even through the caked white paint which disguised her sister's expression. At her left was a woman he did not recognise. And behind them, the tall figure of Pinto Magdalena.

Oh, Christ, he thought. Oh, Christ. But his eyes were misted. Her face, too, was concealed beneath the paint and he could not see into her eyes. But she was the mother of his son.

And the guards were already at his shoulder. Were he to attempt to rise, they would cut him down.

'Anjin Miura is a samurai, my lady princess,' Sanada said. 'He has the right of seppuku.'

'No.' Yodogimi stared at Will, her eyes tiny pools of utter darkness, her breathing so deep it swelled the bodice of her kimono. 'No. This man has no rights. He forfeited all his rights fifteen years ago, on the morning of Sekigahara. I shall kill him, my lords. With these hands of mine.'

The guards moved forward, seized Will's arms. He could throw them off, with a single heave of his shoulders. And yet he knelt, impaled by her gaze.

'But not yet,' Yodogimi said, her voice once again quiet. 'While he lives, they say he is the Tokugawa's fortune. We shall have nothing interfere with the prince's fortune, until he has once again taken his place before us, out there on the plain. On the morning that you lead your army forth, my lord Sanada, on that morning shall Anjin Miura die, and his head will be hoisted high above the battlements, to give cheer to our forces, and to strike terror into the hearts of the Tokugawa. They would fight us, with the aid of the devil. We shall throw the devil back into their faces.'

A guard reached into Will's belt, plucked out the short sword, and threw it on the floor.

'And in the meantime, my lady princess?' Norihasa asked.

Asai Yodogimi's lips parted. No doubt she smiled. 'In the meantime,' she said. 'We shall teach him what it means to betray the Toyotomi. We shall allow his screams to entertain us.'

Of what do you dream, when your body is consumed with pain, your mind with fear, your heart with anger? When life itself is unbearable, and tomorrow is unthinkable. You wish to dream with hate.

A sluice of icy water struck him on the head, cascaded down his face, and he moved. There was folly. Steel razors sliced into his wrists, and no doubt he moaned. Or whimpered. For did not the Princess Asai Yodogimi always get her wish? When she ordained that a man should be made to scream like a child then it must be so.

And there were not even razors, at his wrists. Merely ropes. But he had hung from them for so long now. Only by standing could he take the strain from his wrists, and standing, now, required a supreme effort of will, because standing allowed the blood to return through his arms to his fingers, and this was agony. *This* was agony.

Standing was also a problem for his knees, which were weak. Weak with fear, weak with apprehension, weak with hate?

He watched the man setting a taper to the torches, so that the darkened chamber filled with light, with flaring shadows which danced up and down the wall. Now he stood, and his arms were relaxed. The razors were no longer outside his body, but inside his hands. He looked up, at the low ceiling of the stone chamber, at the rings embedded in the stone. For when he dreamed, sometimes, he dreamed of Samson. He was a large, strong man, and those were but iron rings set in the stone. A supreme effort, a mighty pull, and they might come loose. What then? Might it not be possible, as this room was the bottom of the Asai Tower, to pull away the foundations, and bring the whole edifice crumbling down, tumbling Asai Yodogimi and Asai Jokoin and Pinto Magdalena from their beds, bringing them crashing into this cell to join him. How the Tokugawa would shout for joy, were the Asai Tower to fall.

But the rings were as firmly set now as they had been when he had first come here. God knew he had tried to pull them free, often enough. As when they had thrust the table under his belly to raise him from the floor, for the convenience of the young men. Even *that* day, the rings had not moved, although his heart had all but burst, with shame and anger. So, he was not Samson. For Samson had received his strength from God. And Will Adams had rejected the conception that God interfered with the deeds of men, either for them or against them. Will Adams was alone.

Oh, Christ, that he could be alone. For now all four of the torches were lit, and the room seemed to have grown in size. At the present time there was only one man in here with him. His gaoler, naked like himself, who wandered around in a state of equal filth. A honin, lowest of the low, condemned to live forever in this artificial light, blinking as he came closer, muttering to himself. Really a friendly fellow. Will did not know his name. A man of low passion, as well, fortunately. For here, tied up before him, suspended by his hands with all of his naked body at the disposal of anyone who might take a fancy to it, was the white man. But the gaoler seldom came that close. Perhaps he feared Will's legs. For the first day he had come close, in front. Will even thought it might have been pure curiosity, to see in which way, if any, the white man might be different to himself. And Will had kicked him clear across the room. He had lain unconscious for several minutes, and had even appeared to be dead.

He had not been dead, of course. He had beaten his prisoner with a savage anger which quite surpassed the displays he put on for the princess and her friends. He had made Will scream, far louder than before or since. And it had all been wasted. Yodogimi had been several floors away.

But since that night they seemed to have achieved an understanding. Across the hate-filled no man's land shared by their minds, they had almost become friends.

Now the gaoler busied himself along the far wall, arranging the mats. The floor was raised there, and the mats this day were the best he had. So, today he was to receive a visit from Yodogimi.

She did not come every day. She had done so in the beginning. She had come with her ladies, and one or two of her men, and they had sat themselves in front of him, for an hour's entertainment.

That first day, he had realised the difficulties of hate. They had all been there, even Magdalena. Magdalena, hidden behind her white paint her face expressionless, as she had watched her erstwhile lover firstly raped and then beaten, with thin bamboo rods until the blood ran down his legs. But then, had he ever been her lover? For all the tenderness they had once exchanged. Or had her love changed to hate, when she had discovered how fruitful had been their long day together, and again when Norihasa had put her aside, and yet again as Philip had squeezed his way from her womb.

In any event, seated as she had been, somewhat behind her princess, he had not been able properly to see to her. He had been able to see Yodogimi. So, while he suffered, he had thought, to keep his sanity, he would imagine the Princess Yodogimi, suffering. There was a pleasant dream. But he had been unable to sustain the image.

Instead, he had thought of Shikibu. Of nothing else but her face. It was now near a year since he had seen that face. He knew nothing of the changes which might have swept over it. But no changes would have swept over the face of Magome Shikibu.

Cocks persisted in calling her Mrs Adams. And whenever he did so, Shikibu, with her smattering of English, would look up with an utterly delighted expression. Shikibu, walking in a rose garden, in long dress and tightened waist and ruff and tall felt hat. With a feather. Oh, definitely a feather. A crimson feather, to show off the blackness of her hair.

Shikibu. With every blow of the rod he had remembered every line of her face, every curve of her body. And when the cloying, ugly hands were at *his* body, he had imagined they were hers. Shikibu, who alone could keep a man from madness. So long as he thought of Shikibu, he was surrounded by an invisible wall, through which his enemies could not force their way.

She stood in front of him now, shovelling cold rice into his mouth from a cracked and filthy bowl. The first time he had been thus fed he had spat it back in the creature's face. Then he had been full of anger and defiance. Then.

Now so much saliva filled his mouth he could hardly wait to swallow the rice. Besides, the first time he had made the mistake of looking at the man feeding him. Now he could close his eyes, and it was Shikibu.

There was a great deal of rice. It was no part of Yodogimi's plan to have him become too weak to permit him to understand what was happening to him, day by day, what would happen to him, in the end. And he chewed, and swallowed, because even cold dry rice tasted so good. And because he also wanted to live, to the end? Only thus could he be sure of dying, with Shikibu's face in front of him.

And what after he was gone? Strange that he had not thought of that before today. Perhaps because today his instincts told him the end was approaching. Even down here, in the very bowels of the castle, he had heard the conch shells wailing, yesterday. Wailing close at hand, and wailing in the distance. How long *had* he stood here, and hung here, and suffered here? Several weeks, certainly. The very length of his beard told him that. Several weeks. Perhaps several months. The floor was no longer cold to the touch, his flesh no longer constantly shivered into goose pimples. Several months. Long enough for Iyeyasu once again to summon his vassals and regroup his armies, because the Toyotomi had broken the truce. In despair. With two moats filled, the castle was indefensible. As the Toyotomi knew. So they staked all upon a single battle. But defeat the Tokugawa once more, and victory was theirs. The only alternative was death, for them all. They also knew *that*. But could they ever hope to defeat the Tokugawa again? That was asking too much of the gods.

So what would happen after his death? He would be avenged. Oh, certainly. This castle would be razed, and every man, woman and child in it would be destroyed. So perhaps he was, after all, Samson, who had died, was now dying, to give his lord the time he had needed. Iyeyasu had foreseen this outcome when last they had said goodbye. And *he* had foreseen it too, without yet understanding what was involved.

All would die. Magdalena? Philip? But perhaps death would be merciful, for Philip. And Yodogimi? Yodogimi would be tied to a dog. Christ, he was sweating.

The doors were opening, and there was the rustle of slippered feet on the stone steps outside. Of silk kimonos, too, and the chamber was filled with the scent of freshly bathed and freshly perfumed bodies. How many, today? Six, and three men.

Asai Yodogimi, mistress of Hideyoshi, mother of Hideyori,

woman of the Toyotomi. She wore a pink kimono, decorated, as were all her kimonos, nowadays, as was everything in this castle, with the golden gourds of the Toyotomi. Hideyoshi had taken the gourd as his symbol. In the beginning they had been made of wood, and he had added a gourd for every victory. Later he had had them fashioned in gold, and embroidered in gold upon his every possession. A myriad of golden gourds, for the myriad victories gained by Japan's greatest warrior, greatest man. Whose line now ended in this hate-filled woman and this effeminate boy.

For Hideyori was at her side, today. A Hideyori clad in armour and looking more uncomfortable than ever. And embarrassed.

'There is your enemy,' Yodogimi said, her voice soft. She crossed the room, her kimono rustling, her fan darting to and fro, sometimes in front of her face, somtimes dropping to her side. He would never understand the language of the fan, if he lived to be a hundred. If he lived to be a hundred.

Yodogimi stood in front of him, close enough to touch him. He inhaled her scent. The sweetest scent he had ever known. He could look at nothing but her face, for all the throng behind her, amongst whom would be a fresh set of torturers, certainly, eager to torment him and please him and humiliate him, to display his manhood and his impotence at one and the same time, to satisfy their princess, who remembered too much.

'Your prince has come, Anjin Miura,' she said softly. 'The golden fan flies above the camp of the Tokugawa. It is a beautiful sight, Anjin Miura. All the white scabbards, all the fluttering banners, all the armour. There are many men, out there, Anjin Miura. And they call for vengeance. Because of the death of their Englishman, their fortune. They cry out, Anjin Miura, because they are afraid, supposing you already dead. But this day shall they cry out even louder. Because this day shall they see your head, and it shall still be dripping blood, Anjin Miura.'

His head jerked. This day?

Yodogimi smiled. 'Do you not wish to die, Anjin Miura? After having lived so long and so well? Death comes to us all, Anjin Miura. Even I will die, one day. I am not afraid of it. Why should you fear it? And you will die well.' Again the smile. 'Will you not die well, Anjin Miura? Do not tell me we shall have to drag you, screaming, to your fate. The priests tell me many

Europeans die like that. They have no courage, your people. But I had thought better of you.'

'My death will be a small thing, my lady Yodogimi. Beside yours. This day. But then, you will not die, this day. The Tokugawa will tie you to a dog, in front of his palace, and there enjoy your pleasure.'

Asai Yodogimi no longer smiled. 'You shall not be lonely, Anjin Miura,' she promised. 'I shall set Iyeyasu's head beside yours, and many others. This day. This I swear. Bring the whips.'

'No, my lady mother,' Hideyori said. 'He came as hostage, and we have abused that. He has betrayed us, betrayed you, my lady, and he has suffered for that. Today he dies. Then let him die well. That is the law of the samurai.'

'I give him no right of seppuku,' Yodogimi said, her mouth rigid with anger.

Hideyori bowed. 'So be it, my lady mother. It is fitting, as Iyeyasu beheaded Ishida Mitsunari, that we should behead Anjin Miura. But let him die as a man, not a beast, and with the honour that is due to a samurai. My lord Yuraku, I leave this matter in your hands. My lady mother, you will accompany me to pray before the shrine of my father.'

Yodogimi hesitated, still staring at Will. 'Yet shall I myself raise the pole bearing your head, Anjin Miura,' she said. 'Be sure of that.'

Chapter 5

HE SANK, deep, deep into the deep tub. The water lapped at his chin, threatened to force its way into his mouth. It scorched the still open weals on his back, as if some fresh torturer was scraping at him with a wire brush. It was a delicious feeling, because it cleansed.

He was already clean. The two girls who had washed him remained by the side of the tub, waiting with the soft cloths to dry him when he should have finished. For no samurai could be executed, without first being purified.

His mouth sank below the surface of the near boiling water, and then his nose. Only his eyes remained above the surface as he gazed at the room. Behind the girl waited Oda Yuraku, standing, hands folded into the arms of his kimono. A very old man, who had, no doubt, seen a great deal of death, natural and unnatural. Some said he had been with his cousin, the great Nobunaga, when he had committed seppuku rather than surrender to the traitor Akechi Mitsuhide. Certainly he had been present when Hideyoshi had died at last, his stomach collapsing in a sea of filth. These were the greatest he had seen die. But there had been others. He had been in the pavilion at Kyoto when the policeman, Ishida Mitsunari, had lost his head. He had sat then, not twenty feet from Anjin Miura, had gazed at him for several minutes. With abstract interest, then.

Now they would be together to the end. But Yuraku should not be as interested as he appeared. Having seen so much death amidst so much greatness, what interest had the death of some passing Englishman for him?

What, indeed. He had not seen the old man since the day he had first been brought down here. It was difficult to recall what Yuraku had said that evening, standing at the window, gazing out at the camp of the Tokugawa. But they had been strange words, words which had almost suggested a certain common ground between them. Yet Yuraku had lifted not a finger to prevent his incarceration, and for all the weeks he had hung in the cell Yuraku had not come near him. Until now, when he had been placed in charge of his execution.

Perhaps, after all, his interest was the same as his niece's, concerned with the possibility that the Englishman might not die well. It occurred to Will that they were all interested in this possibility, that he might have to be carried screaming to the battlements, and there held down while they severed his head from his body. They expected him to be afraid. Even the guards, who stood at the doorway to the chamber, expected him to be afraid, gazed at him with interest, as he soaked.

He could, he thought, betray them all, yet again. All he had to do, now, was open his mouth and breathe. And make himself go on breathing. It would not take very long. And yet it would take too long, and then they *would* drag him from the water and revive him. That was unthinkable. It was unthinkable to betray his honour as a samurai in any way. Above all else, now, he must preserve his dignity. He must step from this bath within the next few minutes, and stand quietly while the girls dried him and then dressed him in his kimono and tied his girdle, and then he must walk at Yuraku's side, climb the many stairs, to the battlements of the keep, there to watch the Toyotomi go forth to battle. It would certainly be soon, now. Although he remained deep in the bottom of the Asai Tower, all around him he could hear, and feel, a tremendous stealthy rustle of movement as the army prepared to leave the fortress. And far more than that. This, too, he could feel. There was a plan afoot here. The Toyotomi would stake all upon a single day, and so would they plan, and scheme, to be sure of victory. How would they do that? By bribing one of the Tokugawa daimyo, as Iyeyasu had bribed Kobayakawa before Sekigahara?

He did not think it would do them much good. Nor was he particularly interested. Because before they actually made their assault his eyes would no longer see, however much they looked.

There was a knock on the door, and a guard opened it to admit one of Yodogimi's maids.

She bowed. 'My lady Yodogimi commands you to bring the Englishman to the upper floor, my lord Yuraku.'

'Tell the princess that it shall be done,' Oda Yuraku said.

She bowed again, her gaze searching past the guards for the man in the tub. Then she was gone, and the doors clanged shut.

Time to die. Will thrust his legs down, eased himself to his knees, and then stood up. Water drained down his body, and the girls moved forward with the towels. He stepped from the bath, felt their arms go round him. How small they were. How huge

354

he was. Perhaps it was for this they waited. To see if, in death, he would be different. If perhaps there would be more blood inside his body than inside theirs.

But they never doubted that he would die. The guards leaned on their spears, watching him, with interest. But not with alertness. Because he had been condemned, and he had no hope of survival, and so had accepted his condemnation, and therefore would accept his fate. Was this not the way of the samurai? Of any Japanese, to be sure.

But he was not Japanese. The soft cloth, commanded by the softer fingers, moved up and down his body. He looked down on the two heads of glossy hair, and without raising his own, at the feet of Yuraku.

He was English. So it was also part of the English gentleman's code to die with honour, to kneel and place his head upon the block. To make some witty remark to the executioner, some intelligent remark to the priest. To forgive his enemies and wave at the crowd.

But he was not even an English gentleman. Will Adams, shipwright, of Gillingham, Kent. A man John Saris would not even entertain in his house, in England. What business had he with dying like a gentleman, like a samurai? Were he to die, then why should he not take his enemies with him, force them to kill him on his own terms?

He had no weapon, save the two girls, crouching now as they dried his feet. And Oda Yuraku? Not as a hostage. Yuraku would expect to die, in such circumstances, and the guards would have no compunction. So, only as a human weapon.

He acted without thinking further. His hands reached down, and he picked up one girl in each fist, as if they had been no more than children. As they were. With a heave and a shout he threw them across the room, at the startled guards, and in the same movement himself leapt for Oda Yuraku.

The old man gazed at him with a surprised expression which was, as he had anticipated, entirely lacking in fear. But it was also lacking in disgust or resentment. He retreated, to be sure, to avoid Will's swinging arms, in the same movement as the guards disengaged themselves from the girls and brought up their spears.

'Here, Anjin Miura,' he shouted, and drew his long sword and turned it, presenting the haft to Will's hands.

What a sword. The hilt gleamed even in this dull light, so

closely packed were the jewels. And the cord twined round it was beautiful to the touch, soft, easy to hold. Perhaps Nobunaga himself had once held this sword. Had once used it in battle.

The first spear was already stretching the air as it surged at his belly. He sucked in his stomach as he stepped backwards, swung the sword vertically from above, watched the steel slice through the wooden pike handle while the astounded soldier stared at it in horror. Will followed the blade to the right, and yet was able to turn, balanced on the balls of his feet as he had been taught by Tadatune, hissing as he forced his breath through his mouth and sucked fresh air into his nostrils, to commence his second swing, the great sword now curving upwards. The disarmed soldier desperately reached for his own sword; he stood in front of his comrade, who with equal desperation was attempting to gain a clear field of vision for his thrust.

And so he watched his companion die. The sword cut into the man's left side, neatly missing his breastplate and slicing through the leather thongs securing that to his backplate, to sear through the cloth beneath and into the flesh. Blood gushed from the still pumping heart, and the man died without a sound.

The girls were on their feet, hands pressed to their mouths, uncertain whether to scream or not as they watched Oda Yuraku, still standing against the wall, taking no part in the conflict he had started with his own weapon.

The second guard thrust, and retrieved quickly as Will once again side-stepped. Now he hissed in turn, waved the spear to and fro, and with a quick movement threw it as a javelin. Will ducked, and it passed harmlessly over his shoulder, struck the wall, and fell to the ground with a dull clang. The guard had his sword half out of his scabbard, but Will's was already recovered from his first swing, and was again carving the air, no longer gleaming, but dull and scattering drops of still warm blood through the air as it descended.

The guard took it on his arm, and watched the lifeless wrist drop to the floor in horror. Yet his right hand still swung his sword. Slowly. Too slowly. Will, snorting breath into his lungs and maintaining a perfect balance as he again turned, sliced into his opponent's shoulder, bringing another cascade of blood pumping out like a fresh spring. The soldier's armour clanked as he struck the floor, and in time with him, the two girls sank to their knees by the door, gazing at the blood-spattered naked body of the white man, at the huge sword still clutched in both his hands, at the throbbing chest and dilated nostrils.

'By the lord Buddha,' Oda Yuraku whispered. 'But you handle a sword like some reincarnation of Minamoto no-Yoshitomo.'

'I have been well taught,' Will said. 'But not, apparently, in the ways of the Japanese.'

Yuraku shrugged. 'This castle and all who live in it are doomed,' he said. 'They have been doomed from the moment Asai Jokoin stupidly agreed to Iyeyasu's proposals. You but anticipated my action in setting you free, Anjin Miura.'

'Why me, my lord.'

'You are my passport to the favour of Iyeyasu. And I am close to being the last of the line of Oda Nobunaga. It is my duty to live for as long as possible. Toyotomi or Tokugawa? What business have I with who rules Japan, if it cannot be the Oda?'

Will nodded, thoughtfully. 'Fetch my clothes,' he told the girls.

They hurried forward with his cloth and the kimono he was to have worn to his execution. But he kept his hands on the sword as he watched the doors.

Yuraku smiled. 'There is naught to fear, at least for a while, Anjin Miura. All will be watching the progress of the battle.'

'Yet I am to be executed as it commences.'

'As the final action commences. Which will not be for a while. The Toyotomi have worked out an elaborate plan for this day, which they hope will bring them success.'

'And you do not?'

'You are one of the Tokugawa, Anjin Miura. You tell me if you think it will bring success. The plan is that Sanada, the most famous Toyotomi general, will march forth from the gate of the castle, thereby attracting to himself the principal Tokugawa force, perhaps led by the prince himself. But Sanada will not be in command of the *main* Toyotomi force. This will be making its way through the city of Osaka, commanded by Ono Harufusa, meaning to fall upon the Tokugawa from the flank as soon as the two armies are locked in combat. Yet is this not all. When this happens, Sanada calculates that the Mori and the Asano will hasten to the help of the Tokugawa, thus committing all the besieging armies with the exception of the Satsuma, who have resumed their old position on the east bank of the river, and can take no part in the battle. But there will yet remain a third Toyotomi force: the garrison of the castle itself.'

'Sanada would strip the fortress of its garrison?' Will demanded. The girl tied his girdle.

'Indeed. He is aware that one either lives, victorious at the end of this day, or dies. Hideyori is himself in command of the garrison. Once the last Tokugawa reserve is engaged, then will he sally forth. My lord Sanada holds that it is not just men that decide a conflict, but the opportune arrival of reserves, in no matter how small numbers. And in this case they will number some twenty thousand hand-picked men.'

'And you doubt the success of this venture? A plan so desperate, so total, may always command success, with but the slightest fortune.'

'Therefore must we hurry, Anjin Miura. The Toyotomi fear no assault from the river at their backs, particularly now the spring rains have caused it to flood. We shall make our departure thence. I have arranged a boat for us. Within two hours we may be at the camp of the Shogun, to give him this information and convince him that it will be best to summon the Satsuma to his side, and until their arrival fight only a holding action.'

'Two hours?' Will cried. 'Then by Christ, why are we standing here.' He ran to the door, and checked, looking over his shoulder.

'These girls should certainly be killed,' Yuraku said.

Will hesitated, his breathing once more normal, but his stomach heaving as he looked at the two dead men surrounded by still spreading pools of blood, and at the two girls, crouching by the bath, still naked, still lovely to look upon, still children.

'You may drown them,' Yuraku said. 'That would be best.'

And also in this castle was his son, and the mother of his son. To be destroyed in the coming holocaust. Yet what alternative had he? As a Japanese? As a Japanese had he failed. As a European he had saved his life.

Or would his life have been saved anyway, by Japanese subterfuge?

'We can lock them in,' he said.

'Are you mad? They will make themselves heard the moment we are out of here.'

'Then will we delay the Toyotomi plan, my lord Yuraku. Two of us are not needed, either to work the boat, which will in any event drift with the stream, or to reach the Tokugawa encampment. Indeed, one man may well have a better chance of making his way there undetected by the Toyotomi.'

'And you?'

'I have business here.'

Yuraku pulled at his beard. 'I give you your life, and you throw it away again? To what avail, Anjin Miura? You will never reach Norihasa.'

'Yet is he still in the fortress, my lord?'

'He commands the garrison, with Prince Hideyori.'

Will nodded. 'This is good. Be sure that he will wish to make sure I am dead. Now, my lord, I beg of you. Go while you may.'

Yuraku hesitated a last time, looked at his sword still in Will's hand, its point resting on the floor.

'Oh, take your weapon, my lord. That I have been privileged to use such a blade is sufficient.'

'Then keep it,' Yuraku said. 'You handle it to better purpose than I have ever done. I will keep my short sword, for if I am taken by the Toyotomi that will be all I shall need. I wish you fortune, Anjin Miura.' He opened the door, listened for a moment, and stepped through.

The girls moved, a faint rustle as they huddled closer together. Blood drifted across the floor of the chamber and nearly touched their feet, and these too were drawn up, protectively. They gazed at Will with wide eyes.

'Remain here,' he said. 'And be sure that if you start your screams too soon, then will I return for your heads.'

He picked up the undamaged spear, went to the door in turn, eased it open, listened. Outside was a great deal of noise, but all of it was above him now. The Toyotomi, going forth to war. And what did he intend? Not to stop that conflict, certainly. Nor could he ever dream of interfering with their plans; that must remain the responsibility of Oda Yuraku. So, then, *what* did he intend. His hand tightened on the sword hilt. Only to die, because to live, after what he had experienced, endlessly in the dungeon below here, was impossible. But to die, carrying *her* with him. And others, perhaps. Now he hated. And now he had the means to satisfy his hate at hand. The deaths of the two soldiers had but given him an appetite.

He closed the door behind him, moved silently to the stairs, looked up. There were people there; he heard voices, and the clank of armour. So then, it was to be a quick end. He did not doubt that he would survive these; his very hate would carry him onwards and upwards. But the alarm would certainly be sounded here.

359

He climbed, slowly, softly. He held his sword in his left hand, carried the spear in his right. He reached the landing, and three guards turned to look at him in surprise. Three guards and a fourth man, a large, strong man built very like a suma wrestler, and wearing too, only a loin-cloth. A man who carried a long sword in his hands. The executioner. Waiting for his victim.

Will hurled the lance, and it entered the executioner's belly. He gave a choking gasp and fell forward, hands closing over the wood tearing at his intestines. The haft struck the floor and the jolt drove the spear clear through his body; the bloodstained steel tip protruded from his back. But by then no one was looking at him. The sword transferred to his right hand and closed upon again with his left, Will took the centre of the room where he had the space for his sweeps and cuts, his reverse passes and thrusts. He outreached them, he was larger and stronger than they, and he had the advantage of total surprise. Blood flew and steel clashed on armour, and even once, on other steel. There was a howl of pain and one of anger, and the air filled with hissing grunts. And then became silent.

Blood stained the kimono, flecked his face, matted his hair. Whose blood? Not his, certainly. He ran up the stairs, seeking the upper levels of the tower, gulping air into his lungs, his heart singing with a wild exultation. The last time another man's blood had stained his hands he had felt sick with horror. How long ago? Fifteen years.

Another floor and an empty landing. But now he had reached the surface, and could move cautiously to the great wooden doors, standing wide, and looked out at the courtyard of the keep itself. An emptier courtyard than he had ever seen. There were men at the gate by the bridge, but how few. And how pre-occupied, as they gazed down at the garrison town. Every other man would be waiting by the main gates, for the signal to join the battle.

And now, drifting on the air, there came the renewed wailing of conch shells and the shout of a multitude of men. The battle had commenced. The first battle.

From below him also there came a sound, a thin wailing noise. The two girls had decided he was far enough away. But now it did not matter. There was nobody here to listen.

He mounted the next flight of stairs, his breathing settled. How silent it was, how peaceful, within this tower. He was alive, and would continue living for as long as he chose, now. For there could be naught but women above him. He could continue on his way, and slay, and slay, and slay to his heart's content. Yodogimi. Jokoin. She had visited him often enough. Oh, yes, he would wish her to die. The other women who had smiled at his screams, at his uncontrolled writhings. And Magdalena.

Magdalena. After all, what did he intend by this climb, by this mad, blood-filled venture? Was he not still the romantic dreamer, whose vague idea was to throw the woman over his shoulder and make his escape, cutting his way through all who would oppose him? A dream? Had he not just cut his way through six men as if they had been children? He looked down at his sword, his kimono, at his arms. By God, how blood stank.

He had reached the first floor, where were situated his own apartments, as hostage. The doors stood wide at the back of the hall, and he ran across to the windows, to look out over the plains. It was a magnificent spring day, with only a few fluffy clouds to accent the blueness of the sky, with the mountains to the north showing green in the noonday sun. At Sekigahara he had wanted to be a bird, winging high above the battlefield, safe from spear or sword or arrow, watching and noting. How had his wish been granted. He looked across the fortress and the city and the field, and here he was safe. Why, he thought, close those doors and I can remain here forever. No one will seek me here. Forever. A dishonoured samurai.

In the courtyard of the garrison town a mass of samurai waited, in columns, an endless line of waving banners and bristling pikeheads. On the wall, the outer wall of the fortress since the levelling of the original first defence and the filling of the two moats by the Tokugawa, he could see the unmistakable figure of Prince Hideyori, slight even in full armour. Beside him were Ono Harunaga and Ishida Norihasa, watching the manoeuvres on the plain below them. As were the women and children of the Toyotomi farther to the left, away from the gate. An immense accumulation of fluttering bright kimonos, and how anxious minds? For their fates were also being decided this day.

At the moment there was no fighting. Sanada's assault on the Tokugawa advance guard had apparently been halted, judging by the mounds of dead, but he had been allowed to retreat and regroup in good order, perhaps half a mile in front of the castle gateways, and the Tokugawa army, sheltering beneath their myriad banners of the golden fans, remained some distance away, arrayed for battle, certainly, and facing the castle, but not yet committed.

Will gazed at the town. There was little sound from there. The houses clustered close to each other on either side of the narrow streets. Osaka was hardly more than a ghost city now. Most of its inhabitants had either taken refuge within the fortress itself or fled during the long siege. He thought he could make out one or two banners, deep in the forest of roofs. But still very far away from debouching on to the plain. No wonder Sanada had withdrawn. And indeed, might not have withdrawn far enough. For even as he watched, the conch shells wailed, and the Tokugawa started their advance, the spears glittering in the midday sunlight as they moved forward, the lines of armour-clad samurai appearing, at this distance, like undulating leather belts dotted with iron pinpoints, chased by brilliant insects in the persons of their commanders, galloping up and down the lines as they issued their orders and exhorted their men. It was impossible to decide if Iyeyasu was there, but certainly the Shogun would be in command, and his brothers would be at his side. The Tokugawa, this day anticipating their greatest hour.

Farther to the north another huge mass of men was also advancing across the plain. The Asano, obeying the summons of the prince. Iyeyasu was committing his entire force to the destruction of Sanada, careless of the possibility of a threat from his flank. And rightfully, careless, for the Toyotomi lost amidst the houses were lost indeed.

Will watched, breathing slowly and deeply, his entire body tingling as he experienced the euphoria of battle, the combination of humility and pride at the sight of so many men marching on their destinies. No doubt the Toyotomi felt the same, for again as he watched Sanada's army seemed to grow smaller, the wings contracting as the pikes were lowered, to receive the coming assault. And now a swarm of arrows sang through the air. He could not see the bolts themselves, but he watched tiny brown and black dots fall from the foremost of the advancing belts, to remain like grains of pepper on the green spring grass. But arrows would not halt the Tokugawa now, nor arquebuses—he picked out the occasional puff of black smoke rising above the Toyotomi force. As they well knew. Now a group of mounted men detached themselves from the rear of the defenders, whipping their horses as they pounded across the sun-dried mud of the filled moats and made for the gateway of the castle. Hideyori and his officers descended from the battlements to greet them. But it was simple enough to tell what Sanada wanted. He wanted help, and quickly. If he could not obtain the forces at present involved in the houses, he would wish the garrison. For if he was driven back in a general rout, the fortress might well fall in one grand assault.

And yet, so far as Will could tell, no orders were given to the troops waiting in the courtyard. Indeed, now the horsemen had arrived, the gates were being once more shut, and there seemed to be a vehement argument going on between the daimyo, with Hideyori, as ever, plucking at his chin in anxiety, and Norihasa waving his arms, and Harunaga walking up and down.

But he had waited long enough. Whatever was going to happen, the climax of this day was fast approaching. He turned away from the window, reluctantly, for there was the tremendous attraction of the coming clash which might prove the most decisive in the history of this land, and gazed at Philip. The boy knelt in the corner of the room, staring at him. Around him were the drawings Will had made. He must have been there when his father had entered, had remained there, silent, for nearly half an hour.

'What do you here, boy?' Will demanded, his heart swelling.

'I come here, my lord. When they have no use for me, I come here, with my drawings. I was happy here, my lord. With you. But they told me that you would die, this day.'

'So they did,' Will agreed. 'I am not so easy to kill, Philip.' He hesitated, sucking his lower lip. The boy would be only a hindrance in whatever was coming. And if he personally did not survive whatever was coming, then would the boy's life not be worth living, as a prisoner of the Tokugawa. But he had stayed here, in safety, for some time.

He dropped to his knees beside his son. 'Listen. I have work to do, Philip. But I wish you to remain here with the door closed and stay here, no matter what happens. I will come back for you, if I can. If I do not, then when the fighting ceases, you must make your way out of the castle. Go to Miura, south of Edo. There you will ask for the house of Anjin Miura, and you will go to that house, and there you will find my servant, Kimura, and my wife, Magome Shikibu. Go to them, Philip, and say to them, I am the son of Anjin Miura and Pinto Magdalena. My father charges you with my protection and education until I am a man. Can you remember that?'

Philip gazed at him, 'My Lord? How can I be your son? And the lady Magdalena? My lord . . .'

'You will have to trust me in this, Philip. Yet it is true. And Magome Shikibu will know it is true, once she has looked upon you. Trust her, Philip, for she is a most wonderful woman. Trust her, and all will be well.'

'My lord . . . '

'Do as I say.' He got to his feet as a tremendous roar of sound, of human voices and clashing weapons, seeped through the opened window. He ran back to it, watched the Tokugawa surging forward and over the ranks of Sanada's men. Watched, too, the garrison leaving its orderly lines and hurrying to take up position along the battlements, to resist the assault which they knew could be only minutes away, watched too the empty town which had swallowed an army. Not quite. The first of Harufusa's troops were at last emerging from the houses, but too late to affect the disaster which had overtaken the Toyotomi. An over-elaborate plan, doomed to failure by the indecisiveness of its commanders. For had Hideyori indeed led his men from the castle and assisted Sanada's force to stand for only a few minutes longer, then Harufusa might have been in time. Instead of which the Tokugawa had been allowed to destroy each of the three Toyotomi armies, one by one, and were now left with a scant twenty thousand men opposed to them, defending a fortress which needed three times that number to be held.

And where was Hideyori now? No longer even on the outer rampart. As Will watched, he saw the prince come through the gateway of the keep itself, only feet below him, and hurry across the courtyard, taking off his helmet as he ran, throwing it to one side in a gesture of petulant disgust. With himself? Or his advisers. Norihasa ran beside him; Harunaga had stayed to direct the defence. But with Hideyori there ran a woman. Yodogimi had sent one of her ladies to discover why Anjin Miura had not been brought up the tower for execution. And the woman would have found the dead man and the two girls, and hurried to tell the prince that the Englishman was loose, in the castle. Had *that* news influenced Hideyori's decision, or lack of it? Anjin Miura, the Tokugawa's good fortune.

They reached the door of the tower. Will left the window, ran across the room. 'Remember what I told you, boy,' he said, and closed the door behind him.

Feet sounded on the steps beneath. Will sucked breath into

his lungs, thrust his right foot forward, the sword extended from his belly. How slowly his heart beat. For how long had he waited for just this one moment in time.

Hideyori reached the landing, gazed at him in horror. 'Stand aside, my lord prince,' Will commanded. 'Or die.'

'Norihasa,' Hideyori shouted, dropping to his hands and knees and slithering across the floor to the right.

The woman, next in line, screamed, and ducked back down the steps.

Norihasa reached the landing, his brows knitted. 'By the lord Buddha,' he whispered. 'It cannot be.'

'Draw your sword, my lord,' Will said. 'I have waited too long for this occasion. I but regret that my gaolers stole your ko-kotana along with my other possessions.'

'Aye,' Norihasa said. The sword seemed to leap from its scabbard, and the scabbard was thrown to one side. Hideyori regained his feet, sidled round the room, gazing at the men as he made for the steps.

'Do you reach your lady mother, my lord,' Norihasa said.

'And you, Norihasa,' the prince begged. 'Without you, my lord, we are as nothing.'

Norihasa smiled. 'I am still at your side, my lord Hideyori.' His sword flicked forward, and the blades touched, lightly. Yet the daimyo was all the while circling to his left, forcing Will to *his* left, as he had in the garden at Shiba.

Will moved forward, into the centre of the room, sword performing a figure of eight through empty air as Norihasa moved back. The Japanese struck his arm against the wall, and frowned, as he turned, weapon once more raised. Hideyori waited at the top of the next flight of steps.

'You have learned, Anjin Miura,' Norihasa said.

'Enough,' Will said. 'My teacher was Shimadzu no-Tadatune.'

Norihasa nodded, slowly. 'A good blade, Anjin Miura. Yet not good enough.' He came forward again, slowly now, sword point quivering as it thrust out from his body, held, surprisingly, only in his right hand. Will swung, to knock it aside, and it was as quickly withdrawn, to be grasped in both hands and reversed, to come sweeping back from left to right. Once again the body slash. But Will had anticipated that, and turned on the balls of his feet, his blade held vertical and rigid, to take the blow, and it was so powerful it all but drove him aside, and then to come up and itself thrust at the daimyo's chest. The point tore the leather immediately beneath the breastplate, and Norihasa leapt backwards, once again striking the wall, and now he panted.

'Norihasa,' Hideyori wailed.

And now a woman's voice came from above. 'My lord prince? What do you here? The enemy are at the gate, my lord. My lord?' Her voice rose to a scream as she looked past the prince's shoulder.

Norihasa's sword came up again. But now it moved even more slowly, and beads of sweat stood out on the daimyo's forehead. Outmatched for strength, and now for speed around the hall, he was realising that he was, in addition, at least matched for skill. Breath hissed through his nostrils. And now he waited. His hope lay in the riposte.

Will moved forward, also slowly, his blade extended, frowning with concentration, waiting for Norihasa to move. Either way. It mattered not. Tadatune had spent too many hours teaching him the backhanded cut. Now, he thought. Now it is ended. And what else may not be begun? For with Norihasa dead, the tower is mine. Hideyori is no warrior. The tower, and the princesses, and Pinto Magdalena, all are my prisoners.

From the corner of his eye he saw the prince move. Hideyori slowly drew his long sword. It was incredible that he would dare violate the laws of bushido, yet for the moment Will's attention was distracted. He half turned to face the new threat, and Norihasa stepped forward. Desperately Will swept from left to right, attempting to parry Norihasa's thrust. The momentum of his swing carried him round, and he had not known how near he had been standing to the steps. While still off balance he gazed into space.

The great sword of Oda Nobunaga slipped from his grasp, and he was tumbling, head over heels, propelled by his own strength, rolling down the stairs, striking the next landing, losing his balance once again as he attempted to regain his feet and then rolling again, off the stairs, this time to drop through twelve feet of space and strike the stone floor of the ground. All this seemed to be happening around him. Darkness did not cloud his mind until the final drop, and then it was only for a few short seconds.

He heard voices, far away, but coming closer. Screams. Shouts. Loud threats and reproaches.

'I am dishonoured, my lord prince,' Norihasa said. 'There was no need.'

'I would not have interfered,' Hideyori said. 'You must believe this, my lord. I but sought to defend myself in the event of your death.'

'But you expected my death,' Norihasa muttered, half to himself.

'His head,' Yodogimi shouted, her voice strangely harsh, and rippling with hysteria. 'We shall throw them his head.'

'Do *you*, then, believe in such superstition?' her sister demanded. 'Look, my lady, look. The gates are down. Nothing will now stop the Tokugawa. And the tower burns.'

Because acrid smoke was drifting up the stair well from the kitchens and dungeons below ground level, clogging the nostrils, whispering at the mind with its portent of death.

And now their feet were on the stairs. And he was weaponless. Desperately he rolled to one side, saw the stone circle of the well, and rose to his knees. His belly flopped against the uneven stone, and he threw himself forward. Too far. For a moment he hung over endless space, and then his hands caught on the iron rungs of the ladder. Even so he slipped as his fingers would not grip, and he slid down several feet, body hanging, muscles screaming, until feet and hands seemed to catch at the same moment, and he lay vertical against the curving wall, panting, sobbing with anxiety. For what business had he with death, now? He had faced Norihasa, and the honour was now his. And the day was Iyeyasu's. The greatest day in the history of Japan.

Feet and voices, far above him now.

'Gone,' Yodogimi wailed. 'Gone. He is a spirit. An evil spirit. Gone.'

'He fell, but a moment since,' Norihasa said. 'Indeed, my lord prince, he should be here.'

Was Magdalena there? Of course. Where Yodogimi went, so did her maid. What more was there between them than that? How strange, knowing as he did what Iyeyasu felt for him, he had never supposed the possibility of a similar relationship between Magdalena and Yodogimi. But now she was silent. Of them all, only Asai Jokoin seemed to understand the reality of the situation.

'The tower *burns*,' she cried. 'And you stand here quarrelling over the whereabouts of one man?'

But what would they do? Where would they flee? Yodogimi, tied to a dog. The dog was coming closer. Who were there? How many did he wish to save.

Smoke billowed down into the cavern of the well, had him

choking. But they too were choking. And their voices were lost in the churning chaos of his mind, the shrieks of rage and anger and pure vengeance which came from the inner gate, the wailing of conch shells and the dull explosions of arquebuses. All hell had descended upon Osaka this day.

And the castle burned. Or at least, this tower. Memory plucked at his mind, and he thrust himself upwards. His fingers scrabbled at the iron rungs, and he reached for the air, exploded from the mouth of the well like a ball from the muzzle of a cannon. The huge hall was empty, and the steps led emptily upwards. He climbed them, while the red glow of the stairs from the kitchens chased him onwards. On the landing he found the sword, which had accompanied him at least part of his fall.

He picked it up, climbed the next flight of steps, ran along the corridor, tore open the doors to his apartments. 'Philip. Philip,' he called. But there was no one here. Impatiently he kicked mats aside, overturned bowls of flowers which still stood, incongruously, in every corner. The boy was gone, and with him his papers. He had smelt the flames, perhaps, and left. That made sense. And he would have supposed his father dead.

Will paused at the window for a moment; the gate to the garrison town had fallen, and yet the Toyotomi fought, and died where they stood, in ranks of armoured samurai, being assailed on all sides by the eager Tokugawa. Now they fought along the walls as well, and in and out of doorways. And from the houses there had arisen a great screaming and wailing. The women of the Toyotomi, given over to the victorious soldiery, after a siege of such magnitude, so many dead.

And in the strongest possible contrast, the courtyard of the keep was empty. Empty of sound, empty of blood, empty of death, and empty of people, while separated by only a moat and a wall from the carnage. What then, had happened to the Toyotomi? Were they, even now, making their escape by some secret way from the doomed citadel?

He ran outside, was met by a cloud of smoke. He ran down the stairs, reached the ground floor, and staggered through the great doorway, to inhale fresh air, and look at the Asai Tower, now shrouded in the smoke which issued from every window, every floor, obscured the banner of the golden gourds which still fluttered bravely in the afternoon breeze.

Such as it was. It was hot, and the sun was only now declining in the west, and the smoke for the most part rose straight into the air, just as the tremendous clash of battle hung, instead of dissipating. And the gate of the keep was unattended. Closed, to be sure, and barred, to hide the sights and sounds without, and even repel them, but no longer guarded. The keep was at the mercy of any man bold enough to run forward and seize it.

He stood in the centre of the empty yard, gripping his sword with both hands, willing himself forward, and heard a sound close at hand. He turned, the blade raised and thrust forward.

For a moment the woman was strange to him, her white face streaked with dirt and stained with smoke, her kimono equally disordered. Then he recognised the Princess Jokoin.

He bowed. 'My lady princess,' he said. Mockery? Anger? Hatred? Only impatience. 'Tell me where your sister has taken refuge.'

'She is in the armoury, Anjin Miura,' Jokoin said. 'With her ladies, and her son.'

'And Norihasa?'

'He is there also, Anjin Miura. With my lord Ono Harunaga.'

Will nodded, and made to pass her. The armoury, low, squat, with walls of solid stone, five feet thick, and a stone roof, protruded inwards from the outer wall of the keep, at the rear of the tower.

'Wait. They will not permit you to enter, Anjin Miura. The armoury is impregnable. No man, no number of men, may enter there unless the doors are opened.'

'It will not stand before my cannon, my lady princess. They cannot stay in there forever.'

'Long enough,' Jokoin said. 'I would speak with the prince.'

'You would parley, *now*?'

'You will assist me in this, Anjin Miura. Your mistress and your son are also in there.'

'Philip? But . . . '

'He had left your apartments to watch you duel with my lord Norihasa. He chose to accompany us. No doubt he thought you dead when you fell down the stairs, as did we all. Now, will you take me before the prince?'

Will hesitated. She had sat beside her sister in the cell, and smiled at him. But Magdalena was in there. After all, Magdalena was in there. And Philip.

And Asai Yodogimi?

'We had best hurry,' he said, and ran for the gate, the princess at his shoulder. Fists and pike butts were already smashing against

369　　　　　　　　　　　　　　　　　　　　　L.O.T.G.F.—2B

the wood, and the great doors were trembling. He had to put his shoulder to the bolts to raise them, and then the gates flew inwards, with such force that he was swept against the wall, the princess beside him.

Tokugawa soldiery poured through, screaming anger and vengeance, their swords and spears gleaming dully with the blood they had spilled, to pause in surprise at the sight of the undefended courtyard, the burning Asai Tower.

'You have gained the day,' Will shouted, standing before them.

'Anjin Miura.' The words swelled upwards in a gigantic paean of victory. 'Anjin Miura lives. The day is ours. The castle has fallen.'

They parted, to allow the Shogun to enter. Hidetada had removed his helmet, and there was blood on his face and hair. Blood on his sword, as well, and on his armour. His brothers walked behind him, and their weapons too were coated with blood.

'Well met, Anjin Miura,' Hidetada said. 'Truly, you have the fortune of the great. We had long given you up for dead. And have you taken the citadel, single-handed?'

'Far from it, my lord. I think your enemies surrendered it, by their indecision. My lady princess?'

Jokoin stepped from behind him.

'The woman is yours,' Hidetada said. 'And then she belongs to my men.'

Breath hissed through Jokoin's nostrils.

'She wishes to speak with the prince, my lord Shogun,' Will said. 'I have promised her that.'

'The prince my father has retired to his couch,' Hidetada said. 'Now that the battle is won. I command here.'

'Nonetheless, my lord Shogun, I have promised that the Princess Jokoin may speak with him. She acts as emissary for the Prince Hideyori and his mother.'

'They are defeated, Anjin Miura. They can expect no mercy.'

'They would make their peace, my lord Shogun,' Jokoin said. 'All of Japan now lies at the feet of the Tokugawa. They would, also.'

'They would beg mercy, of the Tokugawa?' Hidetada asked in surprise. 'Truly, it is said, a man's ancestry will betray him in the end. Take the Princess Jokoin before my father, Anjin

Miura.' He turned to his followers. 'The castle is yours. And all you may discover within it.'

It seemed the skies would fall.

Torches flared, around the house of the prince. Guards stood to attention, and some wept. The prince was sick. Some said he was dying. It was not possible for a man aged seventy-three, with a wound in the kidneys, to sit a whole day in the saddle, and command his armies, and still live at the end of it. The Tokugawa, the army, perhaps the world, waited for Minamoto no-Iyeyasu.

He lay on his couch, scarce seeming to breathe. But his eyes were as alive as ever in their long life. 'Will?' he whispered. 'Truly had I this time given you up for lost. But you . . . you are indestructible.'

'There is a saying, in England, my lord prince, that a bad penny will always be found.'

The thin lips parted in a faint smile. 'And you can still joke. What did they do to you, Will? I lay awake at night, dreaming of what they might have been doing to you. And they called you a coward, a man who could willingly go, to that.'

'You once said to me, my lord prince, that the past is not for discussion. Only the future. I have with me the Princess Jokoin.'

Iyeyasu's head half turned.

'She has come to ask for the lives of the Prince Hideyori and his mother. And their followers, my lord prince.'

'They still live?'

'They have shut themselves in the armoury, my lord, and have sent the princess with me to beg for their lives.'

'The Princess Yodogimi also?'

'Yes, my lord.'

'And the Portuguese woman?'

'Yes, my lord.'

Iyeyasu's eyes gloomed at him. And no one else? Had he known, about Philip? Did not Iyeyasu know everything that happened, in every castle in Japan? Was this not his boast?

But now the eyes were moving to Jokoin. 'So, your sister begs *me* for mercy.'

'The Princess Asai Yodogimi seeks an honourable settlement of your dispute, my lord prince,' Jokoin said. 'This war is not of the Toyotomi's making, no matter how many times you say so. This war is the result of your own fear of the *name* Toyotomi, of your own hatred for the Princess Yodogimi. Well, my lord, you have fought and won. Now the Toyotomi ask for honour to be shown to them. In the name of the lord Hideyoshi, your friend and master.'

Now Iyeyasu's head did turn. He gazed at the woman. 'The Tokugawa acknowledge no master save the Mikado, nor have they ever done so, woman. Tell your sister, and her son, that as they claim to descend from greatness, let them meet their fate, with greatness. Tell them if they wish they may come forth from the armoury. Any who wish may come forth, and receive Tokugawa justice. Those who do not wish to do so, may remain there for all eternity.'

Jokoin sucked breath into her lungs. 'You would destroy the son of Hideyoshi, my lord?'

'It was Hideyori's decision to break the truce,' Iyeyasu said. 'Let him come out. The Tokugawa will treat him fairly.'

'As you treated Ishida Mitsunari, my lord?'

'I treated the policeman better than he deserved, Princess Jokoin. Now leave my bedside, or I will hand your body to my soldiers. You have my safe conduct back to your sister.'

Jokoin hesitated, glanced at Will, and then performed the kowtow and left the hut.

'I would accompany her, my lord,' Will said.

'Why?'

'My lord, your vengeance runs too hot for me. But if you would be truly just, not all inside that armoury deserve to die. I crave this, my lord, as I have served you for fifteen years.'

'You have served me well, Will,' Iyeyasu said. 'And I have rewarded you well. Do not seek to come between my family and its future.' His voice became softer. 'If you wish to be present at the end of the Toyotomi, then you have my permission. More, I appoint you my witness. But do not think to settle your feud, now. Norihasa will have more urgent things on his mind. As for the Portuguese, as you have brought me fortune, so has she brought you nothing but misery.' The right arm moved, slowly, weakly, the fingers clutched at Will's sleeve. 'Bring me news of Yodogimi's death.'

Torches flared in the courtyard, bright now that the fire had burned itself out. The Asai Tower was no more, a pile of blackened timbers. Down in the bowels of the tower, where the fire had started—no one would ever know whether it had been an accident or a plan—it was still too hot to enter. Down there were only dead men, in any event. Men he had killed, Will thought. And two girls he had refused to kill. Pray to God they had had the sense to leave. For what reason? To be stretched on their backs by the victorious Tokugawa, and have their honour and their maidenheads torn from their bodies at the same time? There had been enough of that this night.

The regiment on duty squatted around its piled spears. There were women here as well, dragged into the inner keep, to be tormented and misused. And he had thought that *he* had suffered. But now all was quiet. It was the hour of ox, and in a little while it would again be dawn. By European reckoning, the 4th of June 1615.

And here, too, there waited Hidetada and his brothers. Mats had been spread on the earth and on these had been placed the generals' stools. Now they sat facing the closed door of the armoury. They had sat here since the previous evening. Perhaps they were tired, but they still sat straight, and their eyes remained open. They watched the last hiding place of the one man in all Japan who could challenge their supremacy. They did not even turn their heads at the sounds of feet. They were content to wait. But they had with them the means to end their wait, the moment their father gave the word; one of the cannon had been dragged into the courtyard, and its muzzle also stared at the door.

'You have my father's answer?' the Shogun asked.

'He gives no answer,' Jokoin said in a low voice. 'Except that they should come forth.'

'Then tell them that we wait for them, my lady princess. And you, Anjin Miura?'

'I have been commanded to act as witness, my lord Shogun.' Will hesitated. To ask a favour, of this man, where Iyeyasu had refused him? But yet to live, himself . . . 'My lord, I well understand your hatred for the Toyotomi. But not all in there are of the blood of Hideyoshi.'

Hidetada's head half turned, a gesture very reminiscent of his father's. 'Bring out whoever you wish, Anjin Miura. The choice is theirs. As for the Portuguese, *I* have nothing against her. You will act for us as well in this affair, as you have suffered so greatly at their hands. We shall wait here. For half an hour, then we shall blow down the door.'

Jokoin was already walking across the yard, her head bowed, her step slow, her kimono fluttering in the faint dawn breeze which had sprung up. It was a cold breeze. The breeze at dawn is always cold. How often had it chilled his face, on the poop deck of a ship. How often would it do so again? But not for Jokoin.

'Who is there?' asked a voice from beyond the door.

'The Princess Jokoin.'

'You have seen the prince?'

'I have come from him.'

The door swung open, and Will followed the princess inside. For some moments he could not see, so dark was the interior, so filled with smoke. There were half a dozen torches fixed to the walls; there were several stands of spears and swords, and one or two of arquebuses. Nothing else. The empty armoury of the Toyotomi. All else had been expended in their fight.

But not quite all. As his eyes became accustomed to the gloom he saw the piles of dried straw, and saw, too, the thin trails of gunpowder, laid across the stone floor. The Toyotomi had prepared themselves for their final act of defiance.

But how few remained, of the thousands who had followed the banner of the golden gourds. Ono Harunaga, standing by himself, still wearing armour, arms folded across his chest. Ishida Norihasa, staring at Will, seated on the floor close to the Prince Hideyori. Hideyori himself, apparently sleeping, his armour removed, lying on his side, his back to the door, a blanket thrown over his body. There were half a dozen other samurai, and perhaps a score of women, gathered in the rear. And there was Pinto Magdalena, seated against the farthest wall, her kimono gathered close, and resting his head on her lap, the boy Philip. Had she acknowledged him, after all, in this extremity? Or was she just being a woman, comforting a frightened boy.

'What does the prince say to me?' Princess Asai Yodogimi rose from amongst her women, and took a few steps forward, the better to see her sister. She had removed her paint and the beautiful face was as serene and as flawless as it had ever been. But there were tear stains beneath the magnificent dark eyes, and her patterned silk kimono was crushed.

'He bids you come forth, to the justice of the Tokugawa, or stay, as you please. It matters naught to him. But the Shogun has given you thirty minutes to act.'

Yodogimi's head turned. 'And you?' she demanded. 'By now you should have been dead. What evil spirit protects you, Anjin

374

Miura, and keeps you whole, to hound me to my death? What do you here?'

'I am the Princess Jokoin's escort, my lady Yodogimi,' Will said. 'I am witness for the Tokugawa.'

'So tell me why I should not have your head, now,' she whispered.

'Because then not even seppuku will save your body from degradation,' Jokoin said.

Yodogimi stared at Will again, for several seconds. 'So in the end,' she said at last, 'am I tied to a dog. Iyeyasu will always have his way. Tell me this, Anjin Miura, what crime have I committed, other than the crime of ambition, not for myself, but for my son? What crime, that I should come to this?'

How he should hate this woman. How he must hate her, if only because of the hatred she bore for him. Yet at this moment he could feel only pity. And more than that, as he watched the swelling kimono, gazed into the endless beauty of her eyes.

'No crimes, my lady Yodogimi,' he said. 'Indeed, will you but trust to the justice of the prince, you will not find it lacking. He speaks now in anger, because so many of his men have died, because this business has taken so long to complete. His anger will pass.'

'I am Asai Yodogimi,' she said, and turned away. 'Is the prince awake?'

Hideyori knelt, scooping sleep from his eyes. 'I am awake, my lady mother.'

'Have you heard the mercy of the Tokugawa?'

'I seek no mercy from the Tokugawa, my lady mother.'

'Then your followers await your command.'

Toyotomi no-Hideyori gazed at his mother and his nostrils dilated. Still looking at her, he spoke in a low tone. 'Ishida Norihasa, you will act for me.'

'My lord.' Norihasa rose and drew his long sword. He moved round to Hideyori's right side and waited there, the point of the blade resting on the floor.

'Wait . . . ' Will said, but Jokoin gripped his arm.

'No man may interfere with one resigned to death, Anjin Miura,' she whispered. 'Not even the prince would forgive you such sacrilege.'

He bit his lip in anger and frustration, and watched in horror as Hideyori rose to his knees and clapped his hands in prayer. Then he slowly shrugged the kimono from his shoulders. How young he was, how slender his shoulders. There was not a hair on his chest; only sweat, and a heaving rib cage.

Slowly the prince took the long sword from his girdle, and laid it on the floor beside him. Then he drew the short sword in turn, removed it from its sheath, and tested the blade on his fingers. There was not a sound in the building, and not a sound from outside either, now. For the Tokugawa would know what was happening.

'Forgive me, my lady mother,' Hideyori said, and plunged the dagger, held in both hands, into the smooth brown belly, on the left side, below the heart. The blade was turned, and brought to the right side, still grasped in both hands. Breath exploded from Hideyori's nostrils at the same moment as blood exploded from his bowels, pouring down his body in a red cascade, like liquid overflowing from the lip of a cup.

'Now,' Yodogimi shrieked, and Norihasa's long sword cut through the air. Hideyori's head slipped forward and struck the floor of the armoury. Blood pumped upwards from the gaping arteries of his neck, and fell back to join the pool forming around his body. Then the body itself subsided to the floor, collapsing on to its mutilated belly.

A sigh seeped through the chamber. Will felt his muscles turning to water. Almost, he had hated that boy as well.

'He signalled,' Yodogimi said in a low voice. 'You saw him signal.'

The samurai stared at her.

She turned, her hair swinging, to face Will. 'He signalled, Anjin Miura. Say that he signalled.'

'He signalled, my lady Yodogimi. I saw his hand move.'

She gazed at him, panting, and then turned, and dropped to her knees in her son's blood, reaching beneath his body for the dagger.

'*Harunaga.*' Her scream echoed through the chamber, again and again and again, reverberating round the vaulted walls and into the armoured roof. Harunaga unfolded his arms and leapt forward, drawing his sword as he did so. But the Princess Asai Yodogimi was already dead. She had pulled the dagger free from Hideyori's fingers and driven it into her own breast with a single movement. Now she knelt, her head falling forward, her midnight hair cascading on either side of her face, her body slumping from the waist, her blood running down her thighs to mingle with her son's.

Harunaga hesitated above her back, gazing down at her. Then he dropped his sword, and stepped past her to reach the wall. From there he seized one of the torches, whirled it round his head, and still without speaking, thrust it into a pile of straw piled close to the bodies. The other samurai each followed his example before Will could drag his gaze from the dead princess. There was a blinding flash of light and an almost solid wall of flame seemed to leap from the floor to the ceiling, driving him back to the doorway, filling the room with noise, even as it filled with gasps of horror and screams of pain.

'By Christ,' Will shouted, and attempted to go forward. But Jokoin gripped his arm. He tried to throw her off, and still she held him. 'There is my son in there,' he cried.

'And his mother, and his master, who is your enemy. They knew this was to be their end.'

He hurled her aside, and stumbled inside, arms held over his eyes to shade them from the unbearable heat. He stared through the flaring red and yellow, and saw Magdalena. She had risen to her feet, driven by fear and pain and shock. And yet there were none of those things in her face. For a brief moment she was again the young girl who had first gazed at the man from across the ocean, and interpreted for her mistress, and been embarrassed when he would have spoken with *her*. And again the woman in the garden at Shiba? And again the woman who had sat behind her mistress, impassively, and watched her lover tortured. Zenocrate, Zenocrate, fair is too foul an epithet for thee.

Jokoin was dragging at his shoulder and the face was gone, shrouded in a pall of smoke. But she would die without a sound, willingly, because she served Asai Yodogimi.

He discovered himself outside, inhaled fresh air.

'Did you suppose that any personal feelings any of them may have had, whether Magdalena's love for you, Philip's admiration, or Norihasa's hate, would rise above their duty to their lord?' Jokoin asked. 'Were you not prepared to die for the prince, from the moment you entered this fortress? At least allow the Toyotomi the same privilege.'

She released his sleeve, and he remained still. And now the flames filled every inch of the doorway; the room had become an oven.

'And you, my lady Jokoin?' he asked.

'Hideyori was my lord as well, Anjin Miura,' she said. 'And

his mother was my sister. I will ask you for the loan of your short sword, my lord Hidetada.'

For the Shogun and his brothers had risen and come closer. Without a word Hidetada drew his sword from his belt and handed it to her.

'All hail,' Jokoin said. 'To the mighty Tokugawa. May their glory never cease.' She turned away from the men and ran into the blazing room, the dagger pressed to her belly.

'Let their ashes be trodden into the ground,' Iyeyasu said. 'The only monument to the Toyotomi will be the monument to Hideyoshi himself.' The prince had been propped upon pillows, but his breathing was laboured, and his face was blotched. His sons, and courtiers, and his pilot, knelt around him. As did Oda Yuraku. The old, come to terms with the new.

'Yet must the entire accursed race be wiped from the face of this earth,' the prince said, his voice stronger. 'You have prisoners?'

'Many, my lord father,' Hidetada said. 'The ronin who fought for the traitor. And some of their leaders. Ono Doken, brother of Harunaga. The lord Chosokabe. The boy Kunimatsumaro . . .'

'Ono Doken,' Iyeyasu said. 'Did he not command the foraging party which burned Sendai?'

'He did, my lord father.'

'Then give him to the people of Sendai. Tell them to be sure he dies slowly.'

Hidetada bowed.

'Chosokabe will be publicly executed. So will the ronin. So will the boy Kunimatsumaro. Nail their heads to planks, and have the planks set up over the gateways to every town in the empire.'

'The boy is but seven years old, my lord prince,' Yuraku said.

'He is nonetheless a Toyotomi.'

Yuraku bowed.

'And do not forget the priests, my son,' Iyeyasu said. All the Portuguese. Crucify them. Cut off their ears and march them naked through the land, and then hoist them high on crosses.'

'It shall be done, my lord father.' Hidetada's eyes gleamed. 'This will be a memorable occasion.'

'Make it so. Now go. Leave me alone. Remain, Anjin Miura.'

The room emptied, slowly. How often, how very often, had that command been given, had he remained, kneeling like this.

But now his heart no longer pounded. There was no emotion left in his heart.

'Your face is sad, Will.'

'I have learned many things, these last few weeks, and even more these last few hours. My lord, I beg of you, rescind your commands. Do not stain your memory and your glory with such a bitter vengeance.'

'Vengeance, Will? Think you that I seek only vengeance? My vengeance is all contained in that blackened storeroom, with the bones of Yodogimi. I seek to warn, and to make certain, Will. This day the Tokugawa are supreme in Japan. They must remain so. I am dying.'

'My lord, that cannot be.'

'It will be, and is, Will. That spear pierced my kidneys, and there can be no hope for my recovery, no matter how many months I may lie here. But the Tokugawa must remain, for always, for a hundred, nay, for two hundred years and more, supreme. For the good of Japan, Will. For too long have we done nothing but fight, each other. When next we go to war, it must be in the spirit of you Europeans, and fight for conquest and prosperity, not for honour and personal ambitions. So when the daimyo, no matter how long they live, look upon the Tokugawa and say, they are grown too powerful, let them also think of Osaka and of the thousands who die there, and of the heads nailed to the planks, and let them be afraid.' The thin fingers closed on Will's wrist. 'Let them learn the ways of peace and the proper management of their lives. Do you remember, Will, how when we spoke, the day before the Edo earthquake, I told you that I would retire from the Shogunate and occupy myself with composing a code for my samurai?'

'I do, my lord.'

'Well, it is done. And more. I have composed a code for every man, woman, and child in the empire. This is in my will, to the people of Japan. By my instructions will they live, and prosper, Will. And this will be a happy land. A prosperous land.'

'I have no doubt of it, my lord.'

Iyeyasu lay back. 'You play the flatterer, Will. And you lie to me. I wonder how often you have done that to make me happy.'

'Indeed, my lord, while I have no doubt at all that your laws will be good laws and just laws, and intended for the benefit of your people, I cannot help but think that laws by themselves are of little avail. It is the interpretation placed upon those laws. And the leadership given through them. And you, my lord prince, will not be here to lead.'

The liquid eyes roamed over him. 'You are afraid for Japan, Will?'

'Who can tell the future, my lord.'

'Yours is safe enough, Will. Be sure that the name of Anjin Miura belongs in the history of Japan, and will remain there forever.'

'I was but present at great events, my lord.'

'Oh, true, Will. But you were present, at my side. And even at the side of my son. And of others, who matter. The Portuguese brought us their God, and He was not to our taste. The Spaniards brought us a wish for wealth, and we found this no more than amusing. The Dutch, and your own Englishmen, Will, brought us a wish for trade. To a samurai, Will, this is almost insulting. Of all the men who have come from across the oceans, Will, you alone brought us yourself, a glimpse of other minds, other manhoods, than those to which we are accustomed. I have written down my codes, my laws, after knowing you, Will. After loving you. And after respecting you. Who knows what part you have played in the future of Japan, Will? Who can say, for certain, save the gods? But now I would have you choose your own future. Be sure only of our eternal love.'

Tadatune rode with him part of the way. He too had thought his friend dead, and was happy once again to ride at his side.

'I do not understand your gloom, Anjin Miura,' he said. 'Perhaps you did not kill Norihasa, but you faced him, sword in hand, and were not defeated. And after all, he died well.'

'And nothing else matters,' Will said.

'Nothing else *should* matter, to a man or to his enemy. You have a mind to leave Japan?'

Will glanced at him, but did not speak.

The hatamoto reined his horse. 'I shall not attempt to influence your decision, dear friend. But should you again come to Kyushu, Will, be sure that the Satsuma will welcome you as a brother.' He turned his mount. Will waved and continued towards Miura.

No dead, on Miura. No sounds of battle, on Miura. No wailing conch shells and no screams of the dying. No roaring of flames, and no crashing of timbers. Nothing but the faint soughing of the wind, rippling across the surface of Sagami Wan, as it had done since time began, and would until time ended.

Yet there were people. The gates stood open and Kimura and his retainers were waiting, performing the kowtow as their lord approached, and beyond the beach the *Sea Adventure* rode to her moorings, her deck crowded with sailors.

And here too was Cocks, waiting at the gate, with Melchior. 'By God, but it is good to see you, Will,' the factor cried. 'We had heard you were dead. So many times.'

Will dismounted, gestured his tenants to rise. 'But never again, I hope, dear friends. At least until the truth of the matter.'

'But, Will, is it true what they say? About the wholesale executions?'

'It is true. The vengeance of the Tokugawa is no light matter.'

'And the priests? They say the Portuguese are proscribed throughout the length of the empire.'

'That is also true.'

'And that the prince is dying?'

Will nodded.

'And then we shall be at the mercy of the Shogun,' Melchior muttered. 'Today it is the Portuguese, tomorrow it will be the Spaniards, the day after the Dutch and the English. Hidetada has no love for any of us.'

'What? What?' Cocks hurried behind Will as they strode towards the porch. 'Do *you* believe that will happen, Will?'

Will nodded. 'Aye. I believe it will. Not tomorrow. Perhaps not even this year. But as Melchior says, the Shogun has no regard for countries other than Japan, and he hates the Christian teaching.'

'My God.' Cocks halted, pulling at his lip. 'After all our work.'

Melchior followed Will up the steps, where Asoka and Aya knelt, and with them Susanna and Joseph. Will swept the two children into his arms and hugged them to his breast. 'How big you have grown,' he said. And how the tears ran unashamedly down his cheeks.

'You were at Osaka, Papa,' Joseph said. 'Where the great battle was. You must tell me of it.'

'And the heads,' Susanna cried. 'All the heads, Papa.'

'What will you do, Will?' Melchior said. 'The ship is provisioned.'

Will set the children on the floor, opened the screen door,

gazed at the glossy black head. The small table was by her side, and the bottle of heated saké.

'Welcome to Miura, my lord.'

He closed the screen, dropped to his knees in front of her, took her hands, and raised her up. Her eyes were shut, and her mouth was open. He kissed her, and saw a tear escape from the corner of her left eye. 'Oh, Shikibu. If you knew how much I had need of your strength, this last year.'

'I prayed to the Lord Buddha, my lord, day and night for your deliverance. And even when they told me you were dead, at sea, and then inside Osaka Castle, I knew you lived.' Her eyes opened. 'And would return, my lord.'

He poured saké, held out the cup, closed his hand over hers as she raised it to her lips. 'Magdalena is dead, Shikibu. And her son. My son, Shikibu.'

She gazed at him as she sipped, and then placed the cup on the table and refilled it. 'And Ishida Norihasa, my lord?'

'He too. But I did not kill him. We fought, and I think I bested him. But then we were separated, and he committed seppuku with his lord.'

Shikibu held out the cup. 'That is fitting, my lord. It is no disgrace to you.'

'And the woman? I would have saved her, Shikibu.'

'She was of your own people, my lord. I understand that. Perhaps her love was greater than mine.'

How watchful the eyes.

'No,' he said. 'No love could be greater than yours, Shikibu. Nor than mine for you. This I swear. She was a madness. And it is the Western mind to feel guilt, to feel responsibility. Yet even these were not enough. It was when I saw my son. And yet he was not my son. Norihasa had made him into a creature, intended for my destruction.'

'My lord has suffered much,' Shikibu said. 'And is weary. But now he is home. And the wars are finished. There is no reason for him ever to leave Miura again.'

But she was asking a question. The ship remained at anchor just off the beach, and no doubt Cocks and Melchior had been speaking with her. He got up, and walked to the window, to look up at the Hakone Hills, and beyond, at the perfect dome of Mount Fuji. What will you do, Will? What will you do?

'I shall see to your bath, my lord,' Shikibu said. She rose, and the dagger slipped from her girdle to the mat with a soft rustle. Hastily she reached for it, and then checked, and glanced at him.

'There is no need for that now, Shikibu,' he said.

'Not now, my lord.'

'But you would have used it?'

'Had I been certain of your death, my lord. I have no use for life, without my lord.'

'Aye,' Will said. 'I should like a bath, Shikibu.'

She rose, and bowed, and left the room. Will went on to the porch, where Melchior and Cocks waited.

'There is even a fair wind, Will,' Melchior said. 'We could be hull down within the hour.'

'And you, Richard?'

Cocks sighed. 'I have been placed in charge of the factory here, Will, and I must remain until further orders from England, or until the Shogun himself bids me leave. But I wish you Godspeed.'

'The ship is yours, Melchior,' Will said.

'Eh? What do you say, man? You would stay here, in this barbarous country?'

'Barbarous dear friend, certainly. But it is also *true*. Here at least there is honour, unto death, and duty, unto death, and beauty, unto death. There is a savageness, to be sure, but it is a simple human savageness. It lacks the sophisticated hypocrisy of Europe. Yes, dear friend, I shall stay. My wife and children belong here, and to expose them to the sickly sweet stench of Europe were a greater crime than any even I have committed. Besides, I have played too large a part in establishing the Tokugawa rule. I would truly play the coward were I to sail away.'

'But you, Will. What of you?'

'I have been happy here, Melchior. Despite all, I have been happy, where in England I but dreamed of happiness. For this is a country where dreams come true.'

'And nightmares, Will.'

'Those too, Melchior. Those too. But if a man may not learn to accept his nightmares, then he has no right to enjoy his dreams.'

He went inside, to his bath. Shikibu was waiting.

Osaka Castle fell on 4 June 1615. In 1623 the English abandoned their factory in Hirado, because they could obtain no profit from their trade with Japan. In 1624 the Spaniards were expelled, and the Portuguese in 1638. In 1641 the Dutch were limited to the islet of Deshima in Nagasaki Harbour, where they remained virtual prisoners. But as Prince Iyeyasu had prophesied the Tokugawa Shogunate grew and prospered and lasted for over two hundred and fifty years. When at last it fell, in 1868, it was because of the appearance of a foreign battle fleet in Edo Bay, on 8 July 1853, again as the prince had prophesied.

Will Adams died on 16 May 1620. But for him also Prince Iyeyasu proved an accurate prophet. To this day there is no more honoured European in the history of Japan.